2025 HIGH CALIBER AWARDS

Elaine Midcoh
Jacob Sharp
Michael Craig
JP Johnson
Re Gwaltney
Rob Nisbet
Anthony Rudd
Edgar Soto

Contents

Don't Mind Us

Elaine Midcoh

Hello Javon and Anita,
This is Lizzette Turro, your Intro to Sociology instructor. I'm sending this email because I have a special assignment for you. It will be worth more than an A+ grade. Meet me tomorrow, Mon. 10 a.m., at Dr. Wells' office (Sociology Building, second floor, room 215). If I'm not there, remove the small envelope taped to the door. There will be a key inside. Use the key to open his office. On his desk is a manila folder. Read the paper inside. Javon, Anita, you must show up. Do you like clichés? Here's one: the fate of the world is in your hands.

***

Javon, Anita — If you are reading this, then I am dead. Or maybe I'm not. Maybe I had car trouble and couldn't get to campus for our appointment. Try my cell phone. No answer? I'm so sorry. It falls on you then. Read the paper. Stay healthy. Good luck.

Understanding the Benushians: A Sociological Response to the Invasion of Earth
By Lizzette Turro, PhD Candidate-Sociology, Oberdine University

Preface

I was Dr. Anton Wells' student for six years. My first class on my first day at Oberdine was with him, *Introduction to*

Sociology. I loved that class and I loved Dr. Wells, not in a weird young female student/older male teacher infatuation, but just loving his knowledge and the way he taught. I loved how he would get so excited when lecturing that his arms would flail about until he would shove his hands into his sweater pockets. His white hair had an Albert Einstein-type messiness that seemed right for him, with the wild fluffs bouncing in emphasis whenever he discussed an important point. I majored in sociology and took every class I could with Dr. Wells. When I was accepted into the PhD program I asked Dr. Wells to be my advisor, even though by that time he was semi-retired and had accepted '*Professor Emeritus*' status. For my dissertation, I was researching how access to virtual reality drug simulations impacted drug addiction rates in rural communities. But then the Benushians came to Earth and no one cared about anything else.

As Dr. Wells would say, when writing a paper you must assume the reader knows nothing. Thus, please forgive me if I recount facts that are familiar. This will be the last paper I write for Dr. Wells. Even though he's dead I want to do it right. I dedicate this paper to him.

***

At 9:49 a.m., Eastern Standard Time, on Wednesday, February 9, 2033, these were some of the stories highlighted on various news web pages: American Samoa referendum to secede from the U.S. and join China passes by wide margin, Brazil conducts test launch for missile with capacity to reach Miami, President to visit Africa in new economic initiative, Electric cars projected to outsell gas cars for first time, "Seinfeld" reunion project a no go, and Seventy year old woman gives birth to twins. By 9:52 a.m. there was only one story being broadcasted around the world: the Benushians had come to Earth.

Initially, we didn't know they were Benushians. All we knew is that, seemingly out of nowhere and without warning, there were dozens of alien space craft roving the skies of Earth. They were of different sizes and shapes, with the smallest being a long oval about the size of three football fields and the largest being triangular with a length from point to opposite base of approximately two miles. By 9:57 a.m. the aliens had parked their ships and were holding positions over every nation with nuclear weapons, from the United States to Russia, China, India, Pakistan, England, France, Germany, the two Koreas, Japan, Israel, Iran, Saudi Arabia and, much to everyone's surprise, Iceland, whose Prime Minister later acknowledged that they had been a secret nuclear power since 1998. By 10:03 a.m., Iceland's secret didn't matter because every nuclear bomb in the world was gone, seemingly disappeared. While the general population was not informed of this event until two days later, the reaction of the world's leaders has since been well documented; an attempt at immediate absolute secrecy, followed by cautious confirmation that all other nuclear powers were similarly impacted.

At 10:14 a.m. came the first broadcast. It appeared on every television station, every radio station and every computer, tablet and cell phone. The Benushian was seated on a simple wooden chair. He had a human like body, with two arms, a torso and two legs, but he was quite thin, willowy and blue, almost rubbery, as if someone had grabbed one of us at head and foot and pulled stretching us out. Each of his hands had three fingers. His head was so typical of our many imagined versions of aliens with the elongated face and large eyes, that some speculated that the Benushians presented themselves not as they truly appear, but in a form we would find acceptable. This theory was reinforced by his clothing; a long Hawaiian shirt with a bright floral design. (Note: We still have no idea regarding Benushian gender and/or genders. I refer to the Benushian as "he" for ease of reading.)

5

When the Benushian spoke it was broadcasted in the language of the recipient. In the United States, the Benushian spoke in Spanish on the Spanish language television channels and English on the English language channels. In Ireland, the Benushian spoke English with an Irish lilt. French tourists in Manhattan heard the broadcast in French on their cell phones, while native New Yorkers received it in English on their phones. For purposes of this paper, I will be quoting from the English language broadcast received in Milton, North Carolina, home of Oberdine University.

"Howdy," the Benushian said. Despite a strange vibration, it was a cheery voice, the sort of friendly bellow you might get from a neighbor across the street. "We're from the planet Benushia. Don't worry about us. We'll do a little bit here and there, but mostly we won't bother you. Go on with your lives. Don't fret. Everything's fine." The Benushian raised a glass that appeared to hold a margarita and gave a toothless smile as the image disappeared.

Needless to say, the governments and people of Earth did indeed fret or, to use the term employed by Dr. Wells, everyone went *nutso extremis*. Here in the U.S.A., there was the usual reaction to any potential catastrophe: food hoarding and fights in grocery stores. Children were kept home from school. Gun sales, church attendance and alcohol consumption rose. There were "Kiss Your Butt Goodbye" parties, frantic "we may never get another chance so let's make love now" hook-ups and the immediate creation of Benushian related businesses: Benushian action figures, t-shirts, costumes, masks, toys and board games. In Albequerque, a special Benushian Balloon Festival was quickly arranged with dozens of hot air balloons taking to the air with words "Howdy" and "Welcome" and "What's Up?" painted on the sides.

The rest of the world wasn't much different. In Paris, more than ten thousand people gathered on the Champs Elysses to form a peace sign that the organizers claimed could be seen by the Benushian ship hovering over the city. In a small Nepal village, the residents herded a group of goats to a cliff's edge and loudly proclaimed they were inviting the Benushians to dinner. No Benushians showed and the villagers went home leaving two goats tied to a bush in case the Benushians came down later.

In the meantime, world leaders called for calm and called up military units. Two days after the Benushians' arrival the Secretary-General of the United Nations made a welcoming statement promising that, "friendship will be met with friendship and peace shall be met with peace." One hour later the President of the United States, the President of Russia and the Premier of China along with the leaders of forty-three other nations signed a mutual defense pact, stating that if one nation was attacked by aliens from space, then all forty-four nations would respond.

And how did the Benushians react to all this? Nothing, no reaction at all. For five days there was not a single additional communication or action.

And then, on day six, a terrorist group called "The Red Spirit" apparently decided that space aliens were no reason to stop activities. Using drones, and broadcasting live on the internet, Red Spirit operatives released a deadly toxin in the heart of Rome. They called it "Righteous Wind" and claimed that they had created it in their own chemical laboratory.

Hundreds of security cameras captured the attack: men, women and children falling to the ground, bodies arched in seizures, writhing. In one video that went viral, a small child lies on the ground clutching at her mother's dress and foams at the mouth while blood leaks from her green eyes. Multiple investigations later determined that if the attack succeeded, at least eight thousand people would have died and the city's center would have been uninhabitable for several weeks. But no one was killed.

Exactly two seconds after the attack a Benushian ship appeared over Rome. Its appearance was as sudden as when the Benushians first arrived. This ship, commonly referred to as the "Rome ship," removed the Righteous Wind toxin from the air.

Even after the Benushian Rome ship cleared the air, the people exposed to the toxin suffered terribly. There are countless videos of the survivors rolling on the ground, clawing at their necks and eyes, ripping at their clothes and gasping in a desperate attempt to breathe. Experts in biological warfare estimated that sixty-five percent of the victims should have died, even with two seconds of exposure. But no one died. Instead, the Benushian ship began to wobble and shift in small movements as if slow dancing across Rome's sky. In less than twelve seconds the people of Rome stopped gasping, stopped pulling at their clothes, took deep breaths and sat up wondering what happened.

The Benushians healed them. This realization that the Benushians had healing powers — and would use them — rocked Earth. Speculation was rampant. Whether in private conversations, on the cable news channels, across the internet, or in Dr. Wells' office, the questions were the same: Why were the Benushians here? They had eliminated nuclear weapons, stopped a major terrorist attack and healed the injured. But why? Were they here to save us from ourselves? What else could they heal? Who else would they heal?

The next morning I was with Dr. Wells in the Sociology department's faculty lounge. As a PhD candidate I was teaching one freshman level *Intro to Sociology* class and was thus granted faculty privileges including access to the lounge. Despite the old furniture, stained carpet, flea market paintings on the wall and musty smell I was proud to be there and proud to sit at the same table with Dr. Wells, not just as his student but as a colleague. We were the only ones in the lounge. Most of Oberdine University was deserted. As soon as the Benushians arrived frantic parents ordered their children to come home. The Oberdine administration recognized the futility of running live classes with a ninety percent student absentee rate and announced that all on-campus classes would convert to the web for the remainder of the semester. Without live classes to teach most professors stayed home too.

My boyfriend of two years, Cal Ortega, an English Lit major going for his Master degree, decided that this might be the end of the world. He told me he was headed for England. He wanted to see a Shakespeare play at the site of the original Globe Theatre and visit Dickens's London and walk in the land of Keats, Shelley and Browning. Cal wanted me to go with him. He said, "It will be beautiful and we might not get another chance."

I thought about it. I really did. But then I talked to Dr. Wells. His son and three grandchildren lived in San Diego and I asked Dr. Wells if he was going there. Dr. Wells peered at me like I just said something stupid. He replied, "Now, with so much to learn, so much to do?" Dr. Wells never asked me to stay, but his response settled it for me. Despite Cal's sweet invitation, despite my own parents' objections, I stayed at Oberdine. I would work with Dr. Wells.

Like everywhere else in the world, the television in the lounge was broadcasting news where all the talk was Rome, Rome and Rome. We were flipping channels and had been watching for about two hours. For the umpteenth time we saw again the video of the little girl with blood coming from her eyes and then a later interview with the girl smiling and happy on her mother's lap.

Dr. Wells clicked off the TV and threw the remote on the table. He was biting his lip and staring at the blank screen.

I said, "Maybe the Benushians are here to help. So far they've only done good things."

He turned to me and frowned. Then he got up. "Come with me," he said.

He led me to an empty classroom, went to the podium and put on the computer and the overhead projector. Leaving me at the podium, he took a seat in the front row.

"Do you read Italian?" he asked.

"No, but the computer can do translations if we need it."

"Of course," he said nodding, his tufts of hair bouncing up and down. "Find me some Rome newspapers. I want local news, community news, not anything about those terrorists or the Benushians."

As I logged on, I asked, "What do you want in particular?"

"Find crime reports. Tell me what crimes happened in Rome yesterday. "

Understandably, the Rome newspapers were mostly focused on the remarkable events of the previous day. Still, we soon found articles on two separate armed robberies of stores, the mugging of a tourist, a domestic violence murder where a woman stabbed her live-in boyfriend and a workplace shooting where a man used a hunting rifle to kill five of his coworkers. That last one would normally have been a big news story, especially in a European city, but with the Red Sky terrorist attack and the Benushian response happening on the same day it was just a two paragraph article.

Dr. Wells stood up and paced in front of the classroom. "Interesting," he said. Then he went to the podium computer and did a search, "Accidental Death." Many stories came up. Dr. Wells clicked on one from Springfield, Illinois, where a family of three, a husband, wife and their fourteen year old daughter, died of carbon monoxide poisoning. They lived in an older home with a furnace and something went wrong. At least they died in their sleep.

"Can you figure out when they died?" asked Dr. Wells.

"The article says it happened yesterday."

"Yes, but was it before or after Rome?"

We had to find another article to get the approximate time of death and then had to calculate the time difference, but we figured out that they must have died after the events in Rome.

"Ah," said Dr. Wells. He rubbed the top of his head and his eyes focused on the corner of the ceiling.

"Ah, what?" I asked.

He looked at me without really looking. "Fresh air," he said.

We walked outside and headed toward the north part of the campus. Dr. Wells didn't say a word, his face a frozen frown. His hands were clasped behind him and he was going so slowly that my back ached from the unnatural pace. After twenty minutes of random wandering, he stopped, glanced around and pointed at a bench in front of the Student Union building. "Let's sit."

It was a warmer day, especially pleasant for February. With most of the students and faculty gone, the College had closed off all the cafeterias, restaurants, kiosks and recreation centers on campus, except for the ones in the Student Union. Dormitories had been shut down too, with the few remaining students moved to two dormitory buildings near the Student Union. As we sat there, three students played Frisbee on the grassy area in front of the building.

"So, what do we know?" This was Dr. Wells' favorite question. Whenever he asked that in class, it was always a prelude to a lively discussion. I was more than willing to play.

"We know the Benushians got rid of nuclear weapons and that they stopped a major terrorist attack," I answered.

"But they didn't get rid of conventional weapons," he said.

"True."

"Why?" he asked. "Conventional weapons also cause massive death and destruction. Look at the allied bombing of Dresden during World War Two. It caused a huge firestorm. The impact on Dresden was similar to the impact of the atomic bomb on Hiroshima. So why get rid of nuclear weapons, but not other weapons of mass destruction? Or, more succinctly, if you are an alien looking at how humans destroy themselves, what is the primary difference between Dresden and Hiroshima?" He raised his eyebrows at me.

My PhD candidate cockiness evaporated and I felt myself transform back into an eighteen year old freshman. I took out my phone and connected to the internet. Dr. Wells politely averted his gaze rather than acknowledge my need for external help. Dresden was not the equal of Hiroshima. In Dresden

11

about twenty-five thousand people died over the three days of bombings, while in Hiroshima there were approximately a hundred and fifty thousand deaths, though I'm sure to the dead in Dresden the numbers made little difference. Both cities suffered extreme damage, with large areas completely destroyed. So what was the difference? And then I saw it. I put my phone away and cleared my throat. Dr. Wells turned to me, a small smile on his face.

"It was time," I said. "Dresden was destroyed over a period of days, while Hiroshima was destroyed in an instant."

Dr. Wells nodded. "My thought too. And we know it took the Rome ship about two seconds to stop the terrorist attack. So though the Benushians eliminated our nuclear weapons while leaving us conventional weapons, it's possible they would stop us from using them too. But…" he said.

I had to think a moment. "But they don't want us to know that." My words came in a rush. "It's what they said: 'Don't fret, just continue with your lives.' They eliminated what they possibly couldn't stop in time, nuclear explosions, but allowed us to keep what they can control, conventional weapons. So they want us to continue doing what we do, but if we ever use conventional weapons they'll probably stop it, just like they stopped the Rome attack."

"But not all conventional weapons use…" Dr. Wells said, again waiting for me.

What? I thought. But then I got it again and experienced the headiness I always felt with Dr. Wells as a teacher. He never gave you the answer. He always had you figure it out; he let you have the sweet joy of discovery. How I loved Dr. Wells. How sorry I am that he's dead. I said, "The murders in Rome, the girl who killed the boyfriend and the man who shot his five coworkers. The Benushians won't allow mass casualty killings, but they will allow little killings. 'Don't fret, continue what you do.' And we sure do that, we do kill each other on occasion." I was on a roll now. "And they'll allow accidental deaths too, like the family that died from carbon monoxide poisoning. But maybe they won't allow a mass casualty accident, like a big airliner crash."

"Well done," Dr. Wells said. I was soaring. I just earned an A grade.

Over the next ten hours, by monitoring breaking news from across the world and while subsisting on stale doughnuts and peanuts left in the faculty lounge, we came up with the "Rule of Six." I helped Dr. Wells write the paper. It was less than ten pages, but provided a detailed and well-articulated argument for the theory. Dr. Wells posted it to the "Sociology Today" website the next morning. I was surprised and moved that he added me as coauthor rather than student assistant. When I thanked him he waved his hand and said, "The Rule of Six is as much yours as it is mine."

Within an hour of Dr. Wells posting the paper, the Associated Press picked up the story and then the Rule of Six was everywhere. Dr. Wells became an instant celebrity and I a minor one, a Robin to his Batman. That day and the next, Dr. Wells gave a series of interviews, often with me by his side. I dressed up, but Dr. Wells wore his same old sweater. I figured he wasn't nervous at all, though I did see him try to pat down his hair a few times. In each interview he concisely explained the Rule of Six. I always knew Dr. Wells was a great teacher. Now the world did too.

"It's very simple," he would begin. "By looking at various incidents around the world since the initial Rome attack, we've confirmed nine times that the Benushians have interfered — in a positive way — to save human life. The most significant, of course, was when they interfered in Rome. Another time involved a bus accident outside New Delhi. The bus went off an embankment, rolled over, hit some rocks and burst into flame. More than forty people were trapped inside and many would have probably burned to death. Yet, within seconds a Benushian ship appeared and put out the bus fire. The assumption is that they momentarily removed all oxygen from the bus, just as they removed the deadly toxin from Rome's air. More than that, they healed the injured just like they did in Rome. The other incidents also involved high numbers of people facing death: ten construction workers trapped in a building collapse in Sydney, a factory chemical leak in Helsinki endangering seventeen employees, and so on. However, we developed the Rule of Six by looking at two specific incidents, one in Duluth, Minnesota and the other in Tokyo."

Here Dr. Wells would pause and lean forward. "In Duluth there was a head on collision between an SUV and a small school van. The SUV carried the Backus family: mother, father, grandmother and three kids. The school van had seven people: the driver, a coach and five middle school students returning from a tennis tournament. We don't know which driver caused the accident, but we know the result. The Backus family, a family of six, were all tragically killed, including one child who died a few hours later in a hospital and the grandmother who was alive when paramedics showed up, but who died at the scene. In the school van, which had seven people, no one died or even suffered an injury. However, the bus driver, coach and all the students recall being hurt and in pain, just like the people of Rome recall gasping for breath. Also, if you look at photos of the accident, you see that the school van is as crushed and damaged as the SUV. We also know that witnesses in Duluth saw a Benushian ship appear in the sky the same time that the accident occurred. So, it's safe for us to assume that the Benushians saved the seven people on the school van, but did not save the six members of the Backus family. Why?

"Now let's go to Tokyo. For this incident we actually have footage." Here Dr. Wells would open his laptop and play the videos that I downloaded for him. "What you see is a twenty-four-year-old man, later identified as Hiro Namasuko, walk into a crowded pedestrian area in downtown Tokyo. It's lunch time. You see him go by an outdoor café. Then he pulls out a large machete and begins to attack people. It's hard, but watch this. He stabs and kills the young man and woman sitting at a table. Here he injures the waiter, slicing him deep in the arm. Then he enters a clothing store. We have video of this too from the store's surveillance cameras. Fair warning, this is pretty awful. The people in the store don't know what's happened outside and they're just going about their business. Namasuko walks to different areas in the store and stabs four more people. They die too.

"Now here's the important part. Watch this video from the store surveillance cameras. At this point he's killed six people and injured one. By this time some people in the store realize something is happening and a manager leaves the payment kiosk and goes into the main store aisle. Namasuko walks toward him, holding the machete behind him. When he gets close he stabs the manager. The manager falls to the ground and suddenly — watch the video now — Namasuko's machete disappears. It's gone, just like the toxin is gone from Rome. Namasuko runs away. He'll be arrested later. But for now look at the manager. He's bleeding on the floor. From the look of it he was stabbed in the chest, maybe even the heart. But watch this — wait for it — here it is — he suddenly sits up. He looks down at his chest and just like the people of Rome, just like the kids on the school van, he's fine. The Benushian ship over Tokyo saved him. But the waiter, the one with the slashed arm, he's not healed. In fact, later at the hospital, the doctors had to amputate his arm. Why didn't the Benushians heal him, like they healed the manager? In Duluth, the Benushians saved the seven people on the van, but why didn't they save the Backus family? Or even just the grandmother and little girl? They were both still alive when the paramedics showed up."

Now Dr. Wells would lean back in his chair. "It seems clear that for some reason the Benushians have a 'Rule of Six.' If only six or fewer of us are in trouble the Benushians allow fate to take its course, even if it means people dying. But if more than six of us are in trouble then the Benushians intervene and save us. And by trouble, I mean facing death.

The Benushians didn't include the waiter with his sliced arm in the Rule of Six before deciding to intervene. That was a serious, but non-fatal injury. It was only after Namasuko killed six people that the Benushians made his machete disappear. In Duluth, the Benushians allowed the six members of the Backus family to die, but saved the seven people in the school van."

The Rule of Six became a sensation. Why allow six to die, but not more? Religious scholars thought six must be a holy number to the Benushians. Astronomers guessed that the Benushians came from a system with six planets and that's why the number is important to them. Mathematicians argued that since the Benushians have only six fingers, they most likely have a base six number system. For them, six would be a nice round number, the way ten is for us.

Also interesting was the ordinary person's response. A new game emerged: Pick Your Six. At dinner with family or in conversation with friends or while chatting with strangers, people continually challenged each other to "Pick Your Six" — name the six people you would kill before the Benushians stopped you. This pastime caused much commentary, including *America Now* columnist Jorge Fredreico's viral editiorial: "Why We Need the Benushians (Because Earthlings are Sick)."

Of course, Dr. Wells was continuously asked why he thought the Benushians had the Rule of Six. He always responded, "How should I know? At this point, how can any of us know?"

The morning after our last interview Dr. Wells and I were back in the faculty lounge watching the TV. It was strange seeing ourselves on the screen. I thought I appeared young and insecure, but Dr. Wells said I looked like a scholar.

We were watching CBT news when our interview cut off and the camera went back to the morning anchor, Michael Olinskowa. (Dr. Wells and I were among those who saw this live.) Olinskowa's eyes were wide and a tear leaked out and trickled down his cheek. My stomach dropped thinking that something horrible must have happened. But then Olinskowa smiled and broke the news story that forever caused this day to be known as "Miracle Day."

Though an experienced reporter, Olinskowa's voice cracked. "My mother has Alzheimer's — had Alzheimer's. She's in a nursing home with other dementia patients. But she's better now. My sister's with her. All the patients at the nursing home are better. It's a miracle, a miracle."

A few minutes later came the famous on-air phone interview with his mother where she said, "Mikey, you did it, you made it, you're on TV. Mikey, I'm so proud of you."

Olinskowa burst into tears and said, "Mama, Mama," over and over again.

Within two hours the news became clear. Throughout the U.S. and the world dementia/Alzheimer patients regained their memory, Parkinson's disease patients regained control over their body movements, stroke victims were no longer paralyzed and could speak clearly and comatose patients woke up. Victims of traumatic brain injuries, whether caused by war, violent crime or an unfortunate accident, were suddenly healed. As one Johns Hopkins' doctor of neurology stated to a reporter, "I guess we're out of business now." An hour later another stunning development; brain cancer patients were cured with no signs of tumors or other cancerous growths. No one doubted that the Benushians had done this. But why?

Dr. Wells turned off the television and stood up. "C'mon, we're going to the hospital."

"Are you okay?" My anxiety about his age jumped to the surface.

"I am perfectly fine," he said as he strode out of the lounge. "Hurry up!"

Oberdine University has a medical school and next to it is the Oberdine Teaching Hospital. It took us fifteen minutes to walk there. Dr. Wells headed straight for the Emergency Department. There were four people in the waiting area, an old man and woman holding hands and a mother with a little boy on her lap.

We were greeted by a triage nurse, a woman in her fifties who looked tough and capable, like she had seen everything at least twice.

"Can I help you?" she asked.

"Yes," Dr. Wells said. "I want to know about your deaths over the past two days."

The nurse stared at him. "Excuse me?"

"Tell me about the deaths that happened yesterday and today. I need to know." Dr. Wells pulled at his hair leaving one tuft sticking out like a highway extension.

"Uh huh," she said. "We don't share patient information." She returned to her paperwork.

Dr. Wells pursed his lips. I put a hand on his arm and said. "Ma'am, this is Dr. Wells of the Sociology department. I'm a graduate student there. We're working on some research. We don't need specific patient information, just the causes of death."

The nurse glanced back at us. "Sociology department? You're the Rule of Six professor?"

"He is," I answered. Dr. Wells straightened and pulled down on his sweater. I realized he was trying to appear dignified. I almost laughed, but the nurse's indecision stopped me.

Finally she said, "Wait here." She walked into the back office area. Less than a minute later she returned, along with two other nurses, one a young girl who could pass for sixteen and the other a man in his thirties with a huge thick moustache. The male nurse was holding a piece of paper. The tough triage nurse took it from him and handed it to us.

"We've been keeping track," she said. "Since Rome we've had two deaths here in the Emergency Department, a heart attack and a car accident where the patient's femoral artery was pierced. She bled to death. We also had a stroke victim. That stroke was massive, catastrophic and the patient was home alone for half a day before her daughter found her on the kitchen floor. That lady should have died or at least have serious complications, but she completely recovered. We released her forty minutes ago."

The young kid nurse spoke up. "Upstairs on the hospice floor — do you know what hospice is?" Dr. Wells and I both nodded. It's where those who are close to death are taken for end of life care. The idea of hospice is to ensure that the terminally ill don't suffer and have an easy and painless death. Dr. Wells' wife died on the hospice floor three years earlier. I remember feeling so inadequate when I brought flowers and lasagna to his home afterwards. The kid nurse continued, "Well, in hospice they've had three deaths, one leukemia, one liver cancer and one congestive heart failure." She glanced at the male nurse. He frowned.

He said, "But we have one patient up there with lung cancer that spread to his brain. The guy should have kicked off days ago, but he's still hanging on. So after this morning when the Benushians did the miracle thing, the doctors checked him and his brain cancer is all gone. But get this, he still has the lung cancer. And it's still terminal. The man is still going to die, but now has a few extra weeks. That's all. What kind of miracle is that?"

The five of us stood in silence. Miracle Day was no miracle, only a puzzle. Finally, the tough triage nurse said, "So, Dr. Wells of the Sociology department, what does it mean?"

Dr. Wells didn't answer her. How could he? We didn't know the answer, not then.

Miracle Day was the ninth day since the Benushians arrival. On days ten through twelve the Benushians performed more "miracles," almost all of an environmental nature. The northwestern "dead zone" in Japan created after the Kowasua nuclear power plant accident showed no signs of radioactivity. The so called "Lake of Poison" near the eastern city of Tressata in India no longer had any trace of contaminants.

What had been a completely dead lake destroyed by years of toxic waste dumping now had water so fresh and clean that locals began to bottle and sell it as "Benushian Pure." The most significant "miracle," of course, was the little island country of Merisbatil. Grossly over populated, poverty-stricken, pummeled by cyclones and earthquakes and plagued by poor government environmental policies, Merisbatil suffered from a limited and mostly contaminated water supply and had land so arid that it made the American dust bowl of the 1930s look fertile and rich. The Bunushians cleaned up and restored Merisbatil in less than an hour.

By day thirteen the news people were finished with Dr. Wells and me. His continual refusal to speculate as to why the Benushians performed these "miracles" had bored them into finding more lively commentators: philosophers, comic book writers, late show comedians and former government officials who felt free to speculate, as opposed to the current government officials who answered every question with stone faced optimism. Of course, there were always the man on the street interviews, the more crazy and absurd the better.

Day thirteen was also when my boyfriend Cal left for England. For the first week after the Benushians arrived all commercial flights were cancelled. But when it became clear that the Benushians apparently weren't here to kill us — at least not immediately — and that they weren't going to zap planes out of the sky with some alien energy beam, commercial flights slowly resumed. The first ones had military escorts. By the time I drove Cal to the airport all flight operations had returned to normal. Our Rule of Six had convinced people that flying was safer than ever and that if a plane did get in trouble the Benushians would save it.

After Cal checked in his luggage, I walked him to the security line. Cal's hands were full, one holding his carry-on and the other with his book bag. I pinched the tail of his leather jacket, using it as my tow rope so we wouldn't be separated in the crowd. I wish now that I had taken his arm. I wish I had carried his book bag so that we could have held hands. I loved how his big long fingers would overwhelm mine. Instead, we had one hurried kiss. "Remember," he said, "you can still come. I want you to come."

"Maybe later," I responded. How could I know what would happen? How I wish I held his hand.

As I drove back to campus I was already missing Cal. I was too depressed to listen to the radio and I always keep my phone off when I drive, so I missed the Benushians' second broadcast. I did see drivers pull their cars to the side of the highway, no doubt to give full attention to the Benushians, but I was absorbed in my own misery and didn't make the connection. When I reached the university, it was around 9 p.m. and I saw clusters of students outside the Student Union. They were standing close together, looking at their phones then at other people's phones, as if for verification. I pulled over, rolled down my window and called out to the nearest student.

"What's going on?" I asked.

The boy walked over to my car, trailed by two girls. He had peach fuzz on his face and I guessed he was a freshman.

"The Benushians are coming."

"They're here," I responded.

"No," he said. In the street light I could see he was perspiring despite the cool night air. "No, they're coming down to us, on the ground. They're coming down." One of the girls handed him a bottle of water which he guzzled.

"Look." He held his phone up to my face.

"No, thanks anyway," I said. Ignoring the university speed limits, I raced to the Sociology building and parked in the dean's spot. I pushed open the door to the faculty lounge. Dr. Wells hadn't gone home. He was on the couch watching the television. A breath I didn't know I was holding left my lips and I realized I didn't want to be alone for this. Dr. Wells muted the TV and smiled at me.

"How did it go with Cal? Are you all right?"

Considering that Benushians would soon stroll the Earth, I was touched he asked. "It was okay. What's happened?" I sat down next to him.

He gestured toward the TV. "Another Benushian broadcast. They're replaying it now." He put the sound back on and the news was just switching from the reporter to a video of the game show "Cyber Buckaroos." As the host introduced the contestant, the screen went black and was replaced with the Benushians.

This time it was two Benushians, the one (same one?) in the Hawaiian shirt and another wearing a black tuxedo coat, with a high collared white shirt and bow tie. Their physical appearance was the same as before: human-like, but long, thin, stretchy and blue with the stereotypical alien face that you would find on a "Welcome to Roswell" tourist t-shirt. To our eyes they appeared to be twins with only the clothing differentiating them. This time they were standing. They did not wear pants, but their tops were long enough to cover the upper part of their legs. In the U.S.A., these Benushians came to be known as Aloha and Tux.

Aloha gave his toothless smile. "Howdy," he said, his voice vibrating. "This is the Benushians. We have good news. We have reached the time for inspection. We're coming down for a visit."

Then Tux spoke. His voice vibrated too. "Don't mind us. No need to disrupt your lives. Continue doing what you do. We'll just look around."

Then, in a synchronized movement, Aloha and Tux waved their right hands and together said, "See you soon." This was followed by the playing of the chorus from the hit song, "It's All Fine, So Smile, Smile, Smile." As the chorus repeated Aloha and Tux swayed their bodies in a rubbery dance that kept the beat of the song. When it ended they gave a final cheery wave. The TV went back to the news anchor. He looked like he had just sucked a lemon. Dr. Wells muted the sound.

"Most important word?" he asked.

"Inspection."

He nodded. "But inspecting what and why?"

There was no answer to that. So I said, "That dance was weird. Maybe they really don't want us to worry."

"Or maybe they want us to smile," Dr. Wells answered. He stood up. "I can be ready in an hour. What about you?"

"Ready for what?"

He frowned, disappointed at my slowness. "Hilton Head. We're going to Hilton Head."

I grinned. Of course, we were going to Hilton Head. During the so-called "Miracle Days" the Benushian ships had appeared and disappeared in skies all over the Earth. For example, the Rome ship that responded to the terrorist attack was spotted over Cairo, Egypt, Fairbanks, Alaska, and the small town of Plotznik in Slovenia. Only one Benushian ship remained stationary, always in the sky, never moving: the Hilton Head ship. If the Benushians really were going to leave their ships to do their inspection, then Hilton Head, South Carolina, was the only possible predictable location. We just had to hope that the Hilton Head ship wouldn't suddenly disappear from the sky and go elsewhere.

"I'll drive," I said.

It took us eight hours to reach Hilton Head. Along the way we kept track of reports of the Benushian inspections. From Finland to Nigeria, from Madison, Wisconsin to Auckland, New Zealand and in dozens of other places around the world, the inspections all followed the same pattern: A Benushian ship would pop into the sky, then Tux and Aloha would suddenly appear on Earth, approach the nearest people (of those who didn't run away) and then Aloha would say, "Hello, we are the Benushians. Are you happy?" Some were too stunned to reply and those who did always said yes. Then Tux and Aloha would smile, wave goodbye, disappear and show up somewhere else on Earth. Sometimes they would show up seconds later, sometimes minutes later. By the time we arrived in Hilton Head there had already been eighty-seven separate

Benushian inspections. With each inspection Dr. Wells grew more anxious, worried we wouldn't get to Hilton Head before Tux and Aloha showed up there — if they showed up.

When we did finally arrive the sun was beginning to rise. Despite not sleeping, I felt wide awake and alert as we spotted the Benushian ship. Hovering slightly over the shore line and mostly over water, it was an uneven octagon shape, the sort of flying saucer that might appear in a dreamscape Salvador Dali painting. The Hilton Head ship was among the smallest of the Benushian vessels and many felt it must be their command post because it was the only ship to stay in place. Others thought it might be a supply ship or communications center. The local chamber of commerce took advantage of the ship's permanent presence and began an ad campaign to attract visitors: "The Benushians stay at Hilton Head — Why don't you?"

The campaign must have worked because even at that early hour Hilton Head was packed with tourists. On the beach people filled every space, with almost all looking to the sky at the Benushian ship. It took twenty minutes to find a parking space.

As Dr. Wells and I pushed through the throng to get closer to the Benushian ship, someone shouted, "Hey, it's the Rule of Six guy!" And then others said it again and again, "It's the Rule of Six guy; it's the Rule of Six guy." People pushed against us, but also cleared a path so we could reach the shoreline and the ship.

I said to him, "You're a rock star. You're the fifth Beatle."

He responded, "I'd rather be Elvis."

For me the eeriest moment was when we approached the shoreline and the shadow of the ship blocked the rising sun and fell upon us. Somehow at that moment, despite the optimism, despite all the good things the Benushians had done, I felt fear. The people around us must have felt something too because they grew silent and were all facing Dr. Wells. I don't know what they expected or what Dr. Wells thought they expected, but he cleared his throat and nodded to the crowd. "You know —" he began, but then he stopped.

Looking back now, I wonder what he was about to say. Whether he was going to provide comfort or warning or perhaps tell a joke. I'll never know, for as he was beginning to speak, there in the water, wading slowly to the shore were the Benushians, Tux and Aloha.

As if in a choreographed dance the people closest to the water and those around us moved inland, leaving the Benushians a clear path to two people, Professor Wells and me. I have watched the cell phone videos of the encounter and cannot explain my apparent state of calmness. Inside my stomach was flip-flopping and I could feel my knees trembling, but on the videos, I am a solid rock by Dr. Wells's side. As for Dr. Wells, he appeared as relaxed as if he had just run into a colleague at the faculty dining room.

Tux and Aloha approached and, like the eighty-seven previous inspections, this one began the same way. Aloha said, "Hello, we are the Benushians. Are you happy?"

And then Dr. Wells gave the answer that the Benushians had not yet heard. "No, we are not happy."

Aloha jerked his head slightly to one side. "You are not happy?" he asked.

"We are not happy at all," Dr. Wells said.

Neither Benushian spoke or moved. Dr. Wells raised his voice. "We are not happy." Then he glanced at me.

I thought I would swallow my tongue, but managed to say, "We are not happy." Then I repeated it louder. "We are not happy."

Around us some of the people moved away, the way folks slink out of a bar when a fight's brewing. But a few took up the shout, "We are not happy. We are not happy." It almost became a chant until Dr. Wells made a small cut-off motion with his hand and the beach fell into silence.

Tux took a step toward Dr. Wells. Tux's voice vibrated. "Why are you not happy?" he asked.

"We don't know what you want and we dislike not knowing. Not knowing makes us unhappy." Dr. Wells stood slightly slouched, his hands in his pockets as he spoke. "We are unhappy because we do not know why you are here."

"You would like to know why we are here?" Tux asked.

"Yes."

"And that would make you happy?"

Dr. Wells shifted his stance. "It would make us happier."

"Then we shall tell you," Tux said, his voice jaunty. "We are here —"

"Wait," Dr. Wells interrupted. "All the people on Earth want to know this. We should do an interview, a formal interview where we can ask questions and you will answer those questions."

"This would make you happy?" Tux asked.

"Happier," Dr. Wells said.

"Then we will answer your questions and make you happy." As Tux spoke a weird echo effect began and I realized that Tux's voice was coming from the cell phones of the people around us. So began the third Benushian world-wide broadcast: Dr. Wells' interview with Tux.

Dr. Wells didn't hesitate. "Why did the Benushians come to Earth? Why are you here?"

Tux didn't hesitate either. "Human head colds."

"Head colds? What about them?"

"Humans produce mucus when they are ill." I could swear that Tux smiled a little, though when I reviewed the broadcast later I didn't see it. "When you are sick, when you have a head cold, when you have congestion, you make mucus in your sinus areas."

"And why does that interest you?"

"Sinus mucus is tasty," Tux replied.

Dr. Wells' eyes widened, but his voice was calm, as if talking with an alien about mucus was as normal as talking with a neighbor about weather. "So when we are sick, when mucus comes from our nose, you want that?"

Tux cocked his head to one side. "No, that is expelled mucus. We harvest fresh head cold mucus."

"Fresh head cold mucus," Dr. Wells repeated.

"Head cold mucus is best."

"How do you harvest it?" asked Dr. Wells.

"Like this," Tux's blue, rubbery body seemed to expand and stretched past me to a teenage girl. She wore a t-shirt and shorts and, in her hand, she held a tissue against her running nose. A moment later her headless body fell to the ground. Seconds after that, the body itself disappeared. "She has been harvested." Tux said.

Christine Berry, age seventeen, trumpet player, co-editor of her high school paper and life-long resident of Hilton Head, South Carolina, USA, was the first person on Earth confirmed to be killed by the Benushians.

Several of the people around us screamed and ran, but Dr. Wells didn't move, so neither did I. My legs would not have worked anyway.

"What did you just do?" Dr. Wells asked. His hand was shaking in his sweater pocket.

"She has been harvested," Tux said. "Are you happy?"

Dr. Wells shook his head. "No. More details, please."

Tux cocked his head to one side again. "Her mucus-filled head has been harvested for consumption. Her body has been discarded on your moon as excessive waste."

"Why head mucus? What's so special about it?"

Here Aloha stepped forward. "Human head with mucus is yummy, yummy good." Tux nodded and together they did a swaying little dance, like they were in a commercial. I couldn't take it.

"But you can't just take our heads and eat them." I said.

"Why not?" Tux asked. Both aliens shifted their attention to me, which was not what I wanted at all. I turned to Dr. Wells, but he nodded at me. Now I was to represent the human race to aliens who thought of us as cheese on a cracker.

"Because we are human beings," I said. "We are sentient like you. We think. We have feelings. We want to live."

"Cows, pigs, lambs, goats, bison, elk, birds and fish wish to live. You eat them." Tux said.

"But those are animals. We're human beings."

Tux nodded. There was no mistaking the toothless smile on his face. "Yes, you are human beings," he said. "And we are Benushians."

Tux and Aloha gave their synchronized friendly wave and disappeared.

And thus was announced the new food chain on Earth.

Dr. Wells and I tried to get off the beach, but crowds of people were running and screaming around us. Some kept grabbing at Dr. Wells and I kept shoving them away. My head started pounding and I felt a whopper of a headache coming on. By the time we hit the street where I had parked the car I thought I was going to pass out. Dr. Wells put his arm around me. "It'll be all right," he said.

As I unlocked the doors to the car a local news crew approached. They had gotten to the beach just as the Benushians disappeared and said they had been looking for us "like crazy" to get an interview. I wanted to leave, but Dr. Wells leaned against the car trunk and waited as they set up their cameras.

The entire seven minute interview can be found online, but what went around the world and was endlessly repeated, was Dr. Wells' response to the reporter's first question, "What does this mean?"

Dr. Wells responded, "What do we know? We know the Benushians stopped mass killings and cleaned up our land, water and air. And we know they want to consume our heads — if filled with mucus — by 'harvesting' us when we're sick. So what does it mean? It means we're like free range chickens. We're not confined in an overcrowded filthy chicken coop. We get to go where we want, cluck around in a healthy environment and peck away, living our happy lives… until it's time to be eaten."

This is what happened on our drive back to Oberdine. In the first two hours every radio station was broadcasting our talk with Tux and Aloha, or describing Christine Berry's murder or playing Dr. Wells' free range chickens comment.

By the third hour the United States, China, Russia and the United Kingdom launched fighter jets against Benushian ships. Dr. Wells and I heard the roar of the U.S. fighter jets as they flew south toward the Hilton Head ship from bases near Washington D.C. Each attack had the same result. The jets disappeared from the sky, presumably to be deposited on the moon as "excessive waste." Likewise, ballistic missiles fired from submarines and ground silos.

In the fourth hour the United States, China, Russia and the United Kingdom each issued statements blaming the attacks on a conspiracy of rogue military officers and thanked the Benushians for their restrained response.

By the fifth and sixth hours there were numerous reports from across the United States and the world of panic buying. Cans of chicken soup were selling online for three hundred fifty dollars (by the next day they would sell for twelve thousand, five hundred dollars). Store shelves were being stripped of soups, tea bags and over the counter cold remedies. A gang of armed men in Pahokee, Florida robbed a pharmacy at gun point taking their entire stock of antibiotics.

It was the soup story that got to me. I had a strong urge to get off the highway at the next exit, find the nearest super store and stock up. We were down to half a tank and could buy fuel too. When we pulled off I saw a sign for a Mega-Deals store. I asked Dr. Wells if he would mind stopping there. He shrugged. "If you want to," he said.

Though the parking lot was easily the size of several football fields and had hundreds of spaces, we couldn't get in. Cars were backed up into the street blocking lanes of traffic and we could see a line of people waiting to get into the store.

Police officers were trying to control the chaos. Dr. Wells shook his head. "Not necessary," he said.

"No?" As a would-be sociologist I knew panic was catching, its own special virus, but at that moment my immunity was low. I eyed the line and wondered if there was a way to slip through.

Dr. Wells stretched his arms and yawned. "Think about it," he said. "If you were a livestock farmer, what concerns you the most?"

I tore my eyes from the line and glanced at Dr. Wells. He took a granola bar from his pocket, unwrapped it and began munching.

"The health and well-being of the livestock," I said.

"Right. So will the Benushians let us go hungry or suffer from shortages?"

I felt my shoulders relax as I rested my hands on the steering wheel. "No. But they will kill us if we get a bad cold." I focused on the line again. "From an individual perspective, buying chicken soup and cold medicine makes sense."

"Do you think so?"

"You don't?" I was too tired to play student.

Dr. Wells said, "Do we wait for cows to die naturally before we turn them into beef? Or pigs before they become our pork?"

I turned to him. He had on his teacher smile, the one he used in class to encourage students, but his eyes were serious.

"They're not going to wait for us to get sick on our own, are they?" I asked.

"No."

And I knew he was right. The Benushians would make us sick whenever their harvesting required it. Hot tea wasn't going to help. I pulled out of the line for Mega-Deals and drove back to the highway. We turned off the radio.

When we were forty-five minutes away from Oberdine we really did need to gas up. I pulled off at an independent station and convenience store called, "Molly's." It had a big sign that said, "Truckers Welcome." After I gassed up the car we both wanted to stretch our legs, so I parked and we went inside. The super stores weren't alone in being hit by panic buyers. Molly's was stripped. About the only items left on the shelves were plastic rain ponchos, baseball caps and a small section with magazines.

To the far right was an alcove that housed a sandwich place, with a few tables, a counter and a menu hung on the wall. It was empty except for the woman behind the counter. Hanging high in the corner they had a television set mounted. Of course, the news was on. They were showing a video taken in London of a fighter jet streaking toward a Benushian ship, then disappearing from the sky. Cal was there. Though it seemed like a century since we said goodbye, he had left for London only yesterday. As I watched I felt my heart thudding.

"Let's get some lunch," Dr. Wells said.

The human race had just become an alien delicacy and he wanted a sub sandwich? I shook my head no. We had to go. We had to run, though I didn't know where.

"Oh c'mon," he said. "If the Benushians taught us anything, it's that everyone has to eat." He wiggled his eyebrows at me.

I laughed. "Okay."

We got our foot-long subs and sat at one of the tables where we both had a good view of the TV. Dr. Wells always ate faster than me and finished up just as I started on my second half. He excused himself to go to the restroom. After he left, a special bulletin came on that the President would address the nation in a few minutes. It was only when I finished my sandwich that I realized he had been gone for a while. I didn't want to miss the President's speech, but thought something might be wrong. Just as I stood up to check on him, he came out of the restroom. He walked with a quick step back to our table.

"Are you okay?" I asked.

He sat down. "Fine." He gestured toward the TV. "Anything new?"

"The President's going to speak," I said.

"I'm sure she'll have a marvelous plan." We both laughed.

In her speech President Margolis announced that she was activating the Pandemic Protocols as allowed by the Pandemic Emergency Powers Act of 2029. But then the President paused. She swallowed a few times and her right hand clenched into a fist.

She said, "I'm sorry to report that here in the United States and in other parts of the world, it appears that people are falling ill at high numbers. This illness comes upon the victim rapidly —" she took in a deep breath, "— and it has all the symptoms of a bad head cold."

"So we passed inspection," I said. Dr. Wells gave me a sharp look.

He started to say something, but stopped. Then he pointed at the TV. "Let's listen."

"We are calling it the Benushian Flu," the President said. She promised that all resources would be devoted to finding a cure or vaccine.

I shook my head. "Why bother? If we find a cure for this flu, they'll send us another."

Dr. Wells said, "Human nature. When you can't do anything, you still try something."

An hour later we were back at Oberdine. I headed toward the Sociology Building to drop Dr. Wells off by his car. As we passed the Student Union, we saw about a dozen students in the front lawn. They were in a circle holding hands, already breaking the Pandemic Protocols. I assumed it was a prayer circle, but most of them were crying.

"The chickens aren't happy right now," I said.

Dr. Wells grabbed my arm with such force that the steering wheel turned. I slammed on the brake. Fortunately, no one was behind us.

"What?" I asked.

"What you said. 'Unhappy chickens.'"

"What about it?"

He stared at me, lips pressed tight. Then he let go of my arm and leaned back into the car seat. "Just an idea," he said. "Let me think about it."

The Benushian Flu killed people in about eight hours. To be more exact, the Benushians killed people about eight hours after the infection took hold. By that time, the sick person was producing so much mucus a continual thick drip would clog the throat and emerge from the nose. Some people who got infected streamed their misery live on the internet, even adding a timer clock so viewers would know when they were close to the eight hour mark. Then the head would disappear, followed seconds later by the body. Another Benushian snack, another moon dump.

Though it is impossible to determine an exact number, based on available data the World Health Organization estimated that during their first two days of "harvesting," the Benushians killed approximately a million, six hundred fifty thousand human beings. The U.S. government estimated that ninety-five thousand Americans were harvested.

And I think Cal is dead.

The last text he sent me said, "I'm at the Globe Theatre. It's a replica built where Shakespeare's original theatre stood, but I pretend it is the real thing, that Shakespeare is in the wings wringing his hands, and the premiere of MacBeth is about to start. And that I wait for you and we will watch it together. There's a tickle in my throat and my head feels stuffy. I think I have IT. I love you. If you don't hear from me in eight hours, please call my parents."

That was yesterday. I didn't hear from Cal. I did call his parents. I can't write more about that.

On television, the U.S. Secretary of Agriculture, Jefferson Hemming, became a star. He asserted that the Benushians won't kill all of us, their livestock, but would leave enough people alive for breeding and the continuation of the species.

"Our population will go down, but this isn't the end of the human race," Hemming said.

As for Dr. Wells, he didn't come to campus for two days. I assumed he was tired after our trip or possibly depressed like so many. I called him at his home and offered to bring supplies. Cal had left me the key to his apartment and his cupboards were full, so I wouldn't have to fight the craziness at the stores.

Dr. Wells said, "Don't bother bringing anything, but come over tomorrow. There's something I'm working on. You should know about it." I pressed him for details, but he said, "Just come over."

I showed up at his house around 11 a.m. Cal had four chicken soup cans in his kitchen. I put two in a bag for Dr. Wells and filled it with other goodies, the granola bars he liked, some other soups, instant hot chocolate packets, a half filled orange juice container from my refrigerator, apples, bananas, canned fruit and several tuna cans. Cal also had chewable multi-vitamins and over the counter cold medicine, some zinc lozenges and liquid medicine. I split those with Dr. Wells too.

I was holding the bag with both hands so I kicked on his front door instead of knocking. There was no response. I did it again. Still nothing. So I swung the bag to one hip for support and tried the door knob. It turned and the door opened. *Damn*, I thought. I dropped the bag on the floor near the front door and bolted inside. "Dr. Wells," I called. No answer.

The front door hallway went by the kitchen and led to the living room. Since his wife died, Dr. Wells had converted the living room to his home work space. It still had a couch against one wall and a large screen TV hanging on the opposite wall, but protruding into the middle of the room, facing the window overlooking the backyard, was Dr. Wells' old fashioned large wooden oak desk and a smaller rolling desk with his computer and printer. He had also dragged in one file cabinet and bookshelf which he stuck in the corners. Most people would think it was crowded and messy, but I considered it a great use of living room space.

I was about to yell, "Dr. Wells," again when I saw him. He was lying on the couch, propped up by pillows. Sheets of paper were on the floor and on the couch. A roll of toilet paper was resting on his stomach, with several crumpled pieces scattered near him. His eyes were red-rimmed and teary.

As I entered the living room he raised his hand to stop me. He tried to say something, but coughed. He held a piece of toilet paper to his mouth and a big glob of mucus came out. "Oh no," I said. "No."

He said, "Don't come any closer," but his voice was low and strange, like he was speaking from a phone that was underwater. Then he coughed again, but this time couldn't stop. It went on and on. His face turned a bright red, with his tufts of hair bouncing with each spasm.

My brain screamed at me to stay back, but my body rushed to his side. I straightened him up, leaned him against me and pounded between his shoulder blades. It didn't help. Back in my junior year I took a CPR class. The first rule is to clear the airway. I rested him back against the pillows and said, "Open your mouth."

He shook his head and tried to push me away. But then he had an explosive cough and I forced my fingers inside his mouth. "Don't move," I said. I felt a sticky blob of mucus and with two fingers began to slowly extract it. It was thicker than normal mucus and stretched out like an endless piece of bubble gum, long and unbroken, and had the consistency of pizza-top melted cheese. I kept gently pulling and more kept coming, enough to fill a cereal bowl, until finally it stopped. Dr. Wells began to take short, fast breaths. I didn't want to leave him alone, but I knew I had to wash my hands. At the bathroom sink I forced myself to be thorough, making sure soap soaked all across my fingers and hands.

When I returned to the living room the red splotches on Dr. Wells' face had faded. "I wish you hadn't done that," he said, his voice hoarse. "You're exposed now." He was right, but it was too late now. I sat on the edge of the couch next to him.

For a few minutes we didn't speak. He had small coughing fits, but not like before. Finally, I asked, "How long?"

"Pretty soon, I think," he answered. I began to cry. He smiled and squeezed my arm. "No tears yet," he said. "There's work to do."

He tried to get up, but sagged back against the pillows. Then he pointed to a legal sized pad of yellow paper that was on the floor near the couch. I picked it up and handed it to him, but he pushed it at me. The notes were all in his handwriting, messy but legible.

In big letters he had written four lines across the top page:

"Molly's Tues. 2pm, B-room"
"BETH."
"2nd Inspec final – When?"
"Fail??????"

I glanced at Dr. Wells. He stared at me. He was clogging up again and his breathing was growing ragged. I reread the page. The third line had my attention.

"Second inspection? A second Benushian inspection? A final one?" I asked.

He tried to speak, but sneezed instead. Then he began hacking. When it finally stopped he nodded his head.

"How do you know?"

This time he managed to whisper, "Beth."

"Who's Beth?" I asked.

He could barely speak, but choked out, "Peter." I glanced down on the legal pad. The only names listed were "BETH" and "Molly's."

"Who's Peter?"

He shook his head and his eyes got watery. He tried to lift himself, but couldn't. Then dragging out both syllables, he said, "Pee-ta."

"Pee-ta," I repeated. Then it hit me. I jumped off the couch. "PETA — People for the Ethical Treatment of Animals?"

They were one of the world's best known animal rights organization and had been around for years. Their protests and activism were part of the reason chicken farms now had free range chickens.

I peered down at the yellow legal pad still in my hand. "*BETH*? Benushians for the Ethical Treatment of Humans?" I looked up at Dr. Wells. He was smiling and nodding his head. "And Molly's… the gas station?" I remembered how he had spent so much time in the restroom — no, the "B-room" — the bathroom.

I leaned down next to him. "Did you meet a Benushian in the bathroom at Molly's?" Dr. Wells took my hand and using his finger as an imaginary pen, he wrote, "A+" against my palm.

He had a coughing fit then and it was a bad one. When it ended he collapsed even deeper into the couch. He began taking deep sucking breaths. I knelt next to him.

"I love you, Dr. Wells." With his thumb he caught one of my tears and wiped it away. Then with his other hand, he took the legal pad from me.

He smiled and whispered, "My best student." A moment later his head disappeared. Then his body vanished, off to the moon.

I stayed on the floor a long time. When my eyes finally cleared I saw that the legal pad had fallen on the floor face up. I studied it, the last words written by Dr. Wells, and traced my fingers across the letters. Then I traced the letters again.

Something wasn't right. My fingers paused on the first line. Dr. Wells had written, "*Molly's Tues. 2pm, B-room.*" But the day we were at Hilton Head and stopped at Molly's was two weeks to the day after the Benushians arrival, a Wednesday.

I straightened and felt my eyes go wide. Dr. Wells had made an appointment! He was supposed to meet a sympathetic Benushian three days from now: Tuesday at Molly's, men's bathroom, 2 p.m. He'd nicknamed her BETH, comparing her to our own animal rights advocates. I glanced back at the legal pad. *"2nd Inspec final – When?"* Was BETH going to provide him with the date of the Benushians' second inspection, the final one? Like a good academician, I tried to come up with alternate and better explanations, but no other interpretation made sense.

I stared at the paper again. The last line was the most important: *"Fail??????"* Knowing the date of the final inspection would be meaningless if we couldn't fail it. That must have been what Dr. Wells was working on. But he died before he could tell me his idea — if he had one. Then I noticed there was a smudge on the paper. I held up the pad and angled it so the paper would catch the light from the window. It was water, a tiny little drop of water, spread across the last two question marks; my teardrop on Dr. Wells' thumb. I leaned back on the floor, turned my face to the heavens and sent a mental thank you to Dr. Wells. The man was brilliant.

We can't beat the Benushians with bombs or jet planes or anger, but we can use empathy. Some part of Benushian society has a conscience or else they wouldn't have focused on our happiness during their first inspection. And BETH, apparently acting in secret, would not have reached out to Dr. Wells. How many Benushians feel like BETH? How many do we have to convince? We can't throw fists or rocks or missiles, but we can weaponize our tears.

When the Benushians' final inspection begins, we need a world-wide cry-in, with everyone involved. We must burst into tears and wail and rip at our clothes. We must cry for the lost and humanity's fate; cry for the Benushians' failure to recognize us as relevant. We must be so sad that even hungry Benushians will refuse human heads. Through our falling tears we'll force them to acknowledge that Earth people deserve dignity and consideration; that we too are part of this universe and worthy of life.

So Javon and Anita, on Tuesday afternoon, will you go to Molly's and meet BETH? (2 p.m., men's restroom.) I would go, but I have a tickle in my throat and my head feels stuffy. Try my phone once more, but I doubt I'll answer. I'm calling on you because you are my only students still on campus. I checked your social media pages. You were both still posting yesterday, so I'm hoping you are alive now.

You'll need to find out the date of the final inspection. Think carefully before you tell people. There's a reason why BETH chose to meet Dr. Wells in secret. Maybe Aloha and Tux would cancel the final inspection if they knew she leaked the information to us. Ask her about timing. When you decide it is best, post this paper on the "Sociology Today" website and attach Dr. Wells' name to it. That should get it around the world.

There are four cans of chicken soup and some cold medicine in the bottom desk drawer. They're yours. If you do get sick, hand this assignment off to someone else.

Good luck. And remember, everyone has to cry.

Elaine Midcoh Biography

Elaine Midcoh loves reading and writing science fiction short stories. She's a past winner of the Jim Baen Memorial Short Story Award and "The Writers of the Future" contest. Her sci-fi stories have appeared in the anthologies, "Writers of the Future, Volumes 37 & 39" (Galaxy Press) and "Compelling Science Fiction Short Stories" (Flame Tree Press) and in the magazines *MetaStellar, Escape Pod, Galaxy's Edge* and *Daily Science Fiction*. Before jumping into writing, she worked as a college professor where she spent many happy years teaching criminal justice and law courses. She lives in South Florida.

The Graveyard of Empires

Jacob Sharp

When you're wounded and left on Afghanistan's plains,
And the women come out to cut up what remains,
Jest roll to your rifle and blow out your brains
An' go to your Gawd like a soldier.
 - Rudyard Kipling, The Young British Soldier

***

Nothing ever happened on tower guard.

Specialist John Richard Bustamante, (Dick to his friends), stared through the thick bulletproof glass that ringed the pre-fabricated watch tower. The glass, somewhat comfortingly, showed evidence of previous gunfights, the spider-webbed impacts obstructing his view.

"Fuck this fucking shit, man," he said out loud.

The Pine cigarette cradled between his fingers grew hot as the cherry blazed ever-closer to the filter. He looked down and raised it to his lips. Taking a quick puff, he savored the last blast of weak nicotine before plucking the next cigarette from the crumpled pack. Using the dying cigarette's tip to light the fresh one, he inhaled deeply, savoring the brief nicotine hit before remembering how shitty the Pines tasted compared to good old-fashioned American cigs.

"Fuck this fucking shit."

He looked up, scanning the Afghan countryside through the dust-crusted glass. The land would be beautiful if it wasn't for the war. The pristine slopes of the adjacent mountain, rising defiantly above Combat Outpost Springbok, would be the source of millions of dollars of good old-fashioned greenbacks, if the right investors were involved. Being mineral rich, the mountains would be prime real estate for some greasy investor back in the States. He adjusted his gaze, the sweat-crusted Advanced Combat Helmet with its attached night vision grinding into his skull, reminding him that he was a soldier with a job to do. He looked nearly straight down at the entry control point below him. The HESCO bunker held two soldiers, their presence indicated in the darkness only by the occasional flaring of their own cigarettes, which reflected off the long barrel of the M2 .50 caliber machine gun that guarded the serpentine barricades denoting the Combat Outpost's entrance.

"Well, they're still fucking there. Must be nice to have heat." Dick shivered as he remembered the icy mountain air that gusted through the COP. "We checked nearby. Now let's expand out."

He raised his head slightly, following the serpentine entrance to the access road that enabled traffic from Afghanistan's bustling 'Highway 1' to enter the COP. At this time of night, it was empty, *dead empty*, the NATO-funded contracted drivers who frequented it having long since holed up in the safety of American combat outposts, hiding by night from their Taliban adversaries. Road secured, he looked further out, observing the small hills that dotted the countryside between COP Springbok and the mountains beyond. On the nearest hill jutted the old British fort, a relic of the second Anglo-Afghan War. By day, the fort practically blended in with the countryside, historical set-dressing for a nation stuck in the nineteenth century. The only eye-catching portion of the fort were the fluttering flags of the adjacent Afghan grave site, the bodies resting there likely dating back to the very war that resulted in the walls nearby. By night, however, the fort took on a completely different appearance, looking like a giant grave stone in the darkness, its dark gun ports gaping maws, strange glimpses into the past.

Specialist Bustamente frequently found himself staring at the fort, whose name had vanished over the last century. He thought back to his two misspent years seeking higher education, *get a degree in anything*, they had told him. He took their advice (and their loans), and invested sixty-three credit hours into a history major before he realized he wasn't cut out for evaluating the role of female property investment in the thirteenth century and its impact on medieval society. He had dropped out and joined the Army one month into his sophomore year. The dated recruiting videos didn't sway him, but those gunfight videos on the internet sure did.

Despite not getting the degree, the knowledge he gained hadn't yet leaked out of his brain. The Anglo-Afghan Wars had been covered in depth during his History of Colonialism course. The Brits' many overseas endeavors had always been interesting. While knowing a thousand fun factoids about the Sepoy Mutiny and the Boxer Rebellion may not have gotten him any girls at Joe's Tavern back in Watertown, it sure made for fun conversation with his enlisted friends.

Eighteen-year-old Privates were easier to impress.

The wind picked up, howling through the incomplete seal provided by the shoddily constructed tower door, the military industrial complex's shortcomings on full display. His teeth chattered.

"Fuck this fucking shit."

He scanned even further outwards, taking in the empty countryside, but the old fort always drew him back in. *How fucking crazy is it that those guys were pulling their own guard shifts just over there. Fucking nuts.* The glow that illuminated his green night vision goggles stopped his thoughts short.

"What the fuck was that?" he whispered, his eyes narrowing as he concentrated on the irregularity.

Nobody lived in the fort, he knew that. The Afghan National Army commander himself had told the commander to respectfully fuck off when it was suggested at the beginning of their deployment, their tribal superstitions outweighing the tactical advantage it offered.

Who the fuck was in there?

The brief glow appeared again, this time from an adjacent gun port. *It was so short, almost like a... a pipe? A cigarette?*

He had seen that glow before. Somebody was smoking in the fort. Were they watching him? Waiting on a good opportunity for an attack?

Bullshit.

There was no fucking way. Nobody entered the fort, not even the enemy. The ANA commander had said as much. Bustamente squinted into the darkness, the grainy green glow of the night vision feeding the migraine that had started hours earlier.

"Fuck this fucking shit. Nothing ever happens on fucking tower guard."

He looked down at the Pine, which had burned nearly to the filter without him even taking a puff. "Shitass fucking haji cigarettes," he cursed, flicking the butt to the ground. *Let's get some American nicotine going.* Bustamente pulled the can of Copenhagen Wintergreen from his right ankle pocket, then smacked it against his hand to pack the contents. He had never learned to pack it properly like the southern boys in the company had.

Who the fuck cares, he thought, *nicotine is nicotine.*

He pinched the moist tobacco between his thumb and index finger then shoved it into his lips; the nicotine hit spiking into his brain. He reclined into his chair and looked back at the old ruined fort, half expecting to see another light. The structure was dark, just as dark as it had ever been, its mud-brick walls seemingly bone white in the reflection of the moonlight.

Bustamente saw the flash before he heard the deep booming report. The gun port that had previously housed the light source erupted, flame belching outwards towards the COP.

"What the fu —"

The incoming explosion rocked the tower, sending a mound of dirt and debris swirling into the sky. The P25 radio, used for COP-internal communications, flared to life, the Sergeant of the Guard rattling off questions.

"TOWER ONE THIS IS SOG, BREAK, WHAT THE FUCK WAS THAT, OVER?"

Bustamente realized he was on the ground. He stood quickly, scanning the horizon, then ducked again as a fresh spiderweb appeared on the bulletproof glass before him, the fat slug of an incoming round seemingly stuck in the thick pane.

"SOG this is Tower One, we are taking incoming fire from the fort, RPGs and small arms, over."

The P25 beeped as he let off the button. He raised up slightly, finally remembering the MK48 machine gun which rested on the window's ledge. He slid the firing port open and aimed outwards towards where the flash had been, then yanked on the trigger and let the gun eat.

ACK ACK ACK, ACK ACK ACK ACK ACK

The visible tracers streamed out of the gun towards the fort before impacting rock and streaking upwards into the sky. He kept firing, round after round hitting in and around the firing port where he had seen the flash. Below him, the entry control point began firing as well, their sympathetic actions sending hulking .50 caliber rounds roaring through the countryside.

"TOWER ONE AND ECP, THIS IS SOG, CEASE FIRE, I SAY AGAIN CEASE FIRE, OVER."

Specialist Bustamente ripped through the rest of the MK48's one hundred round belt before coming to a stop. The entry control point followed suit, and soon enough, the echo of the outgoing fire receding down the valley was the only perceivable sound. Bustamente examined the cracked bulletproof glass, seeing the massive slug still stuck where it had impacted. He reached his arm through the open firing port and pulled it out of the glass, the fat chunk of lead still warm to the touch. He flipped up his PVS-14 night vision goggles and turned on the Petzl headlamp that hung around his neck to inspect it.

This is fucking massive! he thought, turning the round slowly between his fingers.

The slug was unlike any he had ever seen. Unlike modern bullets, the slug appeared to have been cast from a solid chunk of lead, its large diameter appearing closer to a .50 caliber round than the 7.62 that Taliban normally fired out of their AK47s. The bullet's conical nose had been smashed flat by the impact, but the deep-cut ridges on its base were still clear.

He had seen something like this before.

Bustamente closed his eyes, thinking back to the vacation his dad had insisted on dragging the whole family on during his youth. The trip had gone through Amish Country in Pennsylvania, trailing through a series of Civil War battlefields, and ended in Washington DC, with full tours through the Smithsonian museums. He concentrated, thinking back to the exhibit at Gettysburg that discussed the weapons used by both North and South.

This is a fucking Minié ball!

The massive chunk of lead was a dead ringer for the old conical bullets of Civil War fame. *How the fuck did this get here?*

He shoved the bullet in his pocket then quickly reloaded the MK48, slamming the feed tray cover closed over the fresh belt of ammunition.

"SOG this is Tower One, no more incoming fire at present, over."

The radio crackled to life in response, "Roger Tower One. I'm in route to you to get a debrief. We're spinning up a quick reaction force to go check it out. Were they *in* the fort, over?"

"Roger SOG, the fire was coming from the top level, over." With the communications complete, he settled in and watched the inevitable show.

The QRF spun up like a well-oiled machine, mounting vehicles and rolling through the entry control point. Bustamente watched through his night vision as the platoon cautiously approached the old fort. The men dismounted from their vehicles, their infrared lasers moving vigorously across every possible enemy hiding spot. They entered the fort's rotten gate, vanishing temporarily before reappearing on the fort's ramparts. The men looked around for some time before leaving the structure and remounting their vehicles, which filed back into COP Springbok one by one.

The shaking of the shoddy steel stairs and the movement of the cut up HESCO barricades which shielded the entrance long-preceded his relief. Private First Class Hargrove poked his blonde head through the door, the fat dip in his lip noticeably obstructing his speech.

"Heard you got into a fucking gunfight up here, Dick!"

"Hell yeah, man," he responded. "Those pricks launched a fucking RPG or something at us."

"Fuck yeah, brother. That's some good shit. Well, hopefully that's all of it for tonight. I'm trying to catch up on my reading." Hargrove grinned deeply, then flashed a book from under his uniform blouse, as if he was a drug dealer showing off his wares. The dragon on the cover reflected the light from his headlamp.

"They're making an HBO series about this motherfucker and I plan on being spun up!" he said, smile widening.

"Nice. I'll have to get to that one next." Bustamente grabbed his assault pack and walked to the door. "Have a safe shift, man," he said.

Arriving at the Tactical Operations Center, Bustamente saw that the normal TOC-roaches were on duty. The motley crew of tired lower enlisted stared meekly at the door, averting their gaze as quickly as it landed on him. The Sergeant-of-the-Guard, a fiery Puerto Rican named Jose Acevado, stormed towards him, his heavy footsteps shaking the plywood floor of the hut.

"What the FUCK were you shooting at, Specialist?", the Sergeant demanded.

"Wha — I was shooting at the enemy? Sergeant I'm not su —"

"You're god-damned fucking right you aren't sure!"

The attack was completely unwarranted. Here he had just survived a rocket attack and now he was being questioned? The SOG came at him again.

"I'll ask you one more time, Specialist, what the fuck were you engaging?!"

"I —" he paused, confused, *I literally called up the fucking contact,* "I enga —"

"You know what?" the Sergeant interrupted. "I don't give a shit what your excuse is. Do you think it's acceptable to blast up the God damned countryside just because you fucking feel like it? Is that what the fuck we're doing here? The fucking QRF cleared that whole fucking fortress and didn't find shit. They didn't find shooters, they didn't find cartridge casings, they didn't find cigarette butts, nothing! In fact, they walked through spider webs getting into that fucking place. Afghans don't go to the fort, not even Taliban, they're fucking scared of it! Not only that, but the ECP tells me they didn't hear a God damned thing until you started ripping off with that MK48. No incoming, no explosions, not shit! So tell me again, Specialist Bustamente, what the FUCK were you shooting at?"

Bustamente was floored.

"Sergeant with all due respect, not only was I being shot at, but I have an incoming round in my pocket."

The Sergeant stopped, looking curiously towards the hand that slowly moved into the pants pocket.

"Oh? Show me then."

He slipped his hand into the pocket where he had put the Minié ball.

It was empty.

There was no hole, no possible way the round could have escaped, his pocket was just *empty.* His face paled. The Sergeant, noticing the change in his demeanor, grew flush with anger.

"You fucking bullshitter."

"Sergeant I —"

"Don't say a fucking word to me. You're gonna get fifteen-sixed over this shit and you'll be fucking lucky if you make it through without catching a charge. Hope you enjoyed that free rank while you had it, college boy. Get the fuck out of here."

Bustamente left the TOC in a daze. As the door slammed behind him, pulled close by its water bottle pulley system, he felt the crisp night air hit his face. He was flush with embarrassment and shame. He instinctively lit a cigarette with shaking hands, inhaling the acrid smoke deeply before stepping off towards his platoon's hut. Had he been mistaken? Did he really imagine incoming fire?

There's no fucking way, he thought, *I felt the tower shake. I saw the flash. There was the bullet!*

The bullet. Where had that gone? It must have fallen out on the walk from the tower to the TOC, but how? He pulled open the door to the third platoon hut and made his way to the small room he shared with Hargrove. Third Platoon was on force protection cycle this week, so they hadn't been on the QRF. At this hour the hut was mostly quiet. He could vaguely hear hushed voices arguing over a video game in the room across the hall.

Bustamente stripped off his armor and helmet and hung it on the cross they had built out of scrap wood. He took off his uniform top and unlaced his boots, then sat on his bunk, dejectedly brushing the 'moon dust' off his M4 carbine, his last task before bedding down. Someone knocked softly on his door.

"Dick, you in there?" The door cracked open, and Sergeant Brad White, his team leader, poked his head in. "Got a minute to talk?"

Fuck me running, "Yeah Sergeant, come on in."

White shut the door softly behind him and glanced around, flipping own the camouflage field stool that had leaned against the wall. He sat.

"Drop the Sergeant shit, Dick, what happened out there?"

Bustamente's shoulders sagged, "The tower got hit, I swear to God it did. Something, *someone* in the old fort shot a fucking RPG or recoilless at the tower then apparently dipped. I called it up and shot back, just like we're supposed to!" He felt his heart pounding in his chest, "I'm not lying about it! You know me Brad, why would I make some shit up like that?"

White sat silent for a moment, bringing his spitter to his lips. "If you say you got engaged, I believe you. I just wanted to make sure you were okay."

"Yeah, well Acevado said I'm getting investigated and losing rank. He tore my ass open in front of the whole TOC, called me a liar, said there wasn't anything there at all."

"Fuck Acevado," White said, grinning. "That motherfucker wouldn't know what a gunfight looked like if it happened in his lap. He's the landing zone NCO for a reason...."

"Yeah, well, I'm still worried about it. I had a bullet and everything but it must have fallen out of my pocket. I can show you the tower glass where the round hit tomorrow, *it was real, Brad,* I swear to fuck."

"Calm down, man. I said I believed you. SSG Robertson already talked to the platoon leader, you're fine. Don't worry about it. Clean your shit and get some rest, we go back on mission cycle tomorrow and we've got a presence patrol planned. I'm gonna need you as a dismount."

"Okay."

White stood and turned towards the door, "These stools fucking suck by the way, I never understood the appeal."

"Yeah, yeah, see you tomorrow, man."

As the door closed behind his team leader, Bustamente stared at the wall.

It was real. I know it was real.

***

The smell of diesel exhaust mixed with fine, talcum-like dust was overpowering. The high Afghan sun pounded COP Springbok's rudimentary motor pool, its hot rays warming the bustling, camouflage-clad soldiers as they made their final checks and preparations. Six months ago, when they had arrived in-country, the heady eighty-three foot elevation paired with the wildly foreign sights and smells were dizzying to the point of incapacitation, but as their deployment had drawn on, they became the norm. Bustamente hauled himself up into the back seat of the MATV and did a cursory check of its contents.

Tied-down ammo cans for the truck's .50 cal? check.

Cases of water? Check.

Case of Rip-It energy drinks? Check, check, check.

From the passenger's seat up front, Sergeant White flipped switches and turned knobs, checking the truck's various communications and tracking systems. "Roger Baker Six Romeo, I've got you lima charlie, over," he said. From his swinging canvas seat in the turret, Hargrove poked his head down into the truck's cab, a wide grin plastered across his face.

"You shoulda said lickin' chicken Sarn't." He stuck an invisible handset to his ear and changed his voice, "Roger Baker Six Romeo, we have you lickin' chicken!" The youthful private's mischievous giggle contrasted with his faded helmet and the dip spit that stained his lips.

"Yeah, that's exactly what we need, Hargrove," White responded, "more fucking attention. I've been your team leader for a year now and you still haven't learned the most critical lesson of being a grunt."

Hargrove looked thoughtful. "Snitches get stitches?"

"No, you fuck, this isn't prison. Well, not technically. The most important rule is don't rock the fuckin' boat. Glide in, glide out, be the gray man, whatever you wanna call it. Speaking of gliding, did you lube that gun?"

Hargrove stood up, retrieving something, then popped back down, pointing the white spray bottle of CLP lubricant at his head, "Roger Sarn't! She's wetter than, well —"

"Stop before you embarrass yourself, virgin." Bustamente chided playfully. Hargrove flipped him off and vanished back up into his turret. Bustamante sat with his legs out of the truck's open door, watching Third Platoon's three other armored vehicle crews finish their final pre-combat checks. Soldiers patted each other down, counting loaded magazines, checking eye protection, making sure Camelbacks were full and batteries were fresh — and laid hands on all the other critical sundry required to perform combat operations in the desert. Only a portion of the platoon would be going out for this mission.

Bustamente looked down to light a cigarette. Raising his head, he came face to face with Doc Reyes, Third Platoon's medic, who had crept into his space while he wasn't looking. "Hey Dick, you were a history guy, right?" he asked.

"Jesus Christ, Doc, are you trying to give me a fuckin' heart attack?"

"Wah, wah, candyass mofucker. Anyways, answer my question, you studied history or some shit, right?" Reyes reached for the open pack of cigarettes in Bustamente's hand without asking, plucking one of the Pines out of the pack and sticking it in his mouth. "You got a light?"

"Shit man, you want me to smoke it for you too?" Bustamente lit the cupped cigarette. "Yeah, I studied history a bit, did a couple classes at least before I dropped out. Why, what's up?"

Reyes took a deep drag on the Pine, "Fuck these are nasty." He gestured with the cigarette towards the other soldiers checking each other's equipment. "You think the Greeks or the Romans or whatever did all this bullshit? Or what about those fucking French dudes or whatever that were here."

"French dudes that were here? The fuck do you mean."

"You know, those old colonizer assholes." Reyes pointed at the old fort. "You think they jumped through hoops every time they went out on a mish like we do?"

Bustamente had avoided looking at the fort all morning, instead keeping his head down and staying busy. He stared at the shadowed gunport where the incoming explosion had originated. In the bright light of the day, the large port looked like the eye socket of a sand-colored skull, staring down in judgement at COP Springbok.

Staring down at me.

"I'm talking to you, Dick, hello." Reyes flicked Bustamente's knee, "You okay, asshole? You need me to check you out or something? If you're going down from heat just let me know baby, I'll hit you with the old silver bullet to get that core temp reading, eh?" Reyes intimated the action with his thumb and forefinger.

Bustamente shook his head, breaking his eyes away from the fort, "Yeah you would like that, wouldn't you? Fuckin' fruitcake."

"MOUNT UP! MOUNT THE FUCK UP, WE'RE ROLLING!" Lieutenant Fredericks, the Third Platoon leader, waved his hand over his head from the front of the convoy.

Reyes took a final drag off the Pine and threw the half-smoked cigarette onto the ground, "Yeah, yeah. Anyways thanks for the smoke, professor. Maybe I'll get an answer next time." Slapping Bustamente on the knee, he turned and jogged back to his assigned truck.

Sergeant White turned back towards Bustamente, "Hey where the fuck is our driver, Dick? Check the back of the truck and get Fritts up here, we're fuckin' rolling."

"Yeah, rog," Bustamente replied. Standing on the truck's running board, he leaned towards the vehicle's bed where Specialist Fritts, the team's rifleman, was digging through his rucksack. "Fritts bro, we're rolling, leave that shit and get up here."

The darkhaired Specialist looked up, "I can't find my fucking Cope, man! I don't know where I put it. You want me to do a mission without Cope?"

Bustamente rolled his eyes, "I'll spot you some. Holy shit you people are beggars." Fritts smiled thankfully and jumped out of the bed and into his driver's seat. Bustamente pulled his headset over his helmet and shut the massive armored door, making doubly sure not to catch anything in it, a painful lesson best avoided. He leaned to his right and looked out through the thick front windows. The roar of the vehicles was dampened by the headset somewhat, but convoy operations were still exceptionally loud. The four truck convoy roared out of the gate, slithering through the serpentine barricades and onto the highway.

He thought back to the CONOPS brief. Today's mission was straight forward, ostensibly just a presence patrol. Third Platoon would take their four trucks and head down the main highway for about two miles before turning off onto one of the region's many unimproved back roads. They would follow this for another mile or so until the hit a small, unnamed village that they hadn't yet been to. Intelligence reports said it was a relatively safe area, but IEDs and the usual opposition wouldn't come as a surprise to anyone. Bustamente hoped it would be a quiet trip.

The roar of the engines turned into a drone as the convoy rolled down the recently cleared highway, leaving COP Springbok and the shadow of the old fort behind them. They weaved in and out of civilian traffic, the nearly identical white cars and Toyota trucks indistinguishable aside from the occasional Bollywood star or political figure's face plastered onto the back of a cracked rear windshield. He reached behind the seat and fetched out four Rip-Its, handing them out to the rest of the team. Cracking his own stubby can of caffeine and sugar open, he stared out the window at the passing countryside. As the terrain rolled on and the engines roared, he thought of his first time leaving the wire six months earlier.

Their very first mission in-country was supposed to be an easy one too.

The CONOPS for it was not much different than the one they had received today. Drive down the road, visit the out of the way town, and pull security while Lieutenant Fredericks conducted a key leader engagement. *Easy shit.* They had rolled out with a mixed platoon that day, with members of the outgoing unit doing 'left seat, right seat' rides to help acquaint the cherry platoon with their new area of operations.

He would have never considered zoning out on that first mission. From his turret, every Afghan they passed looked like an enemy. Every shadowed corner and dip in the highway looked like it was surely going to be the end of them. In this way, that mission was anticlimactic. Despite being on edge, the mixed platoon had made it to the KLE without any issues. The meeting went well; babies were kissed, hands were shaken, and they'd all hopped back on the highway and headed home, a job well done.

Bustamente remembered the radio call that had changed his life. *"I've got one adult male on the roadside, two hundred meters northwest, break."* The radio paused while COP Springbok's TOC relayed information from the live drone feed to the convoy, *"He's kneeling behind a berm, has a cellphone in hand, lead truck should be seeing him shortly, over."*

Sergeant White had grabbed his pant leg from below, jerking it to get his attention, "That's you, Dick, keep your fucking eyes open!" Bustamente's heart pounded under his armor. He scanned the horizon, noting the distance and direction that the TOC had called out.

There!

Bustamente could just see the man crouching, his white robe and black vest contrasting against the mottled rock and sand of his surroundings. White called out a command to the driver and the truck slowed. Bustamente cranked the turret around, facing the distant man, and placed his cheek on the stock of the mounted M240B machine gun. He squinted through the glass of the M145 scope and focused on the target.

"Sarn't White, he's holding something in front of his face," the man, seeing the convoy at a halt, appeared to grow frantic, looking quickly from side to side. "He's acting weird Sarn't, what do I do?"

"Wait one, Dick, let me confirm."

Bustamente could hear a radio conversation, but his attention was fully on the man in white. At this relatively short distance and through the magnification of his scope the details of the man were clear. His bushy gray beard fell to his chest, blowing from side to side in the heavy crosswind. The man's head and eyes darted from side to side, looking from the trucks back to the road, as if he was waiting on something to happen. He looked like any other old Afghan man, shriveled under a life time of poor nutrition and sun. Bustamente wondered what his name was, wondered if he had been alive when the Soviets were here. Had he been mujahideen? Was he a grandfather? Where did he live? Why was this old guy squatting in the bush instead of sitting on a recliner back in his house?

"Dick, hey Dick!" White pulled at his pant leg again, "Can you hear me? We're clear, shoot his ass."

He leaned forward against the gun, centered the scope's reticle on in the open section of his black vest, and pulled the trigger. Time seemed to slow. Bustamente rode the burst just like he had been taught, *die motherfucker die,* the seven round burst's report seemingly quiet thanks to auditory exclusion. At first the man didn't seem effected and Bustamente thought he had missed, but then the old man crumpled directly backwards in a heap, as if the strings had been cut from a puppet mid-show. The truck had erupted in cheers.

"First fuckin' kill of the deployment, bro!" Hargrove had said, handing up his pack of Marlboro Reds. Bustamente had lit the cigarette, his hands were completely still. He felt calm, at ease. Was he supposed to feel something? Wasn't killing a man supposed to be a life changing experience? Later that night in the platoon's B-hut he had asked Sergeant White, a veteran soldier with a prior tour under his belt about his own time in combat.

"I've never lost a minute of sleep over killing a man," White had said. "Think about it this way, if you hadn't stitched that fucker up, we'd all be dead. That truck would have been a smoking hulk. You saw the IED they pulled out of the road afterwards? That fuckin' thing was huge. If you kill somebody out here and they deserve it, you don't have a thing to worry about, or at least that's my take. You did the right thing, Dick. You did your fuckin' job."

The hand that reached back from the driver's seat and grabbed his helmet brought Bustamente back to the present. The swaying of the truck and the changing terrain outside the windows indicated that they had long since left the main highway. "Where's my dip, asshole?" Fritts said over the headset.

"Oh Jesus, you guys are fucking worthless." Bustamente reached into his cargo pocket, fishing around for his can of Copenhagen. He handed it forward and leaned as far back in the cramped seat as he could, stretching his legs out. As he brushed against the confines of the poorly designed seat, he felt something hard poking into his thigh. *What the fuck?* Fishing around in his pocket, his fingers closed around the distinct shape of the lead Minié ball. "I found it! Sarn't White, I found the fucking round from last night!"

"What?" White was leaning forward in his seat, craning his neck to better hear the radio chatter coming across the net, he held a hand up to indicate silence. "Fritts man, we're stopping here, this is it." White pointed to a section of the road, "Pull in over there. Hargrove, you're gonna be covering our six, shift your .50 towards the road in case anyone pulls up while we're dismounted. Dick, we're getting out. What were you saying?"

Bustamente dropped the bullet back into his pocket, grabbing his carbine from its spot wedged into the seat.

"Nothing Sarn't, I'll show you later." The truck came to a stop and the two men dismounted. Hargrove dropped down from his turret briefly to combat lock the doors behind them. When his head reappeared, he shouted down to Bustamente.

"Don't do too much work out there, asshole!" The young private smiled wide, returning Bustamente's one fingered salute.

"Lazy ass Hargrove, always in the turret. You're the private, you should be out here walking!" Bustamente left the two soldiers in the truck and jogged up to join White and the rest of the platoon, who were assembling near a low, mud-brick wall.

"It's kind of nice not being nut-to-butt in a MAXPRO, huh?" White said, nodding towards the platoon's larger vehicles, their rear ramps raising after having disgorged the remaining rifle squads. The squads acted automatically, the combat-seasoned soldiers instinctively moving to positions of cover while waiting on Lieutenant Fredericks' direction.

"Sergeant White," Fredericks said, "since your whole squad isn't out today, you and Bustamente will hang out here with one of First Squad's SAW gunners. Set him and the trucks up to cover this field to the east as well as the remaining roadways. I'm taking everybody else into town. This field looks like a decent MEDEVAC landing zone if we need one. It looks much better in person than it did on the aerials."

"Roger, Sir." White responded. White quickly pushed and pulled the men and vehicles into position, and Bustamente watched the tiny element as it stepped carefully into the village. The village wasn't large by any stretch of the imagination, but the conjoining qalats and their thick walls formed a myriad of winding alleyways, connecting the compounds and the road to the small district center building in its midst. Unlike the arid landscape around COP Springbok, this village was in a low 'green zone', built alongside a babbling stream. The verdant landscape was downright relaxing compared to the chaos of the dusty market towns that thrived closer to the highway.

Bustamente settled in for a long stretch of pulling security. He counted buildings, then having made quick work of that, moved on to staring at a group of distant goats to pass the time. After an hour or so of solitude, the platoon could be seen returning. Looking across the field, Bustamente noticed movement at the wall of the leftmost compound that he could see. "Hey White, Sarn't White, I've got something!"

White jogged over. "What are you seeing?"

Bustamente squinted, then raised his ACOG-equipped carbine to his face. He glassed the area where the movement had been, using the scope's magnification to get a better view. "There it is, looks like a couple of males. Looks like —" Bustamente stopped, frozen.

"Go on, what is it. Give me a direction," White said.

The uniforms the distant men were wearing weren't normal Afghan clothes at all. Bustamente blinked, then rubbed his eyes. He refocused on the toiling men, who seemed to be working feverishly around a wheeled object of some sort. *Red coats, blue trousers, and what are those hats?* The men milled about a central point, the glint of painted metal in the sun shaking Bustamente back to earth.

"INCOMING!" He yelled, pulling White down behind the wall. White smoke plumed forward from the red-coated men, and the zooming roar of a massive projectile screamed over their heads. With their backs to the wall, the two soldiers were able to watch their truck take the full brunt of the round. The armored door seemed to cave in, the flash of an explosion sending chunks of hot armor plating flying high into the air. The blast pushed the heavily armored vehicle nearly two feet to the side, and its giant wheels crumpled into the low ground that ran beside the road. With its balance disrupted, the truck slowly toppled over, coming to a rest on its side.

"Fuck! Hargrove! Fritts!" Bustamente screamed, then remembering the first rule of combat medicine, he raised up over the wall and began rapidly firing his carbine towards where the strange crew of men had been. White rose up beside him and followed his lead, as did the First Squad's SAW gunner. White stopped firing long enough to relay information to the rapidly approaching platoon, who quickly moved on line and began advancing forward towards the compound wall behind a fusillade of hot lead.

"Go, go! Check on them!" White screamed over the gunfire. Bustamente threw a fresh magazine into his carbine and then sprinted back towards the toppled and smoking truck. Doc Reyes, having remained behind to form a casualty collection point, beat him there. Reyes had climbed to the top of the vehicle, and was pulling on the driver's door, but being combat locked from within he was unable to open it.

Seeing Bustamente approach, he yelled down, "The turret! Go in through the fucking turret!" Bustamente ran around the vehicle, heart racing. Hargrove was there, his motionless body half buried under the steel plate of the turret. He had been thrown from his position and then crushed by the rolling vehicle. Only his legs were visible, limp and lifeless.

"Hargrove!" Bustamente kneeled by the half-obscured corpse, but he knew in his heart there was nothing that could be done. Tears streamed through the moon dust on his face as he crawled over the top his dead friend into the overturned vehicle. The interior of the truck was hell, with flames and black smoke belching from everywhere at once. He didn't feel the heat, the heat wasn't important right now. He had to keep moving, he had to save Fritts, he had to save somebody.

The smoke stung his eyes and lungs, and he finally found the lean Specialist crumpled against the passenger's side door, covered in ammo cans and water bottles. He dug the man out and, gripping the shoulder straps of his body armor, ripped him free with a strength he didn't realize he had. He jerked the man's body back towards the open turret, bit by bit. The two men fell backwards from the inferno in a heap. Doc Reyes had jumped off the burning vehicle and helped drag the unconscious Fritts away, leading the blinded and retching Bustamente with his other hand.

"Hargrove is dead. He's fucking dead, Doc! They fucking killed him," Bustamente screamed, rubbing the smoke from his singed eyes.

"I know, I know. Help me with Fritts. Focus on Fritts." The medic worked by rote, stabilizing and assessing the badly burned Specialist. As Bustamente's vision returned, he saw the extent of Fritts's injuries. The man would be disfigured for life at the very least, assuming he survived. His own burns were extremely minor in comparison. The gunfire in the background slowly came to a stop, the fight having been won by the aggressively maneuvering platoon. Sergeant White jogged up to the group.

"Hargrove, is he —" as if on cue, the ammunition and remaining fuel within the burning truck began to cook off. Flame roared from the turret, the black, toxic smoke filling the roadway. "Dick, are you hit?" Bustamente looked down at his uniform pants. The pattern was indistinguishable, they were covered in thick, dark blood.

"It's not," he took a deep breath, "not mine."

White nodded in understanding. He wrapped his arm around Bustamente's shoulder and pulled him close. "It's okay buddy, it's okay. You did good. There's nothing we could have done differently here." The men sat in silence for a moment before helping relocate Fritts closer to the field designated as the MEDEVAC point. The platoon's radioman was already calling up the 9-line request, and the returning platoon took up positions of security around the landing zone as they prepared to evacuate their friends. Lieutenant Fredericks, accompanied by a small fire team, strode towards them, the enlisted men looking like hunters, their eyes feral, their rifles half-raised as they assessed the land around them in the fading high of combat.

Bustamente sat quietly as Fredericks discussed the logistics of recovering Hargrove's body with one of the squad leaders. The overturned truck would have to be pulled off the mangled and burned corpse with a tow cable. Bustamente wanted nothing to do with that detail. He remembered Hargrove as the grinning, goofy young private. He didn't want to see whatever was left after the rollover.

The blood on his pants was growing cold and stiff against his legs. "Hey LT", he called out. Lieutenant Fredericks stopped his discussion and looked over.

"Yeah Bustamente, what's up?" he asked.

"Did you kill them?"

"Yeah, we did."

"All of them?"

"Every fucking one."

"Can I — can I see them?"

Fredericks looked back at the squad leader, then over to Sergeant White, who both nodded. "Yeah, Dick." The nickname sounded strange coming from the officer, "you can see them."

The four men, *regular Afghan men*, lay dead in a heap. Their earth-toned robes and vests were matted with blood and torn from grenades. Their weapons, he noticed, were laid out in a row that was significantly neater than the organization of the bodies. One of their AK47s had taken an incoming rifle round and was badly damaged. The green, Soviet recoilless rocket tube that they had fired at the truck had been hauled to the roadside and destroyed with a thermite grenade, the hole through the receiver was still smoking from the heat.

No red coats. No blue trousers. No black hats. Just four dead Afghan fighters. "Thanks," he mumbled to the officer as he turned his back on the bodies.

The MEDEVAC helicopter had long since taken off, and the platoon rapidly made its way back to COP Springbok. The body recovery had gone quickly, though Bustamente didn't have the heart to watch it. The thick black body bag had thankfully gone back with the MEDEVAC bird. He didn't even want to look at it. In the back of the crowded MAXPRO full of somber men,

White reached across the aisle and tapped his knee. "Hey, wasn't there something you wanted to show me, before — earlier?"

"Oh, shit, yeah," Bustamente reached for the Minié ball in his pants pocket, trying not to think about Hargrove's dried blood that was beginning to flake off onto the truck's floor.

It was gone. Every fucking time.

"Never mind sarn't, I must have lost it," he said despondently.

White nodded, "No big deal, man. Maybe you'll find it later." The convoy returned to COP Springbok as night was falling. Bustamente stepped off the ramp of the MAXPRO and cupped his hands around his cigarette, shielding his lighter from the mountain winds. He took a deep draw and then stood upright, stretching. The wind whipped his sleeves, but his pant legs didn't move as he expected them to in the gusts. *Right, the blood.* He looked up, over the HESCO walls.

The old fort sat on its hill, watching the men unload.

***

The sun had long since fallen below the distant, snow-capped mountains by the time Bustamente had finished cleaning himself up and packing Hargrove's gear. He didn't have to do it, in fact Staff Sergeant Robertson himself had insisted on helping, but Bustamente needed some kind of closure. He wasn't sure if he got any.

Robertson's thick southern drawl had breached the silence of the act, "Mission for tomorrow is canceled, bubba. I'm gonna pull you off all duties for the day, sleep in and take it easy, okay?"

"Roger sarn't." The grizzled squad leader gripped his shoulder and then turned to leave, "Hey, Dick?"

"Sarn't?" Bustamente found himself staring at Hargrove's empty bunk, the place where the two had sat on so many nights, talking about guns, games, girls, and all the things they would do when they got home.

"You need to talk? Chaplain is flying in as soon as he can to do the rounds."

"Negative sarn't, I —" The white plume of smoke and the red uniforms played through his head, "I just need to think about things for a while." Robertson nodded, paused for a moment in the doorway, then stepped out. Bustamente could hear his heavy footsteps receding as he walked down the B-hut's plywood hallway. Despite the room's sudden emptiness, it felt stifling. He needed fresh air, needed to walk around. He put his name on the white board next to the door that showed the platoon's soldier's locations on the COP and then, slinging his carbine, stepped out into the night.

The dusty USO tent was unusually quiet at this hour. Normally on a night like this it would be jam-packed with soldiers making phone calls and browsing the internet on its rows of donated computers. The soldier that sat behind the desk on detail acknowledged him as he walked in, "Sorry man, River City. Everything's offline until, well, until the family gets notified."

"Oh," Bustamente looked around, the silent tent blurring into the vision of Hargrove's limp legs underneath the turret. "Right." He walked through the rear of the tent and back into the night.

Fuck.

There was nothing to do, nothing to take his mind off the day. He didn't want to talk, didn't want to do anything except to fixate on something meaningless until his brain melted away. Remembering the HESCO bunker behind the tent, he stepped in and took a seat on the crude bench that ran down its walls. He lit a cigarette and took a drag, then held it in front of his face, staring at the cherry for what must have been minutes until it burned his fingertips. The sharp pain shook him out of his daze.

"Ah, fuck," he said, flicking the Pine to the ground and pulling out a fresh one. He shifted on the bench and put his feet up on the one opposite. He couldn't see the old fort from within the tomblike walls of the bunker, but he formed a vision of it in his mind. As the tobacco smoke wafted towards the opening, he wondered how many other countless soldiers through history had spent a night like this, sitting on its battlements, smoking their pipes while comprehending the horrors of war.

What was it they had called Afghanistan in that class? *The Graveyard of Empires, that's right. Pretty fucking accurate,* he thought.

The war had never much bothered him before. It might shock the people back home, and he would never tell his family, but getting shot at was a *thrill,* a rush, an adrenaline dump that couldn't be matched. The feeling of raw emotion, the *realness* of combat made everything else in his life seem bland. What was he going to do after this, get out and work retail? Flip burgers? Go back to school? *What the fuck do those people know?* He hadn't thought about the man he had killed for months; *White was right, it was either him or us, this is war.*

Hargrove's death was changing that. *Wasn't it?* He wasn't sure, and that's what scared him.

What *was* the point of all this? Greeks, Brits, Russians, God-knows whoever else, now America, what difference could they possibly make here? So many great powers had tried and failed to achieve their aims in this barren, beautiful, terrible land, and for what? They bled, they died, their stories went into the books, and the Hargroves of the world were forgotten by everyone except for their family and friends, and sometimes even by them, their memories buried in the Graveyard of Empires. "I'm fucking losing it," he whispered.

"Dick, there you are," Sergeant White's voice came as an unforeseen relief, breaking through his spiraling thoughts. "Saw your name up on the board, wanted to talk to you."

"Oh shit, hey sarn't."

"Fuck you, we're in the bunker, it's Brad," he said. Bustamente's half-smile came unbidden. "Give me some of that garbage," White said, reaching towards the pack of Pines. Bustamente handed them over. Everyone in the Army was a smoker, the difference being mostly frequency. This was the first cigarette he had seen White smoke since his wife had left him before the deployment.

White coughed, "Fuck these are awful." He blew out the smoke and took a seat opposite Bustamente. "Anyways, I wanted to ask you something, unless you don't wanna talk. If not, I get it."

"Yeah man, shoot."

"Earlier today, before, you know," White trailed off, "you saw the recoilless team. You were calling them out, but you paused."

Bustamente cringed, the distinctive red jackets and gleaming barrel reappearing in his mind's eye. White noticed the immediate change in his demeanor, "I'm not here to correct you, you've never let me down on a contact before, I'm not mad or anything, there's nothing any of us could have done different. They had us dead to rights and somehow, we all fucking missed them, I was just wondering. You've *never* looked like that before. You spotted them and then your face went pale as fuck, like you had seen a fucking ghost or something. Something about you has been off lately. What did you see?"

Bustamente stayed silent, turning the question over in his head. *What the fuck did I see? British fucking soldiers with a cannon? Sure, I'll tell him that. That won't end with me getting hauled out of here in a fucking straight jacket or anything.*

"Dick," White continued, noting his unease, "you can trust me, buddy. You know that. If something's off I just don't want

66

you getting hurt because of it. Shit's been hectic for the last few months. If you need a break or something I can—"

"No," he interrupted, "no man, I'm good. I just, I don't know, I thought I saw something that I didn't. I couldn't tell what they were manning, I don't know, fuck," he leaned forward, "Brad, you're gonna think I'm a fucking lunatic."

"You dropped out of college and joined the infantry. I already know you're a fucking lunatic," White said.

"Yeah well, this is worse than that...."

The pack of Pines slowly emptied as he bared his soul. The fort, the tower, the red uniforms, the vanishing bullet. "So there, I'm fucking nuts. I'm losing my God damned mind out here and it got Hargrove fucking killed, Brad, that's what the fuck is happening." He didn't intend to be so aggressive. He took a deep breath, shoulders slumping as he resigned himself to his fate.

White nodded his head in the darkness, face unreadable, "Here's what we're gonna do. You're right, if I tell higher that you're seeing fucking ghosts out here, British soldiers or whatever you said they looked like, you're gonna be at a nuthouse and on your way out of the Army before your contract is up. I think that's a pretty safe assumption to make." Bustamente put his head between his hands, "HOWEVER, we're not gonna do that, because you're a damned good soldier and I don't think you're crazy, I think you need a break."

"We have six more months left, Brad, how the fuck am I going to get a break in this mess?"

"Easy, baby. You haven't taken mid-tour leave yet, right?"

Bustamente perked up, "Not yet, but I'm not scheduled to go until late, like eight months late."

White smiled, leaning forward and lowering his voice conspiratorially. "And who makes the mid-tour schedule?"

Bustamente paused, thinking. "First Sergeant?"

"Uh huh," White clucked, "and who drove First Sergeant home from the battalion ball when he was shitfaced drunk and trying to fight the battalion commander?"

"You... you did?"

"Uh huh." White reclined, crossing his legs and looking altogether pleased with himself. "So, here's the deal. Since tomorrow's mission is canceled that leaves us with one planned patrol for this mission cycle. We're up for that one, but it's supposed to be short. I mean fuck, they're all supposed to be short, but this one is legit supposed to be short. We do a dismount to the bazaar down the road, shake some hands and make sure the local police aren't robbing anyone, then head back. We finish that out, I whisper in somebody's ear that your leave needs to be pushed up for, I don't know, family reasons or some shit."

Bustamente nodded along, "Okay, so that gets me out for two weeks at least, but I'm still coming back, what's to say I don't keep seeing weird shit and get people killed?"

"Oh, ye of little faith. All that education and yet no vision." White loved bringing up his college. "What's to say you don't, I don't know, slip and fall on a relaxing hike? Maybe your drunk uncle runs over your foot on his way home? Maybe you get a concussion when your pile of textbooks falls off your rich mahogany shelves? You're a smart guy; you can figure something out." White lit another cigarette, looking victorious. "Anyways, you go on leave, sort yourself out, maybe you catch a little *totally unavoidable* injury that keeps you from redeploying, and boom, Bob's your uncle, no more deployment."

Bustamente felt a glimmer of hope, but he reeled at the thought of abandoning what remained of Third Squad. "What will you do without me? I can't just — just leave."

"Oh fuck you, you're a good guy but you're not that good of a soldier," White said, laughing. "We already deployed at reduced strength; it's not like the bad old days after the invasion. If you get hurt on mid-tour, there's gonna be thirty fucking assholes back at Drum with slick sleeves and a wild hare up their ass trying to catch the next hulk smoking to get over here and get their war on. We'll be fine without you."

The soldiers sat in silence for a moment, wreathed in smoke. White's voice grew compassionate. "Listen, Dick, you're a great guy and a shit hot soldier. Yeah, I'm gonna miss you, we all will, but we'll make do, trust me. Nobody will think a thing about it. I don't want you getting hurt, but I especially don't want you getting kicked out of the fucking Army because Big Green can't figure out how to take care of people who have seen the elephant. One more mission, and you're out. We'll see you on the flip side and I'll do whatever I can to help you catch a new assignment or get out, whatever you want. Shit will work out mint, I promise." He stuck his hand out. "Good plan?"

Bustamente met his eyes and gripped the hand. "Good plan." *One more mission.*

***

Hargrove's memorial ceremony went as well as it could, given the circumstances. Bustamente held it together through the chaplain's brief devotion, but Hargrove's inverted rifle and boots with the old fort looming in the background was almost too much for him to handle. He was glad when the formation broke up.

One more mission. One more fucking mission.

White had held true to his word, and within twelve hours of their night time scheming, Bustamente's mid-tour leave date had been shifted left. Two weeks from today, Bustamente would be on a bird back to the states, what he did from there, he would have to figure out as it happened. White's blackmail likely did play a role in convincing the First Sergeant, but Bustamente figured his teammates recent death had far more impact than any history the two may have had.

One more easy mission, then a week of quick reaction force, during which Bustamente, given his upcoming leave date, wouldn't be on the roster. He'd be packing his bags and floating from the COP to FOB Shank, or maybe even Bagram, where he would catch anything he could find that had wings on it going west.

White really had saved him. His mood, in contrast with the last few days of gloom, bordering on despondency, was elevated. He smiled easily at the jokes and wisecracks of his fellow soldiers, and while he thought of Hargrove's death and the visions more often than he cared to, the light at the end of the tunnel was just ahead.

One more mission.

It *really was* an easy one. The platoon, fully manned this time, stepped off from COP Springbok mid-morning. Too early or too late and they would miss the bazaar traffic, defeating the whole purpose of the presence patrol. The monsoon season was quickly approaching, which acted to cool the otherwise arid landscape. The monsoon season marked, in a way, the end of Afghanistan's fighting season. The heavy downpours would turn the moon dust into thick, all-consuming mud, and would pose constant challenges to NATO forces' air assets, which were grounded for days at a time due to the weather. Grounded air meant no missions unless they were absolutely necessary. The rain would eventually dry up, followed shortly thereafter by the bitter cold of winter. Whether they wore camouflage and an American flag or sandals and robes, nobody liked fighting in the cold, and so they largely didn't.

Today's patrol would likely be one of the last of the season, and the shift in gears was palpable. The soldiers chatted lightly as they walked, only growing quiet when the men at the platoon's lead, waving their scanners from side to side, indicated possible hits on wires or explosive devices. Luckily, none of the hits today ended up being real. False alarms were welcomed, compared to the alternative.

The bazaar was teeming with activity as Third Platoon arrived. Shepherds directed screaming herds of wobbling goats past old, reconfigured shipping containers-turned shops. There was little rhyme or reason to what the shops sold, with all of them hosting some variety of food, drink, textiles, and other sundry. Wizened old men sat on the roadside, shouting incomprehensibly at passersby as they hawked their fruits and vegetables. Cuts of meat, accompanied by flies, hung from every conceivable stall. Wildly colorful signs with both the local language and barely passable-English displayed a wide array of largely absurd shop names like *Ahmed K-Mart Store,* or *Mountayn Afghan Inn.*

Bustamente took it all in, savoring the image, cherishing what would likely be his last memory of the country, if everything worked out to plan. He really would miss Afghanistan. Aside from the war, aside from the horror, aside from the adrenaline dumps and the hectic firefights, it really *was* a damn beautiful country. *If somebody could open a ski resort up here they'd make a fuckin' killing,* he thought, not for the first time. He remembered the research he had done leading up to the deployment. People *did* visit Afghanistan for leisure, once. Was it the 70s? He thought back to the old pictures of hippies, posing for photos in streets that looked much like these. The west had changed with time, but this land hadn't.

Afghanistan was eternal, it seemed. Nobody could change the place, neither with money, nor influence, not even at bayonet point. If Alexander the Great had been transported into the future and dropped on patrol with Third Platoon, it's likely that the Americans would be the only thing he didn't recognize.

Aside from all the white Toyotas, I guess.

Lieutenant Fredericks called a halt from the head of the patrol. Things would get tight now that they were in the bazaar proper. Proper intervals were far more of a suggestion in an environment like this then they were a strictly enforced precaution. White leaned his head towards his shoulder, listening to the hand mic clipped to his body armor. "We're stopping here, PL wants to drop in on the police station and see what they're up to." He leaned down again, squinting in concentration over the unceasing cacophony of Afghan life. "First Squad is staying with him, second is pushing out north, we're going south, and weapons squad is staying here with the platoon sergeant."

Bustamente scanned the crowd, noting that everyone around him seemed calm, most of them outright ignoring the Americans in their midst. A good sign. Staff Sergeant Robertson caught the attention of White and the other team leader, Sergeant Smith, and circled his bladed hand in the air before pointing it south towards a wide road which bisected the market town. The team leaders relayed the signal to their men, who moved that direction.

"We ain't going far, fellas," Robertson said to the gathered soldiers. "PL wants us to push out to the edge of town, sit there long enough to burn one, and then head right back. Let the locals see us so they know we aren't just looking at the market. After that, we're out of here." Third Squad "Roger'ed" in unison.

The overstimulation of the market street made the side road's serenity all the sweeter. Within minutes of leaving the bazaar, the packed dirt road turned into a walled alley, just wide enough to fit a donkey cart, or maybe a single white Toyota. The mountains in the distance rose above the qalat walls around them, their snowcapped peaks marking a jagged line of separation between the ruddy brown world of mud-brick walls and animal dung, and the clear blue sky above.

The compounds that lined the road were smaller than those of the more rural villages, but still mirrored the same basic layout. The thick brown walls were breached by wide wooden doors, some of which had been left open for visiting neighbors or family. Bustamente walked past one of these and saw movement from the corner of his eye, he froze, turning his head rapidly.

The piercing brown eyes of the little girl that met his gaze stopped him in his tracks. You rarely saw women in Afghanistan, being largely relegated to their compounds, and not being taken in public without direct male supervision. The girl grinned widely, waving her little hand, and Bustamente responded by sticking out his tongue. The girl's giggle drew the attention of her mother who rushed into view from the compound's interior. Seeing the soldier, she quickly grabbed the girl and ushered her into the house behind them.

Hearts and minds, he thought, as the woman reappeared and closed the compound's gate. Bustamente reached into his pocket, fishing for the pack of Skittles he had saved from an earlier MRE. The red package in his hand was accompanied by a conical lead bullet. *One last fucking mission.* Bustamente gently leaned the Skittles against the compound door, hoping they'd stay there long enough to be found by the occupants, and then caught up with the patrol, rolling the Minié ball around in his hand. As they reached the town's edge the qalats petered out. The town's end was marked with a stacked stone wall that ran along the edge of an irrigation ditch, feeding the fields that lay beyond.

"Smoke 'em if you got 'em, fellas," said Staff Sergeant Robertson. The men of Third Squad kneeled and squatted, finding comfortable positions while still maintaining some semblance of a security posture, and then passed around dip and cigarettes. While they smoked and cracked jokes, Bustamente sat silently on the wall, facing the fields. He stared at the heavy bullet in his hand.

"Fuck you," he said, and then threw the thing as far as he could. The bullet skipped across the packed earth before plunking audibly in an unseen irrigation ditch beyond.

"What was that?" Sergeant White asked, walking up and taking a seat beside him.

"Nothing, just a relic." Bustamente stared out at the mountains, the beautiful countryside unfolding before him.

"Hope it wasn't worth anything."

"I doubt it," he said. "Hey, you want a smoke?"

"What are you trying to do, kill me?" White laughed, smacking him on the back of his armor. "I'm still coughing up the last pack you shoved down my throat!"

White stood and walked off, checking on the rest of the men. One by one the soldiers stomped out their cigarettes and waited for Robertson's command. Before he knew it, they were heading back up the quiet street towards the market. *Towards home.* "Take rear security, Dick," White said. Bustamente fell into line at the rear of the squad, turning every few paces to walk backwards, checking behind them for unseen threats.

The noise of the bazaar grew in intensity as they neared the intersection. Lieutenant Fredericks had radioed up a successful meeting. The local police hadn't abused anyone recently, or at least they were hiding it better now than they had during the first few missions to this town. Bustamente's step lightened, every bit of forward movement propelling him towards the flight home. It was the best he had felt in weeks.

He wondered what he would do when he landed. His parents wouldn't expect him back this early, that's for sure. *I won't tell them, that would make for a helluva surprise,* he thought. What food would he eat when he got there? Six months without anything that wasn't boiled in a bag was a long time to think about your favorite meals. Hell, even fast food sounded good to break up that kind of monotony. *Milk. I want ice cold milk.* That was a sudden craving he didn't expect.

As he spun to check the rear, an opening to his right drew Bustamente's attention. The compound door in question looked the same as all the others. He couldn't quite tell where on the street they were, the bazaar's raucous noise was his only real gauge of distance in the midst of the identical qalat walls. Seeing a flash of color, Bustamente heard a girl's laughter from the doorway. He glanced back at the squad, checking their pace and position. *I've got a second,* he thought. He jogged towards the doorway, smiling at the thought of the girl eating the Skittles he'd left. She wasn't immediately visible, so he stepped just inside, following the noise, *can't take all day.*

As he rounded the corner, the smile melted from his face. Within arm's length stood a red jacketed soldier. Slightly shorter than Bustamente, the lean figure's high waisted blue trousers were held up by a slim, white leather belt. A broad white strap ran across his chest, holding the scabbard for a cavalry saber. The red coat was well-fitted, but clearly worn, held together by threads in some places. The moon dust that coated his own uniform was present here, too. His eyes flew to the soldier's plumed black hat, its golden gilding long since having faded in the brutal Afghan sun. The saber in the figure's hand, cocked behind its head, point forward, should have been more concerning, he thought, but his eyes were drawn to the soldier's face.

He had avoided it for as long as he could.

The man's face was startlingly normal, at least where the qalat wall's shade ended. His fair skin was tanned and beardless, the thick mustache on its upper lip of a style rarely seen outside of textbooks or paintings. The shaded portion, however, was altogether different. The chalk white bone there too had been worked over by the sun, the long teeth seeming more feral than a human's teeth should ever be, being exposed all the way to their root. The empty socket where the eye should have been stared at Bustamente, emitting a sense of red malice that pierced him to his core. A feeling of overwhelming dread overcame him as the saber was driven noiselessly into his chest, the blade's tip skipping off the ceramic plate in his body armor and driving deep into his shoulder. The pain was immediate and overpowering. The skeletal being's vile grin was the only thing he could see.

Bustamente screamed.

When White and the others arrived, Bustamente's blood surrounded him in a pool, the dry ground below him absorbing it as quickly as it flowed.

"Dick! What the fuck happened!" White shook Bustamente, who continued to scream. "Dick, Dick! Where are they? Where are they?"

"I TOLD YOU! IT WAS THEM! ONE OF THEM!" Bustamente cried out in pain, pointing with his unwounded arm, his words becoming increasingly unintelligible. Staff Sergeant Robertson sprinted into the midst of the group as they took control of the wounded man's flailing arms, "IT WAS HIM! HE'S RIGHT FUCKING THERE!" White followed his eyes, fixated on the empty wall beyond. The two sergeants looked around. The dead-end alley Bustamente was in was surrounded by twelve-foot walls on all sides.

As Sergeant Smith and one of his soldiers began packing Bustamente's bleeding wound, White caught the glint of something on the ground. He reached down, standing back upright and holding the bloody pocket knife wordlessly between himself and Robertson.

It was Bustamente's knife.

"Oh, Dick," White's voice grew soft and pleaded as he met the bleeding soldier's tear-filled eyes. "Dick, what did you do buddy, you were almost home."

***

The monsoon season arrived with an unexpected fury. All air assets were grounded for days at a time, but that didn't prevent a single convoy from leaving COP Springbok. Specialist Richard 'Dick' Bustamente sat silently in the back of the armored RG33 truck, watching the combat outpost and the fort above it fading into the distance. They made him wear armor for this mission, but he still felt naked without his carbine. He hadn't been allowed to touch that since the day *it* happened.

No, this wasn't a mission. He had done his last mission. This was something else.

The sun may have been falling, but it was hard to tell in the gloom of the storm. He had nearly slipped getting into the truck, as walking in boots with no laces was something he had never trained for. The soldier assigned watched him averted his eyes any time Dick looked his way.

That was fine. He didn't really feel like talking anyways.

The drive to the nearest FOB with an airstrip was a long one, especially in this weather. It would take a day or two at the very least, and that was assuming they didn't hit any IEDs. Bustamente looked at his wrist to check the time, remembering too late that his watch had been taken too, along with his belt and the tourniquet that lived in his ankle pocket.

What the fuck am I going to do with a strap that short, anyways?

Hargrove would have laughed his ass off at this. Hargrove would laugh his ass of at anything. He leaned his helmet against the armored wall of the truck, but he wasn't tired enough to sleep on this rough of a ride. *At least they let me keep my dip.* That was White's doing, probably. White was a good guy, he always watched out for his joes. Withdrawing his hand from his pocket, he wasn't surprised to find that he was holding the Minié ball instead of Copenhagen.

He wasn't surprised by much anymore.

He looked out the window, squinting to get a look at the mountains that had brought him such calm in the past. In this weather, he couldn't quite make them out, their peaks hidden by the low-hanging clouds, but he could see *them.*

Their horses seemed mostly intact, at least from here, but he suspected they weren't altogether whole under their heavy saddles and blankets. Steam snorted from their massive nostrils as their riders dug in their heels to keep up with the convoy. The legs seemed to move in slow motion, but that had no impact on their speed. The red-coated lancers sat erect, unmoving, their forms floating unnaturally atop their phantom mounts. Only the movement of the pennants at the tips of the lances showed any natural flow, but the contrast between the two was jarring. The lancers stretched out behind the convoy, never losing ground or showing any signs of slowing, an escort, or maybe a patrol.

Bustamente put the ball back into his pocket and sighed. *One last mission and then home.*

Jacob Sharp Biography

Jacob Sharp is a six-year Army veteran who served in 2nd Battalion 503rd Infantry Regiment within the 173rd Airborne Brigade, as well as 1st Battalion 509th Infantry Regiment at Joint Readiness Training Center. After leaving the Army in 2016, he has worked as a park ranger, police officer, and investigator. Sharp holds a bachelor's degree in international relations and a master's degree in recreation administration from Western Kentucky University. Sharp resides in Kentucky with his wife, Emily, and his two loyal basset hounds.

The Road To Frozen Dog

Michael Craig

Idaho Northern Railway 1890s

Ed Hargrove dropped all his coins on the table and glanced up through the haze from his cigar. "I'll raise you a hundred, if you've got the stones for it."

A moment of silent observation passed as our eyes locked. Inside Ed's private compartment, the shades were drawn against the light from outside, casting the room in a soft gloom. The only sounds were the gentle rocking of the southbound train and the rhythmic clack of the rails.

This wasn't my kind of case. This was stuff Pinkerton and his boys handled. I couldn't fathom why Teddy had written orders for me to be on this cursed train to nowhere, Idaho.

"You gonna call, 'Mysterious' Dave Mathers?" Joseph Green said in mocking tones. He burst out laughing at his own jest and looked at his friend for support.

Ed looked up, smirking, "What makes you Mysterious, anyway? Why did Bat Masterson call you that?"

"Good question. Maybe I should've asked," I said, not bothering to look up from my cards.

Ed managed a sly grin and groped at a leather pouch hanging from his neck. He'd been pawing at it all night, mostly when holding cards.

It wasn't so unusual. Gamblers tended to be superstitious. A rabbit's foot, a lucky coin, some Indian charm bag, they'd cling to anything they thought would give them an edge. If I was right, that pouch was a bit more valuable than other charms.

Ed Hargrove was no George Pettibone. But according to Charlie Siringo, a reported Pinkerton agent, he'd had a hand in the bombing at the Frisco Mine near Coeur d'Alene. His actions got him a Union job, possibly moving money to the South. My guess was that a portion of that funding was in the bag around his neck.

He was a dapper man who spent more time waxing his mustache than most women on their makeup and hair. Despite that, he was no slouch, and the scars on his knuckles spoke volumes about how he earned a living.

Roosevelt sent me, so there had to be more to it. He didn't send a Pale Rider to help bust up unions.

Joseph was a gold assayer and as crooked as they came on Cripple Creek. There were whispers around the Gem Mine that he'd been sharing union secrets with the Pinkertons. It wasn't true. But, true or not, once the whispers started, even someone quick with their irons couldn't stop it.

Compared to Ed, the man was generally disheveled and didn't consider personal hygiene worthwhile. His sense of humor not only put me off a pleasant evening of cards, but I was also sure he was shooting signals to Ed.

I didn't care much for being outnumbered in a small carriage compartment. There were many ways to dispose of a body between Horseshoe Bend and Emmettville.

I stroked my mustache, feigning thought, as I drew my Colt but kept it low to my side.

"A hundred?" I asked.

Ed nodded, a smile twisting the frayed edges of his waxed mustache, sensing an upper hand in the game.

"I am down three hundred already. I have, what?" I sat tall in my chair and gave the pile of chips and coins a measuring look. "Another two fifteen in the pot? Another losing hand and I'll become a laughingstock."

"Call or fold, damn it." Ed grinned a humorless smile. "Let's get on with it. I want to get to the sleeper car for an hour or two before we hit Emmettsville."

I let my gaze travel up the wall behind him to the Orientalist images of voluptuous nymphs as if considering my options.

"What do I do?" I mused. I intended to rile the man up, and it worked like a charm.

"Fold or call, damn it. Make a decision, Mathers!"

His gaze flicked between Joseph and me as he stroked that charm bag around his neck. Would the Union bosses forgive him when I took his gold?

"Call me insane, but I'll raise."

"Raise?" Ed said with shock in his voice.

Tucking my hand into my breast pocket, I fished out a roll of bills and tossed them on the table. "Is your blood thick enough for another five hundred?"

"Five hundred? No one carries that kind of scratch on them!"

"I do," I said evenly. "You playing? Or surrendering the prize?"

Ed's eyes shifted toward Joseph, but the loudmouth suddenly found his nails interesting. There was no help to be found there. He went bust early in the game.

"Take my IOU," he pleaded.

"We agreed on a cash money game," I shrugged. "Unless you got something else worth the wager."

"Not on me!" Ed slapped the table in frustration. "Buying the pot is a chicken shit move, Mathers."

"So, win it from me." I motion to the bag around his neck. "What's that little bobble? Is it worth anything?"

His hand shot to his neck on reflex, then he dropped it a little too fast as he tried to cover his mistake. Eyeing me, he frowned and shook his head, "Family heirloom, it's not up for discussion."

"No faith in your hand?" I smirked.

Looking at the pot, I raised my brows, ready to put my cards down. "Been one hell of a game, boys."

Ed shot to his feet, gripping a small, wicked-looking knife. "I'll gut you if you touch that pot!"

"Bet or fold, that's the game."

"My father-in-law, Colonel Jebediah Ferguson, took this from the neck of a Shoshone Shaman after the battle at Almo. Dozens of settlers died at the hands of those savages!"

"You mean the Rock Creek massacre? I believe the other side was slaughtered, not that it's any of my concern," I said conversationally.

I lowered my cards enough to show him the barrel of my Army colt. I wasn't a big man; some would say I was rangy and lean like a coyote. Still, looking down the barrel of a forty-four-caliber revolver has some persuasive qualities.

Ed agreed, dropped the knife onto the table, and sat back down. "You going to shoot me in cold blood?"

"Ed, I don't care about how your wife's daddy ran down some helpless women and children. I'm here to play cards," I said. Then, like I hadn't a care in the world, I set the gun down in front of me.

I smiled and motioned to the cards. "So, what is it? Play or fold?"

His anger burned hot for a few more seconds; a slow, dark smile crept up his lips. His eyes were on a slight tremor of my hand.

"You spooked or something?"

I let the amusement show in my eyes, "Just a little souvenir from the war. Grip a saber long enough, and the muscles forget how to relax."

The Rough Rider's charge up Kettle Hill was brutal and bloody. The tremor wasn't the only thing I'd carried away from that war. I didn't want to think about that or what other things happened there.

"Ed Hargrove. You in or out?" I said, allowing irritation to creep into my voice.

"I'll play, railroad man. But this," he patted the bag, "it's worth more than the whole pot. What will you put up to match its value?"

"How do I know that?" I asked. "Let's see this heirloom."

"I'll let you see it, but if you can't match it's worth, I win."

"Very good," I agreed and sat back in my chair.

Triumphantly, he pulled the thong around his neck and pulled the leather bindings from the bag. He dropped an object heavier than lead onto the table with a dull thump.

It was an infernal thing, and I loathed to touch it. When the light struck it, the air in the small compartment stirred, a gas lamp flickered, and shadows danced like a hanged man on the gallows.

The amulet seemed to thrum as if imbued with a life of its own. The gold, aged and darkened by time, had a sickly sheen that caught the dim light and refracted it unnaturally. It was a predatory glimmer, as if the metal was more alive than inert, watching and waiting for those foolish enough to touch it.

Twisted designs adorned its surface, carved into shapes that defied immediate comprehension. Carapaces, eyes, and forms that might have been mouths but were too alien in their geometry merged and overlapped, creating a chaotic artistry. Each engraving seemed to shift if looked at too long, like whispers caught at the edge of hearing.

A sense of dread pressed heavy on my chest, and I knew they felt it, too. This thing was as enchanted as it was horrible.

Well, at least I know why I'm here, I thought.

"In gold alone, it's worth over five hundred," he said. His face was a mask of victory and arrogance, and I let my expression fall.

"Oh my, that is a peach," I said. Then I swallowed back the dread building inside me.

"I win!" He grinned and reached for the pot once more.

My spirit roiled at the idea of him possessing it, but words came to me quickly. "I said it was a peach, but you already said it was only worth around five hundred dollars."

"I said it was worth OVER five hundred!" he raged.

I cocked my head, judging its worth. "How much more? Joseph, you're part of that honored brotherhood of assayers, right? How much is that lump of gold worth?"

Joseph looked to Ed, but with me looking right at them, they could only exchange glares and hope that the other got the intent.

Joseph swallowed, "At least eight hundred."

Everyone knew that was a lie, but it didn't matter. The only truth that mattered was what could be read in the cards.

"I'll take your bobble at what he claims it's worth, eight hundred," I said. Then I pulled off my cufflinks and tossed them on the table. "Diamonds, easily worth three hundred."

Ed's eyes bulged, and the vein in his forehead swelled.

"I call," I said. As I fished out my flask, I motioned to the lump on the table. "What is that anyway, some miner's charm or something?"

"It doesn't matter." Ed's grin grew wider as he slammed his cards. "Full house. Take that, you bastard!"

Reaching for the pile again, Ed chuckled. I lay down my own cards and then took a pull on my flask.

"A hell of a hand, Ed," I breathed past the fire in my throat, "but my four little eights give me the win, I believe."

Ed's jaw dropped. His gaze once more flashed to Joseph. "No... That's not right!"

Reclining in my chair, I smirked. "Not what you expected?"

Joseph shook his head a touch as his eyes darted to me with a meaningful accusation.

"You dirty chiseler!" Ed lurched to his feet, "You pulled a card from your sleeve or something."

He didn't reach for the cash or iron, but I knew he was thinking about it.

Sighing, I leaned forward. "Why, Ed, you mean something like using your chum to send you signals? That kind of cheating?"

Joseph moved away from me, clearing the way for the move I was sure Ed would make.

"I guess it's your word against ours." Joseph suddenly jerked his Army Colt and cocked the hammer back.

Ed looked between us and laughed, "I'd wager you won't be saying much."

The carriage light faltered, and so did my mood.

"I'm sure you're right." I nodded. "The word of two living men over a silent corpse has a way of settling affairs."

"That's right, two upstanding citizens, Union men," Ed grinned.

"Are you sure he's your chum?" I tilted my head toward Joseph. "You know what they said about him up at the Gem mine. Now he shoots you bad signals at the card table."

"What?" Ed shouted. His gaze shot to Joseph, betrayal burning behind those brown eyes.

"Seems to me like he's my chum."

Joseph glanced at Ed, shaking his head. "I'm no yellow dog, Ed! You know that."

My bluff worked. As they glared at each other, I grabbed my gun from the table.

Every sense suddenly sharpened, every breath shallow and deliberate.

The sound of my heartbeat rushed in like stone tomb doors closing on the last seconds of a life. The trigger yielded just where I knew it would, and a lethal click resonated as the cylinder rotated, aligning the chamber.

The hammer snapped back and fell with a sharp metallic crack. The world condensed into that instant — a fierce and bright spark ignited the dark confines of the chamber. The explosion shook my bones as the muzzle flashed a blinding light. The compartment was bathed in white-hot fury for a heartbeat, illuminating the hard lines of stone and steel.

I didn't wait to see the impact. I knew my shot would hit Joseph, causing his pistol to go off too soon. As his bullet splintered the wood by our feet, Ed tried to jerk his own pistol and gun me down. I didn't let him.

Kicking the table up in front of me sent the pot rocketing into Ed's face. Ed stumbled backward. The door to the car slammed open, and a lean, tan-skinned young man stepped in, his shotgun held high and fixed on Ed's center of mass. "Don't move, Ed, or your brains will paint the wall."

Ed turned his eyes to the massive bores of that ten gage and froze. "Easy, Jack."

I scooped the amulet off the floor. "Where did you get this amulet? What's it for?"

I held up the damned thing, but his eyes never drifted toward it.

"It's a family heirloom, I told you."

"What's it for?" I barked.

"What's going on here, Mathers?" Jack asked, his gun still leveled at Ed.

"You can't shoot me, Jack. I didn't draw a gun," he said smugly. "Point your gun at Mathers. He's the murdering, cheating son of a bitch who shot Joseph."

Jack eyed me and raised a brow. "That true boss?"

"You know me, Jack," I said pleasantly. "My moral compass always points toward magnetic north."

Jack nodded, "You always said True North was for maps and preachers."

"Indian Jack? You trade in horse flesh," Ed said and then peered at me. "I never would have believed you were dogging a train agent's heels like a kicked dog."

"Yeah, well, I sold him a line of horses, and he hadn't paid me in full yet," Jack said. "Till he does, I'm protecting an investment."

"Where the hell have you been, Jack?" Scooping up my bowler, I shoved the winnings and the amulet inside and looked around the room. I was displeased that blood speckled the exquisite painting of the nymph on the wall behind where Ed once sat. Still, the silver was a balm to my distress.

Jack's expression took on a guilty quality, "Dining car."

Ed sat up, suddenly more interested in what Jack had been up to than the gun pointing at his face.

"Again, with your pencils and paper! Who are you sketching now? The grumpy ass conductor?"

Jack's eyes went to Ed, then back to me before muttering. "The scenery."

"You better not be ogling my ladies, you red —"

"Enough of that!" I shouted over his insult. Both men glared at each other, but their mouths stayed closed.

"Now, put the body in the carriage with the hogs. We'll drop it off with William McConnell's people in Emmettville."

"What about me?" Ed asked, his eyes hard.

"Oh. You're free to go, Ed Hargrove. Losing at cards isn't a crime. But, why don't you leave those colts on the table for now?"

♠ ♥ ♣ ♦

The world blurred past — a chaotic rush of indistinct shapes and colors — as the cold, hard metal of the carriage wall pressed against my back, mirroring the frozen landscape of my emotions. For a time, I just stood there breathing, summoning my senses to regain their full faculties.

From my bowler, I pulled the pouch that contained the amulet and peered at it, tempted to expose it once again. A wave of dread rolled through me, heavier than the weight of my revolver. That sense of doom I picked up in Cuba was a frequent companion if an unwelcome one.

"Not now," I said, trying to push down the panic threatening to overtake me. My pulse pounded in my ears like the sound of rifles and cannons, but beneath it, faint echoes of screams threaded through the air.

"Mathers? You, okay?" Jack's voice jerked me back to my senses.

Tucking it into my pocket, I pulled my flask to mask my reaction. "Why the hell were you sketching out 'the scenery' when I was counting on you?"

"There was this girl, she…"

"A girl? You're supposed to back me up!"

Jack shrunk back. "I did back you up."

Turning, I glared into his dark eyes, "Being a Pale Rider means suffering. It means being cursed to never love, or if you do, it's likely to be taken from you. You can never be one of us if you're hung up on a pretty girl in a pretty dress."

Jack's face burned red, and there was rage in his eyes.

"Do you understand?" I asked and grabbed his shoulder.

Jack took in an angry breath. "Yeah, I understand!"

For a few seconds, we just stood there, both fuming, both for the wrong reason.

My gaze fell first, and shaking my head, I turned away from him. "That's not fair, Jack. I just killed a man, and I'm out of sorts."

"You've killed more men than the Shoshone. Why does this one bother you?"

I couldn't tell him why; it just did. It was as if I'd done more than liberate the world from another putrid vermin and instead taken on a burden that I could not fathom.

"I don't know, but I'm sure Lucifer has a list of sins for me to pay off in Hell if I ever get there." I sighed. "That's my problem. Not fair to put it on you."

Another few heartbeats passed, and then Jack patted my shoulder and chuckled. "I wish it wasn't fair. She does have a beautiful dress and eyes the color of warm caramel."

I chuckled and shook my head, then turned toward Jack again.

"I take it you are acquainted with Ed Hargrove?"

Jack nodded. "Up north in Frisco. Though he was drunk at the time. I'm surprised he remembers me."

"How did that play out?" I asked, taking a flask from my vest, and taking a swallow, then offered it to Jack.

Jack shook his head. "I just started my line of ponies and sold some to him and his men. He kept apologizing for the

Rock Creek massacre. Seemed to think he wronged my people."

"Did he?"

Jack shrugged, "I didn't know my tribe. I don't see how it matters. He was involved with the church at the time. His family was sending orphans east to be civilized. Though I got the idea that he made the orphans, and it was his wife that helped send them to be converted."

"What a mess," I mumbled.

Jack squeezed my shoulder, a concerned look on his face. "Why don't you get a drink in the dining car? I'll take Joseph to the hogs' carriage and meet you there in a few minutes. Okay?"

Nodding, I wiped my mouth, then turned away from the shadowy passage.

♠ ♥ ♣ ♦

The Idaho Northern & Pacific Railway spent thousands on a leg that led to the mines. It felt like a road to nowhere. Aside from the river, which the train carefully followed, the terrain was barren. The hillsides were covered in sage and bitterbrush, where the coyotes and badgers hunted whistle pigs and ground squirrels.

I'd been on the rail for days, and I'd seen enough to last me a lifetime. I sank into a worn but plush red velvet seat and sat my hat on the polished hardwood table. "They should have sent Masterson."

"Bat Masterson? You know him? I heard he shot Billy the Kid," asked an old-looking steward with pronounced sideburns.

"It was Garret that shot William Bonny, not Masterson. But, in essence, you're correct; they're both rogues."

I realized that this was no standard steward. He was too refined. Dressed in a white shirt and black vest, he'd worked somewhere fancy before something set him on the tracks. He had a reason to keep moving, a debt, a woman, a crime. I suppose all of us did.

I motioned to a bottle with a yellowed label. "I don't hear much talk, but I hear that Old Crow whiskey calling my name. Why don't you pour me three fingers?"

The steward scowled and nodded as I dug silver out of my hat and placed it on the table. He wanted a story to pass his time, and I wanted whiskey to pass mine. Bat Masterson could go to hell, but the gods know why he sent me to Idaho.

"You headed to Silver City because of that mess in Frisco? Democrats and Republicans, Union and company, there are a lot of people fighting in Boise County right now. I suppose that would be reason enough to send someone."

I shrugged, hoping he would shut up.

The steward missed the hint. "If those boys from the Gem Miner's Association ever find Charlie Siringo, they'll bury him. I wouldn't advise going against the Union around here."

Ed's guns weighed down my belt, and I unburdened myself of them on the bar, then scooped up the whiskey. "Stow those, would you?"

"Not much of a conversationalist, eh?" The steward scooped up the guns, stuffed them under the bar indignantly, and then glanced up suddenly as the carriage door opened. I looked up as well. We were taken aback by how elegantly the woman slipped into the car, like liquid silk.

She walked into the carriage like she owned it. Her hair moved as she did, thick and heavy, swaying against her back like the mane of a wild mustang.

I could feel my pulse quicken at the sight of her. An unmistakable glint of emerald in her eyes locked onto mine for just a heartbeat before flicking away, disinterested.

I shot back my whiskey and watched as she made her way to a booth, pulling a girl behind her.

"Another," I said and set down another coin.

Those eyes — bright, sharp enough to slice through a deck of marked cards — made me feel like I was being read and no aces left to hide. Then there was her smell — a faint hint of rosewater with a touch of something bitter and metallic, like gunpowder if you knew where to sniff.

She was my kind of woman. I wasn't her kind of man.

"What will you be having tonight, Mrs. Hargrove? Tea, perhaps wine?" the steward asked.

The girl who followed Mrs. Hargrove spoke up. "I'll have wine."

She followed the red-haired woman like a shadow, but nothing was subdued about her presence. Raven-dark hair caught the flickering afternoon light through the windows like polished obsidian. It framed her face — a mix of high cheekbones brushed with a natural rose hue and a proud jaw that looked carved from stone as old as this barren land.

Jack's girl, I realized.

Her eyes were indeed the color of warm caramel, wide and watchful, like a doe stepping onto unfamiliar ground. They took in everything at once, the strange confines of the carriage and the glances from the surrounding men, yet they didn't linger as if avoiding any stare that might root her in place.

"Water or tea," Mrs. Hargrove said stiffly as she seated the girl. "The last thing you should do is turn into a drunk. There are enough of those around already."

The girl scowled. "I'm old enough for a poke by some smelly old rich bastard but not old enough for wine?"

Mrs. Hargrove raised an imperious brow. "When you're with the old rich gentleman, you can get good and drunk before your poke. Then he can clean up red wine stains when you vomit all over your dress."

The native girl crossed her arms, "I guess any red stain on our wedding night will do."

"No, it won't! Only blood will consummate the marriage, so there better be no accidents between now and then, or they'll call the wedding off!"

The steward was gawking, a leer on his face that was as rude as it was unavoidable. He, too, was struck dumb by these fair creatures; I'd just had the good sense not to be obvious about it.

Turning my back to them, I fixed my gaze on the steward.

"Fetching scenery for Idaho," I said, snapping him out of his reverie.

Turning back to his bottles, he made quick work of grabbing a pitcher of water and filling two glasses. "Proper ladies. We are honored to have the daughter of Colonel Ferguson again."

"Again?" I asked. "They ride often?"

Shooting them a spurious glance, the bartender leaned in. "Mrs. Hargrove comes a few times a year. She escorts ladies from a finishing school in San Francisco."

Confused, I narrowed a brow. "Escorts them to where?"

"To the men who ordered them," he said conspiratorially.

We both just looked at each other for a long pause, and then the gears kicked into place, and I got it. "Mail-order brides?"

"Only the best. One is married to Sheriff Opdyke, and the other to the brother of Governor Willey. Clara Bell Hargrove has been a chaperone for the would-be wives and consorts of the most influential men in Idaho. I've never seen her with a bride-to-be who was anything less than stunning."

"I thought she worked with the Church orphanages."

"Yes, the nuns raise the kids. The Ferguson Commemorative Finishing School gives the bright ones the potential to further their education and opportunities. Like the young lady there."

"That's a pretty impressive name for a school run by a unionizer and his wife."

The steward arched his brows and tilted his head toward Clara Belle. "The daughter of the hero of Almo Creek is as formidable as her father, and she has twice the business sense."

The tracks rattled beneath us as he gathered the cups and pitcher to a silver tray. Then, with a worn cloth over his arm like the finest maître d, he scurried over to them subserviently.

Mail-order brides. I'd heard of the practice. Those I'd met ended up being brides of the evening, not of any single man. What the bartender described was wholly different. I'd never seen a whore with bonafides.

Perhaps it was because Idaho was new, and the leaders weren't from the old establishment. Who better to make a newly wealthy and powerful mine owner seem refined than a lady who could culture him?

Still, something seemed unusual about it. I could see a Union thief and a cultured madame bumping into each other. Still, these two were from totally different worlds. There had to be a connection. I was guessing he was part of the regional militia. Perhaps someone under the command of the Butcher of the Rock Creek Massacre, Colonel Ferguson. The real question was how did the amulet fit into all this? Why would they have such an arcane piece, and to what end?

"Is what they say true?" a breathy voice said from my elbow.

Turning, I looked at the buxom young wine connoisseur as she breathed excitedly.

"Depends on what they said. There are many things a man might say to charm a pretty lady out of her skirts."

Her mouth dropped open, but there was a smile in her eyes. She was aghast, offended, and charmed near to the bone.

"They say you're invulnerable. You feel no pain and fear no man."

"I feel things just fine," I said, reaching out to run the back of my finger over a curl tumbling over her ear. "For good or ill."

A furtive glance sought her chaperone, even as she slid a shapely thigh over the bench as if to slide in. "My governess would kill me if she found out I was spending time with a man who runs in circles with notorious figures like Bat Masterson and Pat Garrett."

"They don't actually hang about one another." I scowled before my brain could tell my face to ignore the references, and her countenance pinched at my reaction.

"You don't know them? The bartender said you…"

Waving her off, I slugged back my whiskey, but she stayed half-perched in my booth.

"I know them. They're braggarts and curs. Men who would show a lady like you no respect past breakfast."

"Breakfast?" she asked.

Her eyes were wide, innocent, and naïve. Despite her bluster, I knew she was just a kid. Feeling a little unclean suddenly, I motioned toward Mrs. Hargrove. "You better get back. She can explain it to you in a delicate way."

Leaning closer, she smiled and said, "I have a mystery about me as well."

Raising a brow, I waited to hear something inane.

Eyes wide and playful, she leaned in and whispered, "My father was a powerful shaman. He taught me to talk to spiders and said I would marry a mysterious man."

"Mysterious, or Mystery? Seems you're on course for nuptials with the latter," I chuckled. "What was that about spiders, anyway? What do they say?"

She laughed then, sweet and musical. "Nothing, silly."

"Oh?" I asked.

She batted at my arm, "They're spiders. They just listen."

Pausing, she narrowed her eyes as if thinking, then said, "Though a man in our village, a half-breed, said he could hear them."

"Well, don't go talking to strange men about wedding a mystery man. They'll likely take you up on it."

She was pretty, yes — the girl was pretty in a way that made one think of wind over wild plains and sunsets over woodland hills. The faint scent of cedar and crushed sage followed her as if her very presence carried the wildness of her homeland into the sterile, iron-shod world of the train.

"No one I wouldn't want to. Besides, if they do, I have this."

Lifting the hem of her skirt, she flashed me a pale thigh. For a second, I was lost in the rush of heat in my cheeks. Then I spotted the small pearl-handled derringer tucked into the garter belt.

"Lily! You asked to refresh yourself. While Mr. Mathers might smell like the privy, you won't be refreshing yourself in his presence. Put down your hem!"

Lily let her skirt slip back into place and sighed heavily.

"So that's your name," I said with a smile. "The Lily is a pretty flower."

Mrs. Ferguson stepped closer. "You'll be leaving her flower alone."

"Nice to meet you, Lily." Taking her hand, I brushed my lips across her knuckles. "You might want to be on your way before your wicked stepmother strikes us down with her sharp words."

"Enough of that!" Clara Belle snapped, but she seemed amused.

Lily purred a slight hum, then withdrew, her sultry expression slipping away as she glared at her chaperone.

"I don't blame her for wanting more than one man," sniffed Mrs. Hargrove. "But how can she start her own tribe if she's with someone like you?"

"Some women like a man with experience," I said, giving her a crooked smile. "Makes them seem dangerous, I suppose."

Mrs. Hargrove shot me a sidelong glance. "I have my duties, Mysterious Dave. There's no time for experiences of any kind."

Now, this woman was just at the right age. A grown woman and a fierce one at that.

"I have the feeling you're the kind of woman who gets what she wants when she sets her mind to it. Maybe you want to explore some mysteries?"

Her eyes drifted to the side, and a soft hue of red-tinted her cheeks. Her lips parted a fraction as if to respond, and then the car door flew open, cutting her off.

"I am a married woman!" she objected a bit too loudly, but there was a twinkle in her eyes.

"Clara Belle!" came a voice from the car's door, and I turned to see Ed Hargrove scowling at us. "Get the girl, I'm tired of seeing this cur's face."

Mrs. Hargrove nodded curtly.

"Ed's a might sore about losing at cards. Don't be too rough on him," I said.

"Reginald," she shot a side eye to the steward. "We will take our dinner away from the abrasive elements in the room."

She rose like a raven from a kill, shifting her gown as she herded Lily back toward her carriage.

I watched them retreat, catching the dark glares that Mrs. Hargrove shot back my way. Ed Hargrove glared at me again, then followed them into their carriage.

♠ ♥ ♣ ♦

My sleep was troubled, filled with dark images and sick desires hidden in the depths of the jungle. The walls of the mine seemed alive and wet, glowing faintly with some greenish light that only made the shadows deeper. The air reeked of rot and copper, thick enough to choke on.

And then there were the things. They crawled out of the dark like spiders, pale and shriveled, their skin so thin you could see every bone, every twitch of muscle.

Their eyes — God, their eyes — were vast and cloudy, but they saw me, I know they did. They moved wrong, too, all jerking and twisted like marionettes pulled by drunken hands.

All around, bodies littered the landscape and hung from tall rocks near the river. It had been a massacre. The prints from iron-shod horses were everywhere. Not U.S. Cavalry, but an organized force. Settlers, militia, something.

This wasn't Cuba. It was here. Idaho.

Mrs. Hargrove had been there. Exposed to the elements, her once ravishing skin now looked lurid and clay-like as spider-like insects scurried into her mouth and between her fingers. Her nails no longer looked stylish and polished red; instead, they looked like cracked dark carapaces from a beetle.

Her eyes were crystal clear, like chips of emerald. I would have sworn she still had life except for the spider. The spider that cut into the white of her left eye, its tiny mandibles spilling ocular jelly onto her cheek.

From the river, a large hairy creature, dark as night, pulled itself up on the bank. A man's face, its features obscured by the shadows. His eyes were wide, and his mouth formed a perfect O as a scream ripped its way out of his throat.

The mound had a mouth like a gaping abyss, a black hole of teeth and muscle, and I saw the man was only a tiny speck in its horrifying grasp. The creature cast the soldier aside as if he were nothing more than a worthless, broken bone.

A hiss, hot and foul, emerged from its gaping maw, and the single word it spat out struck me like a blow aimed at my very essence. *"Sinner..."*

"Wake up, Mathers!" Jack shook me awake. "You're moaning like you're gutshot. What's going on?"

When I came around, I thought I was still dreaming.

A man, or something like one, loomed over me. His shadowed face seemed to hold something ancient and furious within.

It wasn't the kind of thing you see in person. It was deeper, older like the land itself had risen to condemn everything we'd done to it and its people.

"Mathers!" Jack said again. The spell was broken, the shadows were gone, and the young man stood looking at me with concern.

"Dreaming of Cuba again? The war?" he asked. "You kept saying something about the tribe and the sinner. What's that all about?"

The dreams of the jungle that once haunted me now seemed unthreatening compared to what I'd just seen.

Though the Spanish war left me scarred, the nightmares were a constant I knew, a strange sense of familiarity in the face of my trauma.

"Yeah, sorry," I said.

I rolled out of my cot, noticing the persistent sway of the rails was absent. "We stopped?"

Absently nodding, Jack muttered, "Water station."

"Oh, that makes sense."

Jack sat with his satchel and paper tilted toward the window, the light of the moon cast on an image he drew.

"Who is that? The girl with the Hargrove lady?"

"Lily," Jack said dreamily. "She said her people were from here. I think she is from somewhere near The City of Rocks."

I gave him a confused look. "What does it matter where Lily came from? If you like her so much, make your own if it suits you."

"She said she was the daughter of a tribe elder. She was sent back east to learn the white people's ways."

"You think?" I asked.

Jack grimaced. "I doubt she went willingly. A lot of those tribes were decimated, like mine. More likely that she and the other kids from the tribe were taken in by the missionaries and converted."

Standing, I fished my flask from my bag. "How did you get her alone? Mrs. Hargrove keeps her eye on her like a hawk on a rabbit."

Jack blushed a deep shade of red and swallowed. "She caught me coming back from the conductor's booth. Snuck me into her private compartment so she could ask questions about you."

"About me?"

Jack nodded. "She wanted to know the mysteries of 'Mysterious' Dave Mathers."

"Then why the blush?" I asked.

"It was a long conversation. Topics wandered."

I gave him a stern look. "That the only thing that wandered?"

A grin split his face. "She let me draw her while Ed played cards. I don't know where Mrs. Hargrove was."

He turned the paper toward me, and the image of a girl was shown in the pale light. "Look, she is just amazing."

The sketch was as good as any I'd seen. Each stroke breathed life into the image of the native girl. Her gaze, soft yet profound, captured the melancholy of her predicament.

The gown she wore — a blend of the frontier's rugged grace and the ballroom's opulence — hugged her figure with a quiet elegance. Shadows from her hair spilled over her shoulders like ink on silk, framing her face in a cascade of contrast.

There was something sad in her expression, grounding the ethereal beauty of the moment. It was a portrait not of a girl but of a dream caught in motion, a fleeting glimpse of something ethereal.

"She looks sad. Worried about the nuptials?" I asked.

"Didn't want to talk about it. It was like she thought she was going to her death, not to a rich husband's bed."

The drawing caught my eyes once more. The detail had me gobsmacked. There was a faint mark on her pale shoulder, barely noticeable against her skin. A birthmark or a spider-shaped pockmark, it was so subtle, yet it brought an unmistakable feeling of reality to the sketch.

"Damn, son. You could sell —"

A noise from above made me jerk my gaze to the car's ceiling. It was like nothing I'd ever heard. The hair on my arms rose as the skittering, shuffling sound continued down the length of the car.

"Something is up there."

Jack was looking up as well, inquisitive and not concerned. "Maybe the conductor wanted to check some of the trunks stowed up there?"

In answer to his question, a shot rang out, then two.

"What the Hell? Who's shooting?" I hurried to the window and craned my neck, trying to get a look up the side of the train.

Jack went to speak, but his words were cut off by a brisk rap on the door.

Jack closed his satchel and picked up the shotgun. I picked up the Army colt from where it hung in its holster, then crept to the door.

"Who comes?" I said and stepped to the side of the door.

"Mr. Mathers? Mr. Mathers, it's Clara Belle Hargrove. I need to talk to you. That savage, Jack Wood, ran off with Lily!"

"Lily's gone?" Jack asked.

I jerked the door open. I leveled the pistol at waist level, ready for Ed to be standing there, ready to reclaim his losses.

What I found wasn't at all what I expected. She stood there, framed by the flickering light of the corridor lamp, her fiery red hair spilling over her pale shoulders like a river of flames.

Her wide green eyes shimmered with desperation, tears threatening to spill, and her trembling hands clutched the doorframe for balance.

"What did he do with her?" she pleaded.

Jack was on his feet, his shotgun forgotten as the barrels drooped to the floor. "I didn't do anything. What happened to Lily? Is she alright?"

Clara Belle looked at Jack, then me, in confusion. "She had to be with you. If not, who has her?"

"Hargrove," I said, frightened about what the man might be doing with her.

"Ed? No, he took a few shots at the man she was with. We thought it was Jack. Ed went after them," Clara Belle stuttered.

"Did you see this other man? Or did Hargrove just tell you he was out here?"

Turning, she fled back into the passage and toward their car. Jack pushed past me and followed close behind.

I followed along, pistol in hand.

Clara Belle and Jack burst into the dining car and out the other side. The conductor's startled voice shouted out in confusion as I rushed in as well.

The conductor was scrambling to his feet, some sort of logbook falling to the floor in a hiss of paper on wood. "Who was shooting? We don't have time for game hunting, we're on a schedule."

"Did anyone get off?" I demanded.

Confused, he shook his head. "Why would anyone get off? It's a water station. There's nothing here."

Jack erupted back into the dining car, his eyes wide, face pale. "Hargrove is gone! I think he took Lily."

"Why would he take Lily?" I asked. The girl was already with them. Why steal her off the train?

Clara Belle reddened, her eyes going hard. "That son of a bitch!"

"What?" I asked.

Jack's hands balled into fists. "He took her because of me."

"Because you two..." My gaze shifted wearily to Clara Belle.

Clara Belle's face was as hot as the boiler on the locomotive. "I should have known he wanted her for himself!"

♠ ♥ ♣ ♦

"Of course, I'm going with you. Don't be daft. I'm going to murder Ed."

Taking a pull off my flask, I shook my head. "I don't think that's a good idea."

Clara Belle Hargrove donned her dress and pinned back her hair. Her lips were thin and pale, as if they were carved from porcelain. I'd seen that kind of mouth before — soft as a whisper until it wasn't. Until it spoke with the cutting cruelty of a snakebite.

"Like I'm going to leave a vulnerable young girl in the company of scoundrels."

She was breathtaking, a storm wrapped in satin and lace, and when she turned those eyes on me again, a shiver skittered down my spine. Beautiful, yes, but cruel enough that the thought of crossing her made the whiskey burn sharper in my throat.

"Why would he take her here?" I asked and put my flask back in my vest. "The conductor said there is nothing around here."

Jack was kneeling in the sand, his eyes narrow. "There is nothing here, not anymore. But there used to be."

His hand lifted, drawing both of our eyes to the water station tank and a small board nailed to it. "Frozen Dog - three miles."

Confused, I shook my head, "Frozen Dog? What the hell is that?"

Standing, Jack clapped the dust from his hands and glanced at us, "An old mining settlement. I thought it was deserted, but the buildings might still be there. Makes sense. Ed would know about every mine between Lewiston and Silver City."

The conductor dropped off the train's iron stairs, his head shaking. Clad in a crisp uniform with gleaming brass buttons, he was a steadfast figure. His strong hands were calloused from years of labor, and he possessed an air of authority which he tempered with a forced smile.

"Frozen Dog isn't real, Mrs. Hargrove," he said. "It's a story of a ghost town. Bill Hunter made it up when he came this way from Alaska. Don't follow these men because some clown hung a sign here to further the legend."

"Real or not," I cut in, "their tracks lead down the road to where that sign is pointing. If we want to get Lily back, we need to follow where it leads."

The grouchy old conductor shook his head. "You do what you want. I have a schedule to keep."

"You can't just leave her out here," Clara Belle said. "As a conductor, don't you have some responsibility? A code?"

The conductor jerked his thumb toward me. "No! I have a rail agent. He gets paid to handle things like this. I get paid to make my stops on time. Besides, you got the horses. It's not like you're stranded."

I stepped in close and wrapped my fingers in his collar. "And I'm telling you to wait for us. It will take no more than a few hours to go to this Frozen Dog and get her, then come back."

"My schedule!"

Jack lifted his shotgun. For a second, I thought the boy was going to shoot the conductor. Instead, he jerked the shotgun to the right and aimed for the swing arm that was feeding water to the engine.

Two barrels worth of buckshot turned it into scrap and steam and sent the conductor sprawling in the dust.

"Looks to me like you have an unavoidable delay," I said with a grin.

♠ ♥ ♣ ♦

Along the road to Frozen Dog, granite monoliths clawed upward, defying nature itself. Their silhouettes were jagged against a sky ablaze with an alien crimson hue.

The stones, ancient and eroded, bore a sinister aura, as if they harbored the memories of eons long past epochs predating humanity.

Shadows danced unnaturally under the eaves as if cast not by light but by something stretching and writhing as if alive. The sign above the gate — Frozen Dog - Est. 1871 — seemed carved not by human hands, something alien, something that did not know wood or the weight of tools.

"Well, this is practically Eden's gate, isn't it?" Jack muttered.

Doubting its divinity, I muttered, "The other place has a gate, too."

The wind carried not just the bite of autumn but a faint and fetid musk, too distant and too old to place.

Clara Belle turned her fretful eyes to me and breathed out a near whisper, "I guess it exists."

"Should it?" I asked.

Steeling myself, I stepped forward, determined to be done with this dark business. "If some outlaws are squatting here, Lily can't wait. Let's get moving."

Clara Belle muttered a prayer under her breath while Jack clutched his shotgun tighter, his knuckles pale. He tried to speak, but his voice seemed swallowed by the vast, oppressive silence that clung to the place like cobwebs spun by an unseen spider.

We strode three abreast down the damp road. Mud clung to our boots with every step we took. Not a rodent stirred, not a bird roosted in the barren cottonwoods.

Clara Belle lifted her chin, trying to summon that old imperious strength, but her voice quivered. "I think you might be right about it being a ghost town."

The wind whispered through the air, carrying the sounds of a distant wind chime, which seemed to transform into an ethereal song. From a building on the right side of town, I heard a sound that made me think of a child fumbling with a piano, the strings all out of tune and some even missing.

"Seems someone's at the saloon," I said and angled toward the music.

Clara Belle's hand shot out, grabbing my arm roughly. "Wait! We don't know who's in there."

My instincts were warring with my good sense. Every piece of me that had ever known fear demanded I flee this accursed place. My sense of duty to what's right and decent said I had to go in that saloon.

"We're in a ghost town in the middle of nowhere, Idaho. Of course, we don't know who is in there. But if anyone has been through here, I doubt it escaped their notice. Hell, it might even be Hargrove himself."

The saloon's door creaked open with the sound of a coffin lid, and the stench hit us like a corpse that yet lingered. A sickly blend of rotting meat, spilled blood, and something more profound, fouler. As though the very walls soaked up the suffering of ages.

"Jesus," Jack breathed and brought his sleeve to his nose.

Inside, the gloom was near absolute, broken only by the faintest flicker of a lantern hanging askew in the far corner. Shadows clung to the place like parasites, shifting and writhing in ways that defied the weak light. There were figures — four, maybe five — seated at scattered tables.

"Who do we ask if they've seen Lily?" Clara Belle asked in a voice that was a little too loud.

The patrons turned their eyes toward us. Their faces hovered like pale masks in the dark, drawn and unnatural, their skin stretched too tightly over sharp, almost alien features.

"I think you just did," I breathed into the silence.

Their eyes gleamed faintly, catching the light in a way no human eyes should. I felt the weight of their attention pressing down on us like a physical thing.

Clara Belle stepped closer to me, her hand brushing the hilt of a revolver I hadn't known she carried. I could only stare, rooted by the terrible stillness of those patrons who seemed more part of the decay than any living thing.

"My name is Dave Mathers; this is my partner, Jack, and Mrs. Clara Belle Hargrove. We're looking for a girl who might have come through here with an ugly bastard named Ed Hargrove. Anyone seen them?"

Not a soul moved. Their yellow eyes followed us as we stepped further inside.

Jack piped up, his words making my stomach sink. "I've got silver for the first person who gives us a solid lead. The girl's pretty, native like me, goes by the name of Lily."

From the bar, a toad-like voice with a French accent spoke up. "A pretty flower is lost? We lost a flower once, a beautiful rose."

Tall, thickly built, with long spidery hair, the man speaking made me want to hold my Army Colt for company. He looked somewhat native. My guess was that he was a half-breed, a French father, most likely.

"You seen her?" Jack stepped forward, his eagerness putting him outside of easy coverage.

"Jack," I warned. But my tone didn't slow his pace.

The bartender wiped a dirty glass with a dirtier towel. The greasy rag left streaks across the surface before he set it on the counter. He then uncorked a bottle with liquid as muddy as the puddles outside, the smell of stale liquor wafting up, and poured a drink.

The monotonous hum of a fly filled the empty room. The faint sound was the only evidence of life in this desolate place. The bartender watched the fly with the focus of a bobcat.

A low haze settled in the saloon, curling around the base of the bar like some living thing, clinging to the ankles of patrons and creeping toward the corners of the room. The dim, oil-lit lanterns on the walls sputtered weakly, their flames licking at the air as if starved of oxygen.

"As you can see, a lot of people come and go around here." The bartender's voice was thick and slow like molasses, but his eyes were sharp under the brim of his hat. "I'd have to think about it. Why don't you sit and have a drink? I'll try to recollect your pretty flower. You said she's a red skin?"

His hand shot out suddenly, quicker than I thought a man his size could move. His thick fingers snapped around a buzzing fly, silencing its frantic wings as his hand closed. He grinned, a predatory gleam in his yellowed teeth, and brought his fist to his ear as though listening to the insect's final struggles.

"Been through an eastern finishing school," Jack said again, though the bartender's scowl was hard enough to pound railroad spikes.

Suddenly, violently, the bartender shook his fist and flung the fly into the shadows. It didn't hit the floor, as I'd expected, but vanished into a darkened corner where something caught my eye. A web stretched between the wooden beams, trembling faintly as its occupant — small but unnervingly deliberate — skittered toward the trapped fly.

The bartender's gaze shifted back to us, unblinking, heavy with something shy of menace. "Drink," he insisted, his voice a low rumble. I slapped a coin onto the counter and took the glass myself.

Acrid and vile, the liquid seared its way down, the heat building in my stomach. It was more akin to a poison then a drink. That was the reason they called it rock gut, because it took one to digest the foul liquor.

I glanced back toward the web. The spider was already at work, wrapping its prey in silk with swift, efficient movements. The sight unsettled me more than it should have, and I couldn't shake the feeling that we were all caught in some unseen web, struggling as the spider approached.

"Dear god, what was in that?" I asked, gasping.

The bartender grinned a rotten, yellow-toothed smile, "It's good. I use it when I get a sour tooth."

The laughter that followed the bartender's crude joke was low and unsettling, like the rumble of distant thunder. It seemed to come from everywhere at once, bouncing off the warped wood of the saloon walls.

Jack's face was infused with heat, and like a viper striking, he seized the larger man's lapel in his tightly balled fist. "We're wasting time! Where's Lily?"

Clara Belle gasped, "Jack, no!"

As if brushing off an annoying child, the bartender broke Jack's grip and shoved him to the floor, knocking his shotgun into the dust. Around us, the patron's chairs scraped on wooden floors, and glasses thumped as they were dropped onto their tables.

My gun was out in a flash, and I thumbed back the hammer. I covered the unmoving bartender. "Easy, everyone. No need to get salty."

The bartender's lip curled in disgust. "Your boy ain't got no manners."

Jack struggled to his feet. Humiliation now added to his frustration and anger. I knew if I didn't cool him off, things were going to go bad fast. As much as it rankled me to do it, I had to take Jack out of the situation.

"Jack, why don't you go out and watch the street. Make sure the horses are okay."

Jack's face turned toward me with shock, hurt, and anger. He knew what was going down, and it was salt in his wounds. "No, Mathers, I got your back."

"You can cover me from outside. I don't think your being in here is going to make getting answers any easier."

Silence hung between us for a second as the patrons looked on, and the bartender fumed, his outrage only just contained.

"Go on now," I said.

Stepping to Jack's side, Clara Belle put a hand on his shoulder and squeezed it. "Jack, please. For Lily."

Glowering, Jack scooped up his shotgun and headed for the door. "I'll be within earshot."

The moment he was outside, the patrons settled down. Their mood was soured, and they'd lost the taste for recreation. Squatters, outlaws, rogues, or miners were the dregs of society, and I was positive every one of them was familiar with violence. Now that they had the smell of it, they liked the aroma.

"Okay, boys," Clara Belle narrowed a brow, "now that the entertainment is over, can we discuss what the information is worth to you?"

"What makes you think you have anything we want?" the bartender shot back.

Clara offered her imperious smirk, and I saw a glimpse of what had made Ed so successful.

As perilous as her father indeed, I thought.

A loud *thump* echoed from the ceiling above us.

Clara Belle yelped, her hand going to her chest. "What was that?"

The sound was followed by a slow, deliberate scraping, something heavy and sharp dragging across the boards. Every head turned upward, eyes straining in the dim light. The air thickened, the haze rising higher as though whatever was on the ceiling was pulling it upward with its movement.

Behind us, the door slammed open with a violent *crack*. A chill swept in, cutting through the stifling air and carrying the unmistakable stench of rot. Clara Belle screamed, her voice thin and brittle, as the shadows beyond the doorway writhed and shifted. A figure staggered forward, half-collapsing into the room.

"Mathers..." The voice was a rasping whisper.

"Jack?" Her voice trembled as she stepped toward him.

Jack stumbled inside and collapsed to his knees, his hands clutching at the floor as though trying to anchor himself to reality. "There's...."

A thick fog rolled in, tendrils snaking through the open doorway and chilling Jack to the bone as they curled around his hunched form. The air grew heavy and still. A tremor ran through him as his words faltered. His eyes darted over his shoulder to see something that contorted his features in a grimace of pure, unadulterated terror.

"Something's out there," he gasped. "It took the horses."

As the last word left his lips, he jerked violently as though yanked by an invisible force. He screamed, the sound raw and piercing, and was dragged across the floor toward the doorway.

"Grab him!" I shouted, lunging forward, but my boots slipped on the fog-slicked floor.

Jack's body twisted, his head snapping back to reveal bulging eyes and a mouth frozen mid-scream. With a clatter, his shotgun went tumbling to the floor, and he shrieked as he scrambled for it, to no avail. His voice was suddenly drowned out by an unnerving *skittering* sound, a chorus of tiny claws scraping against wood.

From the shadows beyond the doorway, something moved. Shapes — too many to count — spilled into view — hundreds of them, maybe thousands. Spindly legs glinted in the faint light, their owners crawling over one another in a writhing, endless tide.

"Spiders!" Jack screamed, his voice cracking with panic. He managed to regain his feet just outside the door.

I stumbled backward, pulling Clara Belle with me as the swarm surged. Jack's attempts to stomp them away were futile; the spiders climbed him like a living tide, their long legs clinging to his clothes, hair, and skin. He screamed, flailing wildly.

"Get inside!" I barked, shoving Clara Belle toward the bar. The fog thickened, and the shadows seemed to deepen, their edges sharpening into something alive, something waiting.

I turned, only to feel a sharp, explosive pain in my skull. The last thing I saw before the world went black was the bartender's grinning face, an ax handle in his hand.

♠ ♥ ♣ ♦

In the darkness, everything spun, a disorienting lurch like a boat tossed in a hurricane, or maybe it was just my head swimming. The pain blazed behind my eyes, a hot, jagged shard of agony that spread down my neck like liquid fire. Blinking, I could barely see through the stinging sweat and blood dripping into my eyes.

Clara Belle's unmistakable voice washed the fog from my mind. "I think he's waking up, Maurice."

So, she was behind it all along. When will I learn?

My arms were bound, pinned tight against my body. I flexed instinctively, but the sticky threads dug deeper, biting my skin. The smell of damp earth and something faintly rotten hung in the air, turning my stomach.

Maurice must be the bartender, I surmised. *He must have been the one who grabbed Lily.*

The clattering of iron wheels on warped rails rattled in my ears, steady as a funeral drum. I squinted through the gloom, the swaying lantern casting long, flickering shadows along the walls of the narrow tunnel we were riding through. A mine cart. They'd thrown me in a damn mine cart like cargo bound for hell.

The deep, resonating voice of the bartender confirmed my suspicions. "Doesn't matter. No one can escape those bindings."

Ahead of me, silhouetted in the flickering light, Clara Belle sat prim and straight as though she weren't in league with monsters. Maurice, the bartender — or whatever he was — sat beside her, his greasy voice carrying over the din of the wheels.

"Where's the girl?" His tone was low and guttural, though the undercurrent of anger was unmistakable.

Clara Belle didn't look at him. "Ed has Lily at the cave."

"And the boy?" The sound echoed sharply in the tight confines. "The spiders came for him. Why?"

The tension between them crackled like static, but they weren't paying attention to me. Good. I shifted slightly, testing the bonds. They held fast, unyielding as steel.

"I don't know," she said, her voice bitter and brittle as hoar frost on barbed wire.

Maurice muttered a curse under his breath. "If the sacrifice is not delivered, there will be no forgiveness. A Priestess should know that."

Priestess.

The word struck like a hammer on a pike, sending a jolt of clarity through my pounding skull. Whatever Clara Belle was — and whatever I'd thought of her — it was a lie.

"He will provide," she said. Though she looked at Maurice like she'd already considered her options.

The cart jolted suddenly, nearly tipping me to the side. The movement sent a flare of pain through my head, but it was nothing compared to the anxiety churning in my belly. I glanced toward the end of the tunnel, where the darkness seemed alive, shifting and coiling like something waiting for us.

The cart's rhythmic clatter began to sync with another sound — low and guttural, like whispers from a crowd that wasn't there.

And then the memories hit.

Cuba. The temples. The gods we weren't supposed to see.

I squeezed my eyes shut, trying to block them out. The jungle heat. The strange carvings. The curse. The things that crawled in the dark, half-seen but wholly felt. Roosevelt called his battalion the Rough Riders, some of us were more than that. Pale Riders were chosen to hunt what no one else could.

The Charge on Kettle Hill was more than it seemed. Our war, our disrespect, was our undoing. Misfortune was the price we paid for our victory. The god Eshu stood at those crossroads, his mad laughter striking with the din of steel on steel. It was his temple we defiled, and for our ignorance I paid the price.

My curse would be with me all my days. It was one with which I'd grown familiar. But this? No god from this realm was worshiped here. This was alien.

I forced my eyes open, staring at the pair before me. They didn't care that I was awake or thought I couldn't understand. I did. I understood all too well.

We weren't just heading into the mine. We were heading into the mouth of something ancient. Something hungry.

The air changed the moment we left the rickety cart behind. It was heavy, clinging to my skin like damp wool, and thick with a smell that turned my stomach — a blend of rotting meat and stagnant water, rank and warm as the breath of a dying beast.

Maurice guided the ponies ahead with his lantern's flickering light casting jagged shapes on the walls. His confidence, so sharp and biting before, faltered. I could see it in the way his shoulders hunched, the way his gaze darted toward every sound, every faint shift of the shadows.

"It's too quiet," he muttered, almost to himself. His voice wavered, a far cry from the snarling bark he'd used earlier.

Clara Belle's laugh was soft, almost kind, but it carried a sharpness that made my skin crawl. "Afraid, Maurice?" she asked, her voice echoing faintly in the cavernous space. "You, of all people, should trust the path. After all, you've walked it long enough."

"My people understood the balance —"

"Your people?" Clara Belle laughed. "You were born of a cast-off and the fur trapper who raped her. Don't try to tell me anything about The People."

He shot her a glare over his shoulder.

I trailed in silence, my arms still bound, the sticky silk holding fast against every attempt to wriggle free.

"You are quiet, Mathers," Clara said, her tone light and mocking. She turned to look at me. "You always were a delightful conversationalist. Don't stop now."

I bit back a retort. She wanted me rattled, desperate. I wouldn't give her the satisfaction. Instead, I watched. I listened.

"Let's hope you're as good a replacement as Joseph was supposed to be," she said, almost wistfully, her voice carrying a note of amusement. "Poor Joseph Green. He tried to hide, you know. Bless his foolish heart. It took a long time for Ed to track him down."

Maurice grunted, his steps slowing. "Ed," he chuffed a laugh. "Ed is just as foolish. Gutsy, maybe, but foolish. That's why he failed."

Clara Belle's features were sharp and scornful in the lantern light. "I would have been the mother of his new people. The Spider's bride bound up in her web forced to birth god and demon alike. It would have been an eternity of agony, despair and pleading for a death that would never be granted."

She was supposed to be a sacrifice.

"Ed spared me," Clara said, "I've paid Atlach-Nacha for his kindness every day since."

The name hit like a hammer to my chest, a sharp spike of recognition stabbing through the fog of confusion. *Atlach-Nacha*. The spinner of webs. The weaver of worlds.

Roosevelt's files mentioned the name once, a footnote in a report half-burned before we could finish reading it. A god — or something close enough to it. Something ancient. Malevolent.

"And now it ends," Maurice said. There was little conviction in his voice. "Do you really think He will allow another substitute?"

"He has to! How would I know Mathers would shoot Sergeant Green over a game of cards?

"It doesn't matter," she sniffed. "Bringing the last of the tribe to their god will prove my devotion."

"You're bringing Mathers as a substitute? That's going to be trouble."

"You should listen to him, Clara Belle. The Pale Riders will come for me."

Clara Belle smirked. "You should be honored, Mr. Mathers. Tonight, you'll see one of the genuine mysteries of this universe. Atlach-Nacha will love you, and you will love him. The weaver is good to his children. He devours his enemies."

I met her gaze with as much defiance as I could muster despite the bindings cutting into my wrists. "Spare me the sermon, sister," I said. "You think I haven't heard the ramblings of zealots before? You're no different."

Her smile was sharp, predatory. "Oh, I am," she said. "I was chosen, Mathers. Atlach-Nacha saw fit to enlist me."

She laughed, low and bitter. "My husband, Captain Ed Hargrove, and I were supposed to be on our honeymoon when my father and his irregulars massacred their tribe. Instead of sweet dreams and lovemaking, we suffered terrors in the night and whispers that stuck in our minds like bugs on a spider's web."

"It wanted retribution for the dead?" I asked.

"No," she laughed. "It wanted an accounting. My father's irregulars all had to pay the price for what they did. We knew we'd have no peace until they were all sacrificed."

I shook my head. "What do young girls have to do with it? Why the mail-order brides?"

"Atlach-Nacha isn't a patient god." She gave me a baleful look, "His hunger is immense, and without a tribe to bring him sacrifices, someone had to sooth his hungers, or he'd have driven us insane."

She shrugged, like murdering all those innocent women meant nothing. "The soldiers were enough to keep away the whispers at first. As they learned of the fate of their compatriots, they fled and became harder to find. So, we turned to alternatives."

"You started sacrificing young girls."

"Only those no one would miss. Year after year, blood for peace. It was never enough. He always wants more."

Clara Belle looked sad, resigned, and beautiful at that moment. I almost pitied her until she looked up and smiled. "Eventually, so did I. Now I want the power."

"And you think giving him Lily will satisfy him?" I asked, forcing the words out through clenched teeth.

"Oh, no," Clara Belle said, stepping closer, her face illuminated by the lantern's glow. "Lily must live. She will be his bride, as she was born to be."

Her eyes took on a distant look. "I will be her mother. Ed, a father both to her and her children. Our tribe will rise and serve. We will grow and spread till, like Brigham and his Mormons, we can establish our own land. A land where I would be The Queen Regent and Voice of Atlach-Nacha."

"Atlach-Nacha is no benevolent god! His kingdom will be bathed in blood to rival the Aztecs in Mexico. You couldn't possibly hope to get away with it," I said.

"I can, and you could have joined me. We know you're cursed by that pretender god from Cuba, Mysterious Dave Mather. We could have freed you from your curse and given you power."

"You know nothing of my curse," I spat.

She laughed dark and ruefully, sending a shiver up my spine.

"We had just one more life left to take. You went and messed that up when you shot Joseph Green."

I shrugged. "He's dead. What does it matter where he died?"

"Now you must take his place, and," she said reverently, "if you're lucky, the god will use you to help bring about his eternal glory."

The blood in my veins turned to ice, "You're insane."

"I'll have my kingdom." Her words echoed in the cavern, a chilling finality to them. I stared at her, at the calm certainty in her eyes, and felt the pieces clicking together. The hints, the innuendos, the strange dance of power between her and Maurice.

Lily and Maurice are from the tribe.

The tribe and the sinner. My dream of the Rock Creek massacre back on the train.

As the realization settled over me, the surrounding shadows seemed to deepen, the rotten warmth of the air pressing closer, suffocating.

Clara's eyes narrowed as a sound rippled through the cavern — a faint, rhythmic clicking, like claws on stone. It echoed from the depths, growing louder, closer.

Maurice stiffened, his eyes wide, his lantern trembling in his hand. "What is that?" he whispered.

Clara's smile returned sharper than before. "The god is stirring," she said, her voice low and reverent. "He knows we're here."

The sound wasn't coming from the shadows. It was coming from above. I craned my neck, catching the faint glint of movement — a shimmer of silk, threads descending from the cavern's ceiling.

Clara didn't notice. She was too enraptured by her delusions, too focused on the power she believed was within her grasp. Maurice saw it, and so did I.

Something small and dark fell on Maurice's shoulder, making his eyes go wide and then narrow like he was listening to something.

"Clara Belle, are you sure?" Maurice said, his head shaking.

She waved him off, stepping further into the cavern. "Nothing's wrong," she said. "Everything is exactly as it should be. The God will take what's owed, and we will be free. His children will walk this land consuming any and all who get in their way!"

"Where's that flask of yours?" Maurice said. Then he dug at my vest like the drink owned him. In seconds, he had my flask out and greedily gulped down several mouthfuls.

Tilting the bottle again, he spilled liquid that soaked the bindings. The alcohol's sharp scent froze me in place. Maurice briefly looked at me, his face revealing nothing. Something changed. I was sure of it.

He glanced down at his shoulder, where I noticed a small spider-shaped scar. A scar, like one I'd seen so perfectly rendered in a sketch not long before.

He knows she's going to kill him.

Clara Belle didn't notice. Her frantic pacing drowned out her words. My thoughts swirled. Whiskey-soaked fibers glistened in her lantern's light. The silk creaked under the pressure of my movement.

Maurice sat his lantern down beside me and stepped back. His gaze lingered on me for a heartbeat longer than necessary, and then he kicked the lantern.

The silk flared as the fire raced across it, and I screamed in agony. The pain was like a blazing fire inside me, obliterating all thought, but I couldn't stop, couldn't slow down. Straining with every ounce of strength, I fought the ropes biting into my flesh until, with a sudden break, I tumbled to the cold, hard ground.

Clara called out, her voice high with anger and panic, "Maurice, get him! Don't let him die. Not yet!"

I rolled till the flames went out, leaving my skin searing with pain, but I was used to pain.

Rolling to my feet, I leaped away and ran till my legs burned with fatigue. The air in the cave was stifling, almost tangible, and vibrating with a low hum that felt alive, pulsating with the heartbeat of something ancient and powerful.

Behind me, Maurice ran as well, though I did not know his intentions. Had he been trying to kill me or release me? Did he know my curse? Clara said she needed me, so why?

"It has to be you, Mathers! It's the only way," Maurice called behind me.

As I ran, the darkness of the cave seemed to give way to memories brighter and more alive.

Cuba.

The fever dreams clawed their way into my consciousness as I ran. Cuba, hot and thick with rot and smoke, pressed itself against my senses. I could taste the rum-soaked air and feel the dense heat wrapping around me like a shroud as I chased the Spanish soldier through the dense growth.

And there it was, standing at the edge of the grove. Eshu's temple and dark statue were long lost in the jungle. His dark, angular form was draped in scarlet and black, his grin wide and gleaming like a crescent moon. The courtyard had long ago been reclaimed by the vines, but the walls were standing, ominous and bleak.

It was like a gateway to another realm, a gateway guarded by a malevolent trickster. Time and again, I tuned in from that dark place, only to find myself facing that Spaniard and that dreadful altar once more.

The saber in my hand felt so heavy then, as if it knew what I'd done — and what was coming.

The Spanish soldier had been lost, just as I was lost now. Stumbling through the sacred grove, our blood defiled soil where we never should have tread. We fought with blades, rocks, teeth, and claws till we were both bloody forms, trying not to die. As it turned out, my fortitude was the greater of the two.

When I cracked his skull, Eshu wasn't even angry. No. He laughed. A cruel, musical laugh that danced on the edges of my hearing long after I left Cuba behind. It wasn't until weeks later that I realized the truth. I was cursed to suffer until age claimed me or Eshu grew bored with my screams.

Reality came back to me as the ax handle, I'd used to smash Maurice's skull slipped from my bloody fingers. Laughter echoed in my memory of the amused God, and I wondered if he found this amusing as well. It looked like Maurice played a role he hadn't even known he'd auditioned for.

It had to be me.

Turning away, I found Ed Hargrove looming over me.

I was in the altar room, but how I got there I could not say. Behind him, Lily stood, hands bound, a dazed expression in her eyes.

Ed's hand shot out, slamming into my temple. I slumped, agony becoming my world.

"The amulet was a game changer, Mathers. But you know what? You raised the wager. Now you have to play the hand you're dealt."

Ed grabbed me and dragged me toward the altar, tearing burned flesh over rough stone. A laugh escaped my burned lips as my own sanity tried to flee. Because the joke was on me. It always had been. One God wanted me dead. The other insisted I stay and suffer.

Lily put a finger to her lips. There was something in her eyes, something as cool and soothing against my fevered mind as cold silk on a summer's night. Her eyes darted to a mass of web and a limp form strung up within.

"I told you, I speak to spiders," she winked.

Jack, I realized. The spiders brought him here. Lily had something to do with that?

Biting back the pain, I controlled my mewling moans as Ed dropped me to the ground.

"Stay with him!" he commanded, then shoved Lily down beside me.

A familiar voice whispered in my ear, "Easy, Mysterious Dave, okay?"

The dazed look was gone as she glanced toward Ed's retreating figure and my burnt form. "If you kill Ed before we're wed, we can stop this. Ed is his vessel."

"Lily!" Clara Belle called with a delighted tone. "Ed, I knew I'd find you here. Let's consummate this marriage and begin our new kingdom."

Lily ignored Clara Belle and smiled down at me sadly. "I'll ensure he gets close, then shoot him in the heart," she said. She reached down inside my shirt and grabbed the amulet, jerking it free. "He won't kill you till he finds this. He needs to complete the ritual."

Quickly, she lifted my hand and pressed her lips to my knuckles. "It was nice to meet you, Mysterious Dave Mathers," she said, a twinkle in her eye. Then she pressed something small, cold, and metallic into the palm of my hand.

Ed's footsteps faded away, and I was left alone to suffer at Lily's feet.

The silence was deafening, and that's when I noticed it. Perhaps it was the pain clouding my mind, but Ed's movements were hesitant, lacking the usual vigor he always exhibited. No longer was he able to move with the same ease and grace, his body now stiff and heavy, jerked with a puppet-like motion, as if controlled by unseen strings.

I swayed, my eyes blurry as I watched him move toward the altar, and as if in a daydream, I found myself unprepared for the vision that met my gaze. The back of Ed's skull was missing, and inside the hollow, a shining, long-limbed spider sat, its legs twitching as it peered out of his dead, empty sockets.

It was only a vision, but what I saw would spawn new nightmares.

The skin on the back of his legs appeared sliced and flayed, with muscles exposed. Inside, sticky white webs were strung down to his knees and feet and more up to his arms. The closer I gazed at the vision, the more the strands stood out, and each gained its own unique horror. The strands weren't web at all, but the countless souls of the many sacrifices offered to the dark God.

For his efforts, the creature was treating Ed like a sock puppet. He had been entirely consumed by the evil of the spider god, and nothing could save him now.

Clara Belle moved toward us; her steps confident, imperious. She'd disrobed and drawn arcane symbols on her skin with mud, and somehow, she was still regal and in command. She had every right to feel victorious. There wasn't much I could do to stop her now.

Firelight flickered off the walls, casting jagged shadows across the thick webbing draped over everything — the altar, the floor, even the ceiling. I could feel the God's presence, heavy and oppressive, like the air before a storm. It was awake now, watching, waiting. Ed stood at the center of it all as Clara Belle moved to his side like some hellish consort.

Clara Belle's lips were curled in that smug little smirk of hers, the one that always made my skin crawl. She thought they were untouchable and that their hold over me was absolute. Then, as if to prove it, her followers from the saloon in Frozen Dog followed her into the cave and lined up like priests at Mass.

Disrobed, their actual forms were more horrible than I'd thought. Their limbs were long and thin, with too many joints and too little muscle. I saw on them the marks of war, slavery, and abuse and knew at once they had all been sacrificed. No wonder they were so quiet. The dead don't talk much.

Around me, the ritual took shape, nuptials binding one world to another as the minions summoned Atlach-Nacha.

Clara Belle led Lily toward the altar I lay against and guided her onto the stones. "You'll be the mother of a new tribe, a new nation in a world ruled by Atlach-Nacha. You have no idea the honor you've been given."

"No. Please, I'm afraid." Lily said, her voice timid, a little terrified.

The God's presence was close now, and Clara Belle presented a blade that shone like lightning just before she sliced into Lily's dress, laying her bare to the cold cave air.

Ed grinned wickedly as he fumbled at the bottom of his own shirt. I heard Clara Belle's words echo in my head and shuttered as I realized what was about to take place.

He'll be her father and the father of a nation.

Moving toward Lily, Ed's hands worked his belt, hunger in the hollow behind those eyes.

Lily will be the gateway. This is how Atlach-Nacha avoids the pathways between worlds. He will be born to her. This is why Eshu wanted me here, to stop this.

"Do you have the Amulet?" Clara Belle demanded, turning to look at Ed.

Ed looked puzzled, confused.

"The amulet is the key! You can't spill her blood unless you are adorned with the amulet!"

Ed then looked over at me with a scowl. "Where is it, you dirty, cur?"

In quick, jerky movements, he was by my side, his hands in my shirt and searching each pocket. The more he searched, the more frantic he became. Frustrated, he slammed a fist into the side of my head once again. My head collided with the stone of the altar, and lights flashed in my eyes.

His knife came out, that small, wicked little dagger he'd brandished at the poker table.

"Don't kill him! We need him for the sacrifice!" Clara Belle shouted.

"Where is it! Do you know what's at stake?" Ed screamed and started cutting my burned clothing from my body.

Around us, the chants grew louder, and the heavy demonic presence grew till my nerves felt like fibers pulled too thin. The God was near, and it was angry.

"Hurry," Clara Belle screamed. "It's upon us!"

"Lily!" Jack yelled, awakened from his stupor.

A roar filled the chamber, making Clara cover her ears. Her gaze searched the chamber and grew wide with horror as the shadows coalesced into long, thin appendages. The God was pushing its essence into the world, reaching for its host so that Ed could shed the blood of his bride.

Lily yelped and hopped off the altar, her nimble body crowding in toward Ed.

"NO!" Clara Belle screamed.

Ed turned, his instincts kicking in. His hand went out like a flash, the blade gleaming into the lantern light.

My hand seemingly moved on its own accord, rising and pointing, what I realized was a small, nickel-plated derringer with a pearl handle. Lily's derringer.

"I know the stakes, Ed," I said pulling the trigger. "Call me a fool, but I'll call."

Ed stumbled as the bullet exited his back and sprayed visceral matter over Clara Belle.

Unhindered, he attacked, driving a razor-sharp blade into Lily's ribs until the brass hilt was buried.

"It's done," Clara Belle said, breaths ragged. "The blood is spilled; the last soldier must die to consummate the marriage."

Ed smiled wickedly. As if all the sound in the world was cut off, silence reigned at that moment.

We failed...

Ed's expression fell as Clara Belle, blood splattered like the voluptuous nymph who adorned the wall of the train car, slumped to the ground. Blood leaking from her lips as she cupped her stomach.

The bullet went through Ed and hit Clara Belle!

His face now a mask of rage, Ed lurched toward Lily, his knife slicing the air between them.

"Lily!" A fresh voice called. Jack ripped free, the remnants of the web slicing his skin as he unleashed a furious roar as he escaped his confinement.

"Jack!" Lily sighed and nearly lost her feet. At that moment, Ed dove at her with his knife. Jack's shotgun roared as if it were an awakened dragon. Somehow, he still had it. Ed was the one who felt its fire. The buckshot tore into his body, sending him down into the throng of chanting worshipers, who scattered into growing chaos as the dark God's presence grew.

"You have to die!" someone screamed, and I realized it was Clara Belle. She crawled up my blistered husk, her red talon-like nails sinking into any soft tissue she could find. The nails broke and chipped, looking like they'd been in my dream.

I screamed as my skin came off in burned shreds, leaving torn, bloody wounds all over my arms and chest. She was trying to literally tear me apart, and there wasn't much I could do about it.

"If you die, he'll accept you as the last soldier. I know he will. He has to!"

Close the passage. A voice said in my mind, and I knew it was Eshu who spoke.

Pain. Pain, like I'd never known, raked my soul and demanded I succumb to a reaper who didn't know my name. My fingers had grown numb. Somehow, I managed to lift the derringer and cock the hammer once again.

"Why won't you die?" she screamed.

My own chilling whisper snaked through the air. "My curse… Do you really want to know my mystery?" A hollow ache echoed in my chest, the unspoken grief in my voice as I spoke. "The truth is, I can't die. No matter how much I suffer, I'll survive so Eshu can laugh at my agony."

Through the pain, I heard a hollow, choking laugh. I fired the second round from the derringer right into Clara's heart.

Incredulity, then panic and fear flooded over Clara Belle's features as she drew back. "Please, no. Don't take me, I can serve you. I can bring more…"

Her legs crumpled as her soul was claimed, and the last look on her face was terror at seeing her God in the afterlife.

Nearby, Jack was holding Lily close and weeping openly. Her color was mostly gone, her eyes losing their luster.

"I'm sorry, Jack. I wanted to save you, so I spoke to the spiders."

There was panic in his eyes as Jack pressed his hand to her wound, the blood seeping between his fingers. "Easy, Lily, you'll be okay."

Her bemused laugh turned into a cough. As she tenderly tried to wipe web from his hair, she smiled. "I guess I did… in the end. It can't… can't be born if I'm dead."

"Lily, no!" Jack howled.

The dark God screamed in rage as his victory slipped from his grasp and back into the abyss. His wail was nothing compared to the heart-sick despair in the sobs of Indian Jack Wood.

Like all of us Pale Riders, Jack would have his share of nightmares and grief. Some things just can't be unseen, unlived.

All I could do was lay there and try not to move as Jack carried Lily to the surface, then gathered the bodies of the dead and stacked them like cordwood. I didn't want to think about the flames that would follow. I had my own burns to occupy my mind.

"Is it always like this, Mathers?" Jack pushed me out of the mine in the mining cart.

"No," I said through clenched teeth. "Sometimes we don't get to bury our dead."

Behind us, the stink of burning flesh caught up with us just as we broke into the open.

Jack looked around for a moment, then at the spot where Lily lay. "Once we get her buried in Emmettsville, I'm going to come back and collapse this mine. Bury them all inside and make it like it was never here."

"You can bury it deep, son. But it will always be here," I said. But I didn't just mean the mine. Like the horrors in this world, the road to Frozen Dog, and others like it, would always exist.

Michael Craig Biography

Michael Craig is a lucky SOB with a supportive family and beautiful lady at his side. He is an author, and father of one son, two unruly goats, chew toy to three dogs, and a stupidly big horse. A retired Army Medic, who has dedicated his life in service to American veterans, he currently spends his time either in his garden, fishing or penning the occasional yarn.

Across the River

JP Johnson

Children were a nuisance. It's not that he hated children, he just found them to be irritating more times than not. When children found something they wanted, they had the persistence of a hungry dog when you had a sandwich in your hand. This particular group was a pack of hungry dogs.

He was busy, and this wasn't a distraction that would help him get his current series of projects done. He had a new cooling mechanism for the city's cold house to design, and several new weapons that needed to move from drawing board to something held in your hands. After a second of consideration he decided that it was best to give them a morsel, and maybe, just maybe, they would leave him in peace.

Setting the small metal part for a new rifle design onto the cluttered work bench, he turned to his erstwhile distractors, "What is it you want exactly? I am too busy for foolishness today."

Doctor Otto Messer fixed each of the six children with his most stern look before leaning back to rest against his workbench. A short man, and slightly stooped, the bench came up to just below his shoulder blades. He pushed back a lock of gray hair with a hand covered in soot and dirt, leaving a smudge on his forehead. His square face and gray eyes looked at this latest bunch of pests. They were perhaps eight or nine years old; he had a hard time telling anymore. Time was hard to measure when you had lived as long as he had.

"We want to hear a story about the old days, Uncle Otto." Part request and part command from the ring leader. She was a wisp of a girl with long brown hair, her head held high, mustering up as much gravitas as could be generated from a child. He had no doubt that this one would wear a braid one day, and ride with the women of the 1st Cavalry when she came of age.

Every child in town called him Uncle, a small irritation in a world of much larger problems. The people of this town were as close to family as he would ever have again, taken in that context, the nickname wasn't so bad really. He had learned to accept such things as they were intended.

"A story? That is no simple request. Stories are always about more than words." The scowl softened, and the short man took a seat at a stool near the bench.

A boy stepped forward, "My Pa said you were there during the River War. Is that true, Uncle?"

"It is true. I was here from the beginning to the end." The memories were always there for him, just below the surface.

The River War, he shuddered to think of how close a thing that had been, and how much it had cost them in their young city/state of Lexington. These children wanted to know about the return of magic, and the great heroes. They always wanted stories about heroes and the great battles fought for the very survival of man by those men and women.

"What part would you like to hear? I will give you some time but then you must go, I have work to do." He rubbed some of the dirt from his hands with a rag from the bench.

He saw her then, standing in the back of the group. She was always so quiet. She would be a thinker like her grandmother and father. A person who let deeds speak for them. Right now, she was a pencil-thin girl with unruly dark blonde hair and a shy demeanor. Her eyes looked to the ground more than anything else.

"Little Sophie! There is no truth to be found on this dirty floor. Look up and tell me what you would like to hear." So many years and he still had an accent, most thought it was German, but it was far older than what modern man thought of as German.

He looked like a man in his seventies but his voice was still hard and steady. He had lived here for years before anyone had finally asked him why he never looked any older. People had more pressing issues to deal with at the time. The collapse of civilization brought everyone back to more crucial and basic concerns.

The girl seemed to think for a moment, and then looked up toward the man the adults called the Builder and the children called Uncle Otto. He remembered the girl's grandfather, a good man, and a bad end. Otto also remembered her great grandmother. She was a woman he could not forget.

He remembered everything that he had ever encountered, every detail both good and bad. It was a curse of sorts. Memories he would like to forget, as fresh today as they had ever been. The pain just as sharp. There were good things to remember, but the bad was always louder in his mind.

"I want to hear about the Scout," she said barely above a whisper.

There it was, what he knew she would ask for this warm Lexington morning. He could not tell that woman's whole story in so short a time. The Scout: time had already forgotten her name had been Harper Beardsly, but that's how legends and myth worked. Time morphed and changed them.

"Hmmm how about one short story about the Scout?"

Her face lit up, "I would like that very much. Can we hear about when she fought the demon across the river?"

Otto had to admit to himself, that was a good story. The sort of tale children always wanted to hear about. Adults leaned toward stories about hard decisions, and great movements of men and nations. Children however, they wanted excitement and adventure. They wanted stories that were very clear, this person was good, and this other person was bad. Children do not like nuance or ambiguity.

"Very well," he pointed to a pair of benches along the back wall, "Sit down everyone."

"I will tell you about the Scout and her fight with a great demon in the woods." He reached into a jar on his bench and drew out a small handful of grey powder.

He tossed the powder into the glowing coals of the forge to his right. The grey powder flashed and made an acrid smelling smoke that hung over the coals. Soon a cloud of grey smoke formed above the forge. The cloud's center changed and became smooth as glass.

"You have heard of The Fall, the end of the time before this time; the time when men lived in glorious cities with buildings reaching toward the sky. Man had reached the pinnacle of his science and the heights of his arrogance." As he spoke, images of shining cities and great airplanes flying through the skies appeared in the cloud.

Each child's attention was riveted on the scene playing out over the forge. All knew the stories of mankind's descent from near godhood to a relatively primitive life virtually overnight.

"You see, the old powers, the ones that ruled this world when man still feared the dark, they were waiting for their opportunity to return and dominate mankind once again. Science had driven them out. Each gadget that man created weakened their power little by little until they became nothing but legend and rumor. Each great discovery pushed man further and further from the real truth of this world. Dark forces still dwelt amongst men, things that wanted to regain their power over humanity, but men no longer feared the dark, and believed themselves the masters of the world. That arrogance made humanity weak." He sat back on the old stool.

The image in the smoke changed with Otto's words. Airplanes and skyscrapers were replaced with statues and images of ancient gods. Many of the statues portrayed dreadful things of tooth and nail. Gods of death were followed by deities of nightmare.

"The old powers wormed their way back into the world of men. They sowed dissent wherever they could. We grew fearful and resentful and hateful from their crooked words. An angry man is a man easily manipulated. That fear grew and grew until the nations of man began to make war on one another. First there were small wars that were fought for many years. The final war ended in horrible bombs and the day we call The Fall. The world of man collapsed into ruin and those old powers returned. The dark ones had waited, and now they stepped back out into the world of man. What did they bring with them?" he looked into the transfixed faces.

As one, they all whispered, "Magic."

"Yes magic, and monsters, and things that hadn't been seen by man for many years. But man was not done, was he? We stood and we organized as men always do. Our home here was born out of the dark time of The Difficulties. The hungry years that came right after The Fall. Man had forgotten how to live off the land, he had relied on his machines, but those no longer worked, did they? Those were terrible years, but we persevered, and we learned again how to live a simpler life. We learned how to sow the fields again and hammer the steel. We prospered, didn't we? Soon one of the worst of the old ones saw us and he plotted to destroy us all. The one we called the Prince, he who was the Avatar of Malice." A gasp from the children after he named a being that had become a cultural bogeyman for the people of Lexington.

"The Prince was jealous of what we had built and he set out to undo all of it. He sent people and things to kill us. He made war on us. Children, this is how our story came to be, in that time on the frontier between us and Old Georgia, across the river that was once called the Savannah, into a land of nightmare made real. The Scout was a member of the 1st Cavalry, the Braided Women. She was a great soldier and very clever, but she had become separated from her patrol after they had been attacked by men twisted by the Prince's evil. It was here that our story starts, in that dark time, far away... across the river." The old man waved his hands in the air.

The image in the smoke changed to a lean woman in her twenties with a long brunette braid down her back and sun-tanned skin. She was dressed in brown pants with a black stripe down the legs and a long sleeve brown shirt with Corporal's stripes on the arms; the uniform of the Lexington

1st Cavalry. Weapons hung on a leather belt around her narrow waist. Tall brown leather boots in the stirrups, she rode a light brown horse in a piney wood.

Staring into the image in the smoke, each child could smell the pine and saddle leather, and just as soon, they felt the horse beneath them.

***

She was being stalked. It had become obvious a mile back when she realized that she hadn't seen or heard a bird or squirrel in quite some time. These woods had teemed with small animals when she entered, but now it was absolutely silent except for the sound of her horse's hooves on the old road. Somebody was shadowing her.

Flickers of movement caught her attention as she moved through the trees. A shadow kept off to her right, staying in the trees just far enough for her to be unable to get a good look at it. She was pretty sure it was just one man, but how did it stay alongside her, and yet it kept so low to the ground? Horses make a lot of racket, so she ruled out a mount. The guy was smooth, fast, quiet, and apparently on foot.

Was it waiting for friends to arrive or was it just playing with her? The obvious move for her was to force the situation, but that required some planning. She needed a good spot, one that would maximize her position and weaken or negate any advantages her stalker currently possessed. If it was someone just able to run and move fast, she had one very clear advantage, she was mounted on a horse and a good horse was a weapon unto itself. A horse offered a big speed bonus in the hands of a cavalry trooper.

Her team had been tasked to patrol into Old Georgia. No small thing from her perspective. Once you crossed the river you were in an area of savagery and brutality. Before the fall, the land across that narrow strip of water might have been a great place to live, but that time was now a just a memory.

Radiation from the bombs, chemicals from unattended factories and a host of biological weapons had made the land across the river a hard and unforgiving place to live. Civilization had reestablished itself back home, but not here, and maybe not for a very long time.

Three days after they had ridden from the city of Lexington, in what was once called South Carolina before The Fall, her three-woman patrol had run into raiders at the river crossing. This was a well-used fording site for the Cavalry patrols, a fact the raiders mustn't have known.

The desperate men had tried to stop the three women to levy what they called a tax for crossing into Old Georgia. Their leader had yelled his demands as they rode toward the ford over the old Savannah River. Narrow and shallow, it was a good spot to ride the horses across, which is why the three women were trying to use it.

The filthy man waved a machete in the air and threatened certain death if his commands were not obeyed. She and her two comrades were members of the 1st Lexington Cavalry and no one commanded them that hadn't earned that right. Harper's patrol leader drew her revolver and shot the man in the chest from twenty-five yards away. The .36 caliber bullet had ended the threats. The body dropped into the muddy water to be swept down river, food for the critters that called the rock-strewn river home.

"If you sons-a-bitches don't clear out, my girls and me will kill the bunch of you." Sergeant Adams yelled from horseback, now halfway across the river. She dramatically turned her head so her long braid would be visible to anyone that may be hiding in the brush on the opposite bank.

The women of the Lexington 1st Cavalry braided their hair when they were accepted into the unit. It was both practical and a very visible symbol of the toughness of those that wore it. A woman wore the full braid until time or injury took them out of the unit.

Harper appreciated a little intimidation. Shooting one man and playing off the mythos surrounding the members of the 1st Cavalry was a good technique and saved them wasting ammunition. She had heard, and seen from refugees what effect just seeing the braid had on people. Sometimes it was reverence, and sometimes it was abject fear. She had one very old woman ask to kiss her braid after her patrol had saved the woman's small group from a gang of possible cannibals.

These idiots fell in the category of abject fear. After watching their leader fall, four ragged, skinny men broke cover and ran. It was actually very good luck for them, if a platoon from the heavy infantry or worse a team from the Light Company had showed up here, those four would be very dead. Her brothers on the ground weren't big on negotiation.

The men in the heavy infantry liked to nail a card to the skulls of these kinds of raiders. The card had a laughing skull on it and the words 'Courtesy of the Lexington Heavy Infantry'. Most of the time the raider was dead, but not always.

Once the first hurdle in the trip had been dealt with, the three women crossed into Old Georgia and started their mission of reconnaissance across the river.

They hadn't ridden two hours before running into another group of raiders picking through an old farmstead. Harper saw ten men, lightly armed and reported that to Sergeant Adams. The older woman decided to go around them and avoid a fight. Their mission was to observe and report, and only fight when they had no other option. The detour added hours to the first leg of their mission and forced them to ride through most of the night.

Traveling at night in that land was not the best thing to do for most people. Things walked around at night. Things you didn't want catching you unprepared. Creatures twisted and turned by forces manmade and unnatural. Monsters didn't just come on two legs in Old Georgia.

Sergeant Adams had them catch a quick nap in a cold camp for a few hours before sun up. The Scout was fairly sure the patrol leader had stayed awake the whole time. They were supposed to take watches but neither she nor the third member of the patrol, Private Metz, had been awakened.

Sergeant Adams was a tall woman who had grown up in a place called Texas before The Fall. Her husband had been stationed at a local Army post when everything went to hell. Harper thought of the woman as the perfect example of what a good leader should be. She was decisive and exuded a quiet confidence that Harper tried hard to copy.

Day two had been clear, sunny and very mild as far as the temperature. Summer and its oppressive heat hadn't made its grand appearance yet. When she thought about it, it was a great morning to ride, right until the bullets starting flying by the mounted women.

Harper wasn't sure who was shooting, but they were definitely shooting at the three women. Sergeant Adams cussed loudly and told them to ride, pointing to where she wanted them to go. When you're on a horse and people start shooting at you, people that you can't really see, your reaction is to take off and let your horse get you out of trouble. Harper didn't think of it as running. They were in a bad position, and you don't let the enemy bait you into making an even worse decision. They needed to disengage and make the tactical situation better.

The real problem occurred only minutes later. Another very good rule to remember was to never underestimate your opponent. The patrol rode hard into the woods to break contact with whoever was shooting at them from their right and directly into another group. The second bunch looked like they were waiting for the women to do just what they were doing. They had set up barriers of brush and small trees in front of them, and were firing from behind the hasty barricades. The rough men yelled and jeered at the Cavalry troopers.

The Scout remembered her father laughing one evening and saying to be careful, things can always get worse. The man had lost an arm during the time after The Fall, when Lexington was fighting to get back on its feet. A one-armed man during the Difficulties learned to survive by luck, friends, meanness and adapting a certain level of philosophic sarcasm. That outlook proved true right now. It was, in fact, much worse.

Sergeant Adams kept her head through it all, and yelled to turn to the left and ride like hell before drawing her pistol and firing toward the second ambush party. Visible through the trees was a steep embankment just twenty yards away. The shooters probably thought the embankment would keep the women from escaping.

The Scout wondered if capture had been their real goal. You don't shoot that much and hit nothing nowadays, and raiders did like to capture women. Three women from the hated Lexington 1st Cavalry would be a very prestigious prize. A rumor persisted that there was some kind of bounty on the women's braids, but she didn't know that for sure.

The three galloped toward the embankment. Metz's horse stumbled in a low spot and she spent critical seconds getting it under control, and headed in the right direction. The patrol leader stopped to wait on Metz, her horse dancing around the forest floor, anxious to be out of the danger. Harper started to draw her pistol from the black leather holster at her side, but she heard Sergeant Adams yell.

"Go, damn it, go!" There was a note of desperation that had crept into her mentor's voice, and that alarmed Harper more than any radiation sickened man shooting at her.

Her horse made short work of the embankment, climbing it with ease as she leaned over the saddle to keep from losing her balance. When she reached the top, she paused a second to look back and saw the Sergeant and Private Metz riding along the bottom of the embankment to her right and away from the men firing from the barricade. Maybe the Sergeant thought she could skirt the edge of the two groups. Harper didn't know, and she couldn't wait around. The fire was now directed at her. Bullets impacted tree trunks and branches all around her.

Small splinters filled the air. She pulled her horse around, and rode as hard as she could away from the shooting.

It took two days of running and hiding to finally give her pursuers the shake. She had to admit to a certain admiration for the raider's persistence. They typically weren't this disciplined. Raiders preferred the easy route to get what they wanted. Chasing one woman on horseback didn't seem very easy to Harper. Harper couldn't discount the possibility that this was all related to why she was here right now.

Her patrol team had been sent to confirm or deny the existence of a new warlord in Old Georgia. Refugees had reported a gathering of forces near a town called Milledgeville. The starving and frightened folks said the worst kinds of men were all heading toward that small town. A threat like that posed a significant threat to the city/state of Lexington, and they certainly wouldn't want mounted reconnaissance riding through their area.

Late on the second day she gave them the slip after riding through a swampy area near a small town that had been burned to the ground years ago. Her clothes still stank of that swamp as did her horse. She found an abandoned barn late in the day. It was large enough for her and her horse to stay in for the night. A little rest was past due for them both. The small house near the barn had been burned sometime in the last few years. Harper didn't even check for any salvage; she would just add the persistent stink of ash to the swamp smell.

The sun set and she waited another hour before she set some tripwires, changed into her only other uniform and tried to get some sleep. It was hard to relax after the previous day's exertions but she managed to get some fitful sleep.

Her dreams were bizarre and difficult to clear from her mind even after waking. A man with light brown skin, slicked back black hair and an easy smile spoke to her. He called to her by name, and in the dream, she wanted to go to him. It unsettled her on a deep level. She was a Cavalry trooper, and the saddle made you hard. She was not someone to cast aside good sense for a handsome face.

Some of her rations hadn't been soaked in the swamp so she had a light breakfast of hard tack and jerky on the morning of the third day in this no man's land. Not particularly tasty but it filled your stomach.

Patrols getting separated wasn't extraordinary, it just hadn't happened to her before. She had to decide what to do next. The book, so to speak, said to continue the mission. Usually, a rally point would be established in case something like this happened, but they hadn't set one when the ambush started.

Typically, a rally point would be a terrain feature, something easy to find. The ford was a known factor, but that meant giving up on the mission. She could ride there and wait or she could ride through her sector and gather whatever intelligence she could alone. It was a tough nut to crack. Alone was wasn't an attractive option.

She checked her horse and led him to some grass nearby, letting him get some food of his own. The mission came first, people were relying on her team and the other patrols to fill in the blanks about what was going on across the river. Standing there watching her horse munch on grass, she made the decision. She may be alone, but one cavalry trooper is all it took, and the mission did come first.

***

"She was alone, it must have been scary." A little boy whispered.

The tall girl, whom Otto suspected was their informal leader piped up, "She wasn't alone, she had her horse."

One young man who had remained silent until now added, "They always have their horse."

"The grunts don't." a small voice added from the shadows.

"The Ghosts don't need nobody." The boy's father was in the Light Company where each member was commonly called a Ghost.

"That is all true, but the Infantry have each other. The Light Company is trained to be alone. The women of the Cavalry rely on their horses as a means to move around and a faithful companion. They sometimes go great distances and a companion helps." The small man tossed a little more grey powder into the forge.

"What happened to the other two, Uncle Otto? I liked Sergeant Adams." another young voice.

"That is another story, you asked for The Scout's story. Now, are we ready to continue?" little heads nodded in near unison.

"The woman named Harper, who we now simply call The Scout, was alone, deep in Old Georgia. She knew she had to do her duty, so she rode away from the old barn heading southwest toward a town called Apple where she hoped to find some refugees or farmers she could talk to." He began to wave toward the smoke again but was interrupted.

"Apple is a stupid name for a town," said the third child from the right on the right-hand bench. A skinny little stick of a boy. Otto knew that one's mother, the boy's lack of manners was typical of Mira's brood.

"I will ask the spirits of that town about the name next time I see them." Scowling, he began the spell again.

"She followed an old highway until a group of men caused her to get off the road and ride through those haunted woods. It was there that we go back to her story. She knows something follows her but it must be confronted. Let us see how she solves this problem." The smoke changed again and the children were back on the path through the piney forest.

***

There was a clearing ahead, it looked like it might work for her purposes. Time had come to draw her skulking friend into the open and put a few lead bullets into his head. Random people didn't track you like a dog through the woods. This man meant her ill.

She drew her horse to a stop and stood in the stirrups. A casual observer would think she was simply stretching, but she was trying to figure out how much room she had to work with when she broke into the clearing. As nonchalantly as possible, she tried to determine where the stalker was right now.

A shadow paused in a stand of scrub oak and bushes just twenty-five yards to her right. She couldn't get a good feel for what she was dealing with exactly. It looked like a large man, but when she turned her head in that direction the shadow vanished. When she looked back down the road toward the clearing ahead, she could just see it in her peripheral vision. It didn't matter, she was going to force the encounter before the encounter was forced on her.

Gently pushing her heels back, her horse began walking down the old road toward the clearing ahead. Two years ago, the shod hooves of her horse would have made a sharp, clear noise on the blacktop surface of the road. Today, the old, dark colored surface was no longer visible; it was buried beneath dead leaves and pine needles. She moved her horse slowly down that fading road.

As Harper got closer, she could see the small grassy meadow was perhaps fifty yards across, and round in shape. The old road cut right down the middle with no ditches or obstacles visible. It was a pastoral spot with knee high grass and a mix of pine trees and scrub oaks surrounding it. There were butterflies flittering from blossom to bush, adding to the tranquility of the spot.

The distance to the meadow was growing smaller and soon things would become much more energetic. It would be a very bad time to make a careless mistake. Her horse could step into a hole, but you couldn't plan for that. A small hole in a forest meadow was just bad luck, but finding a weapon missing because it wasn't secured properly was bad soldering.

She tried her best to casually check the leather strap that held her carbine in the long scabbard secured to the right side of the saddle. She could feel her pistol at her hip. The revolver was big enough to not let her forget its presence when in the saddle. The handle of her knife had always rubbed against her left side. The leather handle used to give her a blister, but over time she had developed a callus in that spot. Finally, she scooted her butt in the saddle seat and felt her tomahawk shift at her back where it sat in its belt loop.

She had all her weapons in place. Now things just needed to work out in reality like they did in her head. Her father called it 'go time', the moment when thought turned into action.

She put her heels back hard. Her horse immediately launched from a slow walk to a full run. She let him have his head as they burst into the meadow. The other side of the open space had a thick patch of trees that would serve her plan. A little pressure on the right side of the horse and he turned to the left and that same small stand of very dense trees. Just before the trees, she pulled him around to the right and stopped just past the small stand of young pines and tangle foot brush.

She vaulted from the saddle and when her feet hit the ground she reached up and pulled the cavalry carbine from its scabbard. It had been patterned on a very old design called a Winchester Model 73. The Builder said it was a good weapon for mounted troops to use, and it was easy to keep working. Harper was fond of the short rifle. She wasn't a big person and the gun just fit her better than anything else. She pulled the lever on the bottom of the carbine down and then back up, feeding a cartridge into the chamber.

Turning to the clearing, she took a kneeling position and brought the rifle to her shoulder. She waited to see if her pursuer in the woods would make a fatal mistake. She fought to control her breathing. Sweat ran down her back and bugs flew around her face, but despite those distractions she watched the other side of the meadow through the sights on her carbine. She could hear her horse shuffling around behind her but no other sounds.

Her stalker hadn't done what she hoped he would do. She expected him to dash across the open area in pursuit of her. She knew her plan wasn't perfect, and anyone with any sense would stop when they hit the open area, but she was a good shot and just a few seconds of indecision on the other person's part was all she needed.

No one appeared on the other side of the meadow, no breathless raider trying to keep up and not lose contact with her, no anyone. She told herself to be patient, but it was hard. Her heart pounded in her ears. Harper had been in a few scraps during her two years in the 1st Cavalry but this time was different. There were no sisters to watch her back; this time she was alone.

The first sign of trouble, beside the bad guy not cooperating, was her horse suddenly becoming very agitated. He stomped around and began uncharacteristically huffing through his nose. The horse was not happy about something, and getting less happy by the second. She knew there was no chance for surprise anymore. The amount of noise the horse was making gave her position away as sure as a gunshot. The horse finally bolted, running back to the old roadway and away from the meadow as she watched helplessly. Her problems were stacking up and still no sign of the person shadowing her. She only had the weapons and ammo she carried on her belt, and to compound things, her canteen was still tied to the now distant saddle.

She turned back to the other side of the meadow and across the open ground. A light breeze was blowing, and she could see the tall grass move with the wind. It was a pretty spot to camp or just stop and rest.

A feeling blossomed and grew in her mind until it verged on compulsion, a desire to just put down her carbine and lie down in that tall grass. An urge for rest, sleep, and a break from the mission and the burden that it brought. The grass looked so inviting. The urge grew and before she completely realized what was happening, she dropped the short rifle and stepped out of her hiding spot and into the open.

A voice called to her from the now inviting grassy meadow, "*Harper.*"

***

"When does the fighting start? I want to hear about fighting," said the little boy as he made slashing motions with his hands and a series of sound effects to accompany the combat he imagined should happen.

"You are an odious child," said Otto. These delays were maddening.

"It was a demon dummy. They got magic and stuff." Another voice chimed in on the discussion.

Children. Aggravating little monsters of our own making. A self-inflicted plague of misdirection. Otto didn't regret having no children, and right now he was wishing others had exercised the same sentiment and abstained.

"Battle starts first in the mind. War and fighting are first a matter of will." He was probably wasting his time trying to explain this to these micro assassins of efficiency.

"My dad says a good soldier always attacks." The first critic asserted.

The old man grabbed his head. That was Reynolds boy. He had no recollection of Reynolds ever attacking anything but a beer.

"Yes, well first you need to know what you are attacking. You wouldn't want to jump from the frying pan, into the fire, would you?" Gods, he had things to do.

"I guess." The boy grudgingly acknowledged.

"It warms my heart that a child would validate my opinion." He turned back to the forge.

He raised his hands again, "Now if you wouldn't mind, let us see how our hero handles this problem." And amid more slashing sound effects from the little critic, the image in the smoke changed back to the Scout standing in the tall grass.

***

"*Harper.*" The voice was so inviting.

It felt as if she were floating above herself, and watching as her own body moved. She needed to focus, to concentrate, and try to break whatever spell was being cast on her. It was hard; her mind felt mushy and she couldn't clear her head enough to get control back. She took one step forward. Fighting as hard as she could to regain control, she finally managed to stop. Harper thought she had succeeded in overcoming the strange compulsion, when the horse came running back into the meadow.

The light brown gelding ran back into the clearing, and reared back, iron shod front feet slashing at the air just yards in front of her. The whole thing was strange; why was he doing that? There wasn't anything there that she could see. Seconds passed before she felt as if a great weight had been lifted from her shoulders.

A shadow stood just five yards in front of her. A shadow in the shape of a large man. It was perhaps seven foot tall and very broad in the shoulders. No weapons were evident, but apparently it needed none because it backhanded her horse, sending it tumbling over into the tall grass.

"*Aggravating animal.*" The voice changed from inviting to annoyed.

She stepped back and drew her revolver while her horse recovered his footing and stood on shaking legs. The shadow turned back to her, unconcerned with the horse now. She could see no features in its face but she knew on an instinctive level that the creature was amused by the whole situation.

"*You have been most intriguing Corporal Harper Beardsly, daughter of Ramona and Joseph.*" A voice that sounded as if it came from the depths of the very Earth itself now filled her mind.

"How do you know my name?" she shouted trying to get a good aim at the apparition's head.

It laughed making her ears and head hurt to hear the sound. It was an assault of sound. Trembling, she thumbed back the hammer on her pistol and squeezed the trigger. When in doubt, shoot first, and work things out later.

Fire flew from the muzzle. She pulled the hammer back and fired a second time. The shadow stood unfazed. There was no blood or bone, there was nothing at all but the dark outline of a head.

"*Oh, you are most entertaining, aren't you? Do you think that little machine can hurt me?*" it said with a laugh that made her stomach clench. The thing spoke with an awful surety. She couldn't have missed.

"*Possession is so boring. This is much more fun and interesting, isn't it?*" The thing changed, slowly then more quickly until a man stood in the place of that dark outline.

He was dressed in relaxed clothes, unpatched jeans and an untucked white shirt, leather boots on his feet, a smile on his too-perfect face.

She didn't know a lot about art, but she had seen some in pictures, and this is what those ancients were striving for when they sculpted in stone. Men did not look like that now; life was hard and that deprivation inevitably reflected in your face.

A thin, straight nose sat on a lightly tanned face framed by light brown hair that fell to his shoulders. A clean-shaven face highlighted eyes that had a sort of blue glow to them. She had to force herself not to look into them, for she was certain she would be lost if she did. He looked much like the man from her troubled dreams in the old barn. He wasn't the same man, but they could have been brothers.

"It has been a joy following you, watching you, one of the dread braided women." His hands moved to his mouth as if in fear at the last part, merriment in his eyes at the same time.

"That was clever in the swamp. I liked that a great deal. You made fools of them, and I applaud you for it. Your ancestors would have been very proud." He clapped in mockery.

His manner was almost childlike in spite of her trying to shoot him.

"All games must end, and yours and mine are no different. Your skills have earned you a singular honor." He sat down on a chair that hadn't been there a second ago. "*I am a scout myself, of sorts.*"

She holstered her pistol, which clearly wasn't going to work. Her mind raced trying to think of what would hurt something like this creature.

"Oh, that is a fascinating question, isn't it?" She recoiled. Could he read her mind?

He laughed and held his fingers to his temples, "*Are you thinking about avocados? I see small green, bumpy objects.*" A deep belly laugh now.

From his shirt pocket he drew out a cigarette and match. His long fingers quickly maneuvered the slim paper tube to his mouth and with a quick flick the match ignited. He drew in a long drag and regarded her again.

"*I can't read your mind, but I can read your face. Relax a little.*" Another drag from the cigarette.

She had to think of something.

"Did you know that I created tobacco? Really, I did. It was genius if I must say so. The Boss was impressed with that one." That laugh again.

"Anyway, let's get to it, shall we?" he tossed the cigarette away which seemed to just vanish into the air. "*I work for someone very special. I find things for him. Objects and... talent.*"

She needed something, anything to help get out of this. Her horse still looked like he wasn't sure where he was and her pistol was useless.

"A man materializes in the woods and I should believe his words?" She needed to stall until some viable option became evident.

"I need people, people just like you. The kind who will do the things my boss needs done. Now I don't promise fame and fortune, but I do have a very generous benefits package that includes all the best the world has to offer right now. You know, scratch that, the world is kind of messed up isn't it, not much really to offer there at all." He looked into her eyes before she could turn away.

"You have nothing I would want. I have been warned of your kind." Harper straightened to her full five-foot four-inch height.

She had been told to be leery of things that may not be altogether natural. All the girls had laughed at that until a patrol returned with firsthand experience. The women had run into some kind of ghostly thing in the ruins of Atlanta. None of the women on that patrol were the skittish type so their words were taken to heart. The world had boogeymen now; be on your guard.

"I'm sure you have never heard of me. How about a little immortality? You would never get sick again or grow old. You would be the same healthy young woman you are now." The man leaned forward in his chair.

Harper had to admit that was an attractive offer, but she knew better than to trust such a creature. The things that were now appearing across the land of Old Georgia after The Fall practiced deceit like a human breathes. Not many years ago, things like this apparition would be unheard of, but now the world really was different.

"Oh, come on, it's a lot of fun. I got really drunk once in Rome during the reign of Augustus, you can't beat the Romans

when it comes to a good time." He was so pleasant in his manner that you wanted to believe him.

"I don't know anything about any Romans." She tried to remain steady and defiant.

"Time hadn't started when I was brought into this universe. How would you like some of that? No more patrols, bad food or crappy booze. You could just wait it out until things got good again. They will get better, they always do." An emphasis on that last bit.

"So, what do you say? Want in on the team? I'll even let you keep the horse." He sat back again in the chair and she was able to finally break eye contact.

A huge grin on his face and a confidence you didn't see these days. Below it all was a kind of malevolence. She was sure that this man was perhaps the most dangerous creature she had ever encountered. The man was like many of the old wooden homes still dotting the land. Pretty on the outside, but you knew if you scratched away the paint you would only find rot and decay.

"I will take nothing from you. I am a soldier of Lexington; a trooper of the 1st Cavalry and I cannot be bought by you or anyone." Harper hoped she sounded firm in her conviction and not scared.

Harper was suddenly struck by a strange feeling while she stood there in the meadow. The same feeling you get when trying to remember something important you had forgotten, but this was much stronger. A nagging thought she couldn't clearly see, but it shouted in her mind. It wanted her to remember something very important. Oddly, the sensation felt somehow alien, as if it wasn't her memory at all. It was becoming quickly very uncomfortable. What did she need to remember?

"Truth can be harsh Harper. The truth is you're a little girl, alone in the woods, it isn't the best position to be in right now. I'll give you one more chance to change your mind." The

man leaned forward, the grin falling and changing to something less pleasant.

Harper quickly pulled the knife at her side before drawing the long-handled tomahawk from its loop on the back of her belt. The revolver didn't work, but cold steel might.

"I have to say, I am disappointed, good help is very hard to find right now and I think you would have really fit in on the team. A real asset to the organization." His words began to slur as his teeth could be seen changing, they seemed to multiply and grow very sharp.

The features of his face became more severe and darker like someone had added dabs of black dirt to all the deep spots on his cheeks and eyes. The cheeks expanded to points and the chin narrowed. His hands lost their delicate appearance and become long and tipped with sharp claws. The skin of his arms became a dark gray color and muscles rippled beneath the surface. The casual clothes he wore fell away. He stood and the chair vanished to wherever it had come from.

He continued to change before her eyes. Horns sprouted from his head, growing up before sweeping backwards. His eyes were no longer blue, they had a reddish hue to them now.

"Oh, you are such a treat. I really hate to do this but you aren't buying what I'm selling. I can see it now. I'm afraid you've got to take what's behind door number four." He grew more bestial as his last clothes fell away revealing course fur and clearly defined muscles.

It was as if a great and terrible horned wolf-like creature was standing on its hind feet in front of her. Harper watched as he grew taller, now towering over her. Slobber dripped from his large fangs.

"In Hell we like to say, sell them till you get to eat them. Guess what part we're on now?" and the man who became a monster started toward her.

The memory that had nagged at her mind bust from its mental confines. She suddenly remembered the day she was given her knife and tomahawk. They weapons were handed out when you finished the training course to become a long-range patrol trooper. All the women got pistols and rifles when they got their braids during the graduation to become members of the 1st Cavalry. Not everyone got the special knife and tomahawk. Those weapons were only given to the best and brightest of the graduates. The women who would become the eyes and ears of the fledgling city/state of Lexington.

Every woman in the 1st carried some kind of knife, that was true, but her knife and tomahawk were forged by the Builder. The little man made all of the weapons given to the few who had shown they could live off the land, and survive to report back what they had seen in far lands. Each woman was handed the weapons by the Builder and told to keep them close. Each girl drew her knife and tomahawk at the end of the ceremony and kissed the blade of each weapon. The act signified the bond between the woman and the weapons.

The weapons glowed for a few seconds before fading to the appearance of plain steel. The only thing visibly different from any other knife or axe was the odd little symbols each trooper's weapon had, near the guard on the knife, and the handle on the light axe. They were called runes and the Scout couldn't read them, but the little man told her after the ceremony, the weapons were sort of blessed.

He told her after the ceremony when she asked about the weapons, "There are things in this new world immune to bullets, Harper. A time will come when these small trinkets may be the difference between life and damnation. You will know when."

She felt a sense of relief, the feeling you get when you remember the thing you had forgotten. She took a wide legged stance with both weapons extended to her sides, inviting him in.

Each weapon began to glow with a faint golden aura. The light enveloping each blade gave no heat, but they somehow felt lighter in her hands. She found herself now feeling less daunted by the thing before her and more confident. If it wanted a fight, she would give it one.

The wolf-like creature stopped its advance and fixated on her axe and knife.

"That little bastard Brokkr is still alive? Oh, I recognize his work. You are no godling or being of the higher worlds. the little elf's toys can't save you from me." His teeth slurred his words, but she got the idea. She wasn't sure what the hell an elf was, or who this Brokkr was, but it didn't matter now.

"I have no idea who Brokkr is and don't care. You keep coming and I'll bury this axe in your head." She stammered a little. It sounded more intimidating in her head.

Her instructor in fighting with blade and axe had said, the fastest man or woman wins. When her group of young aspiring cavalry troopers chuckled, he simply said, that it really was that easy. Be fast and you win. She just needed to be fast.

"Let us put those toys to the test little girl. I will wear your scalp at my waist when this is done. I think I will let you watch me do it." The man-thing charged toward her, his long sharp claws reaching out.

It was overconfident. He relied too much on that initial shock to overcome an opponent. She easily side stepped to her left, twisted and brought the tomahawk down, connecting with his right arm. Black blood flowed from the wound immediately, and he howled in rage and pain in equal measure. She didn't wait around, and stepped off quickly to the spot where he had been standing. She got back into her stance, keeping the blades moving in front of her.

It spun around much quicker than she could have guessed and charged again It came in low and swung its injured hand at her knife hand, its left arm cocked back. She saw the trap. If she came in with the axe on the injured arm again, the thing would stand up to its real height and nail her with that cocked left hand.

He was fast, but she could see what he meant to do, and that allowed her to be faster. The monster had probably counted a great deal on fear to aid him. He was a frightening thing to behold, but she learned to channel her fear long ago. She feared liked anyone else, but she had always been able to compartmentalize that fear till the fight was over. Fear could cloud the mind and she needed her mind clear. Living through both The Fall and the time of The Difficulties taught people to control their fear. The new world taught you things very quickly and brutally. Fear could paralyze a person if uncontrolled and that could get you dead.

She dodged the injured arm and instead of bringing the axe down on the already bleeding forearm, she rotated at the waist and swung it low and into the creature's side. It was risky and she knew it, so when the injured arm reversed and sent her flying, it wasn't a big surprise. Black blood oozed from a nice hole in its right side, roughly below where its ribs should be. She rolled in the grass and recovered quickly. She fought to catch her breath. Her midsection hurt with a sharpness she hadn't experienced before. She had to fight an urge to cough. Maybe the man-monster would stop to talk and let her catch her wind.

She pointed at the wound in its side. "That must hurt. You can run; doubt I could catch you."

She was feeling a little more confident as she watched the black blood flow from its wounds. She just needed a few seconds; the backhand had hurt. A horse had kicked her once a few years ago, the blow from the thing had been like that kick.

There would be no respite today, the thing was on her immediately. Sharp claws raked across her left shoulder. Blood immediately flowed from the deep cuts. Its body had turned with the swing and now she saw that it had exposed itself. The pain was intense but she couldn't play around with this thing. A voice in her head told her that bleeding him wasn't going to work, it was just too strong. She needed to score a big hit someplace critical. Her chest hurt more each second. She needed to finish this now.

Harper reversed her knife and brought it up to where she thought its crotch ought to be. Its swing had opened it to attack, arrogance was deadly in this kind of fight and the creature was certainly arrogant.

Harper felt resistance for only a second and then she felt blood wash over her knife hand. The dark ichor was very hot and it was flowing very heavily from the deep wound. The thing bellowed toward the sky and seemed to draw its body in. Its claws reached down, trying to pull itself from the knife buried to the hilt between its legs. It stood on its toes trying to get away from the knife blade.

This was her chance, time seemed to slow as she swung with all the strength she had, and buried the tomahawk in the creature's neck. The whole six inches of steel had penetrated the thick neck. Blood splashed out from the strike. It shrieked in spite of the horrific neck wound. The sound was a physical thing.

The wolf-like monster that had been a shadow, and then a man, exploded in light and waving tendrils of darkness. The force threw her into the air to crash onto the grass ten yards away. The breath had been knocked out of her and her tomahawk was gone, wrenched from her hand by the violence of the explosion of light and energy. She still had her knife, and she kept it in front of her as she stood back up on shaking legs, fighting to catch her breath. Harper was sure a few ribs were broken. She tasted blood in her mouth.

An amorphous blob of inky darkness, so dark it hurt her eyes to look at it, hovered where the creature had been. Its shape constantly changed and moved. A set of glowing blue eyes appeared in the center of the mass. Then the darkness changed from a round form to man shaped before becoming the handsome man in casual clothes again.

"Damn, but you are a good time. I loved the crotch shot, that was inspired, and the follow up with the axe, absolutely sublime." His voice wasn't sweet and smooth now, it was harsh. His words hurt to hear.

Harper's body was hurting everywhere and the wound in her shoulder was starting to throb. Her horse seemed to have his wits again but he was backing up from the thing of darkness. She found she was resting her arms on her waist, no longer able to keep the knife in the ready position as she had been taught. The backhand and the explosion had hurt her worse than she initially realized. A trickle of blood ran from a head wound she didn't even know she had until now.

"Look, no hard feelings. I got excited and you got excited and mistakes were made. What's a little casual knifing amongst friends, right? I got stabbed by a Mongol warrior once and we still managed to work around it, nice guy that Genghis. Moved on to great things and you can too." The man smiled. His hands moved with each word. He liked to talk with his hands.

"So, last time, and this is the last time, my dear. I am too old to beg and you did stab me in my naughty parts with an enchanted bowie knife. Join the team, we have plenty of openings for someone with your obvious skills." The smile, the eyes, you wanted to like him, you wanted to please him.

She fought the compulsion to go to him and kneel before him. He was a thing of evil, even if the evil was wrapped in pretty paper. She could see the malice in those eyes. The knife in her hand took on an intense golden glow, she had decided, or maybe the blade had made the decision. It didn't matter, she crouched down the best she could into a knife fighting stance. Blood in her eyes and mouth and lungs that couldn't seem to get enough air into them.

"No! Nothing you have is anything I would want. Come on, let's do this." And she tried to look him in the eyes.

"I had high hopes for you I really did, call me an optimist. But no hard feelings. This was just an audition of sorts. The Boss said to try and recruit you and I did, so no sweat off my nose. He did say not to kill you, so you have that going for you." His eyes seemed to focus on her wounded shoulder.

Harper steeled herself for the attack she was sure it was about to start, but the man didn't move toward her, instead he stroked his chin for a second.

"I can fix that." And he pointed at the bleeding claw marks. She felt the cuts contract and when she glanced down, the deep wounds were gone, only red scars where they had been. Her ribs felt repaired as well. Breathing was much easier than it had been a moment ago.

"You know, I can't just let you walk away from this. You have to pay something for sticking me in my favorite spot." And both his hands came up and she felt a wave of something pass through her.

"Every year, on this day, at this time, for the span of our conversation, those scars will open again and you will bleed, and you will know pain. Then you will think about how you spurned my most generous offer." The man was fading before her and the voice grew deeper and more menacing.

"Good bye, my dear Harper, and tell the dark elf bastard that made those blades that Mammon would still see him dead. I have not forgotten him, and you will not forget me or this day." Then the man and the darkness faded to nothing.

She felt like a great pressure in the air had been released, and she drew in a deep, clear breath. She staggered to where her tomahawk lay in the grass not far from her carbine. Retrieving both weapons, she stumbled toward her horse. It was time to head back to do what Scouts do, report what she had seen. She needed to find out what a dark elf was, and who the hell this Brokkr person was when she got home. Scouts ask questions, and she had a lot of them.

***

"Did she get back?" a little voice asked breathlessly from somewhere on the left bench.

"Of course she got back. How else would we know the story?" another one answered, indignant at the question.

"Yes children, she got back and told us what had happened. About the fight in the woods, and all that she had seen on that patrol into Old Georgia." He stood up and stretched, feeling his many years.

"Who was Mammon and who was the dark elf he was talking about?" the ringleader asked, standing now.

"Mammon was the demon, jeez." One virtually snarled. Children could be cruel.

Otto paused, "Mammon is a very old demon and the elf is another story. Now I have work to do and time waits for no one. Not even me."

"But Uncle Otto, don't you make the weapons for the patrols?" It was the quiet girl, the one who wanted this particular story, Sophie.

She walked to stand directly in front him. He crouched down and looked at her face, she looked so much like her great grandmother, as if time itself had rolled back and he was looking at the Scout, the girl Harper, as a child again. He missed her, maybe most of all. She was so alive and he missed that feeling. He was proud of her and what she had become in those days. A kind of daughter he never had. She was a modern shield maiden like few others.

There were so many stories from that war, and the times that proceeded. It saddened him because he may be the only one left who remembered them all. He wondered if he should write all the stories down somewhere. Later though; he had work to do now. His guidance had put them firmly back in the age of steam. He still had many projects to do before sitting down and becoming something as tedious as a storyteller.

Little Sophie still stood expectantly in front of him.

"Yes child, I made her weapons." A gnarled hand touched her cheek.

"Will you make mine?" she asked with a smile on her face and in her eyes.

"Yes child, I will make yours too." And he smiled, because when the day came, he would make her knife and her tomahawk like he had her great grandmother's all those years ago.

JP Johnson Biography

JP Johnson is a retired US Army Cavalry Scout Master Sergeant and Dept. of the Army civilian. He currently lives in South Carolina with his wife of 41 years. When his grandchildren will let him, he likes to fish, hunt, spend time on the range, and write. A longtime history nerd, JP also likes to build black powder guns in his shop. He is responsible for many converts to the muzzle loading cause.

We Are Not Gods

Re Gwaltney

Aithyr's central trade road erupted with vicious shouts, sprays of blood, and the acrid scent of false magic. Under the glaring rays of noonday sun, highwaymen — no, something else — pounced on the guarded carriage like a swarm of ants. They traded lives for those of their victims; for each who fell to the sword, another found an opening for a decisive and lethal spell that gained them a scrap of ground toward their target.

My steps slowed several dozen yards from the carnage, unnoticed despite the loud crunch of gravel underfoot. Though my fingers twitched in the air with intent, I stood my ground. My lips pressed hard shut, face sternly blank, chest rising and falling with deliberate rhythm. The dozens of combatants dwindled, finally, to a mere five.

Ah — one less.

All at once it was over. Chaos fell into stillness as the victorious assailants caught their breath in a sea of leaking corpses.

Whatever the reason for this, they would be gone soon. I could be on my way.

One of the men, clearly the leader, reached into the carriage and hauled out a waifish woman with long locks of black hair spilling loose across her shoulders. At first, I tried to turn away; a skirmish I could stand to witness, but I couldn't watch a helpless innocent fall and do nothing. But I glimpsed her face as her palms sliced open across small, sharp stones. Her pale eyes stared forward, vacant of thought and feeling. She showed no panic or pain, nor any inclination to defend herself. My resolve to ignore the bloody clash died when I caught sight of her.

The man left her in the middle of the road and took his place with the others. In unison, they raised their arms and wrapped something long and thin around them. Once again, the harsh smell cut through the wind, only growing stronger as they mimed the slow draw of a bowstring. Vibrant, ugly green shafts materialized, all pointed toward the woman. Then, after a short breath, they all first at once.

With a rough shout, I called on my own power.

Sheaves of steel petals sprouted from the ground, engulfing the pale, prostrate woman just before the arrows struck. The missiles broke into sparks of sickly green that splattered across the chrome with thousands of tiny, hissing whispers. Acid. Had even a drop touched her skin, it would have burned through flesh and gnawed through bone and marrow. That sort of caustic magic wrapped around nerves and spread throughout the entire body. Her death would have been as painful as it was quick.

And yet I still shouldn't have interfered. Thoughtless instincts like this endangered my oaths.

'Stop fooling yourself, Izithia; your vow is holding you back. There are so many more just like her. You wander and wander, and you do nothing.'

I ignored the phantom voice whispering in my ear. For seven hundred years she'd goaded, coaxed, and confided in me. The wisest answer was always to ignore her. It was *my* judgment that summoned the steel rose around the woman, that drove my boots across the dusty gravel to face off with the four humans that cast the carnivorous acid, that set my quiet gaze against the crazed glare of their leader. I was sure of it.

"Hybrid. Traitor. How dare you?" he snarled. "Don't you recognize the Weeping Lady?"

I considered the woman's title. Stories trickled across the region this past decade of a young woman whom some called a prophetess and others called a god. They said she revealed herself a handful of years ago to lead the humans — the ones without magic — to salvation. It would explain this slaughter on the trade road.

'What a find. Dearest, you've stumbled across gold.'

"This is an execution," I said and brought a hand to my throat. My voice sounded foreign to me. It came out soft and hoarse from years of disuse.

"It is," said the man without shame. "Are you new to these lands, woman? If you are, I urge you not to get involved. Travel on, or better still travel back where you came from, but leave the woman with us. I have no wish to kill a fellow magus."

Pouches, pockets, the clinking of small vials, and the smell of chemicals in the air marked them as alchemists, the closest things to mages that pureblooded humans could become. In their narrow minds, that made them magic. I reminded myself that they simply couldn't know or feel the depths of true power. This was as sacred to them as anything worth killing and dying over.

The other three fanned out in a vague arc behind their leader, hands lifted with various reagents twisting between their fingers. I knew little about their strange science and couldn't begin to guess what manner of spells they aimed at me. Perhaps something strong enough to break my rose. Or even to break me.

'Don't make me laugh. Insects, all of them.'

"Worldspeaker…" I released her title in a breathy whisper. My eyes squeezed shut, opening only a moment later with the layered steel petals in my sightline. Flashes of a giant prison of the same shape resting in the center of a barren wasteland played across my mind. I drew in a shaky breath and pressed my palm against the smooth slope of metal.

"Has she raised a weapon against any of you?" I asked.

The man's brief attempt at calm dissolved. "She arms our oppressors with anti-magic tools! She gives them gifts of war and slaughter!"

That was enough.

My fingers sank into the metal and curled. Drawing my hand away, I brought a length of steel with me that formed into a long, thin pole. The stiff metal changed into a supple and balanced form with grips molded along the length, near the center. I stepped between the rose and the mages, twisting my staff through the air.

"Leave," I said.

His eyes bulged. The muscles on his neck strained against his skin. "I knew it. Filthy hybrids never had any sense of honor."

He signaled to his allies. Two of them sprinted to my sides while the third ducked behind him. I had no time to check what they were doing, though the suffocating feel of chemical air blossomed around each.

The leader produced a small vial from a pouch and crushed it in his hand. Hissing with pain, he hurled the bloodstained shards in my direction. Whatever formula he'd concocted elongated and sharpened the shards, and they sang through the air. My staff met them in rapid spirals. Glass shattered with each tight sweep, but a few needle pricks bit past my travel leathers.

With so many around me, I couldn't play defense. Alchemists excelled at coordinated attacks, as each could contribute to a piece of a larger ritual in a fraction of the time. The only way to stop it was to disrupt a part of the machine before it could take form. Confident in the Weeping Lady's shelter for now, I abandoned it for a charging swipe at the leader.

As I hoped, he dove out of the way. Ignoring the urge to pursue, I carried into a second strike for the woman behind him. In one hand she held a gout of heatless flame the color of a cloud. She pulled it far behind her and raised her other arm to take the blow. A crack of metal on bone. She screamed and crumbled to the ground, but her pyrelight still burned in one raised hand.

She met my eyes, then looked wildly past me as the other end of my staff flicked toward her uninjured hand. Just before it made contact, her fist closed around the flame and it molded back over her hand. Weaving, lacing, no longer fire but a thousand impossible white threads. My strike snagged on something and suspended in the air. I couldn't wrench it free.

And still more fine white tendrils like spider thread spun around me, each anchored to at least one of the three axes of the ritual formed by the magi. The more I struggled with my hopelessly tangled weapon, the more it snared me, too.

Something sizzled behind me. I spun, feeling more of the webbing wind around my arms, and saw the leader draw a symbol on the steel rose in a liquid that scarred the surface with each touch. My teeth clenched and a hot lash of malice burned through me. Traps. Trickery.

'They really would let their hate kill a helpless woman. I told you.'

My eyes shut and muscles clenched, and I turned my palms down as far as they would go with the webbing holding them in place. In my mind, I formed a perfect picture of myriad stone slabs the shape of shark fins, their edges so sharp they gleamed. The landscape took shape. When I opened my eyes, it laid over the scenery before me like a second picture. My phantom blades would claim every unoccupied space for fifty feet.

"Don't worry," the man said to me. As he activated his spell, it began to eat a hole straight through the rose. "I have no reason to kill you. If you hadn't placed yourself in the middle of this, we would have greeted you as a friend — after the Weeping Lady is dead, we can have peace."

My tongue clicked behind my teeth. The last vestige of compassion I had left for the humans waned and snapped.

All in the same moment, dozens of razors sprouted around me. They obliterated the webbing and spiked toward the two standing mages hard enough to leave them stunned on the ground. Their spell broke. No new threads formed. Then a needle-like thought flashed through me. I could continue, I could — if I just made my spires a little longer — let them bite into flesh and bone, the rest would be so simple.

I could kill them.

I could.

"...Sentinel."

The voice came small and trembling. I had to turn again to see the woman I'd injured back on her feet, heavily hunched with her broken arm clutched safely against her belly. She stared wide and hard at me, as though witnessing some mythical figure. Something beyond myth. Sentinel. My breath caught.

I halted my onslaught. A cold chill washed down my spine — I'd been recognized, and so easily. Then, glass shattered on metal, a few drops of something hit my sleeve with a scream-like sizzle, and lightning pain shocked my skin below. The burn wracked my mind enough that I lost my mental hold on the forest of spires.

They dissolved into nothingness. I broke the staring contest and turned, throwing my staff like a spear at the leader. No sooner had it thunked into his shoulder than I sprinted over open ground. He tried to hurl a second vial at me, but I summoned a wall between us to clear myself a path to the rose. I heard glass shatter and gout of flame, then nothing.

I let the rose dissolve. The woman still sat where she'd been thrown, staring lifelessly into the face of one of the casualties of this useless fight.

I grabbed her and ran.

***

A few dozen yards from the trade road, the rocky crest of a hill met a sharp, unnatural descent into coarse, pebble-filled dirt. Trees were few and far between in this stretch of the country, and the barren winds from the west stripped the natural wetlands of all life-giving humidity. Yet the city Aithyr found that to be a boon. Over the past thirty years, they pitted their shovels and picks against the ground until vast quarries broke the landscape in all directions. My charge and I barely had to run twenty yards before the lip of a quarry sheltered us from the mages' spells.

I allowed us both a few scant seconds to rest while I listened. Unfortunately, the arrhythmic pattering of boot and raised voices told me everything I needed to know. I adjusted my grip on the Weeping Lady to tug her by a single hand, continuing into the quarries.

Thank Everything, she ran with me. Despite acting like an empty doll on her own, she did as I wished the moment I touched her, as if all she needed was the direction of a higher power. My gaze, in between checking our footing or the path behind us, constantly returned to her. I felt none of the alchemists' chemical magic on her, nor did she show the usual signs of a drugged stupor. Her pupils worked normally and her complexion was clear. But still, she hardly acknowledged the world other than to follow along, step by step.

I couldn't imagine her as a prophetess, much less a god.

Just as the thought formed, she made her first sound. I'd meant to pull us around the most circuitous turns I could find, keeping us out of the view of the shouting pursuers close behind, but she halted before the inky black entrance of a tunnel bored deeper into the earth. She slipped from my grip with a sharp gasp. I stumbled to catch myself.

"I'm trying to save your life," I said, thinking she resisted out of fear. But her hand extended toward the cavern in something like reverence, and I fell silent.

"This…"

She whispered her first word, still so deep in her daze. Nothing else came out.

The shouts grew closer. I glared at the most recent bend in our path.

She entered the cavern.

"It will be a dead end," I called, but it made no difference. The woman I'd recklessly made my charge descended into a pitch-black quarry, so I must as well.

From my meager supplies, I pulled a small lantern that barely illuminated the few feet in front of me once lit. Once past the threshold of the cave, I turned to inspect the entrance. Though I couldn't name the stone, it put me in mind of the dark and sturdy architecture of nearby villages and the walls of the city itself. Perhaps some of what I'd seen came from this very cave; it certainly wasn't natural, given the straight lines and shelves chiseled into it.

I imagined the same stone as a seamless wall across the entrance with all its imperfections, strata, and striations. Just as the mages rounded into view, their dust-lined robes billowing and faces full of hate, I raised my hand and formed the wall between us.

For some time I stood with the gloom, the lantern's warm orange light, and the itch at the back of my mind that was the Worldspeaker.

The Weeping Lady knelt deep in the quarry when I found her, her face pressed hard against the ground. She hadn't so much as pulled her hair from her face. Alarm shocked my system — was she hurt? — and I rushed to her side. Yet, when I grasped her shoulders, she tensed up and fought my efforts to pull her upright.

"No. No. I've found myself. Finally. Here I am."

She spoke with a voice so broken and hoarse, it amounted to less than a whisper. Shocked at the coherent speech, I released her. She nuzzled against the unforgiving rock as though it were a blanket of silk. Her fingers spread and slid against the floor, soaking up every point of contact. I noticed we sat in the center of a patch of differentiated stone; color meant little in this light, but it was pure and pale compared to the rest.

"I don't remember how long it's been. It's been... such a haze, so much fog around me that I can barely see and hear.

This is all I know. This." She turned her cheek against the stone and opened her eyes. Staring at my knee, she bloomed into a sweet smile. "Sister."

Horror wracked through me, so much so that I threw myself back and cracked the lantern against a shelf of stone. The light guttered wildly. I ignored it. My breath caught in a harsh gasp filled with dust and the cool smell of earth, and I took in every spiraling trace of her.

It was not her. It was not my sister. It *could not be.*

The image of a spear plunged into her chest formed in my mind unbidden. The violent impulse overcame me, fueled by hatred so deep and ingrained I hardly recognized it. I rushed toward the precipice with no hope of stopping, only able to watch myself lose my grip.

I would kill her.

Then, something locked me down. The Worldspeaker lacerated the conjured image with her claws in my mind. Her voice came louder and colder than I'd grown used to these past years.

'One thoughtless move and so many could be lost. This is what happens when you fold yourself away from the world. All pent up — reclaim yourself! She is not *me.'*

In that one moment of weakness, I couldn't trust my thoughts. My principles, my purpose. Why would she stay my hand? After so long cajoling me to action, why would she halt the tragedy now? Perhaps she meant to prove to me that if I acted, she would be here to temper my efforts. But she was wrong, wasn't she, if I could slip so easily with just a word? I could not be trusted —

Thin fingers closed around my wrist. My limp palm dropped against the Weeping Lady's pale stone. At once, my mind cleared, the voice of the Worldspeaker so far away I could barely hear it. The woman fixed me with a smile so gentle I sank and sagged to the ground without another thought.

"Sister," she said again. "I am Zijiri from the far south, same as you. I would have greeted you if I could, but my body is so empty and aimless when out in the open air. This —" she pushed her nose against the stone again "— brings my will back to me. For so short a time."

"You're Sanjii," I said. I should have known. Even with her unusually light skin, she had similarly wide cheekbones and a pointed chin. Her hair, like mine, was thick, dark, and far straighter than the locals'.

"Yes."

All my horror had been in vain. Sister in country, not blood; not a trick of my twin to twist and upend me. Whatever brought Zijiri here, it had nothing to do with the great prison in the center of the badlands, the voice in my head, or the battle that raged in my heart.

"What happened to you?" I asked at length. Her hand lay gently atop mine, and I felt no need to displace it.

"Magic. There was a great sickness borne of magic that spread rapidly across the lands. It killed so many, everyone it touched. Our people cautioned against intervening, but I couldn't bear it. I went to quell it with my Hallowed gift, but I couldn't move fast enough to stop it. From the people, it spread into the land, and from the land, it spread deeper. The Everything's lifeblood was at risk."

Hallowed. Those with the gift to nullify magic around them. Rare, but not as rare as my gift. I was an Architect, able to create anything out of nothing. And if I wished, that creation could become permanent.

If I held it too long, the wall between us and the exit would be too.

"That's impossible," I said. "There is no power capable."

"There is," she assured me, her smile turning sorrowful. "So I communed with her and asked, 'Would you take of me my soul?'"

"You gave away your soul?" I asked.

170

"Yes. I spread it far and wide, across the land and deep into its marrow. I am everywhere. Veins of me formed across endless strata. I... am here." She ran a hand along the stone. "...Hollowstone."

The name sparked some faint memory; I'd heard it discussed in passing conversations in my aimless travels, but never lingered long enough to learn its consequence. Was this the weapon the mage spoke of? If it indeed housed the essence of her soul, which contained the gift of the Hallowed, it would be as devastating to mages as described. Humans could dig up her soul-turned-stone and use her power to wage war on the magic of the world.

'This is what becomes of things when we neglect to act. They take our gifts and twist them into horrors. Oath or no oath, you must do more than just walk away.'

I could agree. Seeing Zijiri folded against the floor of a spent quarry, soaking in the scant remaining traces of her soul while she could after her captors had scraped it out for weapons, I could. The Worldspeaker had never made more sense.

"Was it worth it?" I asked Zijiri.

"Of course. I saved so many lives."

"Of course it was," I repeated. "And now they've taken your gift of peace and forged it into weapons of oppression. Your mistake was to act at all, and yet now you do nothing. You have the power to take this back and return things to how they were before. End this —"

Zijiri sighed out, long and slow. "I understand. I did what I had to do to prevent a calamity, and I will never regret it. Perhaps I made a mistake rebelling against the teachings of our people. The leagues of pain overwhelmed me and I didn't understand how we could stand back without helping. But I understand now. I'm fortunate that, out of everyone, I'm the one who must pay for my meddling."

"Did you not hear me? They mine your essence and kill people with it!"

"I'm not a god that can take this back now," she said with more force. "I can't change the way they live, the choices they make, just because I disagree with them."

'But you could.'

***

I'd feared Zijiri would fight me when it came time to leave. She kept one hand planted firmly against the white stone as she rose and looked at me with such an expression of affection and fear — I had to turn away. My stomach squirmed, but I adjusted my gentle hold on her shoulders and pulled her from herself. She breathed out a heart-wrenching sigh. When I looked at her face again, it held no life.

She leaned toward that stone that was her soul, but she walked where I chose.

Unmaking a creation of mine left nothing behind, not even dust. The facsimile of the cavern wall dispersed with a flash of magic as it returned to the Everything. I shielded my eyes with a hand against the sunlight that spilled in, but soon sensed the chemical presence of alchemy outside. I pulled Zijiri protectively behind me.

Loose rocks scattered beneath quiet steps. I flexed a hand, ready to conjure a weapon despite my glare-blinded vision. Would they force me to kill them this time? I wished I had the power to teleport away with my charge and leave everything else untouched.

"By your mercy, permit me to speak. Steel Sentinel, I come in peace," said a woman's voice I didn't recognize. "Please, forgive us."

I froze. Cold discomfort trickled into my gut, but my limbs no longer tingled with the need to defend myself. Blinking my vision back into focus, I saw the woman whose arm I'd broken and no one else. She knelt with her head bowed low.

My teeth ground together. I pulled Zijiri out of the cave and stopped before this mage.

"Where are your friends?" I asked. "Is this a trick? If they mean to ambush us —"

"No, Sentinel. Izithia, Lady of the Steel Rose, Goddess of the Vigil." Her brown gaze lifted, filled with awe and reverence. "That is who you are, isn't it?"

I stepped back.

"I understand — we all understand. It would be suicide to make war with you, Lady. Please accept my apologies. I recognized you too late. You and your wondrous creations could make short work of any of our spells, as you showed us. I simply couldn't catch up to the others fast enough to explain this to them, but once I found them they agreed that they should go and I alone should wait. We need to speak with you. We — I — beg for your assistance."

'Mm, the deference. It feels like home in some ways, doesn't it?'

I clicked my tongue and tried not to sneer in disgust. But with whom? With the humans, who saw something powerful and long-lived and simply assumed it was a god? With the Worldspeaker? Certainly. Yet she wasn't wrong; I found the reverence satisfying, like an echo of the respect my position afforded me in a past life. It was the least they could do after forcing me to fight for my life.

"I won't kill the Weeping Lady," I said. I started to add that I wasn't a god, but stopped myself. Who would it help if that only made them attack again?

'What is a god, anyway?'

"Of course not. Of course, I'm not here to ask that, Lady. May I stand?"

"...Yes."

'Is it a powerful being meant to be obeyed?' the Worldspeaker posed to herself. I struggled not to respond.

Standing, the woman took stock of herself. She wiped fiery, sweat-slicked hair back from a weathered, weary face with her good hand. The other tucked deep into the mess of belts and pouches around her middle, wrapped in a makeshift splint. She must have taken something for the pain to stand it with such stoicism.

"Izithia, we need your help," she said. "Desperation drove us to attack the Weeping Lady. She leads them to the white mineral known as Hollowstone, a substance that can nullify any magic near it. They've forged it into armor and weapons and started hunting us. At first, it was anyone with magic in their blood, but then they started after alchemists like me. We only practice the sciences in peace. They mean to kill us all."

That explained Zijiri's role in all this. The soul-strewn stone she'd created to save the world from disease called to her like a siren, and the humans merely had to follow where she wandered. Even now, she leaned against my hold toward the cavern, longing to meet herself again.

Rage brewed hot in my gut. To have such a wound exploited into a tool for genocide was bad enough, but that the victim was one of my people?

But — No. I quashed the feeling, reminding myself of the consequences of getting involved. An untouchable monument at the center of expanding badlands, a voice in my mind, and this unnaturally long life I'd been cursed to endure. Once again, I paced my breathing to a tranquil and distant rhythm.

"I won't kill them, either," I said. "This is not my war. I'm only here to remove Zijiri from the grasp of both sides. I'll take her and leave, and they won't have their guide to the stone."

Anything more and it would be too far. Far too far.

"That won't work!" the mage insisted, even taking a step closer. "Their champion arrived today to take her under his protection. He's a ruthless hunter and killer, and he bears a sword and shield of pure Hollowstone. None of us can fight against it."

I couldn't help the soft, disbelieving scoff. "They have a champion."

"He uses a new technique that gives him an impenetrable defense against magic. When he finds her gone, he'll lead a crusade and slaughter us all." The mage stepped close enough to grasp my sleeve. "And then he'll follow you to the ends of the earth to retrieve her."

I dragged my arm away. "I will *not* fight a war."

"You don't need to. Don't you see? You're the Steel Sentinel. All you must do is speak with them. Speak with them, Goddess, and take us under your protection. Make the humans stop."

'This is your chance. Are you going to wander without purpose until the end of time? If you have the power to protect people and you don't use it, what are you?'

It wasn't that simple. My sister herself had shown me how devastating good intentions could be. They could kill people. They could torture and scar the world. Yet as my gaze flicked between this injured woman before me and Zijiri's empty visage behind, I felt sick. Torture and death already occurred — more every day.

"What is your name?" I asked the mage.

"Veli," she answered.

"I will intercede for you, Veli — but only intercede. You will have a chance to negotiate with Aithyr's lord for peace. Make it count."

***

The central sentinel tower of Aithyr jutted into the sky like a beacon, inescapable. Without much tree cover, it defined the horizon for miles around; an eyesore, certainly, but an easy point to navigate by as we made our way back to the road. As the afternoon wore on, clouds crowded it, carried by a cool breeze and tinged with the ominous gray of a gathering storm.

The three of us entered the city against the late afternoon traffic. To avoid suspicion, Veli posed as my prisoner with her wrists bound together by a length of leather — yet another reminder of the inferiority of her craft, whose magic could be disarmed so easily. Those we passed largely had little reaction, too consumed by the fatigue of long days at work or hawking wares in the market. Those with the energy to notice Veli's restraints had the wherewithal to grimace, but little more. Now we stood on the edge of the plaza by the open gate, surrounded by high stone walls and black brick buildings that rose in tiers toward the central fort.

Lining the walls on either side of the gates were bodies that had been burned until only their faces remained intact. A sign hung from each: *Magus*. Veli caught me looking at them.

"They let us see the faces of our kin," she said. "To shame them. We learned not to grieve too openly for our mothers and brothers; only a mage could mourn the loss of a mage, after all."

I ignored her and led us through the smooth cobblestone streets, trying to swallow my heart from my throat. I couldn't help but consider it hypocrisy; just as many humans lay butchered and burned on the trade road at Veli and her people's hands.

Attention followed us. Murmurs traveled ahead like an ethereal guide as we made our way up the city's tiers to the central fort. Before long it rose before us in its full majesty across a wide plaza designed for large spectacles. Speeches, parades... perhaps burnings, I mused, as my gaze swept over faint charring on the cobbles. The fort itself was built in typical style for the country: solid, blocky shapes resolved into skillful archways and awnings further up, where defense was no longer as critical a concern.

The champion met us at the fort's entrance, flanked by two guards. I'd pictured a typical knight, but he wore supple leathers with a simple breastplate and bracers, both of gray metal laced with white. He flexed his hand beneath a buckler of pure white and hovered the other near the hilt of a sword whose blade surely bore the same hue. He looked less like a champion and more like a mercenary.

If there was any doubt his gear was Hollowstone, Zijiri dismissed it by drifting forward with a hand outstretched. I snatched her back before she came within his reach. A soft sound escaped her, gentle and helpless. My heart twisted.

Settling his black gaze on me, the champion smiled his welcome.

"I am Rudis. I see you've brought the Weeping Lady back to us," he said. "You have our thanks. Now you may leave her with me; she'll be safe under my watch."

My fingers laced with Zijiri's. I pulled her behind me and watched tension flood back into Rudis' frame. He readied himself to fight me for her. His glove creaked against the hilt of his sword.

But I wasn't ready for another fight.

"I am here to speak to the Lord," I said. "An attack on the road left a dozen of his people dead not three miles out from the gates. If I had not been there, the Weeping Lady would be dead as well. I've saved her life and I've brought the ringleader to face justice. The least I deserve is an audience."

"...Of course," he said after a moment. "Release the Weeping Lady to me, and I will speak to the Lord about granting you an audience."

"No. I must keep her with me until I speak to him."

"This is non-negotiable," he growled.

"I will not release her."

'Do you want him to kill you? If so, by all means. Keep going.'

I shut my eyes tight and gripped my head. A blade scraping from its sheath lured them open again. Rudis leveled it at me, the white blade glinting in the angled light. Coming alive, Zijiri pressed against my back and drove me forward a half step. The tip of the blade nipped my throat.

I remained perfectly still.

Veli hissed, "How dare you —"

"Do not speak," I barked at her, and she fell silent. Something about this obedience hit Rudis strangely, I noticed; he took another long look at me, as if searching for something he missed the first time around.

I met the appraisal with a cool stare. "You're just arrived. I require an audience with the Lord of Aithyr in a room with guards and witnesses. I will be surrounded. If he decides you should kill me and take her back by force, you're welcome to attempt it then."

My heart pounded. My limbs shook with a rush of energy. But I stood my ground. Our impasse lasted a minute, then more. His arm never wavered. Veli shifted but remained mute after my command. This silent battle of wills was the most I would do. Until he forced my hand, I must hold back. I must.

Finally, he sheathed his sword. "Enter, then."

***

Amber light streamed in through windows along one side of the hall while the other clothed itself in the brewing storm's slick darkness. The Lord's audience chamber teemed with various officials, some lining the walls, others perched along rows of tiered benches that flanked the main expanse of the hall. Between meticulously sculpted walls and rich decorations of northern wood, smooth limestone stretched across the floor.

Lord Alderek met us in the center of the room. He clasped ink-stained hands behind his back and flitted a clever gaze to and fro across my form. My simple travel leathers, my scant supplies, and my weathered features. While his champion shifted impatiently beside him, he waited until I deigned to meet his eyes.

"My man tells me you have given no name and no explanation," he began. "But you have brought our precious lady back to us, and I'm grateful for that. Welcome to Fort Aithyr."

"Thank you," I said.

He waited, but I remained silent. So, he continued.

"I assume you insisted on keeping her with you to ensure you received a proper reward. That wasn't necessary, I assure you." He extended a hand. "I'll give you any amount you desire. Funds, supplies, or — if you tire of travel — a deed to a grand new home. Now, please. I'm sure the Weeping Lady is weary and needs rest."

"Her name is Zijiri," I said. As I hoped, this caused a ripple of surprise that stalled their immediate reaction. "She is not a tool, and she's not yours. I came to tell you that I will be taking her with me. Please do not pursue us."

While Alderek kept his smile planted stiffly on his face, Rudis broke into a shocked glower. He shouldered past his lord, and the crack of his boots against the stonework broke the stunned silence.

He bared his sword and the room erupted into activity. Onlookers exclaimed, Alderek admonished his champion, and I retreated with Zijiri in hand. Her thoughtless body tried to meet the sword that was a fragment of her soul, straining against me until I had to grasp around her waist and throw her backward. The blade might have bit into me if Veli's shoulder hadn't collided with mine and sent me reeling.

"You raise your sword against a god! A god!" She screeched. "Stay your blade or face the Steel Sentinel's wrath."

Oh, why hadn't I corrected her?

"Ha! You expect us to believe such a blatant lie?" Rudis scoffed, but hesitated. His attention split between the three of us. Me, stoic. Zijiri, vacant. Veli, zealous. I wanted to silence her but couldn't bring myself to undermine myself among enemies.

"Prove yourself," came the Lord's simple command.

It chafed, but I forced myself to stand calm. I held my hand out toward Veli; the leather that bound her hands together dissipated. Her composure broke, stunned by the relief in her broken arm. She panted slowly and sank to her knees.

Where alchemy used reagents, I had none. Where hybrids created powerful shows of energy, I exerted my will directly on the world. Not many could simply make something disappear. The show of power, small as it was, did the trick. Lord and champion both watched me with renewed wariness.

"I am Izithia, the one they call the Steel Sentinel," I said, walking the fine line between the truth and the utter dissolution of my oaths. "I am the one who created the Steel Rose and stands watch at the edge of the Barrens."

'Ah… finally embracing it! It feels so sweet!'

"…But I am not a god," I added in a lower tone. The Worldspeaker's presence thrummed once through my mind in a distinctly unpleasant way, then receded.

Alderek was silent for a moment, during which time he stepped forward and put a hand on Rudis' shoulder. The sword he still held aloft wavered in the air, then fell in a smooth arc. He sheathed it. And Alderek considered me with a shrewd look.

"Others follow you," He said finally. "Many others keep vigil at the borders in your name."

I winced. "Yes. I do not ask them to."

"Even still, you have a force of your own. People to call on should you ever be in need." He turned the thought around in his mind, adjusting to this new paradigm. He no longer addressed a single, simple traveler. This was no longer a show of decorum and honor for him but a true negotiation. He did not hold all the cards. He might not even be able to take Zijiri by force, if what Veli said was true.

'He could if you let him,' the Worldspeaker mocked. *'Leaving yourself one step behind everything won't work for long. Grow a spine soon, or you will have stepped into the lion's den for nothing.'*

"A goddess needs none of these things," Veli said in between tight breaths. "She stopped us alone with little effort. Four of us. Treat her… with the deference she deserves."

No, Veli. Stop.

He had his angle. The man spread his hands out to his sides, peaceful and inviting. One waved Rudis down until he grudgingly backed away. His teeth poked out behind a sly grin.

"Sentinel, forgive us. If you had identified yourself at the gate, we would have welcomed you with respect and honor. A feast before the last of the evening light faded. But now I find we're at an impasse — you see, the situation is delicate. These mages infest our communities and trade in their magics and deceit. Without the Hollowstone, we'd be defenseless. They would grow until they sent the world spiraling into imbalance again. Another plague — or worse.

"Mages need to be controlled. I heard of the carnage on the road, and you saw it yourself. You see the damage they do. To us." He gestured toward Zijiri. "To our defenseless lady."

I wavered, unable to produce a defense for the mages. He saw my hesitation and approached.

"Without her, we cannot keep the peace. Not unless you help us, Sentinel."

Veli flung her head up. "What —"

"You could stop this calamity. Stop them without all that gruesome death! How much calmer would the populace be with a goddess keeping the balance?"

"I…" I started. "I'm *not* —"

Something reached into my head and tipped my thoughts into a jumble. I made a promise, an oath not to use my power to interfere with mortal business. But where was the line? Had I already crossed it in saving Zijiri from certain death? A war unfolded before me, borne of hate and paranoia after the plague — was that something I shouldn't stop? I had the power to stop it.

"I can't," I said finally. "This is not my home or my war. Both sides *must* allow me to leave with Zijiri in peace. Do this and I will not have to get involved to defend myself."

'That's a little tyrannical, too.'

I clenched my fists and bit my tongue. The hot taste of iron spilled through my mouth.

Alderek's face mirrored my frustration. The light danced across his twitching jaw and gleamed sunset orange in his gaze. Courtly decorum sat steady on his features, and yet it took only a few subtle shifts to turn hateful. The kindness in his tone curdled at the edges.

"I have no intentions of provoking a god," he said.

"My Lord," Rudis growled. "All she's shown us is a parlor trick. I've seen dozens of mages perform seemingly impossible feats with their magic — not only hybrids but mundane alchemists as well. We have no reason to believe the Steel Sentinel has personally involved herself here. More likely this is just a ruse meant to put us on the back foot and steal away our advantages."

Veli floundered to a stand with a weak scoff. Cold perspiration speckled her face, painting faint reflective trails down her throat. "You were willing to believe it when you thought you could turn her to your side."

"I was," said Alderek. He barely looked at her, and no wonder — she made a pathetic picture, hunched over a broken limb. "And I still am. Goddess or no, you are surely very powerful, Izithia. I would be honored to have you by my side, but I also cannot afford to lose an asset. You must prove yourself."

"I haven't already?" My harsh tone shocked me.

"You have not," Rudis answered with just as much ire.

"I saved Zijiri. I did you the respect of bringing her here to speak as equals. I defeated your enemies after a slaughter —"

My chest tightened and I cut myself off. What had I done? In describing my actions this way I'd made myself a player. I'd taken a side, *fought* on a side, approached a ruler, and dictated his actions. My hands gripped my head as riotous laughter shot through my mind. Cursing the Worldspeaker with every fiber of my being, I tried to figure a way out of this room without letting my every promise crumble into failure.

I never should have helped. I should have let Zijiri die. She was only a shell without a soul.

"You did. Yet you are increasingly inconsistent with your stance on this conflict. Are you friend or foe, Izithia?"

I turned and scoured the room. I could see it filling with arches and spires and twisting stone shapes. I could paint out walls like cages for the bystanders and a clear path to the exit. The creation hovered at the tip of my will like an unspoken word, conjured by desperation and stayed by principle.

Uncertainty reigned.

How much was too much? The Worldspeaker's taunts returned to me: *you must act. Tyrant. This is your chance.*

The walls tightened, no longer cages but crushing traps. Blockades sharpened into lethal spines.

'*Do it.*'

A breath clawed against my lips. Electricity traveled down my arms. I would erupt at any moment. And yet I stalled a moment too long and met his eyes again. Alderek waited, alight with curiosity.

My vision of death bled away.

Lord Alderek released a long sigh. "Let's not allow this to descend into incivility. You are magic, that is certain, and no magus can survive against the might of our champion. If you would prove yourself worthy to walk into my home and take what is mine, defeat Rudis in a duel."

There it was — my way out. Relief bloomed through me, weakening my limbs and dropping my shoulders. I could hardly believe the solution handed to me. "I accept."

***

As the sun sunk finally beneath the horizon, the onlookers organized themselves into the pews on either side of the hall. Thunder boomed distantly while heavy rain pelted the windows in a never ending, ever changing rhythm. The room shrunk under the oppressive weight, morphing from a seat of power to a rat trap in danger of being flooded out any moment.

Two guards removed Veli's many pouches and moved her and Zijiri to sit near Alderek's seat of honor. Rudis and I faced each other in the center of the room, illuminated from above by dozens of flickering candles strewn across chandeliers. His malicious smile danced like a devil's, the audience pressed around me like ghosts of amber shadows, and my relief drained from me.

Alderek lifted a hand. "Begin."

I hefted the simple bastard sword, given to me from the hip of a guardsman. Though I never touched a weapon as a child, I'd refined the skill over centuries of boredom. The weapon moved fluidly in my hands and danced into exploratory strikes that Rudis sidestepped or blocked with his shield. My steel made no marks on the Hollowstone.

My gaze flicked to Zijiri worriedly; could this hurt her? A silly instinct, to which I quickly reminded myself of the mining, forging, and shaping of this stone that she had thus far survived. Yet when Rudis flicked his blade forward, I was too slow. He bit a superficial slice into my forearm and I jumped away with a wide swipe to keep him from pressing his advantage.

His sword arced and spiraled through the air in a style I'd never seen, hitting and rebounding into another strike as though my deflections were simply a part of the choreography. He wasted no time with overblown effort. Everything was light and precise. Breath rushed from my lungs and my arms already ached only moments in. Strike, strike — an opening —

I snaked forward for a stab toward his thigh. He blocked it with his buckler and punched it forward with such force that my sword arm flew backward. I teetered off balance, and he pounced. His sword screamed toward my gut.

My snap reaction defaulted to a familiar shape: many thin spines rushing up from the ground. They bit at him from all directions, but none made contact. The true power of his art revealed itself as the Hollowstone blade carved a null path through my creations in efficient spirals. They appeared and were nothing in a single second.

I stumbled to a halt, gaping. So this was the monster the mages feared. A man who could make their magic mean nothing. Who could make *my* magic mean nothing. Rudis offered a single, fleeting moment to digest this. He savored my fear and swelled with the taste of the changing winds. Not a champion, not a knight. A hunter. A predator, wasn't he? He flicked his sword up and down as though cleaning it of blood and approached.

I dodged a swipe and moved around him. When I thrust toward his side, he drew a crimson line across the back of my wrist. I cried out and dropped my sword. He swiftly scattered my conjured projectile from the air and charged forward to drive me further from my weapon. With one sharp kick, he sent it skidding to a halt at the lord's feet.

"Perhaps you're not a god, after all," he said.

He meant it as a taunt, but it was strangely comforting. A tiny claw in my mind pulled out the humor in it. After centuries spent terrified of myself, perhaps my best wasn't so impressive after all. Unthinking and almost delirious, I laughed.

This unnerved him more than anything else I could have possibly done. His grip tightened on his sword.

"Stop that," he barked.

But I continued.

"Shut up!"

'Pull yourself together!'

A force grasped onto my mind. It wrenched me back into focus and the sharp awareness of Rudis' next charge. He flourished his sword outward and swung hard for my throat. Another killing blow. This time, a ready vision answered when I opened my hand. A long, light sword the shape of a needle materialized, and I grasped it.

I willed it into permanence and slammed it against Rudis' sword. Metal screeched across the white stone. A sharp edge dug into the side of my neck, and my vision exploded into painful colors. Hot blood spilled across my shoulder.

"Thank you, Kiera," I murmured her name for the first time in years. It tasted sweet and stale.

'Did it really matter?'

Rudis stared at the sword straining against his, shocked. "How —"

"It's real," I said between panting breaths. "Completely real."

I gave him a moment to process. Perhaps I felt a sense of sportsmanship — or maybe I savored the turning of fate as much as he did. But like me, he didn't recover in time; I slid my sword down the length of his and plunged it deep into his shoulder.

He shouted and jolted away. I dragged the blade upward, and between us, we ripped it through inches of muscle before it came free of the wound. His shout turned to a scream. Rudis retreated from me fully, like a lion from fire.

My hand trailed along the slice in my neck. It came away slick with blood, though that wasn't surprising. My left shoulder was bathed in it, and the only sign my artery was intact was the lack of spray across the stonework. Still, everyone but Zijiri watched me as though they truly beheld a god. Awe filled them. Fear.

Reverence.

I had to end this.

Rudis' arm hung uselessly, able to grip but unable to rise. He dropped his sword and seethed. Wild eyes fixed on me. His buckler became a battering ram, an ax. It wailed on me and knocked my blade aside over and over. I dodged and struck and ducked around it, but new bruises formed, my arms shook, and my grip weakened. I may have mitigated the blow to my neck, but it still weakened me.

Finally, he surged forward for a straight strike with the brim of the shield. I raised the stonework an inch just in front of his boot, which caught and sent him stumbling. Side-stepping, I cracked the hilt of my sword against his skull as he passed. He sprawled on the floor, limp.

***

"She is mine, then," I whispered before my face contorted in confusion. Had blood loss muddled my mind so much? "She is free."

I opened my eyes, almost surprised to find the room wasn't spinning. At some point, I'd dropped my weapon and planted my palm against my neck, where the crimson flow already dwindled. Full night left the room subject to the orange-gold light of the candles and the smell of wax and iron. I wanted to break a window and taste fresh rain — free myself from this stale and disorienting place.

Alderek approached. His voice, at first an unfocused mass, sharpened into words after some seconds.

"...withstand the Hollowstone. You truly are what you claim, and I can only stand and beg your forgiveness. What would you wish of us, Lady?"

'The world at your feet. Or this city, at least. Good job, sister.'

"No, I'm not —" but I was, wasn't I? I bit my lip and centered myself with deep breaths. "I am only Izithia. All I wish is to take Zijiri away, so she won't be used and treated as a tool. Nothing else. Do not treat me as a god, I am not —"

The point of a sword sprouted from Alderek's throat.

Veli clung to the hilt with one shuddering arm. Her eyes were crazed pools of twisted amber shadows, fixed with unmitigated purpose on the back of Alderek's skull. Her breathing rasped and caught with unnerving crackles, each punctuating another second that I — and the rest of the chamber — stared without action.

I watched the light fade from his eyes. Lord Alderek listed to the side and fell, dreamlike, across the unforgiving stone. Just as life returned to the guards with a half dozen swords hissing from their sheaths, Veli spat on the corpse.

"Blessings of the Worldspeaker," she said.

My blood ran cold.

Insipid laughter shrieked through my head. It echoed back and forth and conjured up images from the day with their colors changed. All this time, while she whispered in my mind, the Worldspeaker had propped up her agent beside me. She'd progressed from a voice in my head to a hand that moved the pieces — the people — around me.

This was an artifice. A trap. Veli, the war, all of it.

'Did you think you were special?' she purred beneath the laughter. *'Did you think I only ever spoke to you?'*

A scream ripped from me. This time, no foreign force stopped me from conjuring pillars from the floor that scattered the guards. Two encircled Veli's wrists and stretched them to either side, as far as she could reach and then some. Her agonized shriek fueled me. Sinking the pillars toward the ground, I forced her to her knees.

"Is a thousand miles not enough for you?" I snarled. "Am *I* not enough for you?"

The skirmish on the road just as I arrived to witness it. One of our people in the crossfire, a helpless lure goading me into action. How could I ever think it was a coincidence?

'Somehow you convinced yourself I was defeated, didn't you? An impotent voice in your head, a lesson to learn from. But it will never be over, Izithia.'

Veli's shouts descended into piteous wails as she hung from both arms, one broken and one whole. Incoherent murmurs spilled from her and begged for me to stop. Release her. Apologies meant to appease me and promises meant to motivate me. Around us, humans stood and scattered, and guardsmen hesitated. Those that did not flee dropped to their knees to plead with me, goddess, calm —

"It is over," I said. "It is over. You failed, and your impotent efforts to corrupt the world won't change that. Release them, Kiera. This discord you've sown, end it."

Veli recognizing me was merely a calculation — a thought dropped in her mind. Kiera could not fight or kill me, so she'd done the next best thing: eroded me. Chipped at every weak point and spun me to the brink. I could see her scheme so clearly now, and yet I couldn't bring myself to change course.

Veli's wails ceased. Her body slumped as the pain drained away. For a moment, she looked as Zijiri did: empty. Then a sinister spark ignited in her eyes. Her lips twisted into a satisfied sneer.

"Come now, Izithia. I didn't do this." Veli's voice matched the cadence of the one in my head. "The hatred between them? It already festered here. Mages poisoning mundanes, mundanes cornering innocent young healers in back alleys. A pressure that builds and builds until it scorches the Everything in a wildfire. What's a tiny nudge here, a whisper there, compared to all that?"

I hissed, "Release her!"

"She's already gone."

My arm lashed out. A single spike rose from the floor. She had to lift her chin to keep the point from pricking the soft flesh under her jaw. Yet still she smiled.

"Act, sister," Kiera said. "Act. Wake up from your centuries-long stupor and make a difference. Start here. I've laid it all out for you, first with one leader, then another. Veli's important, you know. And these humans? You've defeated their champion and they've lost their lord. Listen to them."

I did. The cacophonous shuffle of intelligible voices slowly filtered into a slew of phrases and words. They begged for my mercy, they offered me fealty. Sentinel, they said. Steel Sentinel, Goddess, Lady. A city on a platter, one that I could steer away from cruelty if I wanted. No more slaughters on the road or bodies hanging from the walls.

"I'm here with you, Izithia. I feel every moment of your pain and rage at the desolation in this world. A broken world you could fix. Everything we dreamed together all those years ago."

I teetered on the edge, convinced and not convinced. It was all I could do to hold onto that one, clear thought in my mind.

An oath, a promise. And yet in this moment, it seemed only a flimsy excuse to escape any responsibility.

My hand twitched.

"I remember a story of our people," Zijiri said, shocking me from all intent.

I'd forgotten about her. While the rest of the room descended into chaos, she'd drifted to the center of the room where Rudis lay unconscious. Her delicate hands grasped the hilt of his sword. The point dug into the ground where she knelt, and she pressed her face against the pure white blade.

She spoke so softly that I had to hold my breath to hear her.

"Two sisters of great power loved each other very dearly, but the more they learned of the world the more it saddened them. Beyond their village, the humans were wracked with disease, hatred, and calamity. But the elders wouldn't allow them to help because it wasn't their right. One sister agreed, but the other could not let go.

"Over the years, she used her gift as a Speaker to control more and more of the world. First the trees, then the earth and the wind, and even the minds of others. Eventually, she realized that if she learned every language of the world, she would control the Everything. She would become a new god.

"Many tried to stop her, but none were strong enough. Until her sister, the Architect, took action. There was a great battle that killed many and drained the land dry, until the Architect created a prison of many steel petals rising high around the Speaker. Just as her rose was completed, before the Speaker could rip it away, the Everything granted Izithia one final gift. She became permanent and immortal, and her powers grew accordingly. Now she could make the prison immutable and unchangeable, trapping the Speaker inside forever. As she came to terms with her immortality and all that came with it, she made a vow."

Zijiri met my eyes for the first time since we met.

"Never," said Izithia, "will I overreach with this power. I swear to let the world be as it will be, to let kingdoms fall and peoples live and die with free will. I will live as a mortal lives. I will never seek to be a god like my sister."

My hand trembled in the air. The story that had become a ghost in the back of my mind sent spiral fractures through me. I'd nearly forgotten. All these subconscious compulsions and paralyzing aversions to the world — all the shame of walking away. It had a reason.

Zijiri sat like a beacon of peace in the center of the room. No one moved or spoke. Her presence settled any need for it like a warm blanket slipped over the shoulders. The picture of her blurred and came undone, and it took a moment for me to realize I was crying. The hatred Kiera stoked in me drained away, leaving me with a simple realization: I was her greatest weapon. If I let it, my power could be what she used to 'fix' the world.

I would not.

I let the pillars disappear like a long exhale, easing Veli's body to the ground. Kiera picked her up and sat, watching me with silent spite. Turning from her, I addressed the rest of the room. No matter which mind possessed the body, she couldn't hurt me.

"We are not gods," I said, meeting the eyes of every stricken human there. The guards, the courtiers, officials, guests. "Do not treat us as gods — do not allow us to become tyrants. We have the same minds as you, mortal and flawed. No amount of power will give us the right to make you slaves."

"They won't believe you," Veli-turned-Kiera said. "Not after this, not ever."

"I don't care."

I turned from their vacant stares and approached Zijiri. She beamed at me as I helped her stand, then laughed softly when I strapped the Hollowstone buckler tight to her back.

"We're going to travel the world, you and I. And you can leave them your soul," I said. "But that doesn't mean you can't keep a piece of it for yourself."

"I'd like that," she whispered.

Taking her hand, I basked in the rapturous silence as Kiera's presence faded from my mind. Zijiri waited for as long as I needed, and then I led her from the audience chamber. Many watched us leave with so much awe and fearful silence. They may never accept that the ones such as us weren't deities, but we couldn't control that. We couldn't control what they felt and believed.

We were not gods.

Re Gwaltney Biography

A lifelong writer of fantasy and horror, Re ('Ray') Gwaltney loves to dig into the darker things in life and pull out the painful and the beautiful in their inescapable Venn diagram. They write vivid worlds, compelling characters, and unputdownable narratives. When not writing, Re can be found snuggling their dog, practicing witchcraft, and gaming way too much. They live in Raleigh-Durham, North Carolina, and help other authors as a sensitivity editor and writing consultant. Visit www.regwaltney.com for more.

Website: ww.regwaltney.com
Bluesky: @regwaltney.bsky.app
Instagram: regwaltney

Danny's War

Rob Nisbet

August 1944

Startled, Major Stephen Lorimer looked up from the blood-soaked bandage, weary eyes suddenly wide and questioning. He and his team were so close to the front that they'd all heard it: the sharp *boom* of a grenade; sharp as the tang of cordite that crept over the tents when the breeze came from the south. He called for a nurse to take over the dressing of the bullet wound and began to issue orders. He was pleased to see that his well-drilled medical team were automatically preparing for another batch of casualties.

He strode out into the drizzle and along the line of canvas tents, his boots sinking into the mud of this well-trod furrow; his own version, he thought, of the trenches. All around him was swift but organised bustle. Panic helped no one, and he tried always to lead by example. He liked to think of himself as a focus of calm and considered control. Lives were at stake. He ducked under the flap of the receiving tent. A young second lieutenant sprang to attention which Lorimer waved down. "It's Matthews, isn't it?"

"Yes, Sir. Jack Matthews."

"You heard the grenade?"

"We're ready, Sir," Matthews indicated himself and a nurse who was unloading sterilized equipment from a steaming autoclave.

Lorimer nodded his approval. "Your first stint with us, Matthews?"

"Yes, Sir." He paused. It seemed the Major was waiting for something more. "And… well, I sure miss my Mam's roast dinners, Sir."

Lorimer laughed. He sympathised with this youngster. "It's not *all* garlic and frogs' legs," he said. "And there'd be more fresh eggs if we didn't keep eating the chickens." Lorimer was pleased to see the lad twitch a smile. He was barely more than a schoolboy, thrust into the muck and blood of this hell hole; there was precious little to smile about. A seriousness settled over them as they listened to the rain spattering the canvas. Lorimer took the time to find out about the lad's medical background — or rather the disturbing lack of it. He was keen though and knew the basics; thrown in at the deep end like all the other buggers.

It was fifteen minutes later that the truck squelched to a halt outside. Two Tommies carried the poles of a canvas litter into the receiving tent and lay a bloody mass on the raised bed. Lorimer felt his heart sink. There is a basic human instinct to be repelled by gore. He thought his years of service had dulled this response, but now and then, he experienced a sight so terrible that he just wanted to run and scream. He couldn't imagine how this man looked to the young, inexperienced Matthews.

The man's uniform was reasonably intact. But the grenade had exploded at close range, about chest height, exploding upward and taken the man's face with it.

Second Lieutenant Matthews held his nerve, approaching to make his initial assessment. He had been ready to take the patient's temperature, check his pulse and his blood pressure, assess which tent would be best suited to his injuries, but he stood at the bedside and froze. The man was breathing, and mercifully unconscious. In the crater of blood, it was difficult to tell what was missing. There was no nose, flaps of skin had lifted from his cheeks and lay over his eyes like orange peel, and the lower jaw had been blown away leaving a bubbling mess of open throat.

Young Matthews took a breath, then called to the nurse. "Send someone to get the dentist — now!"

Major Lorimer was still reeling from the sight of the injured man, and it took him a moment to register what the lad had said. Matthews was right. The dental surgeon was trained to deal with maxillofacial injuries. The nurse scuttled away, and Matthews began to swab blood from the man's exposed throat. "We've got to keep his airway clear," he shouted.

With the nurse absent, Lorimer realised the boy was yelling at *him*. *Lead by example; calm and controlled; hands on.* He too began to clear the blood and flesh from the tatters of the man's neck.

One of the litter bearers approached the bed. "Major Lorimer," his voice was low, almost apologetic. "We found these…" He handed over a bloody sheet of linen, on which lay shreds of flesh: what might have been a nose, a piece of ear, and a jawbone draped in torn skin.

The dentist, a captain, arrived glistening with rain and, after his initial shock, leant in to make his appraisal. It took him only seconds to straighten again, shaking his head at his superior. "He won't live."

Major Lorimer stood back, but the boy, Matthews, continued to work, having the nurse supply a series of swabs and absorbent dressings.

"Just… make him comfortable," said Lorimer.

For the next twenty minutes Matthews did what he could and administered multiple pain killers. But eventually even he realised the futility of his task. His hands began to shake, blood coating them past the wrists. The man's breathing had deteriorated to shallow barely audible gasps.

"Let him go," said Lorimer.

Matthews straightened and Lorimer saw the resigned despair of a veteran cloud his young eyes. He looked down at the hollowed half-face and picked at the pieces lying on the patch of linen. He placed a piece of ear to the side of the man's head. It made little difference. Then he picked up the jawbone and held it over the shredded throat. The jaw restored some semblance of a normal face. Matthews felt his hands shake again and the jaw slid into place. He left it where it was.

The rasping of the man's breath faded to silence. Matthews bowed his head.

Until he realised the man was still breathing.

The rasping had stopped. Perhaps the jaw was holding the throat in the correct position. The man's chest rose and fell. The dentist came forward, asked Matthews to swab again and folded a flap of the man's neck over the exposed flesh. "Get me some sutures." His voice betrayed his amazement.

They worked on the man's throat for a further two hours. And all the time they didn't expect him to live.

"What's his name?" Major Lorimer asked.

The nurse had found an ID disc embedded in the flesh. "Private Daniel Cooke," she said.

***

Spring 1947

I've heard the cleaners, scrubbing and polishing all morning. Got to make a good impression; everything spotless and in its place. After all, it's not every day that Churchill comes to visit.

Just as well.

From what I've been able to overhear, everyone's in a mild panic. The rehabilitation and ongoing treatments have to be displayed and be seen as worthy of the public purse. And, of course, having the leader of the opposition on side won't do any harm.

Even I have been spruced up for inspection. Private Danny Cooke, aged twenty-one, wounded in action, northern France, not expected to live. Janice, the nurse with the squeaky laugh, has Brylcreemed my hair and combed it out of my eyes, not that that will do me any good. The only benefit of being almost blind is that I don't have to look at myself. I can distinguish light from dark, but that's pretty much it. *Limited contrast vision* they call it. Anyway, I hope Churchill has a strong stomach. My eyelids, what's left of them, never close properly; and my eyes... Well, I heard Janice one day whispering to a new girl that they look like they've been boiled in Horlicks — milky and burnt. And that's pretty much what they feel like too. My throat was the major concern when I first arrived. My face had been blasted from below, I'm told my jaw had actually come away, and even now, if I'm honest, doesn't seem to fit properly. I still have times when I struggle for breath, and I have fits of coughing that bring up globs of blood. But it's *between* my jaw and eyes that is the problem. It has healed enough now for me to feel around. When I think I am alone, my fingers tap tenderly at my broken upper teeth, then reach into the hole. I used to think my nose was too pointed, but at least then I had one.

Nurse Janice accepts what I look like, I can tell by her voice that it doesn't bother her anymore; that means a lot to me. Same with Sir Richard Hardy, no less; he's the surgeon who plans to reconstruct my face — well, do what he can, anyway. But when I was introduced to the new girl, her voice shook, she barely managed to say hello — then I heard her run from the room.

But at least I'm alive. That's what I keep telling myself. *At least I'm alive.*

***

Churchill has arrived, but to me he's just a dark blur against the pale wall. They told me to just sit still. There's nothing wrong with my legs, but they don't want me feeling my way around, knocking things over, especially in front of an important visitor. Sir Richard is giving him the tour. I hear the hesitation in his voice when he introduces me, uncertain, I'm sure, of Churchill's reaction. I sit still through the details: grenade blast, amazing recovery of the neck and throat region, reconstructive surgery, possible graft of skin from the thighs to recreate the cheeks…

The dark blur draws closer. There is a light, and the crackle of a flash bulb. "Do you remember what happened to you?" Strange to hear Churchill's deep earnest voice in person.

I swallow, open my mouth and manage a rasp from the back of my tongue.

Sir Richard is quick to intervene. "I'm afraid, Danny can't speak," he says.

I feel a hand rest briefly on my shoulder. "Poor boy," says that deep voice.

Then I'm wracked by a fit of coughing. A nurse, Janice I think, appears, placing a cloth at my mouth to catch any unpleasantness. And the visitor is discreetly led away.

***

I have nightmares. No surprise. Thing is, I can scream in my sleep. Out loud. A *proper* scream.

"I guess you feel embarrassed," says Sir Richard.

You notice the words people use when you can't see. He's always saying 'I guess' as if hedging his bets; I'd prefer him to be a bit more confident. My screams, though, he sees as evidence that my throat and vocal cords are improving. A miracle, he says, considering the state they were in. The whole throat region, he says, is healing, spreading from the jaw outwards, like new flesh. "We'll get you speaking, yet," he says, but I can hear that he is humouring me. "Better still: we'll have you singing!" He bursts into a wail of Gilbert and Sullivan, but it is too much for him. His breath snags and he coughs violently. Eventually he recovers, but there is a moment of silence, then he tells me, with a tremor of surprise and concern. "I've just coughed up blood, Danny. I guess you know how that feels." I hear him wipe his hand on a handkerchief.

***

Nurse Janice is there to put me to bed most evenings. I don't need help. But she *does* put in my eye drops. They are nothing restorative, no miracle cure, just some balm to stop me scratching at them in irritation.

"Head back. That's right, Danny, eyes wide open."

When she leans over me, with the ceiling light directly behind her, I can make out a vague shape. She's slim.

I like to imagine her perfume when she is this close; something light and flowery. *How old are you, Janice?* The voice is in my head. *Around the same age as me?* She is the only female that has accepted what I look like. *Could you ever bear to touch me, Janice? Or to have me touch you?*

She pauses with the eye drops. I wonder for a brief stupid moment if she has heard my thoughts.

"Sorry, Danny," she says, and her shape straightens. "I had trouble focusing, there." She laughs, that squeaky laugh. "My eyesight will be getting as bad as yours!"

She leans in again, obscuring the light. I feel the drops fall into place. They well over my eyes and overflow like tears. No, she would never touch me, not in the way I want her to.

And then comes the question. I'm sure Sir Richard has put her up to this. "Your nightmares, Danny... you cry out almost every night... I worry about you."

Yeah, sure you do.

"It's not my place to pry," she continues. "I guess you're re-living the grenade attack..."

These are not her words; I know Sir Richard is behind this.

"I'm told it can help — be therapeutic, to share an experience. Perhaps tomorrow, Danny, you could try to write down your nightmares..." She pauses and reverts to her normal self. "Just a thought," she adds, almost as an apology.

They want to know about my nightmares. Psychological rehabilitation: learning to accept things by talking them through — except, of course, that I can't talk. Well, they were bound to probe my mental state sooner or later; they've pretty much exhausted what they can do for me physically. I refuse, though, to write anything. What do I remember of my dreams anyway? Nothing concrete. My conscious mind seems to have wiped out the explosion — but it creeps into my nightmares. I run the vague impressions through my mind, as if telling myself a story. It's odd. I realise that, in my head, I am constantly talking to myself. I'm doing it now. Is that, I wonder, because I *can't* talk out loud? Some need for mental communication?

There. They've got me self-analysing. Talking to myself — and finding some bullshit significance behind it.

Anyway, my nightmares: all I can remember is that I'm out in the open, but I'm trapped. I can see. I can breathe easily. I still have a face — and my too-pointy nose. But I know that there is something there in front of me. I can't tell what it is.

And then I realise there is something behind me too.

I hadn't realised that before; so perhaps there *is* some point in revisiting my dreams.

There are two of them. I want to say they are people, but I can't be sure of that. Certainly, I feel outnumbered. And then, somehow, I know, *just know*, that I am going to be attacked.

And I wake screaming.

***

My nightmares come to the attention of another doctor. Sir Richard brings him in to see me. I am having a good day and manage to stand, hold out my hand — in roughly the right direction — to shake his, and sit again without a nurse easing me back into the chair. This doctor's name is Greenway and he comes from a convalescent centre; some institution for sight-impaired veterans on the Sussex coast.

Sir Richard coughs to clear his throat, then goes through my medical records — pages of them. He glosses over my refusal to write down my dreams.

He coughs again, as if nervous, when he comes to my throat condition. My tongue was pretty much ripped apart when my jaw was blown away. And, in his words, everything south of the epiglottis had been exposed but stitched back into place in the field hospital. He was full of praise for Major Lorimer and his team and had no doubt that they had saved my life.

"The jaw was detached?" Doctor Greenway finds this hard to believe. I am subject to much probing and inspection, even having to open my mouth and say 'Aah' like some kid with tonsillitis. "Remarkable tissue regeneration," Greenway sounds impressed.

"I wish I knew Danny's secret," says Sir Richard. There is one of those long pauses where I can only guess at the exchange of expressions. Eventually he explains in a lower voice: "I've been having a few problems in that area myself. Haemorrhaging of the trachea around the vocal cords." He gives us a forced, painful sounding, laugh. "It's ironic. Danny here is recovering beyond expectations, while I'm falling to pieces."

Greenway sympathises. "I could take a look…"

"No, no, no." I imagine Sir Richard waving him away. "We medics are notoriously bad patients. I have self-diagnosed some debilitative erosion of the throat. Absurdly vague; I guess I don't want to know any more than that."

He, somewhat obviously, changes the subject, moving on to my eyes. Vision, or coping without it, is Greenway's specialism.

"Burns," is Greenway's verdict. Yeah, genius! We all knew that. But he goes on to say that there are signs here too of recovery.

I want to ask him for details! But I only manage a questioning croak. "There are indications," he tells me, "that the damaged area is shrinking. Do you *see* any improvement, Danny?"

I consider, then shrug.

"Still some way to go, clearly," says Greenway.

The examination is over. Sir Richard says that, with the improvement to my throat and breathing, I'm no longer classified as a medical patient. I will receive on-going care, but no further treatment. The priority now, for my rehabilitation, is coping with my lack of sight. Rather than have me bumbling about the furniture here, the centre in Sussex would be better suited to my needs.

"Everyone there is either blind or partially sighted," explains Greenway, as if this is something wonderful. "One thing, though; you'd have to earn your rations. We have an extensive programme of vocational training. We'll do our best to find you a useful skill."

I nod to show that I have understood. Then I realise that there has been a massive omission in the examination: the great ugly hole in the centre of my face. The implication is obvious — nothing can be done about that.

They leave the room. At the door I hear Sir Richard: "While you're here, Greenway, could you take a look at one of my nurses, Janice. She's only young, but she's complaining of eye strain, difficulty focusing. I think she may need glasses."

***

Another night: I lean back for another dose of eye drops. Janice leans over me with the dropper — and misses. She realises and mops at my face. "Sorry, Danny. My eyesight…

203

you won't know, but I wear glasses now." She squeaky-laughs. "My mum says they make me look intelligent, at last!"

She guides my hand up to feel the glasses. They have thin metal frames, round lenses. I want to feel her face; stroke her hair. *Will you kiss me, Janice?*

Of course not; she lowers my hand. Why would she kiss a Horlicks-eyed freak with a bomb crater instead of a face?

She tries again. I have a shadow impression of her leaning closer than usual. This time she is successful. I blink — as well as I'm able. And I see blue. It is Janice's uniform: blue. *I can see blue!* She straightens and becomes a mere shadow again.

"I think I need stronger glasses," she says. "I'll ask Sir Richard about it, when he returns from sick leave."

***

Sir Richard is in some other hospital. He doesn't want to be treated here where people would know him. I can understand that.

He's not doing well. From the gossip, it seems, his throat is pretty much falling apart. Blood seeps into his windpipe and he has trouble speaking. That's something I can sympathise with!

He hasn't neglected his patients, though. Even from his sickbed, he is coordinating plans for my transfer to Sussex. The place is called St. Justin's, on the coast. Apparently, Doctor Greenway is having my room prepared and can't wait to stick me on his programme of vocational training.

***

More eye drops. I can make out Janice's slim silhouette from a short distance now. And she's blue — that wonderful blue.

"Head back, Danny." I have learnt to read people by their voices: hers, now, is ultra-controlled and flat, disturbingly so.

Something is wrong. She gets the drops in first time. Then I hear her breath shudder into sobs. I feel my stomach contract into knots. Her voice collapses. "Oh, Danny — I've just had the most terrible news…" I have to wait for her to sniff back her tears. "It's Sir Richard. Blood in the lungs, they said. Oh, Danny, he died this afternoon."

"No!" I say.

And my world changes.

Janice freezes. I imagine her shocked expression, eyes wide as her round lenses. "Danny. You spoke!"

And we are both crying. It's amazement, and joy, and horrified loss. Janice hugs me and we shake with grief and happiness.

***

"We can talk in here…" Lieutenant Jack Matthews showed his visitor into the white-washed hospital canteen. She was young, pretty and wanted to talk to him about his time in France. She didn't look, to him, like a religious nut: she was from some organisation called Tinderbox apparently. He'd heard a slogan somewhere, "exploding myths…" well, something like that.

He was surprised to have been granted time out for this meeting. But then, he'd learnt that strings had been pulled, between his superiors and a government department he had never heard of. Since the end of the war there were a lot of those: formerly top-secret little offices trying to justify their continued existence.

He collected two coffees from the counter and took them to a quiet table of garish red Formica near the windows. "Powdered milk, I'm afraid," he made a face.

"That's fine." The crimson smile was brief, followed by a proffered hand. "Evelyn Greer. Thank you for agreeing to speak with me, Lieutenant."

"Call me Jack, please." They shook hands and Evelyn sealed the formality by producing a reporter's spiral-bound notebook. Jack's hopes of a pleasant half-hour away from the wards were dashed. Pretty she might be, but she was too posh and business-like. "Am I going to be quoted in *War Cry* or something?"

The smile flashed again, disappearing just as quickly. "I need to ask you about a patient you treated, when you were in the field hospital." Evelyn flipped a page. "Do you recall a Private Daniel Cooke?"

"Poor sod. Yeah, I remember him well — hard to forget."

"Can you..." Evelyn ostentatiously waved a glossy biro, "tell me about him."

"Not much about him, personally, no. But yeah, I remember his injuries and treatments."

Evelyn raised an eyebrow, pen poised.

"As I'm sure you know, this was Normandy. 1944. I think the Jerries already knew they'd lost, so we were just there maintaining the lines. It seemed to rain constantly; let me tell you, there's nothing quite so disgusting as French mud." Jack took a sip of coffee. "I'd actually heard the grenade, but wasn't prepared for the state of him when he was carried in." Jack pointed to the two pips on his shoulder. "I was only a *second* lieutenant then. It was my first week there. And the Major, name of Lorimer, walked in while I was on triage — last thing I needed! But probably a good thing for Danny Cooke. I wanted to make a good impression, see, in front of the Major? So, I never gave up; kept swabbing at his throat; trying to keep him breathing." Jack paused delicately. "You, er, know how badly he was hurt?"

Evelyn nodded. No smile this time. "I'm particularly interested in the explosion site."

Jack shrugged. "Can't help you there. In fact, I'm sure Danny himself said he couldn't remember what had happened — blasted from his memory." He gulped at his coffee, and his eyes lost focus as if seeing into the past. "Actually... yeah, I'm sure one of the blokes who carried him in mentioned a copse of trees. Yeah, that's right. Danny had been heading off towards these trees; don't know why; seen something I suppose. That's where the grenade got him."

Evelyn reached into a bag and pulled out an ordnance survey. She opened it out on the table. "Can you tell me where this copse of trees is?"

"We were based here… near Formigny." Jack prodded the map. "So — I can't be certain — but Danny would have been in this area, here."

Evelyn took her pen and drew a circle on the map. She leant back in her chair, an obvious gleam in her eyes.

"You gonna tell me what's going on?" Jack asked.

"There have been — reports," said Evelyn. "From *precisely* that area."

"Reports?"

"Well, rumours," Evelyn waved her pen. "Tales in local papers, going back many years, but centred exactly where Private Cooke's incident took place."

Jack shook his head. "I'm not following. How is Danny? Still alive I presume."

"Oh, yes, still alive." Evelyn folded her map. "I just needed some corroboration before I took matters further."

"And now you've got it." Jack's eyes narrowed. "What sort of organisation is *Tinderbox* anyway? What are you up to?"

"I'm sure you must be needed back on the wards." Evelyn stood and flashed that smile again, but this time it lingered: she was pleased with herself. "It ended with horrible injuries, but I think Danny saw something. Something that could be extremely interesting…"

***

I am back in my nightmare: out in the open, trapped again. This time I know I am outnumbered, there are two of them, *the*

207

enemy. I want to call them people but, again, that seems somehow wrong. I know, *just know*, that I am going to be attacked. I look around for some way to escape. But there's no way out. There are trees. I'm in a copse, tangled undergrowth, and the *people* are coming for me. A man and a woman, reaching for me. It's horrible. They want me, *need me*, and I can't let that happen. I pull out a grenade…

The grenade is mine! The grenade that destroyed my face is mine!

And I wake screaming.

***

The speech therapist has only got one leg. I don't know why that surprises me.

He swings into the room on crutches; everything is still a blur to me, but I can make out the imbalance of his outline. I am thankful that, little by little, my sight is definitely improving.

I don't ask about his leg — it would only prompt him to ask about my missing face, and I don't want to think about that. It was my grenade! Did I explode it myself? Is that why it was at such close range? I am asking myself impossible questions.

The speech therapist is not a medical man. He doesn't comment on my recovering vocal cords or tongue. He has me sounding long vowels: "Ooooooo" and "Aaaaaah" like some demented yokel. My voice sounds like I have a heavy cold — nasal, which is ironic. He apologises as he hands me cards to read; they have pictures on as well as simple words. They're for kids. He prompts when I can't see the cards clearly enough, and I can see the contrivance in the sounds they require and the awkward lip and tongue shapes I have to make. "Balloon. Princess. Cricket."

"You're doing really well, Danny." He lays down the cards and waits for me to fill the lengthening silence.

"Sir Richard," I say with faltering emphasis, "wanted me to sing."

"I bet he did!" I hear the droop in his voice. "He was quite the champion of the injured: Sir Richard. Funny — I hear his throat, in the end, looked like a battle wound. And yet he'd never seen active service."

***

I lie in my bed and dread falling asleep.

I have no idea how accurate my nightmare is. It is pretty much the same every time I dream it, and the consistency makes it feel like a memory. Perhaps my memory is healing too. Or perhaps it's my imagination, but there is always some extra detail. I like to think that, as my sight improves, I *see* more in my dream. But at the same time, I dread finding out more of what happened to me.

Janice approaches my bed. I can make out her glasses and, of course, that blue uniform. "Danny," she says and stands closer. "It's going to seem so strange tomorrow night. Practically every evening for over a year, I've given you your eye drops. And now..." She sounds like she's half-teasing, half-scolding me, as if the move to Sussex is my fault.

"Last day," I say.

"I shall miss you, Danny." She leans over me; the eye dropper fills my vision then the liquid blurs and soothes.

"Kiss?" I ask. I am holding my breath. Selfishly, I hope that her eyesight is now so poor that she won't be repelled by my lack of features.

"Don't tell anyone," she whispers. I feel her lips on my temple, and her hair on my brow. And I feel alive. So alive! I feel like I am pulling the life from Janice, feeding from her.

She pulls back, slides her fingers up beneath her glasses to massage her eyes. "Sorry, Danny. I've got a sudden ache. Eye strain..."

I blink away the eye drops and can see her tottering unsteadily towards the door. My head drops back on the pillow and, for the first time, I notice a crack in the plaster of the ceiling. I don't want to sleep.

"I'll see you in the morning," says Janice. "Pleasant dreams."

***

It is raining. That's new: I hadn't realised that before. I am crouching in a shallow slit trench, sporadic bursts of gunfire rattle ahead of me and to my right. To my left is the copse of trees, looking like an island rising from a tempest of mud. I see something in the trees. A furtive movement — not one of *our* men. I can't be sure; perhaps there's more than one.

I look along the trench; there is nobody near me. I don't want to call out, that would give me away. I swing the Sten gun from my shoulder and check the grenade at my belt. There are bushes for cover between me and the trees, and the rain would help to conceal me, if I'm careful.

I reach the trees and make my way stealthily from trunk to trunk. There is no sign now of any movement. I keep my eyes peeled, the copse smells of vegetation and rain, so different from the constant stench of mud.

There is a small clearing in the middle, ferns nod to a bombardment of rain. I know better than to step into an exposed position, but then I hear a sound from behind. It's a woman! The most attractive woman I have ever seen. She is like an angel — out here among the shelling and bullets, she is so out of place, so perfect.

She slinks towards me, lithe as a tiger, her eyes dazzle, her lips curve into a sensuous smile. I back away. I am in the clearing, and there in the trees on the opposite side, stands a man. Like the woman, he doesn't seem real, too perfect, high cheekbones, square jaw; they are like film stars plucked from a screen.

They reach out towards me. It's horrible. I know, somehow, that they want me, need me, and I can't let that happen. My hands are shaking. I pull out the grenade…

It is just a dream. Just a dream…

But still I wake screaming.

***

Evelyn had collated her evidence into a leather document case, all very neat and organised. She didn't yet know anyone at Tinderbox well and wanted to make a good impression. Gareth appeared at the door to Jocelyn's office, smiled and beckoned. "Any trouble finding us?" he asked.

The tunnels under the houses of parliament were a bit of a maze. Tunnel One was the worst kept government secret, it linked the Palace of Westminster with Portcullis House without the need to cross Bridge Street — handy when it was raining. Tunnel Two allowed MPs and dignitaries exclusive access to the House from the tube station. Nobody, apparently, knew about Tunnel Three. And Tunnel Four opened onto a series of underground chambers. All the hush-hush war intelligence had been hidden down there as well as those projects of a more esoteric or experimental nature. The Tinderbox chamber, rather than the cellars, was apparently where Guy Falks had stored his gunpowder. The name had stuck.

Gareth seemed pleasant enough, though Evelyn wasn't certain yet of his official role, Jocelyn's personal assistant, perhaps. He was just a few years older than herself — mid to late twenties, and not bad looking either. Their boss, Jocelyn Price, however, was a different kettle of fish.

Evelyn picked up her case and strode into the office, determined to impress.

Jocelyn wasted no time on kindliness. She waved Evelyn to a seat by her desk and cocked her head to one side. "I understand you have made a discovery…"

"I've made a *connection*," corrected Evelyn quickly, hoping she didn't sound too pushy. She pulled several sheets of card from her case and laid them out on Jocelyn's desk. Gareth stood observing to one side.

Jocelyn set her mouth into a grim line and pulled the first sheet towards her. A faded newspaper cutting had been glued in the exact centre of the page. A badly reproduced photograph of a young man in a jacket and high winged collar was followed by a few paragraphs of type. Jocelyn noted the date at the top: 1891. "It's in French," she said.

Evelyn nodded, then realised her evidence might not be as obvious as she had thought. "It's a report of a missing person," she said. "The details aren't important — but the location is."

Jocelyn was scanning the scrap of paper. "Bosquet d'Anges," she said. "Something to do with angels?"

"Grove of Angels." Evelyn pushed forward the next cutting, neatly stuck to another card. "Another disappearance. 1902, same location." She spread out a further five pages. "More mysterious disappearances, the latest I could find was 1933."

"A serial killer?" suggested Gareth, crossing to Jocelyn's side to see the cuttings. "Over a period of forty years, it's not impossible… This is not *necessarily* a matter for Tinderbox to get involved in."

Evelyn reached into her case. "There's more." She produced an ancient crumbling book, its black canvas cover blotched with age. "*The Pandemonium*," she said with some relish. "You know my background. This book comes from my mother's somewhat peculiar collection. Hand drawn and scribed; I only know of two other surviving copies. It's basically a demon-spotter's guide, French edition." She was pleased to see Gareth and Jocelyn exchange a glance of appreciation as she carefully turned the pages. It was a slim book, garishly illustrated with fanged and horned monstrosities. "It's mostly folklore and legend," Evelyn continued. "Loch Ness Monster tales — not to be taken seriously. But here…" She swung the book round. The page showed a man and a woman, draped in simple toga-like garments. The ink had faded but trees could be seen lush and plentiful behind them. There appeared to be nothing monstrous about them at all. *"Les mangeurs de vie,"* announced Evelyn. "From the little hamlet of Bosquet d'Anges."

Jocelyn pulled the book towards her. "Eaters of life," she translated. "And you think there's some connection between this… *legend* and the people disappearing."

It wasn't a question, but Evelyn nodded. "I'm certain of it. When I read the unusual place name "Grove of Angels" I remembered reading about somebody going missing from there." She waved at the pile of cuttings. "With a little research I found all these — and there's one more thing…"

Evelyn could see that Jocelyn had been drawn in. "Which is?"

"A soldier," said Evelyn. "Private Daniel Cooke. About two years ago he was practically blown to pieces on the front line. He claims he can't remember what happened to him, but the records show that the attack occurred in a copse of trees. There is little left these days of Bosquet d'Anges, just a few deserted houses; the title "Grove of Angels" seems to have passed from the village to this small, wooded area. From the military records, I traced the medic who dealt with Private Cooke in the field and… well, I asked the minister if he could get me an interview." Evelyn paused, half expecting Jocelyn to protest. Involving the minister smacked a little of going over her head. But Jocelyn was waiting impassively for the rest of the story. Evelyn unfolded a section of map. "The medic was able to confirm the location of the attack." She indicated the circled area, clearly labelled "Bosquet d'Anges". Evelyn waved at the newspaper cuttings. "I'd like permission to investigate further," she said. "I think Daniel Cooke was going to be another of the 'disappearances', but he fought back. I think he met the 'life eaters'."

***

"So, what do you think of our tame demonologist?" Gareth sat opposite Jocelyn, in the chair Evelyn had recently vacated.

Jocelyn arranged the papers, still laid out on her desk. "She's certainly keen," she said. "And organised; good at research…"

"But," Gareth hesitated, "you don't like her."

Jocelyn gave him a stare and pulled out her glasses. She never wore them, Gareth noted, in front of the staff unless she had to. "I don't know her well enough yet. I don't know how she's going to fit in." She picked up the ancient fragile book and began turning the pages. "I mean… who else would have "The Pandemonium" on their bookshelves? You're much nearer her age than I am, Gareth, what do you think? Is she *too* obsessive, actively seeking out trouble?"

"The minister likes her," said Gareth, sidestepping the question.

"He would." Jocelyn carefully closed the book. "What with her cultured accent; careful dress sense; subtle make up; *precisely*-centred cuttings…"

"Not to mention her flashy pen and expensive document case." Gareth risked a grin. "And she's half your age…"

Jocelyn glared. "Are you suggesting I'm jealous?" She saw Gareth's teasing expression — and managed to laugh at herself. "Cheeky whelk." She placed the book on her desk. "What's her background?"

"An only child. Her father was an RAF pilot; quite a high-ranking officer; shot down three years ago. Her mother had a passion for folklore and demonology, which she has evidently passed on to Evelyn. We actually have an old Tinderbox file on the mother. She's one of the few people aware of demons, and was becoming quite vocal about it."

"Was?"

"No one believed her, of course." Gareth's tone became sympathetic. "Then, as if talking of demons wasn't considered insane enough, the poor woman developed early dementia; she's in a care home."

"She's not one of our *placements*, is she?" asked Jocelyn.

"Oh no, nothing like that," Gareth assured her. "Her dementia is entirely genuine. But having effectively lost both parents, that left Evelyn as the lonely, independent demonologist who came to our attention. Oh, and one more thing, she never visits her mother. She claims there's no point. Gossip, however, says she's scared witless that she'll end up in the same boat — that dementia could run in the family."

Jocelyn leant back in her chair. "She's moneyed, certainly," she mused, "judging by her clothes and hair. It's always the hair that gives it away."

"I know you like your agents to be more... down to earth," said Gareth. "But it might be useful to have someone who moves in different circles — more of an academic. And she speaks French. I say give her the chance, let her prove that she can be a practical asset."

"She's demon-hunting." Jocelyn frowned. "Seeking out trouble. We don't have a policy of provocation." She took off her glasses and hid them in a drawer. "But, yes, I agree. Let's see what she can do; bring her back in."

***

I've got my voice back, nasal as it is. It is such a relief to be able to talk out loud and not have my thoughts live totally inside my head. I still talk to myself, though, like this. It's pretty much a habit now, I suppose. I feel like I'm telling a story to somebody I can't see.

And speaking of not being able to see... St Justin's is one hell of a convalescent home!

A nurse accompanied me on the train, then a taxi, to make sure I got here in one piece. I realise now that I've been pretty much sheltered in hospitals for over two years and the suburbs are still a wreck of blitz damage. From the train, I saw shops and businesses boarded up; there is scaffolding everywhere — either for rebuilding or for shoring up walls that would otherwise collapse. There are occupied terraces with jagged gaps where houses are missing — like my upper row of teeth. Life goes on; people make do and mend; eek out their rations and have faith in a better future.

Meanwhile, I have fallen on my feet. St Justin's is a requisitioned manor house, set into a hill on the outskirts of Eastbourne. The grounds have massive cedar trees dotted like random umbrellas down to a cliff edge, and beyond that the sea. The view is wasted on the partially sighted. I feel a fraud because my vision has improved so much recently. I've been given the tour, but there's so much I have yet to see. There are staff everywhere, and patients too, though here they are treated as house guests. There is a library of recordings; practically any book you can think of on huge spools of tape. There is a small indoor swimming pool; a dining hall which they call the restaurant; there's even a dance area and on Friday nights a bloody cocktail bar.

My room is comfortable, if basic. There are bold pictures on the walls and the last thing I would have expected — a mirror.

I stand at the mirror for what seems like hours, staring at my face. I think that I was better off when I couldn't see my reflection, and I am glad that most of the patients here are blind. The skin of my throat is smooth now, it looks relatively normal. My eyes have lost the burnt appearance they once had — even my eyelids seem to have recovered slightly. But the hole, of course, is still there. My skin seems to have healed well around the edges, but the central hollow still looks raw. I twist my head, trying to see a profile. It is still horrible. I feel my jaw: the bone that had been blasted away. Like my nose, it had once been quite pointed, now it looks square and angular

– an improvement some might say, but to me it looks as wrong as the crater where my nose should be.

Doctor Greenway allowed me a couple of days to settle and find my way around, then he made a start on my convalescent sessions.

My introduction to his much-hyped vocational training is boot repairing! I join a group with an instructor who has us feel old army boots, the heavy kind which bring back unwelcome memories of mud and gunfire. We feel for any deformations and are given blunt tools to tease the leather apart and stitch it back together again with great concentration. I doubt these boots will ever see any practical use, but it keeps us occupied and I am amazed that I feel useful again. *That*, I realise, is the whole idea. I haven't felt useful in ages.

Sessions at St Justin's are all geared towards our mental wellbeing. With allowances for our lack of sight, we are put through a programme Greenway calls 'emotional rehabilitation'. Part of this, it seems, is a weekly chat with Doctor Greenway himself.

He starts with general enquiries: how am I? Is the food OK? Are the staff attentive enough? Then he asks if I still have nightmares about the grenade attack.

"I know I still cry out at night," I say in confirmation.

"And do you remember your dreams, Danny?"

I think back to when Sir Richard had asked me similar questions, asking me to write down what I couldn't say. I am amazed at how my sight and speech and breathing have recovered since then. I nod in answer to the question. Before, I had only vague feelings of oppression and horror, but now I dreamt with greater clarity. "I see more and more details each time," I say, hoping he can understand the flatness of my speech.

Greenway leans closer. "Why do you think that is?"

That's getting deep! I shrug. "It's like my mind is talking to me," I say, feeling like I'm admitting to something foolish; "revealing a little more to me each time."

He nods thoughtfully, careful, I notice, not to ridicule my idea. It doesn't seem farfetched to me though — my mind talking to me. I think about my constant talking to myself — as if to someone who isn't there. I have a stupid idea that someone could be talking back to me, telling me, through my dreams, about that time in the copse of trees with my grenade.

Greenway doesn't press the point, but I can tell he will ask for more details at our next session. "By the way," he says, as if he's just remembered something. "I had a call from someone, asking about you." He consults a scrap of paper. "From an organisation called Tinderbox. Her name's Evelyn Greer and, as far as I could tell, she's researching French folklore."

"What's that got to do with me?" I say.

Greenway spreads his hands. "I've no idea. Sounds like she's from some minor government department that's looking into… that sort of stuff. Anyway, you can ask her yourself; she'll be here tomorrow."

***

I am in the clearing of the copse, backing away from the angelic woman, wading through ferns. The rain drips off my tin hat. The man steps out from the trees behind me. I am surrounded. They are tall and perfect, immaculately dressed in their togas. I shrink from them, battered, tired and slicked in mud.

There are voices in my head. *Relax, Danny. Stay calm. We want you. We need you.*

"Why do you need me?" In my panic I don't know if I have spoken aloud or not.

They reach out towards me. Their perfection is horrible. *Stay calm, Danny,* their lips don't move. *We are sustained by people like you. We need you.*

They touch me

We need to be alive. So alive!

I feel weak. They are pulling the strength from me. Somehow, I know that they are feeding, maintaining those perfect features — and I can't let that happen. I can feel their exultation, and know I have little time. My hands are shaking. I pull out the grenade. They seem to know what I am thinking, but don't withdraw. Instead, I feel weaker; they are absorbing me *faster*. I grip the grenade's lever in my right hand, pull out the safety ring with my left. I have never been so terrified. My weak fingers relax, releasing the lever; the grenade is cooking, the fuse burning.

The man and the woman can't believe what I have done. They slide away, staring back at me side by side in amazement. They are too late. I toss the grenade into the space between them. There is a violent flash of fire. They are blown to pieces.

And I wake mirroring their screams.

***

I am sitting on a bench with a view down to the sea. Even though the sun is warm, I have a tartan blanket tucked around my legs. The staff don't seem to mind leaving me out here by myself, but I'm sure they are not far away, keeping an eye on me. Besides, I need time to think…

The attractive faces of the people in my nightmare keep appearing in my mind. And their voices: '*Stay calm, Danny*'. They had known my name. I hear it echoed now in my head as if they are calling to me from my dreams. I physically shudder despite the warmth of the day. I remember the overwhelming feeling of weakness as if their mere presence had sucked all the energy from me. I don't know why they horrify me, when they look so perfect; that doesn't make sense. Do they somehow represent the *opposite* of my ruined features? Is that why they look like film stars and why I dread them so much? So much that, in the safety of my dreams, I try to destroy them? Sir Richard would have been pleased with me — I'm self-analysing again.

"Danny." The voice seems real, then I realise… A nurse has called me. She is approaching from behind, escorting my visitor: Evelyn something.

I have a sudden urge to keep my face turned away from them. Now that I can see, I am conscious of how I appear to others.

Evelyn walks round in front of me. I can tell she has steeled herself; her face doesn't react. "Hello, Daniel," she says.

The nurse fusses with the blanket, tucking it around me. She asks if there is anything else I require, then heads back to the building.

"Please, call me Danny." I speak carefully so that she'll understand.

Evelyn remains standing, watching the nurse walk away. "I'd hate to have someone fuss over *me* like that." There is an awkward pause where she realises what she has said. "Sorry, I didn't mean…" her words stumble. "It's just that I would hate to rely on others." She takes a breath and indicates the path that winds down between the cedars. "Shall we walk?" she suggests. "Is that OK with you?"

"Nothing wrong with my legs." I stand and leave the blanket on the bench. Evelyn is younger than I imagined. She is wearing a slim-fitting print dress, simple but stylish, her dark hair curls either side of her subtly made-up face. She is not the frumpy scholar I had been expecting. "You're researching French folklore," I say. "What's that got to do with me?"

She gives a brief smile, but her eyes remain serious. I'm used to people staring at me, but her gaze is thorough and appraising. "I'm sorry for your injuries," she says. "Does it hurt?"

She seems genuinely concerned. "Not anymore." I touch my throat. "At first it was agony; I was steeped in morphine. But now… well, everyone I see is amazed at how much I've healed." I snort. "Can you believe I looked worse than this?"

It is an unfair question; I sound as if I'm fishing for sympathy. She says nothing for a moment, and we continue to stroll. "The place where your injuries took place," she says, "is associated with a French legend."

I have no interest in fairy tales, but she is obviously leading up to something.

"You were in a grove of trees, I believe," Evelyn continues. "Can you tell me about it?"

What can I say? I have nightmares about that grove. But, however much the dream feels like a memory, it is still a dream. Nothing reliable; nothing factual. "I don't remember much about it."

She keeps walking, but turns to face me. "The legend that I'm researching, mentions a man and a woman."

I am stunned! Can she see surprise in the ruin of my face? "I have a recurring dream," I admit. "Though — I have never told anyone about it."

"You can tell *me*, Danny." She is persuasive. "I think you know that I have already guessed what you have to say."

And I tell her. All of it. The fear, the feeling of weakness, the perfect featured man and woman somehow draining me, and the grenade I use to destroy them. It is a relief, *such a relief*, to tell someone else.

She nods as if she believes every word.

"But it's just a dream," I say. "Some claptrap my brain has cooked up to cope with — *this*." I wave at the hole in my face.

We have reached the clifftop and stop, gazing out at the sea. Below us, the rush of foaming waves betrays the incoming of the tide.

"Dreams can be the mind's way of coming to terms with an horrific experience," she says. "Do you have any concrete memories that support or refute this dream?"

I shake my head. "Nothing," I gaze out to the horizon.

"France," she says, following my gaze. "Not far away at all." A breeze ruffles her hair, and she seems struck by an idea.

"I wonder, Danny. Is the dream more vivid here, now you're in Sussex, closer to the source?"

I don't see any logic in this. But yes, my nightmare *has* become more detailed. She can see by the realisation in my eyes that this is so.

"That's really interesting," she says.

"The man and woman spoke to me, in my dream," I explain. "They had never done that before. They even knew my name." I look out across the waves, and imagine I can hear them now, calling me. *Danny. Danny.*

"Did they use their voices, Danny?" Evelyn taps the side of her head, "Or is the communication more — mental?"

"I could hear them in my head," I say. It is obvious that she knows more than she is saying. "What is this legend?" I ask. "Why is it in my nightmare?"

Evelyn flashes that smile again. "Just folk tales." She gives a dismissive flick of her hand and heads back up the slope towards the building. "Nothing for you to worry about."

I follow, and behind me I imagine I hear my name again. *Danny. Danny.*

***

"Here at St Justin's, we've always maintained that rehabilitation should be of the *whole* person, not just the injured limb — or, in your case, Danny, your face." Greenway has accosted me in the conservatory, or *The Orangery* as they like to call it, all wicker chairs and pot plants. He leans in closer from the chair opposite mine; his voice lowers slightly. "Your nightmares, Danny... they indicate disquiet. Whether you're consciously aware of it or not, you are worried, and anything we can do to allay that worry would be a step forward in your psychological recovery."

"Not more boot repairs!" He is familiar enough with my face to see that I'm joking. Then I make a connection. "You've been speaking with that woman, Evelyn, haven't you?"

"We had quite a long chat on the phone this afternoon," he admits.

I am annoyed. "So, I've got no secrets anymore. Not even my nightmares."

Greenway straightens and the wicker chair creaks. "I'm going to make a suggestion," he spreads his hands. "You can refuse if you wish; it's entirely up to you."

I have absolutely no idea what this suggestion could be.

"I think it would be therapeutic, Danny," he says, "for you to take a trip to France."

"Go back to France!" I involuntarily place a hand over my face as if to shield it. My palm sinks into the gap where my nose should be, and I am horrified anew.

"Evelyn agrees with me," he continues. "She was full of enthusiasm. We believe you have created your nightmare scenario of perfectly featured people in response to your injuries. You have made them the "enemy" you encountered during the grenade attack."

Greenway's voice makes it sound so reasonable, but I don't know what to believe.

"One of our male nurses will accompany you," he says. "If you visit the site of the attack, it should relieve some of the mystique that has built up in your mind. Being there may even spark a memory. Then you'd have something genuine to cling to, rather than this somewhat debilitating anxiety that drives your dreams."

I can see his logic. But I can't just accept that my nightmares have been some imaginary self-imposed torture.

"So, Danny. What do you say?"

***

Jocelyn had felt the need of a second opinion, so had called Gareth back into her Tunnel Four office where they sat listening to Evelyn's initial evidence one more time.

Evelyn translated the newspaper reports, giving details of the disappearances, and told them again of the folklore behind *les mangeurs de vie*.

"You say you've now met this soldier," Jocelyn prompted.

"Daniel Cooke." Evelyn nodded. "I saw him the day before yesterday. And I'm *convinced* he has met these creatures." She tapped the illustration in *The Pandemonium*. "He has nightmares of his attack, and when I suggested they might feature a man and a woman, he went straight into details. He described them exactly as they appear here. He said he felt weak, and that they were feeding on him, taking his energy."

"He must have been terrified," said Gareth. "I mean, risking his own life to lob a grenade at them. Thank heavens he survived."

For once, Evelyn didn't have an instant comeback. Jocelyn noticed. "There's more, isn't there?"

Evelyn reached into her document case. "I've been doing a bit more research these last few days," she said. "When I met Danny, he could see, he could speak, we strolled through the grounds of the convalescent home. His face is a ruin," she paused as if remembering; "I'd expected that. But... well, let me show you something. I should warn you, it's not very pleasant." She produced another newspaper cutting, again pasted neatly onto card. "While he was in the original hospital, Churchill paid a visit. It was supposed to boost morale among the injured, and would earn Churchill a fair bit of kudos too. The visit got into the papers and even the cinema news reels, I believe. That's Churchill with Danny; the man with them is Sir Richard Hardy, a specialist in reconstructive surgery."

Jocelyn scanned the cutting. And winced. "Poor lad. Good to put a face to the name, though."

"But what a face!" Gareth leant over the desk. "Poor sod, there's not much left, is there?"

"That was several months ago," said Evelyn. "A lot has happened since then. Danny couldn't speak, his throat and tongue were in pieces. But a couple of days ago we spoke together. His voice wasn't perfect, but I could understand him."

"Go on," said Jocelyn, beginning to see where this was headed.

"He was also virtually blind," said Evelyn. "St Justin's, where I met him, specialises in helping the partially sighted. But Danny, so far as I could tell, could see reasonably well."

Jocelyn looked again at the cutting. "Sir Richard Hardy... didn't he die recently?"

"A form of suffocation." Evelyn nodded. "Blood in the lungs. Caused by an erosion of the throat.

Jocelyn and Gareth exchanged a meaningful glance as the implication hit them.

"And the blindness?" asked Jocelyn.

Evelyn consulted her reporter's notebook. "A nurse who was treating Danny's eyes, Janice Milton, is now registered blind. Her sight deteriorated as Danny's improved."

"Horrible," said Jocelyn.

"Nobody made the connection because Danny was moved away," Evelyn explained. "And having just seen him myself, I can confirm that his face is changing too. The hole, compared with that photograph, is noticeably smaller; the flesh of his face is gradually regenerating."

"So," Jocelyn stared at Evelyn, "what are you saying? That Danny has become one of these 'life-eaters'? But that's not consistent with the legend."

"No, it's not consistent," Evelyn admitted. "I can't say *why* this is happening, but it is obvious that he's been affected by these creatures, he is absorbing what he needs from those around him."

Gareth ran a hand through his hair. "Not every day you encounter a life-eating demon. That makes this Danny Cooke quite a danger." He looked to Jocelyn. "One for the asylum?"

Jocelyn was thoughtful. "He *would* be safer kept locked away..."

"That seems harsh," Evelyn leant back in her chair. "I've met him; I don't think Danny is aware of what's happening to him. As far as he's concerned, he is healing naturally."

"Tricky," said Jocelyn.

"With your permission, I'd like to try something." Evelyn had their attention. "I'd like to take him back to France, to the grove where all this took place. I think to take him there will spark actual memories, rather than the one-stage-removed version we have via his nightmares."

"To what purpose?" Jocelyn asked.

"To prove that these creatures *do* exist. To know for certain that there *are* demons out there in the world."

"*Were* demons out there," corrected Gareth. "Danny blew them up, remember?"

Evelyn shrugged. "Even so," again she tapped the page of The Pandemonium, "wouldn't it be useful for Tinderbox to know that at least some of these legends are based on fact?"

Jocelyn drew a breath, coming to a decision. "No, I can't allow it," she said. "Taking Danny to France would be foolish knowing what we know. He'd be feeding from the lives of everyone he encounters — whether he is aware of what he's doing or not."

Evelyn stood. "I've already proposed the trip to Doctor Greenway," she said. "Unconventional, I know, but I sold it to him as psychological rehabilitation. He agrees that it would be beneficial to Danny's recovery."

"No." Jocelyn was adamant. "I appreciate your enthusiasm, Evelyn. But you'd be putting yourself at risk." She picked up the cutting of Danny with Churchill. "Poor lad. We will have to consider how we can best deal with him. Isolation in the asylum is one possibility." She turned to Evelyn. "Contact this Doctor Greenway, tell him the trip to France is cancelled. For your own safety, Evelyn, I forbid it."

***

"Hello. Hello, Doctor Greenway? … I'm sorry to ring you so early; its Evelyn Greer. … Yes, I'm well, thank you. I'm calling about the trip to France. What did Danny say? Is he up for it? … That's great, I knew he would be … As soon as possible — actually I had thought of leaving tomorrow if that's OK; I've started making all the travel arrangements. … One of your male nurses… yes, of course, that's no problem at all. … Yes, yes, I've spoken to my bosses. They are happy to cover the expenses. They think it's an excellent idea; they were really enthusiastic."

***

Evelyn hated the home, hated the flowery wallpaper, the plastic-covered chairs and the constant smell of disinfectant. And she hated her mother for being there.

"Haven't seen you here for a while," said the duty manager, switching on her cheerful-no-matter-what expression.

Evelyn ignored the barb. "I've been busy," she said. "How is she?"

"Oh, you know, much the same." She pushed open the door to the lounge. The room was ringed by high-backed, sponge-clean armchairs. Most were occupied. A couple of faces turned with blank curiosity at the movement. The others hadn't noticed. "I'll leave you to chat," said the manager, nodding towards the woman by the window, as if to indicate to Evelyn which one her mother was.

Evelyn picked up a stool and placed it before her mother. The light from the window fell harshly across her face. She blinked twice, staring into the middle of the room, but there was no other reaction.

"Hello, Mother."

This was ridiculous.

"How are you?"

Like talking to a brick wall.

One of the staff trundled in pushing a trolley laden with small plates. Each held a square of very pink sponge cake. She handed one to Evelyn before dispensing a plate to those able to feed themselves.

Evelyn looked at the plate in horror, and at the ring of faces she imagined were watching her. "Would you like some cake, Mother?"

No reaction.

Evelyn broke off a corner of sponge and held it to her mother's mouth. An instinctive reaction parted her lips and she ate the morsel, spraying her chin with crumbs.

A single tear slid down Evelyn's cheek. She reached out to hold her mother's hand. "I wanted to see you one last time." She glanced around at the blank faces. Nobody could hear her, nobody that mattered anyway. "I'm going away tomorrow," she continued. "A little trip, somewhere in France." She hesitated. "You remember your book – The Pandemonium? I think I've found a couple of the demons."

Evelyn thought she saw a slight change in her mother's expression. As if, behind those blank eyes, she was fighting against the disease that consumed her mind. It broke her heart to see her mother succumb to it. But sometimes there was a glimmer of hope or understanding in her gaze.

"I don't want to grow old, Mother. You do understand, don't you? I couldn't bear ending up in a place like this, fussed over and dependent on others. I don't want to lose my memories — and have nobody believe the few things I *can* remember." She squeezed her mother's hand. "I've been researching for years, continuing your notes. I know that demons exist, *and I'll prove it*. I know you were never deluded or insane — just confused and forgetful."

The harsh light from the window threw her mother's face into furrows of wrinkles. Evelyn reached out to the curtain and pulled it across to shade her mother's face. The half-gleam Evelyn had seen in her eyes drifted away. "I'll miss you," she said, and broke off another corner of sponge.

***

I am on the clifftop looking out to sea. Waves crash onto the rocks below and seagulls swirl through the spray. Out there is France. I'm not certain how I feel about going back there. I don't exactly have fond memories.

Doctor Greenway says it will be therapeutic for me; he should know. And I will get to see Evelyn again so I'm pretty much sure I've made the right decision.

Danny.

The voices are calling to me again; or is it just the pounding of the waves? I'm sure it's not simply my imagination. I gaze out to the horizon. *I'm coming*, I think, *soon.*

Soon.

My words echo back at me as if I'd heard a reply. It is ridiculous, of course. I remember Evelyn tapping the side of her head and mentioning mental communication. She was referring to my dreams, but this is real. Pretty much anything can happen in a dream…

***

My nightmare has changed. I am still in the clearing, in the copse of trees. The perfect man and perfect woman are here again. The rain drips off my tin hat, my heart thuds, and the grenade is cooking in my hand.

You are dreaming, Danny, says the man.

"How do you know my name?" I ask. Not an obvious question when you're exhausted, mud-covered and have a fuse burning, but hey, like he says, this *is* a dream.

We are inside your head, Danny. Inside your body. We feel your life, and we need to be alive. So alive.

I feel that overwhelming weakness. "You are feeding off me. Eating me!" Terrified, I throw the grenade. It turns slowly in the air. Time stretches. My aim and timing are perfect. It passes between them and explodes. The flash is instant, and I know the shockwave will follow.

We need you, Danny, says the man. *We are waiting.*

Don't abandon us, pleads the woman. *We need your help.*

"I'm coming," I say. "Soon." And the shockwave lifts my face away.

***

"I'm not sure how accurate the translation is." Gareth lay a typed sheet of paper on Jocelyn's desk. "I thought I'd research a bit myself, local rumours, folklore, that sort of thing, in the Bosquet d'Anges region."

"And?"

Gareth waved at the desk. "It's from a local newspaper, about a month ago. A young girl, fifteen, says she was chased by monsters. Two man-shaped creatures she claims were composed of bugs and worms. There's very little detail; seems no one took her seriously."

"Bugs and worms?" Jocelyn was dismissive. "Doesn't sound like our demons — the perfect man and woman."

"True. But it's the *same* location."

Jocelyn leant back on her chair, considering. "Get hold of Evelyn. See what she makes of it."

***

It feels strange to be back here in France. Much here is the same as at home: rationing; damaged buildings; it's going to take decades for the world to get back to normal. And there is a wariness of strangers. I don't think it is just my face that attracts looks of suspicion, Evelyn and Mike have felt it too. Mike is the nurse from St Justin's, sent along to take care of my medical needs. He's a couple of years older than me, mid-twenties, and is treating this trip as a holiday.

Evelyn is a bit of a mystery to me still. I know she charmed old Greenway into allowing this trip, and she's paying for it too. But I'm not sure of her motives.

We crossed on the late Newhaven ferry, so we've got rooms here in this rather shoddy Dieppe hotel for a couple of nights. I guess anywhere would look shoddy after St Justin's. Where are the vast grounds, the cedars and the cocktail bar? Instead, we are sitting in a gloomy saloon around a rickety table with a beer each, trying to ignore the stares from the locals.

"I've hired a car," Evelyn explains. "We'll drive out to Bosquet d'Anges tomorrow morning and be back here for supper."

I still don't know much about the organisation she works for. "What's in this for you?" I ask. She has been vague so far, but I figured, now that we're here, she might be a bit more forthcoming.

She produces that brief smile of hers and trots out the flannel she had used on Greenway: "I am hoping to relieve your nightmares, Danny."

Danny. Danny.

My name seems to hang, reverberating in the air. I look from Evelyn to Mike. Neither of them have noticed. I recognise the voices from my nightmares; the man and the woman; the same faint calls I had heard from the Sussex clifftop. But louder now, and clearer. Closer to the source, as Evelyn had once said.

She knows more than she says.

It is the woman's voice, and I know she means Evelyn.

She knows of us, from her studies. She fears us, but she wants to find us, to prove that we are real. Because there is something she fears more…

I am sure my eyes will betray me. It's like I'm secretly talking with someone who's not here. *How do you know this? I ask without speaking.*

231

We are in her head. Like we are here in yours. We can sense her thoughts, like we can hear yours.

You can hear my thoughts! Suddenly, like fitting a piece of a puzzle, I realise something. Since the explosion — when I couldn't speak aloud — I have been talking to myself, I'm still doing it. A constant commentary on what I am doing and thinking.

You weren't talking to yourself, Danny. It is the man's voice. *You were talking to us.*

We could hear you, Danny, says the woman. *But you couldn't hear us, except in your dreams. As you draw closer, you can hear us more clearly.*

I am amazed that neither Evelyn nor Mike can hear the voices. Mike stands. "Another beer, Dan?" he offers. "Evelyn's paying." He sniffs and reaches to his face. His hand comes away with blood on it. "Eeew! A nosebleed." He produces a handkerchief, turns and heads off to the gents.

Evelyn is watching me. Intently.

She knows, Danny, says the man's voice. *She knows what you are doing.*

I reach up to my face. It is my imagination, surely, but the hole feels slightly smaller.

***

I lie awake on my bed. I don't need to dream; I can hear the voices clearly. And anyway, I don't want more nightmares.

My world has been turned upside down. And my mind is full of suspicions. *What is it that Evelyn knows about me?* Instinctively, I know what they are going to say. I dread to ask, but I need it spelt out to me. *What did I do to Mike?*

You are alive, Danny, the man and woman chorus. *You need to be alive. So alive!*

But, and this is where I panic, *at what cost? What have I done?*

You are healing, Danny, says the woman. Her voice is soft and reasonable. *You draw upon the strength in others to rebuild and sustain yourself.*

It *is* as I feared. It started with my throat, my breathing, my voice. Sir Richard had died, *died*, when his throat fell apart. And Janice! Poor Janice, with her uniform so blue, who could hardly see to put in my eye drops. Janice who had kissed me, despite my face. I stare up through the darkness towards the ceiling and feel tears well from my eyes.

There is a plea in the woman's voice: *You are so close now, Danny, and we need your help.*

I feel suddenly angry and defiant. I didn't ask for any of this. *How can this be happening?*

Your restoration will be faster, now that you are closer to us, says the man.

I don't understand. *What have you done to me?*

You are changing, Danny, he says. *You are almost whole; you are becoming one of us.*

***

Gareth pushed open the door to Jocelyn's office. "Evelyn has gone," he said.

Jocelyn looked up from a pile of papers, too startled to reprimand him for bursting in. "What do you mean?"

Gareth waved an arm helplessly. "I was trying to tell her about that newspaper report. But I got no answer from her home, so I tried Greenway." He paused.

"And..."

"She has ignored your orders. Danny Cooke was taken to France yesterday evening, and it seems Evelyn went with him."

Jocelyn looked furious. "Get me a map," she demanded. "What was the name of that village? Something to do with angels...."

***

The landscape around Bosquet d'Anges has changed, but it is still familiar. What a difference peacetime makes! It is a bright day — no rain. The fields are cultivated, but I know where the slit trenches were. Instinctively I want to crouch and keep low. Instead of bullets there is birdsong. *I am very near to you, now.* We leave the road and cross the fields, stepping through rows of sprouting cabbages.

We can feel you, Danny. You are almost here.

I stop, suddenly. There ahead of me is the copse of trees, still rising like an island from the field.

"Are you OK, Dan?" Mike switches into concerned nurse mode. "You don't have to do this if you don't want to."

He is worried about my state of mind; all he knows is that I am here to face my nightmares. He has no idea how true that is.

By Mike's side Evelyn looks suddenly anxious. As if she fears, at this last moment, that I might turn around and refuse to go any further. I toy with the idea of frustrating her plans. I still don't know her motives, but I know she wants to press on. She too wants to meet the voices.

I give Mike a nod and we keep moving.

I am remembering more and more. This could be therapeutic after all. I remember a movement among the trees.

That was us, Danny.

Yes, I know. I imagine the position of the bushes that used to grow here, following the route I had taken, using them for cover, trying to ignore the sound of gunfire. And we enter the cool shadow of the trees. Mike watches me, carefully. Evelyn looks around.

She is looking for us.

We walk into the centre of the clearing, still overgrown with ferns.

"So, this is where it happened," says Mike. He turns in a small circle. "You were ambushed by two of the enemy, so you blasted them with a grenade..." He whistles softly to himself. "You're one brave guy, Dan."

Like Evelyn, I scan the clearing. *Where are you?*

"Shit, not again!" Mike pats his pockets for another handkerchief; blood is pouring from his nose. He leans forward, pinches the bridge of his nose to stem the flow. I reach out to him. Place my hand over his face. He feels so alive. And that is exactly what I need. I draw from him, like breathing in: the deepest breath I have ever taken. The skin of Mike's face thins to the consistency of cobweb, then falls apart. He screams then crumples to the ground. I don't know if he is still alive.

And there is Evelyn, staring at me, at my new face, the ugly hole restored. "You are complete, Danny," she says. She ignores where Mike has fallen. "This is fascinating! How do you feel?"

I feel... I feel whole, and alive, so alive!

Evelyn isn't surprised. She looks around again. "Where are you?" Her face is stern. "Danny said he'd heard voices, so I *know* you survived." She raises her voice to a demanding shout. "I know you are real. You *have* to be real. Where are you?"

We are here.

The ground bubbles up. Two mounds rise through the ferns, straighten and stand. They are shaped like a man and a woman but their surface crawls, they are composed of insects, spiders, beetles and worms.

The woman turns to me. *Thank you, Danny, for coming to help us.* Her squirming head tilts to one side. *You are restored?*

I am. I reach up to my face, to my new nose, and I smile. I have fed off Mike's vitality and absorbed his flesh. I am whole; no longer Danny Cooke, but something more. I glance down at Mike's body and it moves feebly, I no longer feel for him, nor for Janice, nor Sir Richard. They are as nothing compared with me now that I am complete.

Evelyn is staring at the two creatures. This is not what she was expecting. "What has *happened* to you?"

The man turns to her, but gestures to *me* with an arm formed of bugs. *This was a battle ground. We fed here on soldiers that nobody would miss. But one soldier fought back.*

It is obvious that Evelyn can now hear their voices. She looks to me. "Danny blew you apart!"

The woman steps forward. *There is a legend that we eat life to sustain our perfect angelic appearance. That is true. But in these last years we have had only things that crawl through these woods to draw upon — until now.* Her head writhes and turns to me. *Danny is here to save us.*

I reach down and haul Mike to his feet. His head lolls, the centre of his face is gone and oozes gore. His eyes flicker. There is life in him yet.

The man undulates forward, reaches out hungrily, just as he had reached for me that day in the rain. Mike weakens instantly, sagging into insubstantial cobweb as his life and flesh are absorbed. The man's outline improves; the insects are caught in a thin coating of skin. *Aaah,* he exults, *already I feel so much stronger. So alive!*

It is as if the man, the woman, and I have the same thought. We turn as one to face Evelyn.

"I want to join you." Her voice is quick and earnest. "I have studied you. You are everything I want to be." Her eyes are wide with admiration.

You fear us, says the woman. *But there is something you fear more.*

Evelyn looks to me. At my restored body. And there is a hunger in her eyes.

The woman draws nearer. *You fear old age, you fear dependence on others, you fear the erosion of your mind passed down by your mother.*

236

Evelyn is defiant. "Yes!" she says. "Is it any wonder I want to be like you. Strong, whole, young forever." She stares into the woman's face crawling with insects. "Do to me what you did to Danny."

Danny has become one of us, says the man. *But he is not of our making.*

Evelyn's eyes narrow as if she suspects a trick. "What do you mean?" she demands.

The man flexes the bug-spattered flesh of his new arms, enjoying the sensation. *We were blown apart by Danny's grenade. Danny's face was gone. When the medics gathered him up, they found and took my jawbone.*

Evelyn's eyes grew wide.

My jaw latched onto Danny. He was barely alive, but still living. Slowly, very slowly, my jaw restored Danny's throat, drawing on the life around him. And now he is whole and returned to us: Les mangeurs de vie!

The woman seethes towards Evelyn, her body a-crawl with worms and thrashing insect legs. Evelyn backs away and stumbles heavily into the bracken.

You have served us well, Danny, says the woman. *Soon we can be fully restored.* She bends over Evelyn.

Evelyn is shaking with tears. "No," she pleads. "I want to be like you, perfect and young. I don't want to grow old!"

I watch Evelyn fade and wither. "You won't," I say.

***

Jocelyn slammed down the telephone receiver. "The minister says we have no jurisdiction in France!"

It had been three days now, since they'd lost contact with Evelyn, Danny and the nurse, Mike. They'd stayed one night in an hotel, driven away the following morning, and not returned.

"So, we know these things exist," said Gareth. "We know exactly where they are and what they're capable of…"

"And can do nothing about it," Jocelyn finished. She seethed, wandering backwards and forwards behind her desk in agitation. "We will keep an eye on the situation, of course. We can warn the French authorities, tell their local council, but nobody will believe us. Evelyn will be just another of their mysterious disappearances. The legend will grow of the perfect angels from the grove, and nothing will change."

Gareth flicked through the brittle pages of The Pandemonium which they'd recovered from Evelyn's hotel room. "Except," he said, "that there will be at least three angels now; presumably Danny has been converted." He studied the other faded pictures in the book, of horns, fangs and leathery wings. "If the "Life-eaters" are real, what about all these?"

"We are not vigilante demon hunters, Gareth. That's too dangerous." Jocelyn's face sagged. "Evelyn let us down." She took the book and deliberately placed it on a shelf. "For reference only," she said, "if we ever need it."

Rob Nisbet Biography

I have had over 100 short stories printed in magazines and anthologies ranging from romance to horror. A few short stories (based on the TV programme Doctor Who) have been recorded by the audio company Big Finish.

The Duel (A *Battalion X* Story)

Anthony Rudd

The phone rang, the ringtone insistent. The room was pitch black, not even the slightest hint of moonlight seeped through the barely shrouded window. The DO NOT DISTURB feature should have shielded him from all but the most important callers — whoever was calling was on his shortlist of trusted individuals. He reached blindly towards the sound hoping to snag the phone amidst the water bottles, ashtrays and other detritus that covered his 'nightstand' — a blanket thrown over an old backless chair which gave the barest impression that it was a real piece of furniture. He managed to grab the phone on what had to be only a few rings short of going to voicemail.

Turner. What could she possibly want this late? The screen confirmed it was 1:27 AM — he had only been asleep for about a half hour. *This better be good — sleep came at a premium.* "Yeah?" he answered.

"Kieran, it's Imogen. I need your help," her voice was steady but he detected something amiss. He clicked on the small clip-on lamp that hung from the headboard, its weak incandescent glow filling the room with light and illuminating his small space — an efficiency apartment barely bigger than a large closet, the floor littered with trash and dirty clothes — a metaphor for his life if ever there was one

"Are you in trouble?"

"You could say that, yeah."

Kieran sat up in the bed and swept the sheet aside rising to his feet in a swift motion, a surge of adrenaline propelling him. *No one messes with my people.* "Where are you? Are you safe where you're at? What's the threat?" He located a pair of jeans from the floor and pulled them on, followed by a black t-shirt with a bloody skull emblazoned across the front.

"I am at the bus depot, Fifth and Main. I am safe where I am at."

Kieran located a pair of boots underneath an old ratted out hoody and began to pull them on, pausing as she answered. "What's the issue then?" He countered.

"You remember Jimmy Foster? Of course you do, what am I thinking? We were hanging out, reminiscing about the olden days, you know, before they shut us down and set us packing. I'm not sure what I said but something set him off. He's challenged me to a duel. You know the rules — I couldn't refuse."

"You've got to be fucking kidding me," Kieran exclaimed running his hands through his shoulder-length brown hair while cradling the phone between his shoulder and jawline. He located a hair tie and put his hair into a ponytail. "Imogen, is this some sort of joke? I'm really not in the mood."

"No sir. This is serious as it gets," her voice broke, panic rising in its tenor.

"When and where?"

"Sunrise, Washington Dam. He is bringing Camwicz as his second. I told him I was bringing you."

Damn! If Piotr Camwicz was involved this was likely to go only one way. He took a deep breath and composed himself. "Stay where you are. I'm on the way." He hung up the phone, checked to make sure it was fully charged and thrust it into his back pocket.

Kieran grabbed his wallet, keys, and a small backpack he kept hung on a hook near the door. As he reached for the handle he paused and looked back, searching. There it was. He walked back into the room and reached under his couch pulling forth a subcompact pistol in an easily concealable holster. His Glock 33 had saved him more than a few times. He had hoped he wouldn't need it ever again but it looked like circumstances might be changing. He tucked the holster into his waistband, making sure it was secure. He didn't check to see if it was loaded. It was always loaded.

***

He sat astride his Harley Softail, cruising through nearly empty streets toward the bus depot. He mused that the few people out and about at this time of night were likely people coming home from working the late shift or trying to get home after a stint at their local watering hole. The night was warm but not overly so, and he was thankful for the weather, much better than the alternative. The hum of the motorcycle beneath him generally helped calm his nerves but tonight it only served to heighten his anxiety.

As he made his way to the bus depot, he couldn't shake the feeling that he was barreling headlong into something bigger. Imogen wasn't easily shaken; she was a steady performer, well-liked by the rest of the company, but the unspoken things about her interaction with Foster had his mind racing on what could have set him off enough for him to demand a duel.

The bus depot parking lot was almost empty when Kieran arrived. After circling the station to ensure there wasn't anything amiss, he drove his motorcycle into the small adjoining parking lot, ensuring that the bike was not only in a well-lit area but tactically parked in case he had to make a quick exit. The bus depot was a two-story building, the ground floor the ticketing and waiting areas and the upstairs a small café and what he assumed to be offices for administrators. The building itself was clearly the product of a bygone era of glass and steel making it look industrial. At the back of the building was where the buses pulled in to allow for loading and unloading.

Kieran reached for the glass door and let himself into the building, instantly he was hit by the stench of unwashed bodies and old food. Like many places in the city that were open twenty-four hours, the bus depot housed many of the city's homeless — at least until the weekly rousting by city authorities which only served as a temporary fix as the homeless were back generally within hours of being uprooted. It hadn't been that long since Kieran had found himself in a similar situation.

He spotted Imogen on a bench towards the back of the terminal — her back to the wall and with a clear view of all ingress and egress points as well as being close to both cover and at least two avenues of escape — he had trained her well and she had clearly not forgotten any of it. She spotted him immediately and nodded him over to a seat beside her.

Kieran took a second to assess the other people in the building — there was a young family of three on a bench adjacent to Imogen, the woman cradling the toddler in her lap and the man with his arm protectively around her. On another bench a man was spread across all the seats, deep asleep. Finally, there was a bored older man behind the window at the ticket booth, he looked up as Kieran entered and then went back to whatever he was watching on his phone.

Kieran turned back to Imogen, she looked much as she had the last time he had seen her, albeit a little haggard. Imogen was a short woman, barely scraping five foot in stature and stocky — looking more like a young mother than a hardened soldier. Kieran smirked as he remembered how many times her average physique had fooled others, especially in the combatives pit. There were more than a few buff males that walked away humbled after tangling with her. Her dark hair was pulled back away from her face and into a severe braid, her brown eyes alert as she looked him up and down as he approached.

Imogen stood as he approached and opened her arms wide, "You came."

Kieran reciprocated, pulling her into a quick hug, "Of course. You called. I told all of you that our relationship wouldn't end with our 'retirement'." They both sat, side-by-side, choosing to talk while watching their surroundings.

"Tell me what happened," Kieran prompted.

"I called Jimmy last week; to let him know I was coming in town. Not sure if you were tracking, but I had moved back to Boise. Life kinda sucked there, especially after my mother died, so I figured I'd see if I could start over somewhere new. I was passing through on my way to Florida so I asked Jimmy if I could crash at his place. I got in town this morning. We were hanging out, the three of us, him, me, and Camwicz, drinking some beers, and just talking. Next thing I know he is throwing a bottle against the wall and accusing me for everything that went wrong. We were all pretty hammered so I tried to shrug it off but he wasn't having it. He grabbed my bag and threw it out the door of his apartment." She paused as her voice hitched with emotion. "He challenged me, per the ancient rules and sealed it with blood. He said the words."

Kieran leaned forward and put his hands to his temples, rubbing them fiercely. "I don't understand. You two were close. You must have said something."

"That's just it — I don't know what I said. We were talking about the deployment and the team. Everything was good."

"OK, think back to just before he snapped at you — who were you talking about?"

"We were laughing about Samantha Reynolds and that stupid dog we found. I'm not sure if you were aware but there was something going on with the two of them."

Kieran thought back to the deployment — he had suspected that there was a romantic tryst ongoing with between Foster and Reynolds. Soldiers tend to think their leadership oblivious to all the interpersonal stuff but it had been obvious, the glances, Foster offering to take Reynold's guard duty — the signs were there. That didn't bother him in the least, as long as they did their job he wasn't concerned. There was something that Imogen said that didn't feel right, though. "Wait — what dog?"

"The day of the bombing, Reynolds and I found a puppy that wandered up to the guard shack. It was a little brown mutt with a white tail. She thought it was the cutest thing and wanted to show it off. I told her that I would stay there at the gate while she walked down to the TOC. A few minutes after that is when the bomb went off and all hell broke loose. We went all through this in the inquiry — don't you remember?"

Imogen said it all so matter-of-factly that at first Kieran questioned his own memory. That day was burned into his recollection, more vivid than the memory of what he did that morning. He was leaving the Tactical Operations Center or TOC when Reynolds approached. He had wanted to check in on the troops that were just returning from the last patrol and the two had crossed paths — she definitely was not carrying a puppy.

They had never determined where the blast had come from but that it happened at almost the same time that Reynolds entered the wooden structure that had served as their command post. He lost seven good soldiers that day, his command, and his reputation. Brass had also decided to shelve the entire battle-mage program, reasoning that if they couldn't stop a suicide bomber then they were not worth the extra resources.

"Imogen, I walked right past her. She did not have a puppy; in fact, her hands were completely empty. Are you sure what you saw?"

"Captain, I am sure as I am that my name is Imogen Turner and that I am sitting with you here now, but like I said we've discussed this all before."

"Well, either someone has done something to my memory or yours, because I don't remember any mention of a puppy. Is that what set Foster off? When you talked about the dog?"

"Maybe? I remember that I was looking down at my phone while we were talking, just before he threw the bottle against the wall, so I am not sure if it was exactly that or if it was the mention of Samantha."

"I should call him. Maybe we can get to the bottom of this and avert a disaster."

"I've tried a few times. Each time I call Camwicz answers and says Foster doesn't want to talk to me."

Kieran and Foster had been on good terms, especially since they had settled in the same city. They had been out drinking together a few times back when Kieran had been at his lowest point. Jimmy wasn't normally a volatile person — in fact he had talked Kieran out of more than a few potential skirmishes.

"Let me see what I can do." Kieran pulled his phone from his pocket, flipped through his contacts, and hit call when he came to Foster's contact card. The phone rang a total of three times before an answer.

"Captain O'Cairn, I wondered when you'd be calling." Piotr Camwicz answered in his thickly accented voice. He claimed his accent was Polish but something about it never quite sounded right, maybe influenced by his upbringing in Queens. "This is going to happen — there's no talking him out of it. I am surprised that you would even take up her side. She's responsible for so many deaths."

"What are you talking about, Piotr?"

"Think about it. The only way someone could have penetrated our defenses was if one of us voluntarily let someone in. Reynolds was the muscle on guard that day and Turner was responsible for scrying and defenses. The animal that they let in must have been the bomb. Ask her if she scanned the dog prior to letting it in."

Kieran pushed mute on his phone and turned toward Imogen. He could see tears streaming down her face. She had heard everything. There was his answer.

"Imogen…"

She jumped to her feet; fists clenched at her sides. "I am so fucking stupid! I killed them all!" Her sudden movements and anguished cry roused a few of the other people in the station, including the ticket agent who looked like he was about to phone the cops.

"Sit back down, Turner!" To the rest of the people who had been startled awake: "Everything's OK. Sorry." Kieran raised his hands in a calming, apologetic manner. Imogen slumped down on the bench the tears flowing easily, her body wracked with silent sobs. "Give me a second, Imogen."

He pressed the mute button again. "Camwicz, put Foster on."

"He's pretty solid on what needs to happen, Captain…"

"Cut the shit, Camwicz and drop the rank bullshit. You and I both know that if it weren't for the way things happened that day that you and I were headed for a confrontation. I feel your heavy hand pushing this. Let me talk with Foster so I can salvage some lives."

The next voice on the phone was Foster's. "Captain O'Cairn, she did it. She deserves this. For Reynolds, for all of them." There was barely concealed rage and perhaps a little sadness in his voice. He sounded close to tears.

"Listen, Foster… Jimmy, it's me Kieran. You talked me out of some pretty rash things when I was at my lowest. Let's talk through this. I can't let you duel Turner, regardless of what happened. Something about this doesn't feel right and I think you know it." Kieran tried to keep his voice calm and steady, trying to convince his former soldier rather than come off as too commanding.

"Tell her to be ready. Dawn is only a few hours off. Whether I win or not I'll know that I did my best to get justice."

"Jimmy, please…"

"He's done talking." Camwicz again. "He's said the words and spilled blood. She'll be compelled to show up. I will be there as his second. Foster told me she chose you as hers. I am assuming that you will be duty bound to attend — whether you do so as witness to her execution for her crimes or as her supporter will be up to you." The line went dead.

"Prick!" Kieran swore.

Kieran turned back to Imogen who sat with her face buried in her hands.

"Fuck!" Kieran swore again. He had seen too many lives ruined by that day. He was damned sure that he wasn't prepared to see any more.

Imogen, for her part, appeared to compose herself. She had seen combat and had been privy to things that would grind most men to dust.

"What have you done to prepare?" Kieran asked.

"You know the offensive stuff was never my strong suit so I have been studying defensive spells; shields and protections, mostly. I committed a limited number of restorative spells to memory as well. I was going to ask for your opinion on what else I should concentrate on." Now that her mind was on the task at hand, she was all business.

"Before we tackle that, what were the other parameters?"

"Ancient weapons are okay, swords and the like — again not my forte."

Foster was smart, removing any competitive advantage that Imogen could have used. Her natural marksmanship skills were some of the best in the company, only eclipsed by Kieran and their designated marksman, Garcia. On top of that, her defensive capabilities would have rendered his use of projectiles almost worthless. Foster was an offensive specialist, mostly fire-based so he would likely concentrate on that.

"Do you have any spells that will negate fire? If so, concentrate on those. I wouldn't waste my time on any conventional weapons, other than maybe a sturdy knife. If he closes that gap, it will probably be too late." He paused. "How'd you get here?"

"Uber."

"Call another one and get them to take you to my place. Hole up there and prepare. Take my key and keep it on your possession at all times while inside, the keychain will allow you past the wards I have placed. Here's the address." Kieran sent her his address from his phone and handed her the keys to his apartment.

Imogen looked down at the keys, they hung from a keychain shaped like a fat dragon that looked like it had had too much to drink. "Cute. Where are you going?"

"Like I said, something about this doesn't feel right. I need to do some investigating, call a few people. Camwicz has always had it out for me — ever since this program got started. He was convinced that he should be the one leading the outfit. You know he and I were the first two selected into the program. Our little rivalry started then — but between the battery of psych tests and the fact that I'm not an asshole, they chose me."

"I always thought it was because you were the more powerful mage?"

"If that were the case then Taylor would have been in charge in terms of sheer power. It really came down to aptitude, experience, and personality. That's also why Camwicz wasn't selected for lieutenant or as the senior NCO. His personality and leadership capabilities always kinda sucked. Plus, I went to college and did ROTC for a year. They plucked him off the streets."

"Oh, damn. I guess that explains his shitty attitude. I thought it was just because he was weird. You know he used to try and joke around with us and it always fell flat. Stupid illusions and really bad punchlines, like bad dad jokes but worse. I always thought it was because he was a foreigner."

Imogen rose and gathered her few belongings, "Uber's here. I'll see you in a bit?"

"Yeah. Give me a couple hours. If you don't hear from me before the appointed time, just head out to the dam. I'll meet you on the west side parking lot."

"Okay."

***

Kieran watched as Imogen hopped into the Uber and rode away, then he jumped back onto his motorcycle. Before starting it, he pulled out his phone once more and dialed a number from memory.

The phone rang for the briefest of seconds before a gruff voice answered, "I wondered when I'd hear from you again." Despite the time of night, the voice on the other end was alert and robust; either he hadn't been sleeping, or he was one of those people that naturally snapped awake.

"Top, it's good to hear your voice. I hope things are well." Kieran's normally sure tone was reedy, almost pleading, he sounded broken. It amazed him how quickly he slipped back into the military honorifics, 'Top' being a widespread term of endearment across the Army for the company's senior most noncommissioned officer.

"Look, sir — the last time you called me it was to bail you out of the drunk tank. I don't think you know how much shit you got me in."

"I'm clean now, Top. Six months sober. This time I'm not the one in trouble. Foster's challenged Turner to a duel. Camwicz is involved and is Foster's second — Turner has asked me to be hers. There is something shady going on; I can feel it and Camwicz is wrapped up in it somehow."

"I'm the police chief — you know I can't get directly involved. I spent a couple months cleaning up after your *'outburst'*"

"I'm sorry. I really am. I just need to bounce some things off you. I won't pull you into this. For Turner and Foster?" He pleaded.

"Shit. Meet me at Hyperion Lanes, the all-night bowling alley on Seventeenth and Mercury Avenue. Twenty minutes." The line went dead.

Kieran started his motorcycle and pulled out of the parking lot. Overhead a raven circled twice and then took off, following and unnoticed.

***

Hyperion Lanes was the product of a bygone era and at this hour its clientele generally looked like it had stepped out of a time machine. Three AM and the place was relatively packed as evidenced by the number of cars in the parking lot. They hosted what they called the Night Owl League and games regularly lasted late into the morning. Kieran had spent many nights there, whiling away, nursing a beer to get him through the night and to stave off the DTs. When he finally decided to get sober, he swore that places like this would be off limits — too many memories of how far he had fallen after his dismissal. Now, here he was ready to walk back through the doors — the events of the last few hours had him feeling like the old walls were threatening to close back in.

He entered from one of the side doors at the far end of the lanes so that way the entire establishment was laid out in front of him. Some habits die hard.

The first thing that hit him as he walked through the doors was the sounds of bowling; pins crashing, people yelling, either approval or disgust at their roll and the general roar of loud conversation. After that it was the smell of old cigarette smoke, fried food, and stale beer, mixed with a subtle scent of the antiseptic spray the attendants used liberally on the rental shoes. Visually the place was a cacophony of lights, bright colors and eighties patterned carpet and paint. The chairs and booths surrounding the lanes were cheap plastic, someone's idea of an inexpensive makeover sometime in the nineties that did nothing for the overall ambiance.

Kieran spotted his former First Sergeant, now Police Chief, Hector Ramirez, sitting at a booth midway between the side entrance he had just entered, and the main doors which were situated almost dead center of the building. Top had clearly already spotted him, probably from the first moment he entered.

From Kieran's perspective the man hadn't aged a day from when he last saw him. He was the epitome of a military man to this day; tall and muscular, clean shaven, hair kept closely cropped — a far cry from most of the people surrounding him. Top stood as Kieran approached and offered his hand in greeting; as he did, Kieran noticed that he carried both his service pistol and badge tucked into his belt. They both settled into the booth across from each other.

"Thanks for meeting me, especially after the heartache I caused you the last time."

"Tell me what the problem is."

Straight to the point, the proverbial bridge between them was a smoking wreck and his previous actions had nearly collapsed it. They had once moved and thought almost as one and now he sensed that Top didn't want to be in the same room with him.

Kieran told him everything he knew about the current situation with Top rarely interrupting and then only to clarify a detail. When Kieran finished, he expected an immediate visceral reaction to what Kieran felt was clearly an injustice, instead Top sat deep in thought, looking down at his hands. Kieran knew him to be a deliberate thinker but hadn't expected this level of what almost felt like disinterest in the lives of two of his former soldiers.

When he did finally speak, he uttered the last words that Kieran expected.

"I always wondered how the bomb got in. That makes a lot of sense."

"You can't be serious. You blame Turner and Reynolds?" Kieran was incredulous, his voice rising in pitch as he slapped both palms on the table.

"Slow down. I said that it was a logical explanation. I didn't say that I thought they were responsible."

Kieran settled back down and stared at the man across from him, waiting expectantly for him to elaborate.

"Think about it. What is most likely to escape attention and is instantly disarming — a fucking puppy for sure. Hell, I'm not sure if I had been the one at the gate that I would even think to search it for explosives."

"But that doesn't explain how none of the rest of us saw the thing, or how it never came up in any of the endless interviews during the fifteen-dash-six investigation."

"That's a fair point. I never heard anything about a dog until today."

"I crossed paths with Reynolds just before she walked into the TOC that day — I am one hundred percent sure that she wasn't carrying anything." Kieran rubbed his temple — there was a clue here that he was missing, something scratching at the back of his mind.

"Let's go back to what we know," Top suggested, "you know, take it step by step and look at all the factors."

***

As they spent the better part of an hour going back through the events surrounding the incident and its aftermath, two things became evident: they were no closer to understanding how such a crucial fact had been missed by all of them and that there was no escaping the inevitability that the duel would still happen. Kieran felt the slow rise of helplessness start to overtake him — it was a feeling he knew well and what had driven him to the numbing embrace of drugs and alcohol.

"I'm going to call Imogen and see how she is doing," Kieran said, pulling his phone from his pocket.

"While you are doing that, I am going to make some phone calls. I don't disagree that Camwicz is pulling some strings somewhere. I'll see if the department resources can turn up anything about his movements in the last few months." Hector stood up from the booth and moved toward a vacant area in the back side of the bowling alley, adjacent to some old Dukes of Hazard pinball machines, whose constant droning was threatening to make his grip on sanity even slipperier.

The phone rang and Imogen picked up almost instantly. "Hey, you okay? How're preparations going?"

"You're kidding, right? I'm a nervous wreck. I keep picturing the mission in Herat where Foster got a little overzealous. You remember what he did don't you?"

It was a memory that he really didn't want to dredge up. There had been some serious counseling following that one — both administrative and behavioral and he had sent at least one soldier back to the rear who couldn't get over what he saw.

"He burned those dudes from the fucking inside out. We all know they deserved it and it was us or them…" Imogen's voice caught and Kieran could hear her softly crying on the other end.

He gave her a few breaths before cutting back in, "Listen Imogen, neither of us wants this but right now I don't have a way out. I just talked with Top. He is looking into Camwicz's sudden appearance. It all feels connected and I swear there is an almost physical sensation scratching at the inside of my head — it feels like the reason for all of this is in there trying to get out."

"Yeah, I've felt that too — ever since I got to Foster's house."

"Wait, really?"

"Yeah. It flares when I think about my conversation with Foster."

"That gives me an idea. Gotta go. I'll meet you at the dam. Just concentrate on the fight ahead and I will do my damnedest to head this off."

"Uh, okay. It's not like I could run even if I wanted to."

The compulsion of the duel would force her to comply. It was strong especially when invoked with blood. It could be uttered without the blood component but there were ways to counter it. There was nothing on God's green earth that would keep her from showing except the death of either participant or an equal incantation by both participants calling off the duel.

Ramirez walked back over, tucking his phone back into his pocket as he walked up to Kieran, still seated at the booth they had shared earlier. He didn't sit. "Camwicz was picked up here in town a little more than a month ago. Looks like he has been living here under our noses for some time. The fact that he was here and none of us knew it seems very strange to me. I'll keep checking but I've got to go. There's a huge fire down in the warehouse district that looks to be arson."

"I understand. Thanks, Top. It was good seeing you." Kieran rose and offered his hand.

Police Chief Hector Ramirez looked down at the proffered hand and hesitated for a moment before gripping it tightly. "Short string, sir. No huge catastrophes, please." He looked into Kieran's eyes. "It's good to see you sober." He released Kieran's hand and walked away.

***

Kieran, back astride his Harley, drove towards the edge of town, passing light after light, almost absentmindedly as he made his way out of town and to the allotted place. He wanted to scout things out. His role as second during the duel was simple; make sure both sides adhered to the rules and to act in accordance if they didn't. As part of his responsibilities, he was also expected to walk the ground to make sure that nothing would interfere with the proper execution of the duel. He assumed Camwicz was also performing this same task and this might give him an opportunity to confront the man.

The dam was just a couple miles outside the city and reached by a rural road that all but guaranteed that there wouldn't be spectators. Kieran steered his motorcycle up the winding road that led to the top of the dam, flanked on either side by piney woods that dominated the area. If he remembered correctly there was a small parking lot at the top. The dam was closed to vehicular traffic but pedestrians could easily travel from one side to the other.

When he reached the summit, he pulled into the small parking lot and he noticed one other vehicle haphazardly parked in the corner of the lot, a black Honda with all sorts of anime and movie stickers plastered all over the back of the car.

"One guess who that belongs to," he muttered to himself as he parked and dismounted.

He took the time to get his bearings, getting a feel for the area, the night, and its aura. The moon was waning and would benefit neither combatant but there was a subtly fluctuating power to the site, probably due to the water flowing through the dam's spillway gates. He also casually noted likely chokepoints, egress routes and areas that could serve as potential ambush sites.

He walked slowly out onto the dam's walkway, the way marked by softly glowing lights set at ten-yard intervals, to his right was the reservoir created by the dam, to his left what was left of the once mighty river, slowed to a trickle to flow through the city in the valley down below. The dull roar of the water flowing through the spillways created an almost pleasant white noise. In the distance he noted a shape beneath the light that marked the halfway point. The shape, clearly human, sported a dark coat and hat and seemed to be casually leaning against the low wall of the dam walkway.

Kieran stuck his fingers to his lips and issued forth a screeching whistle, causing the man ahead to jump a bit. He tried to hide it by acting as if he was getting ready to leave but Kieran's actions had their intended affect. Camwicz — he was sure it was him — was off balance, not expecting the sudden noise. Kieran quickened his pace, eager to confront Camwicz.

He pulled up short of the man, keeping about ten feet between them. Something told him to be on guard.

Camwicz spoke first. "Sir, I figured you'd be here earlier. I've waited a bit for you to show up. I was getting bored."

Kieran had almost forgotten how insufferable the man could be, his nasally voice grated and his piss poor attitude had made him a horrible soldier — although neither fault could hold a candle to his lack of hubris. He looked the man up and down; he wore a black duster and a hat, some sort of fedora, underneath the duster Kieran assumed he wore all black — he looked like a teenager's version of the quintessential urban wizard. He even sported a wispy mustache and goatee.

"Looks like you robbed the local Halloween shop. Who're you supposed to be, the Temu version of Harry Dresden?" Kieran hoped to keep him off kilter, looking to press any advantage he could get in whatever verbal exchange was about to happen. "You can cut the 'sir' bullshit, both of us know that you have no respect for me or the rank."

"True, true." Camwicz squared his shoulders toward Kieran, no longer acting like a bored teenager but instead doing his best to at least appear threatening.

"What's your role in all this Piotr? You never do anything without something to gain. I remember the day of the bombing, everyone was devastated, but not you. You walked around like you didn't give a damn. I chalked it up to that fact that everyone grieves differently but you showed your true colors as soon as the inquiries started."

"Spare me, O'Cairn." He interrupted; his fists clenched at his sides. "You were never fit to lead and your leadership cost lives. Yeah, I'd like to see you go down but this is about Turner and the role she played in the deaths of my friends. She watched Reynolds carry that bomb straight into the TOC and did nothing. I can't prove it but I wouldn't doubt it if she was working with the insurgents."

"Are you fucking insane? What could possibly make you think that?" Kieran was in danger of letting his emotions get the better of him. He had wanted to get Camwicz off balance but he could feel things shifting. He needed to get control again. He closed his eyes and took a deep breath.

"I am sure that the reason I didn't see you earlier is that you were going back through the inquiry and talking with Turner. She knows she fucked up, doesn't she? You know the guys from Charlie Company had her pegged from the start," Camwicz stated.

"What?" The last comment threw Kieran for a loop. "Charlie Company? What the fuck do they have to do with this? They weren't even working in the same region."

"Fucking uninformed as usual. Did you ever think to look at the big picture? You are fucking hopeless, you know?" Camwicz looked as if he was about to say more and then thought better of it. "Screw this O'Cairn. See you in a few hours. She's gonna pay for what she did and once everyone else finds out the truth…" Camwicz pushed past Kieran and walked towards the parking lot and his vehicle.

The itch in the back of his brain was now like a tiger sharpening its claws on a tree trunk — he needed answers. His battalion was so hush-hush that it didn't even have a numerical designation and was simply referred to as *Battalion X*. Kieran commanded Alpha Company, a motley assortment of soldiers with magical abilities ranging from almost useless to relatively powerful. Bravo Company was the epitome of the term 'freaks' — most of them could hardly pass as human and those that could were pretty fucking scary in their own right. Their company commander was a werewolf and their first sergeant, a vampire. They were working covertly across the middle east, mostly Syria, and Iran. Charlie Company was the big brains — people with mental powers like telekinesis, telepathy, and precognition. They weren't field operatives and as far as he had been briefed and were working in Europe while Kieran and his company were in Afghanistan. Rumor said there was a Delta Company, but if it existed it was kept from the rest of them. Their battalion was headquartered in the Pentagon, behind some serious security measures and buried deep.

Camwicz opened the topic so Kieran decided to follow the lead. He pulled out his phone and dialed the only number he still had that could reach anyone of consequence. The phone rang just once.

"Password."

"Mary Shelley Two Four Seven Eight Kilo Oscar." He answered.

"Hold."

Kieran waited, unsure of what reception he would get or who would answer.

"What is it, O'Cairn?"

Kieran was shocked — he really expected to be told to forget the number or to have the phone blow up in his face, instead he got the battalion executive officer, Major Timothy Slattery.

"Sir... uh... hello. How are you?"

"I know you didn't call this number — the one you were given and told only to use in the most extreme of circumstances, just to say hello. What's the issue?"

At one point in his all too short career, he had considered Major Slattery to be a mentor of sorts. The man didn't have any special powers that Kieran knew of, but he commanded the respect of everyone in the battalion, especially with his no-nonsense approach to operations and running a battalion full of misfits.

"Major Slattery... sir..."

"It's Lieutenant Colonel Slattery now. I took command of the battalion last month. Again, it's nice to trade pleasantries but I don't have the time. Unless you have something important to say I am going to hang up — especially since it's in the middle of the fucking night. Oh, and by the way that was a one-time use password so make it good."

Kieran started from the beginning and told Slattery everything he knew all the way up to the conversation with Camwicz — that he saved for the end. "I just met with Camwicz, at the site of the duel. He mentioned Charlie Company and them not trusting Turner. Have any idea what he means? I wouldn't have turned to you but I feel like there is something that I should remember that just won't come to me." There was a moment of dead silence.

"The conversation we need to have shouldn't be over an open line. Wait one." The line muted and then after thirty seconds went dead.

"Fuck!" Kieran swore. He wanted to lash out at something, it was only a voice from the shadows behind him that stalled his anger. He turned, startled, his fight or flight response triggered.

"O'Cairn! Just because I said I didn't want to talk about it over the phone didn't mean we weren't going to have this conversation."

Lieutenant Colonel Slattery stood before him, hands outstretched to try and calm the situation. He had aged significantly in the last year; there were obvious signs of stress written all over the man. He had once had a full head of brown hair, cut to regulation of course, but now his hairline had receded well beyond simple male pattern baldness; the lines on his face were deep and it was clear that the man had not kept up with the vigorous health regimen that he had been known for.

"Colonel…"

"I had one of the Alpha Company magicians open a portal for me. You didn't think we scrapped the entire program after the incident, did you?" He paused, before continuing. "Look, everything I am about to tell you is off the record. I will deny it to my dying day, which shouldn't be too long in coming." Slattery registered the bewildered look on Kieran's face. "Cancer — or so they tell me."

"I'm sor —"

"Save it," Slattery snapped. "I've made peace with it."

"Uh, Roger."

"Look there is a lot more to the story then even Camwicz knows. He's just scratching the surface, probably trying to figure out what you really know. I'm not sure where he got his info, but that's a leak that will soon be plugged. There was a Charlie Company operative on your team, I'll not say who, so don't even bother asking. After the incident, they helped clean up the mess."

"What do you mean?"

"That scratching at the back of your brain… that's the memories of what really happened trying to reassert themselves. After everything was said and done, we erased some things, all in the name of national security."

"You've got to be fucking kidding me!" Kieran felt his anger rising again.

"The part about the explosion at the TOC, that pretty much happened as you remember it. It's what happened after that we had to wipe."

"After…"

"Your company went fucking crazy! Hell bent on revenge and there weren't enough assets in the country that could stop you short of dropping a nuke on you. You wiped out an entire village; insurgents, men, women, children — there were no survivors. It was a fucking slaughter — at least a hundred killed. There was no way we could let what happened get out. Not just about the deaths but also the fact that we had an entire company of superpowered magicians working for the US government."

Kieran's legs gave out and he nearly went down hard on the walkway; his emotions threatening to overcome him. He pressed his hands to his eyes and let out a mournful wail. Slattery crouched down in front of him.

"O'Cairn, get a hold of yourself. Here's the important part: you and Ramirez, you tried to stop them but they got the drop on you — incapacitated you before they rolled out into the village. You did your best to stop them but in the end it wasn't enough. You were distraught after. It was a kindness to take those memories away from you."

Kieran scrambled back to his feet and backed away from Slattery. "I don't think it fucking worked! I've been a wreck for the last year and right now I don't think any of what you told me makes it any better. If anything, it still incriminates Turner!"

Slattery shrugged; at least he had the decency to try and look as if he cared but Kieran wasn't buying it. The whole thing was a shock to the system and he had a hard time coming to grips with what he had just been told. He wanted to ask questions but none would formulate in his mind.

"If it's any consolation; you and Ramirez — I'd take either or both of you back in the company in a heartbeat. Not my call though." He turned and started to walk toward the shadows that he emerged from earlier. A portal opened in front of him, Kieran could see cold office furnishings behind him — the Pentagon.

"Wait. One question." Kieran yelled after him, Slattery turned. "How'd you cover up the disappearance of an entire village? You couldn't have brainwashed everyone."

"There was a chemical weapons plant. That was the cover. It was destroyed and the entire area was deemed inaccessible due to the lingering threat. All the civilians that 'survived' were evacuated stateside for treatment." He walked through the portal and was gone, leaving Kieran alone.

He paced. There was still an hour before the duel was supposed to happen. His mind was still a jumble of emotions and thoughts. He pulled out his phone searched for the incident. He found a couple articles that quoted an Army spokesman as saying that while it was an unbelievable tragedy and cost the lives of over a hundred innocents some good would come out the horrible accident. The spokesman went on to state that there was a catastrophic incident at a suspected insurgent chemical munitions factory that had been hidden in a girl's school.

Another memory unlocked.

They had staked out that girl's school for weeks based on intel they had received. Kieran had pushed for a female engagement team to check it out but was repeatedly denied. He could never understand why the request was rejected, especially since it seemed that the intel was good. This was getting more complicated by the minute — nothing made sense and everything he learned seemed to contradict something else. He wished there was a way to fully unlock his memories, it felt like there was still something there, something still hidden.

He looked up from his phone and spotted headlights coming up the road and toward the parking lot. Not much time now. It looked like he was powerless to stop what was coming, despite all the new revelations.

The car turned out to be Foster's. Kieran watched as the man got out of his car and made his way to the center of the dam. Foster was tall, well-built, and still looked every bit the soldier. He was dressed in old fatigue pants and a Nirvana t-shirt and wore a Yankees cap turned backwards. He looked like he was getting ready to hit the skatepark, only where you would normally see a skateboard tucked under his arm, he instead carried a small machete. Kieran thought he looked tired and suspected the long hours of preparation might have tempered his anger a bit. He thought about verbally tearing into the man but decided that he'd give diplomacy another try.

"Foster. How are you?"

"Pissed. Tired. Sad. Honestly, I am all fucked up inside. I don't really know how we got here but I do know that I can make things right. So, I'd ask you to save whatever it is you want to say. I've gone over this in my mind for the last six hours and nothing's gonna change it."

Kieran could feel the desperation in the other man's voice, there was an opening there but he'd have to tread carefully. "Not fifteen minutes ago I talked with the head-shed; remember Major Slattery? He stood where you are now and we talked about what happened that day."

"Fuck! You don't give up do you?" Camwicz materialized just over Foster's shoulder. "I told you he would make up some shit to try and get you to change your mind."

Kieran cursed under his breath. He didn't think to even check magically to see if there was anyone else on the dam. For some reason, despite Camwicz's involvement he didn't think that either man would stoop to subterfuge or cheating. He did so now, fully aware that both would be aware of what he was doing, but he didn't care — the three of them were the only ones there, except for some wildlife. As he finished checking another car pulled into the parking lot. Imogen had arrived.

Imogen approached cautiously, because the parking lot was on one side she would have to walk past the other two men to reach Kieran. He had to hand it to Camwicz — their positioning guaranteed another subtle jab at Imogen's psyche before they even started the duel. To Imogen's credit she didn't even flinch as she walked past the two men.

"You didn't get the party started without me, did you?" Her voice was like steel. Kieran's respect for the woman, already high, grew immensely. She was dressed in yoga pants and a sports bra under a loose-fitting workout shirt and actually looked like she just came from the gym, excepting the long knife she wore at her waist. Sensing the question on Kieran's mind she quietly uttered, "Helps me get my mind right. Just a quick workout, some light stretching." She turned to face Foster and Camwicz. "Gentlemen. Let's get this over with."

"When the sun breaks the horizon, we'll begin. I suggest you make peace with whoever. Of course, chances are you'll be seeing them in person soon enough." Camwicz sneered. He grabbed Foster by the arm and moved back about ten feet, ostensibly to talk strategy.

Imogen grabbed Kieran by the arm and pulled him back toward one of the lights on the dam, "C'mon, boss."

"You seem awfully serene considering what's about to happen." Kieran offered.

"What if they're right? What if I am to blame? Maybe this is my penance." The steel that was in her voice earlier lost some of its iron.

"Listen, I talked with Major Slattery about twenty minutes ago. He said that they had one of the guys from Charlie Company wipe some of our memories. That's why we all feel like there is something more that we should remember."

"What? Wait, does Foster know? Maybe they didn't just wipe stuff — maybe they inserted memories."

"I tried to tell him but Camwicz has him all twisted up. He's not listening. I think there is a lot more to this then we know and this feels like a big mistake."

"What else did Slattery say?" Imogen asked, pulling the thread.

"He said that what they erased was all after the explosion, that the company did some things in retaliation for the bombing."

"That doesn't make any sense. Who'd we retaliate against? We had no idea where the insurgents were hiding."

"The girl's school. Remember the one that we tried to get a female engagement team into?"

"What do you mean? We not only sent in a team but we cleared that place magically. I was there, in person. There were no insurgents and no chemical weapons facility or at least that's what I remember."

Kieran felt a dam burst in his head as memories came rushing back. She was right. He was there on the ground when it happened and had personally reassured the local mullah that only women would enter the school to search. "Slattery said that's the story they concocted to cover the company's outburst."

"Well, that's entirely believable. I never trusted those guys at battalion, though."

"But why make this all so complicated?" Kieran muttered.

His line of thought was interrupted as Camwicz suddenly yelled, "Almost time!" across the expanse of the dam.

He was right the glow of the sun had already started to light up the morning; soon the sun would break over the horizon. Once started Kieran wasn't sure that the duel could end without a death.

The magic of the duel was a very specific blood rite used by sorcerers since the dawn of magic. The invoker had only to draw blood and speak the date, time, location, and name of the person they wished to duel — the only caveats were that the other person had to be within earshot or eyesight of the invocation. This guaranteed that someone couldn't compel someone else from a continent away. The challenged individual would be compelled to duel whether they wanted to or not. It was crude but effective. Because it almost always ended in death it was rarely used. The addition of a second all but guaranteed that allies wouldn't interfere. The only way out for the challenged was to duel or to convince the invoker to change their minds. All users of magic were aware of the rite but its use was all but unheard of in modern times.

Foster stepped forward, looking determined, his arms down by his sides. "I invoke the rite of the duel against you Imogen Turner. The time of reckoning is nigh. Will you abide by the terms?"

Turner stepped forward. "I accept."

"Then when the light breaks the horizon, we will begin. My second stands ready to ensure the rules are followed."

"As does mine."

Both assumed fighting stances but Kieran didn't think it would come to physical blows. Foster was skilled and had seen combat against both magical and conventional foes. Imogen's specialty was more geared towards protection and divination. There was a slight chance that her protection spells could see her last long enough for Foster to exhaust himself; magical stamina was hard to gauge. Unless Kieran could somehow convince them to stop, someone was likely to die. He noticed that Camwicz retreated about twenty feet from Foster so he did the same.

Kieran's mind raced. Slattery's story about the chemical weapons at the girl's school didn't jive with his newly restored memory of the incident, but to what end? Hell, there was even a chance that what he and Imogen now remembered was an implanted memory as well. There had to be some way to make heads or tails of everything rattling around in his head.

The sun broke over the horizon and Foster wasted no time. He brought his hands together and then swept them outward, a wave of red fire erupted from his arms and shot toward Imogen. Imogen must have anticipated this first move; she locked her wrists together and watched as the fire parted about five feet before her. Surprisingly, she did not wait for another attack but instantly sent a blast of her own back at Foster who was still concentrating on the fire he had unleashed. The attack caught him off guard and he brought up his own defenses a second too slowly, he succeeded in parrying most of the attack but the sheer force of the energies she unleashed buffeted him and caused him to take a step back. Seeing this, Imogen took a couple steps forward, pressing her momentary advantage.

Kieran looked over at Camwicz, the man seemed to be enjoying the spectacle, a smile on his face and small cheers every time the two combatants exchanged spells. He longed to wipe the grin off the man's face. With their memories damaged, there was a part of Kieran that believed Camwicz actually held to the fact that Imogen was guilty and responsible for the deaths of their fellow soldiers. He needed to find a way to convince them that this was wrong.

Five minutes in and Turner and Foster continued to trade blows. Small explosions, magical fire and buffeting winds flew back and forth — the two combatants were digging deep into their repertoire of skills. The area between and surrounding the two magicians was scarred by their attacks. Kieran noticed that Imogen's attacks were coming at a slower pace and that she was sinking more of her power into countering Foster's attacks. He surmised that this was likely to come to a conclusion soon.

Kieran felt a buzzing from his pocket: his phone — *who could be calling now?* He contemplated ignoring it but then pulled it forth to see who was on the line — First Sergeant Ramirez.

"Hello?"

"Get them to stop!" Top Ramirez yelled. "Imogen's not responsible for the attack!"

"I've tried! If I interfere now Camwicz will too."

"You need to figure out a way to isolate him. You were right. Slattery just called me. Told me some stuff you need to know."

"I talked to him. He came here. I don't think it changed anything. We were still responsible for the carnage that followed the bombing, plus I still can't figure out how Imogen is not implicated."

"I'm two minutes out. Damn it, sir! Do whatever you have to do but get them to stop until I get there and can explain everything!" The line went dead. Kieran thought he could hear a siren in the distance.

Kieran looked back to the two combatants, it was clear they were both tiring and some attacks were reaching their targets. Imogen's hair was singed on the right side of her head and her face was bright red where Foster's fire had gotten through her defenses. Foster was limping, his right foot was missing most of the boot that he had been wearing and the foot underneath looked raw and bloody. There were only a few feet separating the two and it was likely that both would resort to the knives they brought as they ran out of spells to throw at each other.

Kieran went for broke, "At ease!" he yelled at the top of his lungs.

Foster and Turner paused for a moment, their military training temporarily overriding their concentration on each other.

"What are you doing? Don't stop! Stay out of this O'Cairn!" Camwicz yelled.

Kieran could sense the other man preparing a spell. He reacted instantly with the only spell he knew that could bring this to a halt.

It was an ancient and obscure spell that not many knew. He had learned it from his grandfather and then told to never use it except in the direst of circumstances. It was an extremely powerful spell but its side effects were exceedingly harsh on the caster. Kieran didn't think twice. He pulled in all the energy he could muster and directed the energies at the three people in front of him.

A burst of power erupted from his core; he could see the shockwaves as they moved away from him. Within an instant everything around him stilled as if frozen in time, for that is what they were, even the powers that they directed at each other were stuck in stasis. Kieran immediately felt the effects; for every second he held time at bay he would age a day. The concentration required to keep the spell going was tremendous. He hoped that Ramirez hadn't exaggerated his ETA.

The wail of the siren continued to get louder and eventually he saw the police chief pull into the dam parking lot. The man jumped out, not bothering to close the car door or turn off the engine as he ran over to Kieran.

"What did you do to them?" he said as he got closer.

"Time stasis spell. Can't hold it long. Make sure you don't touch any of them, it'll disrupt the spell." Kieran sank to his knees. It had been at least a minute of real time and he could feel his body aging. "Please tell me you have something that can stop all of this."

"Slattery called me — told me he talked to you and told me everything he said to you. I'm not sure why he bothered. I never trusted him. I think he knows that we talked and wanted to make sure the story was consistent. I asked him about what memories they inserted and he started on about the girl's school."

"Yeah, we figured that part out too, complete lie. Doesn't change the narrative on Turner and Reynolds."

"But it does. Sir, think about it. What was our mission? Why were we there? Do you think they are going to send a company of skilled warrior magicians into a village just to keep the peace? There are plenty of normal units that could do that mission."

"If you had asked me earlier today, I would tell you that we were there to find the chemical weapons facility that the insurgents were building but Slattery said that was just a cover for what happened after the bombing."

"That's what I thought too but think back hard, but in your memory when did we get that info? I'll save you the trouble. It was after we were already in country, already in the village — so why were we sent to that damned place from the start? We were there to root out the enemy's magicians, their supernaturals, not for some freaking chemical munitions plant. That whole story is a cover of a cover."

"Okay, but for what?"

"I think we were infiltrated — but not by our own, but by the enemy. And the worst part is that I think it is still going on. I am pretty sure that we found what we were sent to find. After that I think everything else is a lie. I'm not even sure that our fellow soldiers are dead, Reynolds, all of them. Wanna know what tipped me off? It was the description of the dog. Slattery said it was a dirty white dog, not a brown dog like Turner remembers — hell, you didn't even see a dog at all. We need to ask Turner what she remembers. Is there a way to free her and only her?"

"Help me up." Kieran reached out a hand for help and Ramirez pulled him to his feet. "This is going to be tricky. She'll be released as soon as I touch her but that also means the spell she unleashed will unfreeze as well. It's gonna obliterate Foster unless we break him out as well and that means that the duel starts right back up."

"What if I shield Foster prior to you waking her up?"

"That might work as long as you don't touch him directly."

"What do we have to lose?"

"We need to hurry because I can't keep this up for much longer. I've already lost at least a year of my life. If I keep this up for too long, you'll have to sign me up for AARP afterwards." Kieran chuckled as he said the last part, though he didn't really feel the humor he was trying to espouse.

Ramirez moved over to Foster and Turner and looked at the energies of the two spells that were caught in the time stasis. "Interesting, hers isn't even an offensive spell despite looking like one, instead it looks like a healing spell. She is feeding him energy. She must truly believe that she is to blame. His spell, on the other hand, is a concussive blast aimed straight for her heart. Looks like they were both intending to end this in a hurry. We can let her spell hit him after all."

"Nope. Her active spell will dispel the time stasis — need you to block it."

"Okay, seems a waste though." Ramirez waved his hands, and recited some words in his native tongue, and two visible shields popped up between Imogen and Foster. "This should actually block both spells but it's a one-time deal once they're each blocked it won't stop another attack."

Kieran reached out and put his hand on Imogen's shoulder. She stumbled throwing her arms up in front of her; it was clear to both men that she was braced to absorb whatever Foster had thrown at her.

She looked at Ramirez and then at Foster, confusion evident on her face, "Top?"

"Steady, Turner. The good Captain has both Foster and Camwicz in a time stasis spell but he can't hold it for long. I've been doing some additional digging. We think the puppy is an implanted memory but to know for sure I need to know what color you remember the dog to be." Ramirez held her arm to keep her steady.

"It was brown, long-haired and mangy, all except the tip of its tail which was white."

"You're sure?"

"Yes"

"Absolutely sure?"

"Yes, First Sergeant!"

"Stand over there, next to the edge. I am going to free Foster and I'm not sure how this is going to go. We need to make sure that the two of you can compare stories so that he can see that this is the product of someone fucking with our minds." He pointed to the edge of the walkway near O'Cairn.

Imogen moved cautiously to O'Cairn's side. Ramirez turned back to Foster, "Ready?"

O'Cairn, nodded in affirmation, "Let's do this."

Ramirez walked around the back of Foster and placed his hand on the man's shoulder. Like Turner, Foster's reaction was immediate confusion, first at not seeing his opponent in front of him and second at finding his former first sergeant at his side. He lurched back and instinctively launched into a defensive spell, ready for an attack.

"Easy, Foster. I'm not your enemy." He threw his hands up to placate the younger man. "I am here to put a stop to this though."

"What did you do to Camwicz?" He said looking in the direction of his second.

"He's unharmed, just frozen in time. I'll release him in a minute but we need to talk." Kieran said weakly. "We've discovered some things and I need you to hear it without his interference. I don't think Camwicz is allowing you to hear the full story — I'm just not sure why he is so fixated on this."

"This is important — when Reynolds called you from the guard shack and said that she had a puppy to show you — how did she describe it?" Ramirez asked.

"She said it looked like a white dog but that it was so dirty that she wasn't sure." Foster responded looking from Ramirez to O'Cairn.

"Short-haired or long?" O'Cairn asked.

"She said it was some sort of Chihuahua so I would guess short?"

"I crossed paths with her just before the bombing — I didn't see a dog at all." Kieran interjected.

"When she entered the TOC, I was near the back, sitting behind my terminal. Someone, I think it was Lieutenant Jones, yelled for her to get that 'mangy animal' out of the TOC. I stood up and caught a glimpse of her just as the bomb went off. I was thrown out of the building and was lucky to survive."

"Did you see the puppy?" Kieran pressed.

"I... I don't remember. I can remember everything else so clearly up to that point but it's like there is a blank spot where the dog was when I replay it in my mind. Trauma I guess."

"I don't think so. Slattery told me that they had a Charlie Company plant in our company, to help control things and whoever that was both inserted and erased some of our memories."

"That seems a little far-fetched don't you think? Why would they do that?" Foster asked looking at Top for confirmation.

"There's more. What do you remember about what happened after?" Ramirez asked.

"We came home and were debriefed."

"No memories of avenging our losses, destroying a village?" Kieran continued to press the man, seeing the confusion on his face as he grappled to square his memories with the questions from the two men.

"What the fuck are you talking about?" Foster was getting angry.

"How about a chemical munitions factory hidden in a girl's school?" Kieran knew he shouldn't push too hard but he felt like he was nearing a break through.

"Enough! I'm not sure what is happening here, but I need you to release Camwicz. He'll help me get this straightened out." The man started to make his way towards his second who was still frozen some ten feet to his rear.

Ramirez moved to block his way, putting a hand squarely on his chest and holding him at arm's length. "Hold up, soldier. Ask yourself the most important question. Why would we lie to you? What possible motivation could Captain

O'Cairn and I have for all of this?" he paused, waiting for a reaction. Foster's face fell as he struggled with the question. "The bottom line is that there are discrepancies in all of our memories and none of them jive with the others. Don't you think that's enough to drop this until we can get everything sorted?" Ramirez demanded, his hand dropping to his side.

"Jimmy, you know I loved Reynolds — we were best friends. She was like my sister... I don't know what happened, nothing in my head feels real anymore. Please can we just talk this through?" Imogen pleaded, tears streaming down her face. She took a tentative step toward the young man.

Foster looked back and forth at all of them while slowly backing away from Ramirez, his hands curled into fists down by his sides. Kieran tensed as he watched the man slowly move his hand to his waistband and a small knife he had attached to his belt. If Turner or Ramirez had noticed he wasn't sure; they both seemed intent on Foster's face.

Kieran couldn't stop him with a spell, the one that still held Camwicz was requiring all of his attention, so he pulled forth his pistol and trained it on Foster. "Easy, kid. No reason for any more bloodshed today."

Foster raised his other hand, holding it out to his side as he drew forth the knife, he deftly reached across and drew it across the outstretched arm. "Imogen Turner, I release you. Our duel is finished."

Kieran relaxed and lowered the gun. Turner, to her credit also pulled forth a knife and repeated the gesture. For now, the duel was over.

"Now what?" Imogen asked.

Ramirez looked back towards Camwicz. "Now we release him," he said nodding towards the man.

Turner helped O'Cairn to his feet and the four of them made their way to Camwicz.

"It looks like Camwicz had his own spell stopped by your time stasis," Ramirez remarked.

"Yeah, I sensed him about to cast — guess I was faster off the draw. Can you tell what he was casting?" Kieran asked.

"Whatever it is it was aimed at all three of you, sir. Looks like it was something to incapacitate the three of you," Ramirez answered.

"Can you dispel it?"

"Already done."

"How does the time stasis spell work?" Foster asked.

"He will be released either when I drop the spell or someone touches him." Kieran responded.

"Then maybe I should be the one to release him. Why don't the rest of you back off so that he doesn't think that we are about to attack him." Foster responded.

"Be careful, he might not react the way you think he will, especially since his spell was aimed at all three of you." Ramirez warned.

"Roger, Top. I'll be careful." Foster said as he strode forward arm raised to tap Camwicz in the shoulder.

Camwicz's reaction to being touched and released from the spell was visceral, his face flashing quickly from fear, to surprise and then to immediate anger. "What the hell is going on?!"

"Easy Sarge, the duel's over. I ended it."

Camwicz looked over Foster's shoulder and saw Turner still standing. "You released her!" Spittle flew from his lips as he raged over Foster's decision. "What have you done, you moron? She was supposed to die!"

Foster took a step back. Kieran kept his pistol at the ready, Ramirez stepped in front of them both, shielding them slightly should things go sideways, and Turner, despite what she had just been through, took a ready stance, her hands gripping her knife.

"There're just too many holes in our memories for me to be sure that she was responsible. I couldn't go through with it. I think its best that we talk this through so we can figure out what was real. I'm not sure about anything anymore." Foster pleaded with Camwicz.

It appeared that Foster was doing his best to convince the man but Kieran doubted that any of it was getting through to Camwicz. The two men continued to argue back and forth and as they argued, Kieran took in the entirety of the situation. Regardless of whether this ended with Camwicz agreeing with them, they were all fucked. Kieran could no longer be sure of anything in his memory. He looked around and assessed their options — Camwicz and Foster were between them and their vehicles; the other direction across the dam meant that they would have to hike out of the area — not something Kieran deemed possible considering the amount of energy they had all expended. He was bone tired and ready to be done with this — they could figure out the rest later.

The sun was all the way above the horizon and its warmth was spreading across the valley, the area was waking up and birds were singing in the distance, the irony of a new dawn considering what could have transpired brought a smile to his face. They were all still alive.

Camwicz must have noticed Kieran's smile because he pushed Foster to the side and leveled an accusing hand in his direction. "You fucker! People are dead, our friends, and you're sitting there smiling? You're a disgrace!"

"If you'd stop and listen for a moment to what we're trying to tell you, you'd probably realize that even your memory is suspect. I agree with you that someone needs to pay for what happened but I can't honestly say who that is or what they'd be paying for outside of messing with our minds." Kieran replied.

Camwicz noticed the pistol in Kieran's hand, and started to back away. "Foster, would you look at that, he intends on shooting us the moment our guard is down. None of them can be trusted!"

Foster reached out again, looking to put a steadying hand on the other man's shoulder but Camwicz squirmed his way under the man's reach and moved to the side while simultaneously kicking out to knock the man violently to the ground. Kieran watched as Foster's head impacted the pavement.

Three things then happened at once: Ramirez brought up a defensive shield and tried to cover himself, O'Cairn and Turner; Turner threw her knife, aiming center of mass at where Camwicz had been standing and Kieran braced for whatever was next — still too exhausted to bring any spells to bear; Camwicz continued moving away from where Foster was sent sprawling and lashed out with a blast of pure force directed at Ramirez and his shield. The shield held but both Ramirez and Turner were buffeted by the force and went down in a tangle of limbs. Ramirez had done just enough to steer the blast away from O'Cairn, leaving him unscathed. Kieran brought the Glock up and rattled off a few shots, the last of which hit its mark and spun Camwicz around. He went down to the ground, facing away, clutching his side presumably where at least one bullet had struck.

Kieran kept the gun trained on Camwicz while he moved to check on Ramirez and Turner. She was out cold but breathing; Ramirez was holding his head and his right arm was hanging at an awkward angle.

Ramirez waved Kieran away with his good arm and signaled him to keep an eye on Camwicz.

Kieran approached the man cautiously; he was down on his knees, his shoulders heaving as he struggled to breathe. O'Cairn couldn't see any blood from his vantage but he was sure that the wound was significant.

"Damn you, Camwicz! Why couldn't you listen to reason. Are you so hell bent on someone dying today?" Kieran asked as he moved closer to the man. "Despite our differences I never had any intention of hurting you."

Camwicz coughed harshly and pushed himself to his feet. "That was always the difference between us. I always wanted you dead. If it weren't for the information in your head I would have killed you long ago."

"Turn around. Let me see your hands."

Camwicz turned around slowly, his hands held up. Kieran's breath caught in his throat as the man that faced him was no longer Piotr Camwicz but Lieutenant Colonel Slattery.

"Sir? I…" Kieran started.

The confusion must have registered on Kieran's face because Slattery took that moment to cast a spell intending to blind the man with an intense flash of light, seeking to make his escape. Kieran instinctively brought his arm up to safeguard his eyes and fired a series of shots where Slattery had been just a moment before. There was an audible 'thunk' as a body hit the ground.

It took just a second as his eyes adjusted for him to take in the scene. Slattery was down face first, a pool of blood slowly spreading around his still form. Behind him both Turner and Ramirez were back on their feet. Off to his left, Foster was also slowly working his way to his feet.

"Was that Slattery?" Imogen asked. Her question hung in the air as all of them wrestled with the implication.

Foster moved over to the body and flipped it over. Slattery's face was replaced with a visage that none of them recognized, but that carried a decidedly middle eastern set of features, the man was still breathing, albeit shallowly.

"What the fuck?" Ramirez exclaimed. "It's a fucking doppelganger!"

"A doppelganger? I thought they were just a myth?" Imogen asked.

"Yeah, like vampires, right?" Kieran responded sarcastically.

"Uh, yeah I guess," she said, sheepishly.

"This is probably going to be a problem for you as Police Chief, eh, Top? What should we do. I don't want to jeopardize your life any more than we have already." Kieran asked turning to Ramirez. *So much for 'no huge catastrophes'.*

"Don't worry. We'll take care of it." A voice came from their rear, another Slattery, and a few other men, all dressed in tactical gear, stepped out of a portal. The men secured the perimeter, two branching off to tend to the doppelganger, while Slattery, still looking haggard and worn as he had appeared to Kieran earlier, walked over to the four of them. "Good to see you all still standing. We had a feeling that one of you would turn out to be the doppelganger but we couldn't be sure which of you it would be. I should have guessed it would turn out to be Camwicz."

"Wait, you knew that one of us was the doppelganger? Why not just bring us all in?" Foster asked.

"That's just it. We did. All of you were put through a series of tests the minute we pulled you from theater. Bastard passed them all — must have something to do with how they absorb the memories of those they mimic — makes them all but impervious to mental attacks. That's why Captain O'Cairn came up with this plan."

"Wait, this was my idea?" Kieran asked. "I'm not one for overly complicated plans and this ranks up there as the mother-of-all fucked up plans."

"I'd say that pretty much guarantees it was yours," Slattery said chuckling. "Remember I said that there was a plant from Charlie in your company? You knew who he was. He suggested that one of the best ways to figure out the imposter was to make the scenario and memories as conflicted and implausible as possible. As the doppelganger interacted with you and attempted to read your memories, he wouldn't be able to lock in on what was real. It's my guess that he pushed this whole duel idea as a way to ferret out which of your conflicted memories were real — and to get to the information he was really after."

"Shit, my head hurts. What in my memory is real and what isn't? Is the last year all a lie?" Imogen asked.

"When we get back to headquarters, we'll have all that fixed. Our guy will restore everything and we can walk you through what was real, also give you a chance to reunite with the others, Reynolds, Jones, and the rest."

Kieran ran his hands through his hair, fixing his ponytail and massaging his temples a bit. There was a pain behind his eyes that he was sure was going to cause his head to explode. People he thought were dead, had mourned even, were still alive. He had turned his life upside down thinking he was a failure. "What if I don't want to go back?"

"I'm afraid that's not really a choice you get to make. You all still belong to Uncle Sam; besides, we need what's buried deep in your head — what the doppelganger was really after." Slattery explained nodding at Kieran.

"Which is…" Ramirez asked.

"It was only partially true that you went downrange to counter any potential enemy supernaturals. You were really there to find and retrieve an object of significant power before the enemy could find it. You succeeded in finding it but, because we suspected you had been infiltrated, Captain O'Cairn secured the object somewhere and had your memories locked down. No one knows where the item is except you, Kieran, and you had it buried deep. The plan is to get your memories restored and then get you all back into the fight so you can secure the object."

"What about our lives here, on the outside?" Foster asked.

"Are you really going to be missed? Except for maybe Ramirez all of you have done shit with your lives outside the battalion — that was by design. Ramirez being the tenacious fucker he is screwed all that up by becoming police chief in this Podunk town. We'll just have him step down and then he can come back in."

Kieran was torn. There was a part of him that wanted to go back and undo all the damage — to restore his memories, his reputation, but there was a part that wanted to lash out at the Army, his leadership and most importantly his past self, the one that thought this plan was a good idea. He longed to knock the smugness right off Slattery's face too. He had nearly been driven to suicide more than once and wasn't sure that his psyche could heal from all he had been subjected to. He was angry, hurt, and confused — still unsure of what in his head was real.

"Tell me about this object — you don't know *where* it is — that's in my head, but I'm guessing you know *what* it is. If I am going back in, I want to have some idea of what I'm getting into before I agree to go back. And before you say I don't have a choice, consider that I am a capable mage with a trick or two still up my sleeves."

"We can save all that for a debriefing back at HQ. Too many eyes and ears out here in the open. How do you think we knew where you were? You've been watched every minute you've been gone while we waited for them to make their move." Slattery responded.

While they talked the exfil team continued their work, evacuating the doppelganger and erasing all evidence of what had occurred. Before long the site looked as if it had never been the scene of a magical duel that almost cost the lives of one or more of O'Cairn's soldiers. Everyone except Slattery and O'Cairn had made their way through the portal and back to headquarters.

"How about it O'Cairn? Want your command back?"

"Yeah, let's do this."

Anthony Rudd Biography

Anthony (Tony) Rudd, retired US Army signal officer who resides in Dallas Texas and now works as a government contractor supporting the US Navy. Hobbies include reading, writing and expanding my collection of heavy metal albums. Married with three kids, two of which are in college and one still in high school. Hope to one day make a full time go at being a novelist.

The Warden and the Familiar

Edgardo Soto

Potlabi Province, Cisza, Sadon System

"Remind me again why we're doing this?" Devana asked through the nano-comm. *"I feel that there are some serious flaws in this plan."*

As she was staying hidden within her data chip, Sharpe couldn't see Devana. However, based on her tone, it seemed that she was not happy, *"That's the nature of the job, kid. Thought you wanted an adventure. After all, you did give me the idea."*

"Fair point sir. I just wish you wouldn't remind me of that," Devana replied with a frustrated sigh. *"But, if this goes all pear-shaped, you're following my lead."*

"Roger that. I'm prepared to eat my words."

While the digital spirit was still getting used to working directly with a battle buddy, Sharpe was glad for both her company and her capabilities. During their hasty surveillance of their target's compound, the savvy construct had struck gold with her data diving. Thanks to her data diving, the duo had an accurate layout of the objective and could track the hostile guard force. Unfortunately, there was still the matter of breaking into the property itself. It was obvious that their target, Arios Colton, had not hired the best and brightest for his private army. However, the budding warlord had the advantage of numbers. The money he saved on hiring quality shooters seemed to be invested in making the palatial villa difficult to infiltrate. It was on high ground with open areas surrounding it. That wasn't factoring in the physical barriers to entry and automated defenses not yet compromised by Devana. A direct approach would be risky. Thankfully, one of the fruits of Devana's labor had included details about routine deliveries to his mansion. It was as if the bad guys were leaving the front door open for them.

As he slowly stalked through the darkened forests of one of the Independent Zone's many backwater worlds, Sharpe slowed as the trees thinned. Ahead, an unpaved road cut through the bluish firs. He checked his wrist mounted tactical slate and confirmed that he was close enough to his rally point. His tepid pace steadily increased as he made his way to the rally point before crouching behind one of the taller firs at the forests' edge. He waited several minutes before he saw a pair of trucks barreling down the winding road.

With their high beams on, he didn't even need the fused night-vision mode provided by his smart goggles to spot the wheeled vehicles. Moments later, Devana highlighted the convoy on his Combat Integration Network uplink, confirming that this was the logistic package that the duo was waiting for. He remained motionless as his ride steadily grew closer. Even with thermoptic camouflage active and a heavy poncho, moving would only draw unwanted eyes toward him. Not to mention that even the light drizzle of the evening would diminish the effectiveness of his invisibility. Thankfully, that same rain also mucked with the opposition's vision.

"I'm synced to the auto-truck. Thirty seconds until arrival, sir."

On that signal, Sharpe tightened the sling of his CR5 carbine across his body to make sure that it wouldn't hinder his upcoming sprint. With his current position set in proximity to a tight bend in the road, the automated cargo truck would have to slow down to make the turn, which would give Sharpe the chance to climb on board and ride the auto-truck right through the front gates of Chez Colton. If it didn't reduce speed, then it would be up to Devana to make sure it did.

The lead vehicle zipped past his position while the auto-truck slowed at the bend. Just as the unmanned vehicle moved at a crawl, Sharpe began his mad dash. He silently cursed as he nearly lost his footing. His inadvertent stumble had cost him a precious fraction of a second as the escort began to reverse. Just as his ride began to accelerate, Sharpe lunged for the tailgate. He hauled himself into the covered cargo bed, almost falling as he did so. It was close, but he made it.

"See, told you this was the easy part."

Despite his bravado, Devana was not convinced. *"Uh huh, sure it was. Slipping in the mud was all part of the plan then. Hmmm...seems that the escort is continuing forward now that your vehicle is catching up."*

"See, more good news. Now we just wait to get delivered to a tinpot tyrant's fortress. Just another day on the job."

With the first part of the infiltration complete, Sharpe assessed his surroundings. A number of containers secured to pallets were pushed toward the auto-truck's cab, giving Sharpe barely enough room to move or lay down on the bed floor if he needed to. A quick check of the labels showed him that most of the supplies loaded in the covered cargo bed were luxury items such as cognac and cigars imported off-world. It seemed that the wannabe kingpin had expensive tastes. He sat down and listened in on the comms feed from the enemy's operations center, courtesy of Devana. As expected from a bunch of budget mercs and gangsters thrown together to form a unit, they were unprofessional and only semi-organized. However, they sounded more alert. His mind began to race, wondering if he had been compromised but as he continued eavesdropping, he realized that the security chief's tone was more nervous than excited. Then, the other shoe dropped as the big wigs announced why they were getting their asses in gear, a surprise VIP visit.

"Of course this happens tonight of all nights," Devana complained.

"This isn't the worst snag. We just have to get creative. Killing the VIP along with Arios could be a bonus," Sharpe replied. *"Did our distinguished guest bring company?"*

"Aside from a two-person protection detail... no. His air car has remote piloting...hmmm. Anyway, it's also a last-

minute adjustment for the oppo as well, so they probably can't bring extra guns by the time we get there."

The warden was partially relieved by that silver lining, but he still had a bad feeling which was not only caused by his ever-shrinking time table. Aside from the highly sensitive data he currently had, the only reason that Arios Colton was on Section's radar in the first place was his rapid increase in power and influence. The intel boys suspected that he made some powerful friends who had an interstellar reach but couldn't confirm who they were. He couldn't confirm his suspicions, but his gut told him that this mystery visitor happened to be one of said allies.

***

For someone who thought in the span of microseconds, the twenty-minute drive to the lavish fortress was agonizingly slow for Devana, and she had not been idle during the wait. In that time, she had further spread her influence through the compound's security network, searching for more functions and defenses to hijack for her own purposes.

Her initial entry had been disappointingly easy. Colton had thought himself clever by setting up a net-hopping satellite-based mesh grid to encrypt his communications. It might have befuddled the resource starved Ciszan government, but Section had created an extensive intelligence package on the warlord and his holdings. She used that information to identify which satellites belonged to known shell companies and simply targeted that point of vulnerability to slip in the militia's lines of communication. From there, it was a simple matter of exploiting one of the local yokel's love of holographic waifu games and inability to leave his slate at home, and she had the opposition at her mercy. That said, she thought the ease at which she had completed her task was suspicious. But as the auto-truck approached the front gate, she decided that would be a problem for later. While she had enjoyed the pristine wilderness while it lasted, now she was about to be in her element.

She watched the small convoy roll to the last checkpoint using one of the wall's external cameras. Despite their increased alertness, the guards only conducted a perfunctory check of the vehicles. They scanned the IDs of the escort truck's occupants but didn't bother checking the cargo bed of the auto-truck before directing them towards the backscatter scanner just before the entrance. Devana smirked as she hijacked the scanner, showing only the expected goods as Sharpe's truck rolled through. Having passed the final check without incident, Devana flashed her consciousness over to a different camera and watched the escort peel off towards a makeshift motorpool. Sharpe's ride continued, rolling past an ostentatious water fountain and towards the back of the manor to offload its goods.

"There's a patrol approaching in sixty seconds. Once they're past you, you should be good to dismount. I'll handle the cameras."

Sharpe acknowledged her update with a series of three clicks from his nano-comm. The seconds ticked by and before long, the pair of mercenaries strolled past the auto-truck without a passing glance. Once they were about thirty meters away, her human charge made his move. Outlined in blue thanks to his CIN uplink, Sharpe swung his legs over the tailgate and quietly landed on the dirt trail in a smooth motion, the sound muffled by the soft whine of the truck's electric engine. Moments later, he was up and around the unmanned vehicle's left side to hide him from onlookers. It was a good habit but unnecessary as Devana was ensuring that the head security goons watching the feeds only saw their incoming delivery. When Sharpe reappeared on her view, his thermoptic camouflage was off and he strode toward the three-story mansion like he was just another disgruntled merc. Since he was clad in much of the same kit and weaponry as the uniformed troops, aside from a few special tools he kept hidden, no one paid him any mind as he went through a side entrance. Now that they were both in, it was time for phase two.

While part of her focus was keeping Sharpe out of trouble, her multitask routines allowed her to dedicate much of her processing power to finding a map of esoteric technology caches that Colton had somehow found. To her frustration, it was the one thing she hadn't been able to accomplish yet. While she had searched through reams of data that detailed everything from arms shipments to blackmail material, that damned thug and his cronies had decided to be smart for once and not keep any digital records on his new acquisition. Part way through her hunt for a hint of this MacGuffin, she detected a subtle probe towards her presence. She spoofed her signature in response, pretending to be just another native watchdog program doing its rounds. Then the entity probed again. She retreated, leaving behind a hastily cloned signal as a decoy while she reassessed her situation. The entity investigated her distraction briefly before shifting along the electronic pathways, continuing its search.

No bloody way...could it be?

Of all the possibilities, Devana hadn't considered the chance that Colton had an AI. She cursed her carelessness, wondering if she had missed anything else upon her initial breach. She paused and reset, retasking her functions toward tackling this new problem instead of reflecting on the past. With the possibility that her opponent could also be her objective, she saw her fumble as an opportunity. Before she could enact her plan, Sharpe delivered another surprise for her.

"Devana, just saw a civvie come out a side passage I didn't see before. Any idea where it leads?"

She shifted her consciousness to Sharpe's inquiry, her curiosity getting the better of her. She reviewed the CIN feed and sure enough, a section of wall opened as a gaunt Zarhad clad in a chef's uniform walked out. Behind him there was a glimpse of a descending staircase before the door snapped shut. Flashing through the various schematics of the building, she saw no indication of any secret side passages. Then she realized that she had no feeds coming from below the ground floor. If the opposition had a separate network for more sensitive activities, they would be cleverer than she had assumed.

"Standby sir. I'm following a lead."

A ghost of a signal floated through key subsystems, resuming the search for vital intelligence. It wasn't enough to rouse the attention of the already compromised counter-intrusion system but the guardian, already wary of her presence, would notice. She didn't make it easy for her opponent to detect, basing her lure on the tricks of a Jovepenian cracker she had dueled, but they seemed skilled enough to track her lure. There wasn't an immediate reaction, but soon enough the other followed the trail, unaware that Devana was right behind them. The system's guardian initiated another probe against the decoy program, which attempted its own spoofing signal in response. Instead of repeating the probe, her opponent went on the offensive and closed off the pathway. Her proxy attempted to evade, sending its own ghosts toward infrastructure systems to force the pursuer to deal with other dilemmas. The other isolated them and reduced them to raw code with minimal effort. It had delayed the hunt, but the defender AI had smelled the figurative blood in the water and was closing the distance. Her bait attempted every trick in the book, from fading into the background to data denial attacks, but none of it deterred the hunter. Cloaking her presence as she followed; she watched as the guardian finally cornered her lure. Instead of taking the ghost program apart, it began to interrogate it.

"I would suggest you talk quickly, räuber. I do not suffer fools easily, so tell me where you come from, and I may let you go with a warning."

Devana sprung her trap. In an instant, the ghost program dissipated, and its remnant code threw up a barrier around the guardian. To further isolate her opponent, Devana encrypted the pathways, locking it out of its own system. The shadowy silhouette searched for its attacker only to find itself 'face' to 'face' with Devana.

"Game over. You're mine now, so you better start talking before I decide that your code will give me what I want. Let's start with the eso-tech data."

The dark shape stared back, seemingly surprised by Devana's appearance before it unmasked itself, revealing an elderly man clad a tattered brown habit. For someone being threatened with deletion, he seemed oddly calm and almost... happy.

"There is no need for threats fräulein. Tobias Erwin Rasch, at your service. I have the data with me but unfortunately, I can't send it. With its size and my rather... limited connection, I can only defend this network... a task that I do not relish. However, if you have the capability to assist me, I can give you what you want."

Now it was Devana's turn to be surprised. She hadn't expected the man to yield so easily. In fact, he was practically betraying his human charges. She took a closer look at the 'man' and realized she made her second mistake of the night. *"You're not an AI, are you? You're physically here on the grounds, aren't you? If you give me your exact location, I think I can coordinate a hand off. If you copy the data, then no will be the wiser."*

Rasch winced at the proposal. *"Unfortunately, the situation is more complex than you think."*

As the reluctant custodian explained his circumstances, Devana grew more horrified.

"Sir...we have a problem."

***

Already recognized as friendly by the security system thanks to Devana's cyber-magic, the hidden door automatically opened for Sharpe. Underneath his lackadaisical facade, a cold fury brewed within him as he descended towards Arios Colton's secret dungeon. He wasn't angry because Devana's new find had rendered his initial plan moot. In his experience, plans never survived the start of a mission, and that was if the mission even stayed the same. Data retrieval becomes hostage rescue? It was a simple matter of adapting and overcoming. No, his newfound rage came from the additional update that the target was now moonlighting as a sex slaver. Colton was already a deadee, but now the prick was going to die slow.

Down in the subterranean prison, the kitted-up gun monkeys in blue-green hexagonal-pattern fatigues were mostly replaced by Colton's personal goons in their eclectic mix of casual fashion for both humans and humanoids. Despite not adhering to the dress code, no one commented on Sharpe's presence or gave him an odd look as he passed the rows of darkened nano-glass cells on either side of him. After all, he had been let in, so he belonged there as far as they knew. His disguise and their shitty OPSEC had once again been a boon to him. He filtered out muffled cries and cruel laughter as he moved deeper into the house of horrors. He soon found his destination, a small gray lobby sectioned off from the main area, with a large Usroi in a tailored suit standing guard with a Bartledyne 10-gauge automatic shotgun. Unlike the rest of the thugs, the broad tusked alien mean-mugged Sharpe.

"The whores are getting prepped for the buyer and are not to be disturbed. So, get the fuck out humie," the Usroi rumbled.

Rather than be intimidated by the burly alien, Sharpe reacted with a stubbornness that would have made his Krakavian heritage proud, "Idi na khuy! I'm here to escort monk. Chief's orders."

The alien hesitated, his grip tightening on the shotgun. "You? A temp? Boss doesn't like you types in his office."

"Not my problem. The chief is suspicious of the buyer. You want more guns or less if the buyer does some shit?"

The Ursoi started to speak but stopped, pondering on the likelihood of Sharpe's tall tale. Since he didn't dismiss it out of hand, it seemed that it was a possibility that Colton's people feared. Even so, the alien was still suspicious. "And you'll just happen to be in a place where you can leer at the merch, right?"

"Eh, I care more about living than looking at a nice ass," Sharpe shrugged. "I can go to the town to wet my beak rather than worry about something I can't have."

For a moment, Sharpe thought he might have overplayed his act as the brawny guard maintained his glare. After several tense seconds, the suited alien handed him a key and opened the door. "He's in the only blacked out cell. You got five minutes; the girls will be prepped by then and the 'borg goes on display too. The buyer was clear on that. During the meeting, you keep your mouth shut. Got it?"

Sharpe acknowledged the rules with a two-finger salute. He marched inside, maintaining his surly posture as the door closed behind him. He had to put on a show for the clandestine monitoring strips above the cells… for a while anyway. There were six panes of nano-glass, three on either side but larger than the cramped cells he saw earlier. To his surprise, the empty cells' interiors were far from the horror shows that Sharpe had expected. Rather than cramped destitute rooms, they looked more like an upscale boudoir; classy furniture and comfortable beds surrounded by other luxuries. Colton's gang seemed to operate differently from others in the flesh trade, pampering the special captives rather than abusing them, but the end results were still the same. Despite the fancy furnishings, Sharpe saw the displays for what they were; a gilded cage to show a prospective buyer their soon-to-be property.

Despite his discomfort, he made a beeline towards the sole opaque cell towards the back. He tapped a series of commands on the surface of the barrier and slowly slid up with a hiss. He backed away and kept his carbine trained forward, but once he saw the sole occupant, he realized he shouldn't have bothered. Unlike the luxurious cells, this room was empty except for a man wearing a tattered brown habit stained with blood. He was in a forced kneeling position, with his wrists chained to the floor. With his head bowed and hooded, Sharpe noticed a thin cable coming from the back wall connected to the back of his neck. The prisoner slowly looked up, revealing a face of metallic synth-flesh and a pair of electric blue ocular implants.

"Devana, are we clear?"

"Yes sir, I have control of the feeds."

With no prying eyes around, Sharpe dropped his surly merc act and made the sign of the cross. "In this sign, you will conquer."

The cyborg cocked his head, the lenses of his eyes narrowing as he studied him. Then he let out a synthesized chuckle. "You are signing the wrong way."

"I... what?"

"Your sign, its... never mind, it's close enough. You must be the one Fräulein Devana spoke of."

"That's me. Call me Mr. Knight." Sharpe knelt and unlocked the friar's manacles, "You have the data?"

"Ja, in here." Rasch tapped the side of his head with a single finger. "Though it pained me to destroy one of God's relics, I do so to protect the innocent. I also encrypted it to prevent these schwein from trying to steal it from my head." The cyborg gingerly pulled down the collar of his habit, revealing a thick matte black ring of hardened polymer secured around the base of his neck. "Unfortunately, if I try to upload or delete it, I will no longer have a head."

Sharpe winced as he examined the Laptev-made compliance collar. He thought about using his master key trick but decided against it. He had no idea what anti-tampering features this model had and he didn't want to trip them while playing amateur EOD. "Devana, I need you to look at this and tell me if you can unlock it."

Devana's avatar was by his side in an instant, leaning forward to study the collar while ignoring Rasch's shock at her sudden appearance.

"How —"

Devana interrupted him by rapidly snapping her fingers. "Hey, focus. Please pull your collar down more and turn. Have to see what I'm dealing with."

Rasch stuttered, trying to think of a reply before complying with her request, muttering about the rudeness of youths as he did so. The construct scanned the explosive device slowly, taking every minute detail as her subject turned, from slightly squared bulges on the sides to a small segment slightly embedded near the back of the cyborg's neck. At the end of her inspection, she grimaced as she made her conclusion.

"Bullocks, that's a Type Six… with a bloody manual lock. No network means no hacking and jamming triggers a random countdown. It's dumb enough that it can't be hijacked but smart enough to be a bastard. I can block the detonation signal, but I can't disable it."

"Could we disarm it if we went manual?"

"Sure, if you connect your slate's data cable to the collar, I can deactivate the anti-tamper bits. Then, I walk through the disarmament process. Even with your lack of bomb disposal experience, we have a good chance of success. The issue is time…which we don't have."

"Shit… okay, guess plan B got a bit riskier, "Sharpe replied before reaching for one of the pouches on his battle belt. "Hey Tobias, can you hide something for me?"

"Ja… why?"

"Because if you don't," Sharpe replied, a small gray sphere in hand, "Chances of us dying grow much higher."

***

Sharpe emerged from the special cell block well before the five-minute countdown elapsed, his surly persona returned and Rasch in front of him with hands manacled behind his back. The guard now had company, in the form of two young women clad in shimmering backless cocktail dresses that left very little to the imagination. Despite being dolled up, it was obvious they did not want to be there. Though their eyes were downcast, the terror in their eyes was palpable, and the skimpy outfits did more to highlight their discomfort. One of them, a short, freckled redhead who looked to be barely nineteen years old, seemed to be on the verge of tears as she trembled. The taller lithe brunette, who Sharpe realized was a yemarri with the pale gray skin and slightly pointed ears being a giveaway, seemed older and had a hint of defiance in her eyes. That defiance changed to concern when she saw the state of the cyborg friar.

"Brother Tobias, what did they do to you?"

"Quiet!" The usroi bellowed, "You will speak when spoken to! Now move."

Though Sharpe stayed quiet and glowered at the cowed captives, the yemarri's concern piqued his curiosity. The Kurzweilian friar hadn't mentioned he knew the women. As he took a closer look at them, he noticed that the older girl was rubbing a poorly hidden wooden cross in her hands. Perhaps it was a coincidence, but he was beginning to suspect that Rasch had been working alongside one or both. With the likelihood of the ladies being Rasch's colleagues, a small part of him wondered if they also knew what had been found in the wilderness of this quiet world.

He ended his internal theorizing as he took up the rear guard. While information control would be an issue, questioning and memory alteration could come later. He was going into the lion's den, so he needed his head in the game.

* * *

Meanwhile, Devana was not remaining idle. While her partner went headfirst into a plan that he likely thought daring and cunning, she was setting the stage so that the dismally low odds of success could be tipped in their favor. They needed a distraction and some additional firepower. Thanks to Tobias practically giving her the keys to the kingdom, she now had full access to the villa's security subsystems, so she had *plenty* of options.

She looked through the compound's defenses like a kid in a candy shop. She was in a prime position to create a lot of chaos for some evil scumbags. However, she saw them more as tools to enable their escape in the event they were compromised. Then her digital eye caught a particular subsystem labeled infantry drone control.

"Well, hello there. Where have you been hiding?"

She grinned maliciously as she learned about her new toys. The infantry drones, bristling with a variety of weapons, were as formidable as a heavy combat suit. Though there were only six drones at her disposal, two of them were acting as the HVT's personal security. She was glad she could communicate with Sharpe directly when he made his move. She just knew he was going to run into some unknown snag that screwed up his master plan.

Her first order of business was to update their FFI criteria; in a nano-second, she designated every mercenary and minion on the premises as hostile. Sharpe, Rasch, and the two women were not only considered friendly, but also VIPs. Unless their orders changed, the drones would guard the four organics until they were out of the fight. Despite the change to their rules of engagement, Devana didn't unleash her surprise just yet. Instead, she had them continue their current activities until she received the go-word. Once she did, the remaining drones would prove to be *very* distracting.

"Oh, this is going to be fun."

***

Oh, this is going to suck.

As Sharpe stepped inside the spacious office, he began to think that he made a serious miscalculation in his plan. His newfound concern had nothing to do with Colton or his cronies. With slicked back hair and a cream-colored bespoke suit sans tie, he looked more crimelord than warlord. Confident that he was untouchable, Colton cracked jokes while a small group of flunkies off to the side lounged around and laughed at their bosses' quips. The pair of two-meter-tall infantry drones flanking the warlord weren't an issue. Devana already alerted him to their existence, and they were outlined blue on his CIN feed. They were force multipliers rather than targets. No, he was worried about Colton's guest because he recognized the asshole.

Felix Sazar, known as the Butcher of Tamaun, was on the target deck of every player of the Great Game for his acts of terror and infamy, with the Laptevites chief among them. Despite being on everyone's hitlist, the dour corpse of a man wearing an ill-fitting suit had not only survived, but thrived as a facilitator for the worst people in the Orion Arm. Sharpe learned something new about the infamous terrorist; he was a practitioner. Judging by the developing headache, Felix was powerful enough for his senses to automatically warn him. There was also the matter of his bodyguards. The two velin, dressed in contractor chic tailored for their physiology, looked wrong. Though the pseudo-canines looked ready to brawl, their attentive stances were at odds with their slack expressions and flattened ears. There was also something hiding behind the aliens' dull eyes. Something familiar…and hungry.

Nergal Servitors. This just keeps getting better and better.

Three pairs of eyes flitted in Sharpe's direction and he briefly worried that he was burned by the warlock. The fear proved to be unfounded as their attention locked on to the captives hesitantly proceeding towards their captor. Unlike the jeers and wolf whistles from the goons, Felix's entourage was silent and staring intently as the trio sat on a plush couch across from them. But rather than the two girls, much of their attention was on Rasch. The warlock's severe expression remained unchanged, but Sharpe noticed that there was a slight anticipatory glint in his eyes as if he were imagining himself prying open the cyborg's head to get at his secrets. Then Colton let out a bellowing belly laugh and interrupted his guest's reverie.

"You see! What'd I tell you? Your old friend Arios delivers once again." The broad wannabe warlord did a double-take when he spotted Sharpe standing next to the doorway, and his tawny complexion took on an angrier tinge of red. "Hey, who let the fucking temp in here?"

Now all eyes were on Sharpe, with Colton's suited lieutenants looking with disdain and Felix taking a moment to study him. Sharpe returned their stares with indifference but kept his mouth shut. Despite the dicey situation, showing weakness would probably be more suspicious than if acted like he was supposed to be there.

"I'm extra security."

The usroi guard cleared his throat, uncomfortable with the situation. "That's right boss. This is an important meeting. Never hurts to have extra help."

"Well in case you forgot, temps don't come into my office armed. So please, get his gun."

Sharpe mean-mugged his temporary usroi companion, before reluctantly handing his weapon off to the large alien, who slung it across his back. He didn't like being disarmed. He had other weapons on him, but a pistol was the weapon used to fight your way to the carbine you should've had. Still, it seemed that everyone was ignoring him once again, so there was some benefit.

"Eh, must be one of the new jacks," Colton scoffed, "Now, back to business."

He stood up, moving in front of his desk and beckoning the women to join him. Neither moved at first, which only prompted him to frown and motion more intensely. With a nervous sigh, the yemarri woman finally stood, returning the warlord's frown with her own as she helped her companion. The warlord grinned as the girls became his reluctant arm candy and draped his arms around their shoulders. With a cocksure smile on his face as his hands wandered without quite coping a feel, he enjoyed acting like a playboy.

Christ, what a fucking prick.

"The last time we spoke, you said you would deliver one item and the relic data, "Felix said, his melodious tone at odds with his appearance. "You never mentioned that there was a second item or that I would have to extract the data myself."

"We hit a few snags trying to get it out of the 'borg's head. Heavy encryption and the like. I probably could have gotten it out of his head if I had more time…but since you are here now, you'll have to work for it a bit. As for the first issue, I was actually planning on keeping one of them." A lecherous glance toward the yemarri woman made it clear which one he was talking about. "However, I'd be willing to part with her if you're willing to pay up."

Felix didn't reply immediately as seemed distracted. He cocked his head as assessed the headstrong woman, as if he were listening to a voice only he could hear. He finally nodded, seemingly confirming some unknown order. "Unfortunately, I don't have access to my accounts, nor did I bring any hard currency…."

"Too bad," Colton replied with faux-sympathy, his hand sliding down to the girl's waist, "Well if you come back —"

"But I'll take her too."

Colton's head snapped to Felix, staring dumbly before belting out a laugh. When his guest didn't join in, the laughter died out. "You're serious?"

"Of course. I'll take them all. I am the reason for your current fortune, so I think I'm owed a favor."

"I'm not some merchant at a Bhazik bazaar where you can haggle." Though he kept hold of the yemarri, Colton dropped the playboy act, stabbing an angry finger at Felix. "You want the bitch; you pay for her."

A mirthless grin that promised violence appeared on Felix's face as he stood. The ghoulish man towered over Colton, prompting the petite redhead to retreat to the couch in a futile attempt to seek shelter. The warlord forestalled the other girl's attempt to do the same by tightening his hold, which looked like a poorly disguised attempt to use her as a shield. Felix's bodyguards' eyes turned jet black as the demonic meat puppets readied short K30 PDWs and bared their fangs. Colton's entourage stopped shit bagging and drew similar subguns with helical magazines, slowly fanning out to cover more angles. Even the combat bots that Devana controlled repositioned to protect their principals. The friendly meeting had devolved to a tense standoff and in the middle of this soup sandwich, no one was paying attention to Sharpe as he grabbed the two flat optic clusters of his smart goggles and rotated the frame over his eyes.

"Showtime... Dev, I'm going to need that distraction soon."

"With pleasure, sir. One distraction coming up."

As the standoff approached its apex, the lights shut off and plunged the room into darkness. With his smart goggles turning the pitch-black into a faded full-color view of the world, Sharpe watched as shooters and civvies alike blindly scanned the room for new threats. No one noticed Rasch lean forward to drop the spherical object he kept hidden in clasped hands. As the friar warned the two captives in calm Germanic, Sharpe looked away before tapping a command on his tac-slate. The sphere jumped, drawing several eyes towards its sudden movement, and sent a series of bright strobing flashes in rapid succession. Once the seizure grenade finished deploying its non-lethal payload, Sharpe looked up as bedlam descended on the lavish office space.

Colton's lackeys were out of the fight, either vomiting on themselves or caught in violent shaking fits. While Felix's demonic guard dogs weren't completely incapacitated, they were shaking off the stunning effects. It was enough of an opening for Devana's subverted drones to make their move. The first leapt in between the suited gangsters and the hostages on the couch before raising one of its wrist-mounted PDWs and hosing the hapless mooks. The other refrained from opening fire, as Sharpe was down range. Instead, it rushed at the nearest nergal servitor and choke-slammed it. Screams and the crack of automatic gunfire drowned out the shrill screams of the cowering redhead. Not everything went to plan, as several hostiles were fully lucid... namely the usroi guard, who was leveling his Bartledyne 10-gauge at Rasch.

Sharpe lunged and smacked the barrel of the assault shotgun aside, just as the large alien pulled the trigger. The rocket assisted shell shot toward the second possessed velin and detonated just as it hit, unleashing an incendiary payload. The creature thrashed around and let out an unnatural wail as white phosphorus began cooking puppet and puppeteer alive. Before the usroi could react to his spoiled shot, Sharpe delivered a snap kick to the side of his knee. With the force of his blow enhanced by the muscle suit he wore under his uniform, bones broke and the usroi's knee snapped inward, crippling the large alien. Sharpe's left hand shot down to the sidearm hidden in an oversized dump pouch. With a sub-second draw, he had the MH6C smart pistol out and jammed into his target's temple. At contact distance, the thug's defense screen wouldn't protect him. With two trigger squeezes, a pair of subsonic 5.56x30mm ripped through the alien's skull, painting the floor with blood and gray matter.

With the immediate threat eliminated, Sharpe shifted his aim to Felix right as the warlock unleashed a wave of sickly green energy. Not wanting to test the strength of his barrier spell, he grabbed a fistful of the dead alien's mane with his free hand and yanked the body ahead of him. The guard's corpse took the full brunt of the spell which began to dissolve meat, clothing, and firearms in a bloody slurry. Sharpe moved laterally, firing his integrally suppressed pistol as he achieved target lock. The self-guided projectiles zipped toward the warlock's head, only to pass through the air harmlessly as he disappeared in a flash of black smoke. He reappeared a second later, right next to Sharpe. Sensing the new threat, Sharpe pivoted to face Felix, only for the warlock to seize his wrist with surprising strength.

"Good try soldier," Felix hissed as he jerked the barrel away from him, "But not good enough."

The warlock cocked back a fist, gathering more energy for another acidic attack. Fortunately, Sharpe was faster. He broke his grip and pointed his first two fingers at his opponent's chest. A bolt of white-hot energy shot out from his hand and speared Felix through the sternum, flash frying organs as it burned a ragged hole through him. The warlock gasped for air as he stumbled back, a look of shock plastered on his face. Not willing to chance it, Sharpe kicked him down and fired repeatedly in the head, blasting the top of Felix's skull clean off. When it came to the supernatural, there was no kill like overkill.

"Guess I was good enough," Sharpe muttered as he turned to address any remaining threats.

With Felix taken care of and his attention back to the main fight, Sharpe saw that few threats remained. Colton's men were assuming room temperature, each ventilated by 6.5x25mm sabots. The first nergal servitor was reduced to burning meat and bone. The second drone grappled with a horror made up of fur and inky black tendrils that stabbed at its armored chassis. The robot slugged the beast in the face before shoving a heavy laser in its face. With a loud ionized crack, the servitor's head exploded into bloody steam. Now, the last bad guy standing was Arios. Taking him down would prove problematic, as he held the second woman before him in a headlock with a large snub-nosed revolver pointed at her head. Aside from the muted explosions and the distant chatter of gunfire from Devana's ongoing distraction throughout the manor, the only sound permeating the ruined room was nervous breathing from hostage and hostage-taker.

"All of you stay the fuck back or I'll kill this bitch!" Colton yelped, breaking the silence.

Sharpe didn't respond because he was trying to get a better angle on the terrified warlord. Even with the drones' innate accuracy, their weapons were suboptimal for this situation. With only a sliver of Colton's face exposed, there was a high probability that he'd end up maiming or killing the girl even with the holo-dot aid target acquisition. He gradually shifted the smart pistol's point of aim to get a better flight path for the smart pistol's self-guided rounds. Even as his HUD confirmed target lock, he hesitated. He would much rather have Colton live long enough to show him where the key to Rasch's compliance collar was. While Devana could delay a potential dead man switch signal, he didn't know if there were other low-tech measures that Devana might have missed.

Fuck it, I'm shooting this prick.

He was about to squeeze the trigger when he sensed a faint hint of psychic residue. His eyes snapped to the hostage, who had hand outstretched in his direction. As Sharpe's magic senses focused, he saw a frail blue tendril stretching out towards Colton's desk. A short letter opener on said desk began to rattle as the psychic hand struggled to pull it back. Then with a final surge of effort, the impromptu weapon flew into the girl's hand, and she slammed it into her captor's wrist. Colton yelped as the short blade cut into him, causing him to lose his grip on the wheel gun. She tried pulling away, but the warlord tightened his hold, using her as insurance while trying to choke the life from her. She frantically stabbed behind her while barely looking, leaving small angry wounds on her captor's side. Then fate decided to give her a break. With one last jab as she tried to break free, the blade hit the wannabe-warlord below the belt. Colton screamed in pain as his hands shot down to his crotch and fell to his knees. The closest drone was on him instantly, clamping a metal hand around his throat and shoving him against a bookcase.

The former hostage staggered around and dropped to her knees as well, coughing as she gingerly massaged her neck. As Sharpe moved to check on her, her eyes snapped toward him, still wild with fear. The girl scrambled backward until her hand touched Colton's discarded revolver. With fight or flight instincts taking hold, the yemarri snatched the hand cannon up and leveled it at Sharpe. He stopped in his tracks, his weapon pointed up and finger off the trigger.

"Ilanna, nein! Don't shoot!" Rasch shouted.

"Woah, woah! Friendly! See?" With exaggerated slowness, he reholstered the smart pistol in its hiding place before rotating the optic clusters out of the way. While he was loath to lose an advantage, he was equally unwilling to get shot by a hostage. With just enough ambient light provided by the smoldering servitor, he saw that the woman still had her weapon trained on him. Despite the threat, he held out his hand to her. "Ilanna, is it? Are you hurt?"

She stared dumbly at the offered hand, probably because Sharpe was only the second man here to not threaten violence against her. After some hesitation, Ilanna accepted his help... but kept the revolver. "Y-yes. I'm Ilanna. Ilanna Sevania. And I'm... I'm okay."

"Good, because I could use your help," Sharpe replied as he helped her up." I'm going to give you a key for Tobias' cuffs. I need you to free him, then check him and Freckles for injuries. Okay?"

Ilana narrowed her eyes, doubt still touching her features as she took the handcuff key from the warden before marching to her companions. She never saw the murderous intent in Sharpe's eyes as he drew his vibroknife and advanced on Colton.

Pinned against a bookshelf, the warlord's focus was entirely on his blood-soaked crotch and not the robot searching his pockets. Though the stab wound below the belt looked nasty, he ignored the streams of blood coming from the other gashes on his side. The ochre of his fake tan had taken a pale pallor from the steady bleeding. Without medical attention, Colton would expire within the hour. Sharpe didn't need him alive for that long.

"I've searched him sir...and lookee here" Devana said through the drone, gently waving a thin black remote. "Found the detonator but no sign of the key. Backscatter scanners aren't picking up anything... but I think that's due to all the bloody scan-shielding in the room."

"That cunt neutered me," Colton whined, barely registering the world around him, "I need help."

Sharpe crouched before the wounded warlord and tapped him on the forehead with the flat of his knife. The dying man squinted before his tear-filled eyes went wide at the sight of the five-inch blade. "Where's the key to the collar?"

"What?"

Colton's blubbering ended as Sharpe pressed the knife's edge between his legs to show that he was done fucking around. "The key to the collar. If you tell me now, I'll take care of you. If not —"

"Cigar box on the bookshelf. It's in the black cigar box with the Bellissimo logo!"

A quick inspection of the decorative bookshelf revealed the aforementioned box. After a quick check for traps, Sharpe opened it and retrieved a blocky key. "Did you install any surprises on the collar that I should know about?"

"No, no mods. You unlock it, it comes off. I told you what you want to know. Are you —"

Colton's reply was interrupted by a series of rapid thrusts from the vibroblade to the heart. The warlord let out a choking gasp before going limp. Satisfied that his target was dead, Sharpe cleaned his knife on his victim's suit before sheathing it. With nearly all key objectives finished, all that was left was extraction... which would be more complicated with the trio of noncombatants.

"You murdered him," Ilanna blurted, somehow surprised despite the other bodies sprawled throughout.

"I took care of him, like I said I would." Sharpe tossed the key at her. The young woman nearly fumbled the catch but managed to hold on to it. Having overheard the interrogation, she immediately set out on her new task. With that issue being addressed, Sharpe focused on inventory and the next fight. *"Dev, how's it looking in the rest of the compound?"*

"I've rattled the bastards. I've cut off their comms and taken out their operations center, so they're having a hell of a time coordinating... and I've also locked some of them in. OPFOR has taken thirty-six percent casualties, more gangsters than mercenaries. But I'm down to four —" a muffled explosion interrupted her report. *"Bugger. Now three infantry drones... which includes these two. Much of the guard force is back inside the house. They're spread out but can regroup quickly if they need to."*

He acknowledged her with a nod while swapping the half empty magazine in his smart pistol for a long thirty rounder filled with armor piercing sabot rounds. The smart pistol's targeting software would have a delay to compensate for the party mix of ammunition, but he didn't have the time to reload individual rounds. *"What about an enemy reaction force?"*

"Delayed the main force by shutting down the lift. However, a secondary team will be at the door in a minute... at most. I initiated a security lock on the door but if they have breaching tools, it won't hold for long."

Sharpe swore as he shoved the pistol in the holster wedge secreted between a side pouch. He was mildly pissed that the fucking warlock had turned his primary weapon into sludge, but he made do with one of many K30 PDWs lying on the ground. With a quick pull of the charging handle, he confirmed he had a round chambered before putting his smart goggles back in place. He made a quick assessment of his new charges and was not liking his odds so far. While he and his drone wingpeople could move at a decent clip, the group would only be as fast as its slowest members; the Kurzweilian friar and two ladies who were a strong breeze away from a wardrobe malfunction. The practical move would have been to leave the girls to their devices, but at this point he had given 'practical' the middle finger.

Stupid fucking chivalrous streak.

"Okay ladies and gent, get up and ready to move. We're going to catch a ride. You follow my lead, and we'll all go home in one piece."

Despite the injuries he sustained during captivity, Rasch was on his feet in an instant. Before he could move, Ilanna grabbed his artificial hand and spoke in hushed tones. "Brother Tobias, are you sure we can trust him? I know he saved us but he's ..."

"An assassin? Don't judge him mein kind. He may be a killer, but I helped him commit the deed. After all, he needs what's in my head, so he has incentive to get us out alive."

"I'm more worried about what happens after." After a moment of indecision, Ilanna drew up some more courage from her reserves and confronted Sharpe, "Why are you helping us? What are you getting out of it?"

"It's the right thing to do, your ladyship. On the topic of help, you wouldn't happen to have any more power, would you?"

Her defiance melted away as she bowed her head sheepishly. "Ummm, not really. I'm not a powerful psychic...wait, what did you — how did you know?"

"You're yemarri and you've got some psionic juice. Kind of obvious you're nobility. Now we need —"

The rattling of the door's handle and muffled shouting on the other side reminded everyone of the tight timeline. Thankfully, the enemy seemed to lack breaching charges because they continued trying the handle. The drones' heavy lasers snapped up at the door, covering it while Sharpe beckoned his precious cargo toward him. As he guided his charges to the left of the entrance, he saw that Freckles was close to cracking. Between the hyperventilating and repeated muttering of 'we're all going to die,' she was going to become a liability fast. He needed to nip that shit in the bud.

"Hey, miss, what's your name?"

She jumped with a start, blinking at Sharpe before she comprehended his words. "M-my name is Emili."

"Good to meet ya. I'm going to let you in on a little secret. We aren't going to die. Know why? We're too pretty to die. Okay? So, say it with me; we're too pretty to die."

"We're too pretty to die?"

"Good. Now repeat it... preferably very quiet-like. Gotta take care of some assholes now."

With all his ducks in a row and the door covered, Sharpe stood before the door with a breaching charge in hand. As he hastily attached the small brick of explosives to the center, a buzzing sensation began to fill his head. He spun on his heel, searching for the source of his growing headache before he saw Felix's body twitching. His free hand rose at the jerking corpse as he attempted to weave a spell to stop the impending disaster. The effort was futile. The carcass was hoisted in the air by an unseen force as two pairs of talons punched through the torso. The civvies gawked in horrified silence as clawed hands pulled open a portal dripping with gore. Instead of viscera and organs, impenetrable darkness filled the gaping wound. The drones opened up with their heavy lasers, only for their shots to splash harmlessly against an invisible barrier. Six glowing orbs broke through the void and Sharpe realized that they were eyes. Intelligent eyes locked only on him and filled with unmitigated hate.

"Oh, there is no way my luck is that bad."

He was instantly proven wrong when a massive black blur launched itself at him with a booming roar.

As the beast lunged, Sharpe dove to the side. The impact nearly knocked the wind out of him, but he managed to escape by the skin of his teeth. The force of the creature's rush smashed the door off its hinges and bowled over the reaction team. The hapless mooks screamed in horror and pain as the demon began tearing through them. A rainbow of blood splashed the entryway, and severed limbs flew into the air as the eldritch horror reveled in the slaughter.

With gunmen and monster both distracted, Sharpe fumbled with a detonator before squeezing the clacker. The whirlwind of violence was halted by a thunderclap as the breaching charge exploded. Though he was a safe distance from the improvised bomb, Sharpe was still close enough for the dregs of overpressure to wash over him. The force had stunned him and left his ear ringing but managed to keep his bearings. He staggered to a knee with his PDW trained on the opening, seeing only chunky multicolored giblets and a stirring heap of charcoal chitin.

"Move! Dev, get everyone moving!"

The lead drone hustled the ex-prisoners to their feet, giving them an extra push out the door before leading them away from the carnage. Sharpe and the second battle-scarred machine dashed after them before pivoting toward the nightmare made flesh. The demon had fully recovered, rising to its full two point three-meter height. It could have been mistaken for a humanoid from a far distance if not for its segmented tail, the second set of long spindly arms, and the exoskeletal mask around its head. The explosion had hurt it, but it was more than ready for round two.

Before it could lunge, Sharpe held up his hand and began chanting in a long dead tongue. The demon recoiled and froze as the banishment spell held it in place. The drone wingperson took advantage of the thing's helplessness, blasting it with the laser. It shrieked as directed energy scorched its carapace, but the shots weren't penetrating. Then the creature lowered its head and stepped forward as profane symbols all over its body glowed red hot. Its progress was torturously slow, but it was advancing on Sharpe, nonetheless. He surged more effort into banishing the abomination but the harsh snap of laser fire to his rear threatened to divert his focus. Even with his additional power, the demon kept coming and would probably get to him before he could send it back to the abyss. So, he switched tactics.

"Dev, take that bastard out!"

He dropped the banishing spell and unleashed another bolt of concentrated energy that smashed it off its feet. He turned and sprinted back to his tagalongs just as the drone fired off a micro-missile at the downed demon. For a brief nanosecond, he dared to hope that the thing was dead. It was quickly dashed when the cacophony of combat echoed behind him. Amidst the rapid cracks of laser and gunfire, the demon bellowed a challenge.

"YOUR TOYS CANNOT STOP ME MAGI! NO MATTER WHERE YOU RUN, I WILL FIND YOU! I WILL DEVOUR YOUR SOUL!"

"Crapcrapcrapcrapcrap!" Sharpe muttered as he picked up the pace. *"Dev, how are the packages?"*

"Apologies sir, one second." Laser fire briefly intermingled with the sharp retort of subguns before the latter cut off abruptly and Devana continued. *"Everyone's good, moving to the second floor… sir, what was that thing?"*

"Demon and a real tough bastard at that. You do whatever it takes to take it down or delay it."

"I'll do my best… but the drone is close to its last legs."

It wasn't the best news, but it was better than nothing. The demon had gathered enough mana to anchor itself to the material world, so he couldn't banish it. But if Devana fucked it up enough, then he could deliver a coup de grâce. Of course, there were still mortal adversaries to deal with, a fact made apparent as he passed the scorched bodies of Colton's remaining gunmen at the top of the stairs.

"Friendly coming from the rear, hold fire," Sharpe hissed as he rushed down the spiral staircase two steps at a time. He made good time in his haste, managing to catch up to the rest of the group just as they reached the bottom of the gilded staircase. "Keep leading us on Dev. I've got rear security."

The group pushed on, with Devana setting the pace and Sharpe ensuring that no one was left behind. Though the civvies started to slow as their adrenaline gradually faded with no immediate danger, the warden kept them moving at their previous pace. So far, neither the thugs nor the mercs had shown up in force to stop them, but whether it was due to their focus on reaching their boss, their lack of coordination, or Devana's distraction still wreaking havoc, it was a blessing. The only sign of the opposition was the occasional sound of fists bashing a locked door as the crew passed several locked rooms. Their brief peace was about to come to an end just before they turned the corner.

"Sir, we have a squad-sized element pushing up the stairs at the foyer. They'll see us once we round the corner."

Sharpe didn't relish the idea of a firefight in an extended fatal funnel. With no cover and facing a larger force, it would take a lot of luck to survive the battle, let alone win. However, there were other options. *"Kid, I need you to up the chaos. Give them something else to deal with."*

"One descent into madness coming up sir."

With her new marching orders, Devana did not disappoint. Her first action was through the drone, which rounded the corner and launched a micro-missile. As the combined mercenary/gangster element made contact, the micro-missile detonated in an airburst. Shrapnel and overpressure shredded them, dealing with the immediate threat. Before the gunmen could get their shit together, Devana ceased her jamming of their communications to deliver an important announcement from their now deceased don.

"Those temp fucks tried to kill me! Get them!"

To Sharpe's surprise, there was no hesitation on the part of the made men to turn on their mercenary hirelings. Instead of shouting and denial, the gangsters who were not presently engaged immediately opened fire on any nearby mercs. He had severely underestimated the lack of trust between the two groups, but he wasn't going to complain. After all, there was no need to fight the metaphorical city because Devana had made the city fight itself. With additional time bought, the group made their move.

The infantry drone remained posted at the corner as Sharpe dashed to the opposite end of the dogleg. With a quick pivot, he pushed forward, and the bot mimicked him as the civvies followed closely behind the armored machine. Speed was security, especially when it came to moving through the long fatal funnel, and having more guns to cover the angles was always a plus.

There were a few scattered shots in his direction, but their combined fire kept the enemy's heads down. Once the ragtag assembly was a quarter of the way through, their luck started to run out. A burst of 10-gauge slugs ripped through one of the doors just as the infantry drone passed before it. The drone swiveled just in time to blast through said door with its primary, but the high caliber barrage broke past the bot's defense screen and sheared off one of its legs.

Sharpe snapped the PDW toward the murder hole and let off a quick burst, the sabot rounds passing through the door and flesh with ease. The clatter of boots on carpet alerted him to the gaggle of assholes trying to make a push. Seeing the mutilated robot likely made them think that they just had to deal with him. The second micro-missile airbursting among their ranks proved them wrong.

"I've got you covered sir. Drone 3 is headed to your position. Go!"

He didn't need any additional encouragement, and he was glad that neither did the civvies, who dashed across the room right when he motioned to them. He was still a couple of doors away from their exit, but with only one gun in the fight, the time to get out of the fatal funnel was now. In the span of a few strides, the crew reached the closest door. He tore off his final breaching charge, slapped it on the door, and squeezed the detonator. The door disintegrated and he peered around the corner, a smart grenade already primed and ready to toss...

just as a hail of gunfire poured out of the haze. He had exposed himself for barely half a second, but enough of the inaccurate barrage smashed into him to deplete his d-screen, but it held long enough. The explosive surprise sailed through the air, its sensors detecting the gagglefuck of shooters and promptly unleashing the gift of fragmentation in the middle of the crowd. Sharpe chased the explosion, his weapon up and cutting down the few wounded goons in a welter of blood. The K30's bolt locked back as the last goon let out his death rattle.

"In now!" Sharpe yelled as he let the weapon drop and drew the MH6C.

As the civvies hurried in, he became a victim of poor timing once again. No sooner had the prisoners entered than an adjoining door was thrown open and a trio of bloodied and bedraggled mercs burst in. They gaped at Sharpe and his charges, a mistake that cost them their lives. The smart pistol was already up and firing, servicing each with a controlled pair. A soft click from the remaining subsonic preceded the muffled cracks of high velocity tungsten penetrators that tore a ragged hole through the first merc's throat. Though initially befuddled by the party mix, the targeting software soon caught up by the time Sharpe was shooting at merc three, sending self-guided rounds right into the bad guy's face. He was charging forward even before the last body fell, seeking to exploit the new breach. Through the portal, he noticed a lone shooter through a crack in the door, unaware that his buddies were dead. He would remain ignorant as Sharpe unleashed a salvo of sabots. The first few splashed against a d-screen before the subsequent shots perforated the zarhad's skull. After clearing the left-most corner, he continued to the door and slammed it closed.

"Okay, everyone on the balcony," Sharpe ordered as he dragged an ornate side table in front of the door. "This is our last stop."

"Is someone coming to get us?" Ilanna asked, a relieved smile beginning to form.

"Yeah… something like that," Sharpe replied as he shoved open the balcony doors.

As soon as the doors flung open, the faint whine of ducted fans could be heard in the distance. Sharpe's smart goggles cut through the gloom and drizzle, giving him a clear view of a sleek black air car lifting off from a duracrete landing pad. With Devana at the helm, they were going to use the departed Butcher of Tamaun's ride as their own. Ilanna gave a joyful gasp and Emili's manta gave way to a relieved giggle as the aircar drifted next to the balcony, hatch down on top of the railing. They were almost in the clear, so naturally, things went pear-shaped.

"SHIT! Drone Two is down. The demon is going through the floor! It'll be right on top of you!"

An eerie green glow emanated from the ceiling of the previous room, as the nightmare phased through and dropped to the floor. Its battle with Devana's drone had put it through the wringer. Two of its arms were charred stumps and large segments of its carapace were broken, exposing skin and luminescent green blood. Its organic mask was also broken, exposing its skull-like head. Despite the severe damage it suffered, the demon hadn't lost its speed. Sharpe lashed out with his signature bolt of concentrated power as the demon rose a talon simultaneously. His beam of thermal energy struck true, slicing off one of the demon's unarmored limbs. Sharpe was faster, but not fast enough to stop the long quill from spearing him through the shoulder. The projectile retained enough force to throw him back and pin him against the balcony's rail. He bit back a scream of pain, attempting to hit the demon again but the beast was on him. His uninjured arm was seized in a vice grip as the demon's six eyes bore into him. Expecting his opponent to try and eat his face, he groped for one of his frags. If he was going down, so was this fucker. The demon had other ideas; it attacked his mind. He let out a scream.

With its psychic attack, the demon showed him what it planned to do to him; to Rasch; to the women; to the planet. A million images of unending horror flashed into his mind in an attempt to break him. As he grabbed hold of the grenade, he tried to tell Devana to leave him. He missed his chance at martyrdom, because help came from an unlikely source.

"I'M TOO PRETTY TO DIE!"

The mind trap of horror ended abruptly as the loud boom of a .454 magnum slug went off. With the psychic attack halted, Sharpe shook the afterimages out of his head and took in a scene of absurdity. To his surprise, his savior was Emili. She clutched the pilfered snub nose revolver in one hand and one of her ears in the other as she experienced the joy of tinnitus. Rasch and Ilanna gaped, the latter likely with greater shock at her friend's decision to snatch a gun away from her. The demon, with half its face blown off, looked insulted that its food had the gall to fight back. The lull in its attention was all Sharpe needed.

He let go of the grenade, gripped the spike in his shoulder, and pulled. He ignored the intense pain and lunged at the monstrosity. He plunged the spike deep in the demon's chest, shoving it off balance. Before it retaliated, he speared his hand into exposed flesh and unleashed a high yield bolt of pure magic. The blast exploded out of its back, nearly cutting the creature in half. But he had to make sure. He pulled out his vibroknife and channeled his power through it. With the blade glowing white hot, he brought it down into its neck. Glowing green blood sizzled from the wound as Sharpe cut through flesh, muscle, and cartilage effortlessly. The demon's head plopped to the ground just before its body dropped. He nearly fell on his ass as he turned on his heel and made a beeline to the aircar. Exhaustion was starting to take hold, but he would be damned if he was going to die before completing the mission. With Rasch and Ilanna climbing on board, he thankfully only needed to round up one straggler.

"Hey Emili! EMILI!" He shook the short girl to break her out of her tinnitus-induced stupor. "It's time to go, you crazy kid!"

She blinked before comprehending his words a split-second later and scurried after her companions with Sharpe close behind. With everyone on board, the AC accelerated into the darkness.

***

24 Hours Later, Directorate Outpost, Cisza, Sadon System

The day after the raid on Casa de Colton was less than eventful, but Sharpe was not complaining. While Serderius' resources were limited on Cisza, the Directorate of National Security and Intelligence still maintained a mission support site on the planet...something which Devana gleefully exploited. With a hastily concocted cover story and legitimate identity codes, their sister agency provided them with a temporary sanctuary until Section could pick them up. After debriefs, a trip to the site doctors, and a *long* rest period, Sharpe decided it was time to celebrate. He strode through the prefab building's hallways toward his assigned quarters, a bottle of vodka in one hand and two glasses. As he entered his room and locked the door, he was glad that the head of station had given him his own private quarters.

"Hey Devana, you here?"

In an instant, Devana's avatar appeared in the corner with a slight grin on her face. "My, my... I see that you've acquired some high-quality spirit for your post-mission celebration... and two glasses. Who are you celebrating with? Not Rasch... is it, Ilanna?" The spirit leaned forward, her grin taking on a snarky character. "Or is it Emili? I do believe that she fancies you."

Sharpe barked out a laugh as he filled the glasses. "Oh God, I'm going to have to break that poor girl's heart then. I'm not going to special hell for taking advantage of a young maiden's crush. Besides, I'm thirty years her senior. I don't rob cradles."

"Aha! I knew that your service record was lying! But really, who's your drinking buddy?"

"Well, isn't it obvious?" Sharpe paused for effect, "It's you; a reward for a job well done."

The spirit blinked before looking at the glass on the table. "Me? But… I don't drink… hell, I *can't* drink. You know that right?"

"Well, it shouldn't really matter. It's the camaraderie built during post-mission celebrations. The drink is just a bonus." He made a show of examining the bottle as if it were a fine bottle of wine. "After all, this is the finest rotgut from my ancestor's homeland. You don't want it to go to waste."

She rolled her eyes and chuckled before drifting toward the small table. She smoothed out her sundress and 'sat' down. As Sharpe lifted his glass, Devana mimicked the motion sans glass.

"A toast to Devana; for completing her first mission. I promised you a challenge and I gave you one." He downed his drink and winced as a dull pain shot through his wrapped shoulder. "Though I think I had to do the hard part."

Devana gave a snort of laughter before she made a show of downing a nonexistent drink. "About that sir, there's something I wanted to ask you."

He glanced up from his second pour. Though Devana retained her jovial and cunning nature after that surprisingly brutal gauntlet, Sharpe could tell that there was something weighing on her mind. He figured he knew what that was, but he figured that she would tell him on her own time. That time seemed to be now.

"Go ahead kid. Shoot."

She opened her mouth but hesitated, seemingly mulling over her choice of words. "Felix and that demon…what were they doing there? I get that he was Colton's sponsor, but I just don't get why?"

It wasn't the question he was expecting, but Sharpe admitted it was a good one. He scratched his beard, thinking about the various possibilities before settling on a working theory. "He probably selected that piece of shit because he's small time. He doesn't know shit from fuck when it comes to the supernatural. We weren't even looking at Colton until the intel boys heard he got into the eso-tech game. As for why Colton was kidnapping women for them…my bet is that they were looking for sacrifices."

"Sacrifices?" Devana's cocked an incredulous eye at the assertion. "There has to be an easier way to get that than reaching out to some wannabe warlord."

"Oh, for sure. But that demon wasn't looking for easy, it was looking for quality. Something that would give it a bigger boost in power. The innocent and the virginal. Emili and Ilanna fit that bill. Plus, Ilanna's psychic abilities would probably have given it an even bigger boost. That stereotype has existed for millennia for a reason…good thing we stopped it."

"Why's that?"

Now it was Sharpe's turn to hesitate. He prided himself on his mental defenses and ability to withstand psychic attacks, but there were some things that he couldn't get out of his head. "The demon had plans… long-term ones. If you think that thing was tough, it probably could have gotten much bigger with more sacrifices… or worse, bring some of its buddies with it. So, is that all you wanted to ask?"

The chipper and talkative AI was silent in response. She clasped her hands in her lap, her curiosity replaced with dour regret. She wasn't on the verge of tears, there was pain in her eyes. "… No. I… well this is the first time I've killed anyone. I know that I didn't directly kill them, but it was still my actions that led to their deaths. During the mission, I wanted those bastards to hurt… but now…."

"Yeah, I figured that was troubling you. Since you aren't like other AIs...or even other Familiars, you probably process emotions like us..." Sharpe said with a nod, "Well, it's perfectly natural to feel guilty...hell, it can be a good thing as long as you don't let it cripple you or. While ninety-nine percent of our opposition tend to be assholes, don't let that be a justification. Rather, focus on the good you've done."

He leaned forward and looked his companion in the eye. "Thanks to you, we prevented something unholy and eldritch from getting a foothold. Thanks to you, we ended a cycle of slavery and subjugation. Thanks to you, we saved three innocent people. I'd say that those are damn good achievements. Don't you agree?"

The change was slow, but Sharpe saw that his words had gotten to his saddened companion. Sorrow melted away and was replaced by a cocksure smile as the digital spirit nodded in agreement. Then she raised an imaginary glass.

"I'll propose a toast. To Mikhail Sharpe for being a damn good partner and mentor."

"Ha! I like that!" He downed his second drink in a swift pull and let out another laugh. "I think this is the beginning of a beautiful friendship."

Edgardo Soto Biography

Edgardo Soto is a veteran, aspiring author, and father of three rambunctious youngsters. An addict of action packed tales of danger and intrigue, he writes action thrillers of both the modern day and science fiction variety. Raised in Virginia, he currently lives in West Texas."

Facebook: https://www.facebook.com/edgar.c.soto?mibe xtid=ZbWKwL

Instagram: https://www.instagram.com/ecsoto13?igsh=d TR0d2Nsbmg0azcy

Twitter: https://x.com/ECS013?t=DCebTuCMmLPppDlu xzNQpw&s=09

The Judges

After an initial scrubbing by the Cannon staff, the top nine stories are judged on a rating scale considering six different criteria. The judges, authors who act independently of Cannon Publishing, grade each story on the following.

- Plot
- World Building
- Grammar
- Composition
- Ending Characters
- Storytelling

Then the aggregate scores are determined and ranked, with the highest score determining the winner. It's a hard choice sometimes, and one that I'm glad I don't have to make as the editor!

Alex Shaw

International Best Selling Author

Alex spent the second half of the 1990s in Kyiv, Ukraine running his own business consultancy before being head-hunted for a division of Siemens. The next few years saw him doing business for the company across the former USSR, the Middle East, and Africa. Most recently he has spent several years in Doha, Qatar.

Alex is an active member of the ITW (The International Thriller Writers organization) and the CWA (the Crime Writers Association). He is the author of three international bestselling thriller series featuring AIDAN SNOW, JACK TATE and SOPHIE RACINE, and the standalone 'Delta Force Vampire'. His writing has also been published in several thriller anthologies.

Alex, his wife and their two sons divide their time between homes in Kyiv - Ukraine, Sussex - England and Dubai - UAE. Follow Alex on twitter: @alexshawhetman or Instagram @alexshawthrillerwriter or BookBub @AlexShaw or find him on Facebook. He is represented by Justin Nash of The Kate Nash Literary Agency. @JustinNashLit

Kevin Harris

Winner, 2024 High Caliber Awards

A voracious reader, Kevin grew up on fantasy and science fiction, finding inspiration for his writing in the Halls of Moria, with the man-eaters of Zamboula, and on the 'hurtling moons of Barsoom'. His first published novella, 'Mightier than the Pen', is a standalone Military Fantasy story set in an epic fantasy world full of danger and grand adventure. In his limited free time, Kevin enjoys birding and gaming with his son, conspiring with his wife to cancel social engagements, snuggling his dog Freya, and hunting dragons with his half-feral daughter and their insane cat Mumbo.

Amazon Author Page:
https://www.amazon.com/author/bowandbegin

Website: https://www.amazon.com/author/bowandbegin

Kacey Ezel

Dragon Award Finalist

Kacey Ezell is a retired USAF helicopter pilot who writes emotionally charged adventure fantasy and science fiction. She is a two-time Dragon Award Finalist for Best Alternate History and has written multiple bestselling novels published with Chris Kennedy Publishing, Baen Books, and Blackstone Publishing.

Find out more and join her community at
https://kaceyezell.net/the-dragons-horde/

James Copley

Cannon Author

James Copley is a former Non-Commissioned Officer of the U.S. Army, having served over twenty-one years in both Active and Reserve/Guard units, variously trained as Infantry, Communications, and Ordnance specialties before finally retiring from the Army National Guard in 2016. During his service, he deployed four separate times, twice to Iraq and twice to Afghanistan.

He is currently working as a software engineer in Central California with his wife, two children, and two dogs. Reading was his number one passion from a very young age, and more recently he decided to try writing his own. Feel free to join him on his writing journey! You can find him on his Facebook Page

https://www.facebook.com/profile.php?id=100090711964251

Join the Crew!

Sign up for our newsletter for the latest news on new releases and more.

Follow our authors at their Amazon Pages!

J.F. Holmes (2 x Dragon Finalist)
Shane Gries (Dragon Finalist)
Lucas Marcum
Al Hagan
James Copley
Jason Kyle
G. Scott Huggins
Michael Morton
Charles Hackney
Jon LaForce
Jason Weiser
Kal Spriggs

More Books from Cannon Publishing

The Fae Wars

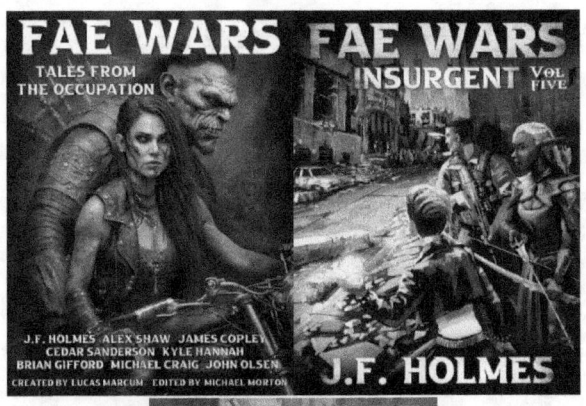

An ancient enemy invades Earth, returning to claim their home world. The men and women of the US Military find themselves matching technology against magic as cities burn and armies clash.

Onslaught
The Fall
Futures Past
Tales from the Occupation: A Fae Wars Anthology
Insurgent
Ghost

Irregular Scout Team One

In July of 2016 a plague swept the world, and the civilization collapsed and fell. For a lone National Guard sergeant, a veteran of the wars overseas who had settled down to a new life, the nightmare began on a hot summer evening at the barricades. Orders and chaos, gunfire and being overrun, his unit dwindles away in the face of the infected.

Months later, living in the ruins, the thud of helicopter rotors followed by a crash and the rescue of a downed pilot leads Sergeant First Class Nick Agostine back into the arms of the US military. From his experience comes the idea of teams, military and civilians experienced in dealing with the undead and barbarism of the wilds. The first Irregular Scout Team leads the way for Task Force Liberty to advance down the Mohawk Valley in Upstate NY, making contact with survivors and clearing out the infected with stealth and firepower.

The Line

When the world descends into chaos and anarchy with an unbelievably swift plague, turning victims into ravenous maniacs, the soldiers of America's storied 1st Infantry are asked to hold the line. From the brutal streets of urban combat to the bloodied, desperate defense on the plains of Kansas, they fight a war against an unrelenting enemy who used to be their fellow citizens.

As civilization falls, can they hold the line?

The Thin Dead Line

Dead Storm Rising
The Big Dead One

Fallen Empire

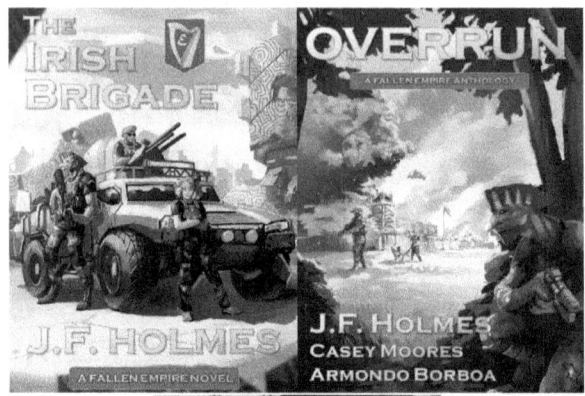

What's a soldier to do when the war is over? When he's only known conflict his whole life? Since time immemorial the solution has been to find another war, this time for pay. Whoever has the credits and wins the high bid gets the experienced fighter. Sometimes, though, the credits aren't enough to cover the price.

Empires rise, but Empires also fall. The Terran Union has spent five centuries under the control of the alien Grausians, like a barbarian tribe under the thumb of Rome. Now, after almost two decades of civil war and succession struggles, the formerly subject races have settled back in their ancient territories to lick their wounds and re-arm, leaving hundreds of settled planets to exist in a political vacuum.

Into that space steps the free companies, mercenary units that fight for gold, honor, power and glory. Veterans who can't get the wars out of their souls, new recruits looking for adventure, corporations with their own agenda.

Join us in a 27th Century that echoes history.

The Irish Brigade
Overrun
Silent Violence

Athenaeum, Inc

The Professor has problems, and not just what decades of soldiering did to his back and his knees. His boss just died, leaving him as CEO of the extremely discreet intelligence contractor Athenaeum, Incorporated. His old buddy the Operations Director is a highly skilled Army Ranger veteran but his finance chief is slightly unhinged and spends her money on highly inappropriate work outfits. The surviving old men on the Board of Directors are stuck in the 1970s. Running Athenaeum out of an old Cold War bunker and keeping their roster of experts together is expensive, but the government contracts are drying up or going to bigger, flashier corporate players.

Door Number Three
Doubling Down

Invasion

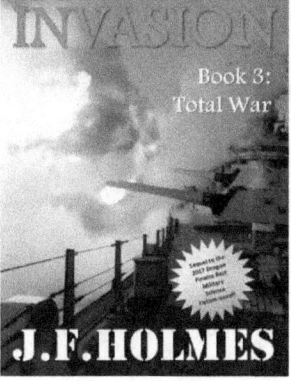

More than a decade after the Confederated Earth Forces were defeated, their commanding general, a boyhood protegee, lives in exile and disgrace. His life on an isolated farm is forever changed when two strangers show up at his homestead, and the war comes crashing back down on him. The problem though, remains the same. How do you fight an enemy that is technologically superior and holds the high ground?

Invasion: Resistance
Invasion: Day of Battle

Invasion: Total War

Offworld

When nuclear war erupts on Earth, the American colony in the Alpha Centauri system is left stranded. As the new day dawns, a furious attack by the native inhabitants threatens to overwhelm the colony's defenses. It's left to the thin red line of the US Army's 9th Regiment to stem the tide and ensure humanity's survival in this harsh new world.

From two time Dragon Finalist and author of the best selling series "Irregular Scout Team One" and "Invasion" comes a new tale that tells of the struggle for survival on a brutal planet.

Offworld: Ragnarok
Offworld: Expeditions

Valkyrie

Humanity engages in a desperate struggle with an alien species for this side of the Orion Arm. Space ships die in instantaneous bursts of light and turn into vapor, but on the ground Marines scream and lie wounded in the mud and blood, praying for the Valkyries to come save them.

They aren't wishing for death and a Nordic goddess to take them to Valhalla, the wounded are praying for the men and women of the '348th Field Hospital MEDEVAC to dive through fire and hell to come save them. Because they know that ...

Valkyries never die!

<u>Valkyrie</u>
<u>Valkyrie: Rebellion</u>
<u>Valkyrie: Attrition</u>

The Cannon High Caliber Awards are an annual contest for new writers. In it we ask them to submit a novella length story of Science Fiction, Military or Fantasy genre to challenge their skills.

2024
2025

The Wishkiller Saga

While on patrol Captain Aethal Paaling discovers evidence that an ancient terror has reached the rich soil of his home: the Lotus, a prolific growth whose addictive leaves devour their victims from within turning their hosts into horrible, terrifyingly violent mockeries of humanity. Created at the dawn of history by the twisted power of a godly relic called the Well, the return of the Lotus may be a harbinger of even more horrors to come.

Carrying the fatal news to the capital, Aethal discovers that even in the face of death itself, the Lords Paramount of Verlaen will fight to keep their secrets and their power. With only the guidance of his legendary Greater Rifle and the aid of the Pheonix Lancers, the soldier must find his way through the halls of a forgotten holy order and into deep dens of crime seeking answers.

He must find the truth as quickly as he can, because the Lotus may have already taken root among those he loves... and fighting it may cost him everything, including his soul.

A Cold and Mortal Spring

Hexen

When nine out of ten people in the world have died in a brutal plague, what do those who remain do to pick up the pieces? Does the creed, "Duty, Honor, Country" have a place any more if there's no country left?

On his way across the devastated remains of Texas, Marine Corps veteran and survivor Eric Marten rescues a young woman from a vicious attack by men who have turned into savages. As Dani slowly learns to trust him, they try to stay alive in the deathlands that America has become, using all their wits to survive a post-apocalyptic nightmare.

90% Death Rate: A Post Apocalyptic Thriller
Angel of Death: A Post Apocalyptic Thriller

Hell Train

A single train carries what might be the last vestige of civilization through a hellish nightmare.

A few hundred alive out of millions, lights going out all across what was once America as the possessed arose from the dead and murdered the living. A few hundred survivors travel across the country in an armored train, seeking some place to shelter in a fallen world. All that remains is a dystopian nightmare marked by rains of blood, impossible horrors, and portals to Hell opening in the skies.

US Army Captain Jack Zamora is responsible for their safety, a self-imposed burden that wears on him every day. Fighting off undead, protecting the survivors, keeping the train running and supplied as his team desperately plans their next moves. Starvation and disease threaten. but it gets worse, because the ancient gods have sent their emissaries, horrific beings of myth and legend that walk the Earth. Things that can drain a man's very life essence or even that of an entire city.

Hell Train: All Aboard

The Path

Sometimes a hero isn't what you expect, and the one you need comes from the castaways of society.

Nearly broken and at the end of his rope, former decorated scout pilot and prisoner of war, Red has finally accepted the inevitable. He and his kin have no future in the Human Confederation of Worlds, being gene mods and barely human themselves. With the help of his friend he flees Terra for adventure and fortune out in the reaches of the galaxy. Along the way he's dragged back into conflict that calls on all his piloting skills and he learns the deeper meaning of Kin, as his crew becomes his family.

Path to Freedom: The Path, Book One

The military experience is timeless, and echoes down from our past and into our future. Along the way, not everything is as it seems. Thirteen stories from established and new writers in the field of Military Science Fiction and Military Fantasy bring you tales of the terrors of combat and the even greater fear of the unknown in Cannon Publishing's first Bi-Annual Military Anthology.

Fifteen classic Science Fiction stories from both masters of the craft and up and coming new writers!

A tyrannical United Nations pulls the strings of its colony worlds, ruling with an iron fist. Corporate interests take precedence, and brushfire rebellions smolder on the edges. One system, home to the only alien species yet discovered, with human allies throws off the yoke and calls itself Independence.

Feedback from the slight pressure of a hand closing sends a powerful mechanical arm smashing into an opponent. A neural link hurls blustering plasma fire from your suit's shoulder mounted cannon. Your reactor levels scream with overload as return fire smashes into your armor, and damage alarms wail while you hurl your twenty ton body sideways for cover.

You're a Mecha, a mechanical fighting machine with a human pilot. The guy that the infantry curse at in training and pray for in combat. The machine that the last hopes of your people ride on. The construct that strikes fear deep into alien hearts as they hear your turbines power up. The one able to pass through hell and come out the other side victorious, or die trying.

In the near future, massive empires rule the stars, and west of the Reach, they are battling for control of new systems. In the no-mans land between the front lines, Captain Nate Meric and the crew of the privateer Lexington fight for prize money, and loyalty to their ship and their friends. Beneath it all, though, runs a hidden dream. To see America restored, and take her rightful place among the stars.

Brian Corel, former slave, gladiator, ex-fiance to an Empress, exiled Captain of the Taland Royal Guard and now owner of the frigate *Widowmaker,* does the best he can to balance the lives of his crew with his own desire to live life as a free man.

Skirting the border between being a privateer and an outright pirate, Corel stumbles into a war with a religious cult intent on corrupting the kingdom of an old friend and has to set things right while grieving over his lost love. Along the way he signs a dragon into his crew and has to risk everything to rescue his brother from the grasp of a demon that has destroyed an entire continent.

Chosen by the Sword

There are some things a PhD doesn't prepare you for, like running two feet of steel through the guts of a flesh-eating monster straight out of a nightmare, while ducking razor sharp claws. Or having the sword critique your fighting style while you do it.

Dave Howard had a problem. Last week, he was out looking for a teaching job in the middle of a wrecked job market. This week he was neck deep in green blood and hellfire. Dragged into it by the very sword, his grandfathers' mysterious possessed blade, that was now walking him through hacking up a ghoul without getting his own head cut off. This wasn't exactly what he had gone to school for, and the University he had just taken a job with seemed to be anything BUT an academic institution. More like some kind of monster hunting bunch of weirdo nerds. Maybe his degree in Personality Psychology might be useful there, at least. The fighting though … as he dodged another swipe of claws and awkwardly tried to follow the instructions the sword was screaming at him, he shot back at it, "Hell, I'm Canadian! Swordplay isn't in my cultural DNA!"

Beyond the Wall: A Novel of Post-Roman Britain

The legions are but a memory, the glory of Rome only a shadow of crumbling ruins and broken walls.

A darkening tide of barbarism was washing across Britain's shores and the lights of civilization were slowly flickering out into darkness, only kept burning by the legendary Red Dragons cavalry unit. Led by their Tribune, Arthur, who serves no kingdom but goes where the fight is hardest and most crucial, they wage desperate battles to keep back the tide. The Red Dragons ride the length of Britannia to fight the invading Saxons, Scoti and Picts, wherever they show, from across the seas or down from the Highlands.

At sixteen years old Peredur of Gwynedd has listened all his life to the stories of his father Pelinor fighting with Ambrosius Aurelianus. When word comes that his older brother has been slain in battle with the Saxons, his desire for revenge leads him to follow in his father's footsteps as a warrior, becoming a cavalryman with the Red Dragons. Along the way he may either find himself a warrior and leader worthy of Arthur or be left lying forgotten in the dust of history.

Two souls collide in the middle of a deadly war.

Sergeant Sylvie Lyons of Her Majesty's Royal Engineers wishes she'd listened to her grandda's advice and stayed away from the military.

USMC Sergeant Hondo Cassidy wants nothing more in life than being a Marine and fighting.

Hondo and Sylvie find themselves thrown together when his artillerymen are assigned to provide security for her engineers deep in the desert of Afghanistan.. Amidst death, destruction, cultural misunderstanding and the inevitable that happens when you mix an all male unit of Marines with an engineer unit that is mostly female, Sylvie and Hondo find in each other a reason to live.

That is, if they can survive.